Contempt For Caution

To Jenny, a patient and tolerant text typist and Colin, a police officer and brave winner of the Royal Humane Society of Australia Silver Medal. No father has ever been blessed with such a wonderful Daughter and Son.

CONTEMPT FOR CAUTION

DUDLEY FLINT

Cover image by Shutterstock

Cover Design and typeset by BookPOD Pty Ltd

Printed and bound in Australia by BookPOD Pty Ltd

Typeset in Garamond Premier Pro 12/15

National Library of Australia Cataloguing-in-Publication entry :

Author: Flint, Dudley, author.

Title: Contempt for caution / Dudley Flint.

ISBN: 9780994151902 (paperback)

Subjects: Revenge--Fiction.
White collar crimes--Fiction.
Detective and mystery stories.

Dewey Number: A823.4

CHAPTER ONE

EVERY ATOM OF THE LARGE thirty one year old muscular body of Erwin Dormunt radiated contempt. He allowed Lenny, his jubilant lawyer to push through a crowd of angry, dismayed and betrayed relatives and friends of the little boy. After a four day trial, Erwin was adjudged by a jury to be not guilty of the hideous rape and murder of an eight year old school boy.

Erwin could still recall most of the two hours of his intense physical and mental delectation as he inflicted horrific sexual atrocities on the smooth skinned pre adolescent.

He recalled how the boy's screams enhanced his sexual performance empowering him to thrust powerfully, repeatedly. When the eyes of his naked, bleeding, living toy focused on the wire noose and the young brain realised he was to be hung, Erwin relished the recollection of his pitiful, begging appeals. But all good things come to an end and the appeals became screams then brief, strangled gasps as Erwin had lifted the bleeding body and attached the other end of the wire to a butcher's hook on a metal rail. Erwin gently lowered the body to prolong the gasping, twisting and writhing. The squeaky noise made by the wire grating on the butcher's hook when the boy was fully suspended and threshing, still echoed joyously in his ears.

His recollections, as his lanky lawyer pushed through the throng, included the feeling of a euphoric inner calm, the outward manifestation of which twisted his lips into a sardonic grin. That grin further fuelled the flame of frustration of the family and friends of the little victim.

Erwin believed in the maxim of "might is right". Being born with a body that benefitted from the genes of large boned ancestors, he dominated any group of same aged children from kindergarten to near high school graduation. This early experience of domination, ineffectually curbed by over indulgent parents, engendered an early predilection towards activities involving physical contact.

As his muscles increased with sports training his physical pain threshold also increased. To the extent that he contemptuously shrugged off normally punishing blows delivered surreptitiously in retaliation on the football field and with calculated intent to injure in the boxing ring.

The combination of a large frame upholstered with large muscles and an above average insensitivity to pain made Erwin a formidable adversary and most sensible would-be opponents backed off. Consequently Erwin became convinced that his might gave him the right to act as he saw fit. And he saw fit to inflict pain on others in ways that normal members of society regarded as perverse. He reasoned that if weaker members of society were unable to protect their own offspring then it was not his fault. Erwin's brain rationalised his murders by laying blame upon parents who inadequately protected children.

Erwin's exoneration by the court of the rape / murder of the frail bodied eight year old boy reinforced his perception of his might and that his unrestricted exercise of it was right. His only self-recrimination was slight and centred entirely upon an act of carelessness that allowed the Victoria Police to connect him with the dead toy-boy. This carelessness had not existed when he indulged his sadistic sex executions on several young boys in other States of Australia. So Police records still carried those names as missing persons. Erwin was proud of his ability to exercise his rights; indeed he fixated on the word "right". Politically he readily defended ultra right-wing causes.

Erwin's intellectual hatred for "leftist" causes and his belief in "right" wing issues were conceived from his limited range of reading. That consisted lately of weekend newspaper magazines discarded by residents of the back packers hostels that he frequented. Erwin also loved to read the jokes found in Christmas crackers. Had he the intellectual sophistication to discern it, Erwin might have realised that his allegiance to right wing beliefs owed much to the "leftish" writers who seem to have a stranglehold on the articles published in those allegedly "arty" weekend magazines.

To Erwin, the "left" was associated with mollycoddle, fuzzy, undisciplined, unrealistic concepts such as the surrender of independence in exchange for the utopia promised by leftish politicians. The principal difference between "right" and "left" ideologies in Erwin's warped personal lexion, was that the right purports to champion self discipline and individual initiative, whereas the left disguises its tyrannical aims behind "smoke and mirrors" supported by two levels of society.

The first being the privileged upper class gullibles, riddled with guilt caused by unearned wealth and magnified by inherent personality defects. The second betrayer of human progress are the so called "workers" and "battlers" an ambiguous mob of misfits and spongers on the social security budget. Their favourite occupation is to constantly denigrate the hand that feeds them whilst allowing union bosses to exercise their thinly sublimated megalomania by dictating how the workers must think. Workers are deluded to be eternally grateful to the very institutions that keep them in a subordinate status. The clarion call of communal cooperation seems so loud as to numb any application of common sense. How the workers consent to the paradox was unfathomable to Erwin.

Erwin's selectively activated mental equipment was sufficient for him to dimly perceive that every "left" movement in the past 200 years led to tyranny, genocide, misery and enormous loss of the human life the left purport to support.

The leftish French revolution of 1789 with its rallying cry of Liberty, Fraternity and Equality metamophosised into the murderous right regime that popularised the guillotine and led to Napoleon seizing the State. With unbound egotism, the former Army corporal appointed himself to supplant the royalty that the revolutionaries strove to bloodily annihilate. Napoleon's wars of ego driven conquest caused millions of deaths. Napoleon abandoned his armies three times, once in Egypt, again in Moscow and finally at Waterloo. This betrayal of their disciples is a characteristic trait of all tyrants.

During earlier, brief, incarcerations, in prison, Erwin had time to watch documentaries on television that showed Germany's path to destruction began with the rise of the National Socialist German Workers' Party in the 1930's and the political system designed to restore dignity to German workers. But instead it spawned a total police state with the former Army corporal, Adolf Hitler, supplanting royalty. With the self imposed title of "Der Fuhrer", Hitler became the Kaiser but with powers that no king dared to assume.

Again, millions of his own people were murdered by bullet; gas chamber and piano wire hangman's nooses, a method that particularly attracted Erwin. True to the characteristic form of dictators, Hitler abandoned his soldiers in North Africa and at Stalingrad. He ensured maximum destruction of his people.

Lenin's Russian socialist revolution of October 1917, resulted in millions being executed, by bullet or starvation and the ascendancy of Joseph Stalin, an egotistical butcher who seized for himself the position of royalty that he promised to eradicate. Stalin's rule was bloodier than that of any Tsar and his wars resulted in millions of deaths of his people. When Hitler unleashed his superbly trained and indoctrinated armed forces on Russia under the plan codenamed Barbarossa, Stalin abandoned his army by cowardly hibernating for week. The Nazi military inflicted millions of casualties on the recently purged Russian Army that initially floundered without proper leadership. Thus Stalin, the so called "divinity of the working class", exhibited the characteristic betrayal of his people.

In China, Mao Tse Tsung gained power in 1949. He professed to save his people from right wing warlords but installed a new royalty with himself as premier warlord. Millions died or were crippled. Intellectuals, ie, those who opposed Mao or were literate, were killed or their talents wasted in back breaking labour to ensure their early demise. China's prosperity disappeared beneath the Red Army's repression and Mao's constant purges displayed again the characteristic betrayal of people.

Erwin believed that a characteristic of the leftish writers in every democracy is that, uncontaminated by facts or rules of evidence, they amplify out of all proportion any deficiencies actual or rumoured of democratic leaders whilst shrivelling the actual, proven, horrendous crimes of the socialist ogres. Erwin was of the opinion that a female journalist in Melbourne must have a perverted Oedipus complex because almost every one of her newspaper articles sought to equate a democratically elected

Prime Minister with the most barbaric personages in history, to make her beloved left seem benevolent by comparison.

In his own personal revolt against the left, Erwin became fascinated with right wing Nazi symbolism. TV documentaries about the Nazi Party had a mesmeric appeal; the red flag with the black swastika in the white circle symbolised power and might. Erwin's early reading of articles by war time authors denigrating the horrendous activities of the Nazi regime had an opposite effect on him. He admired a political party that suckered the workers into believing it would increase their dignity and liberty but achieved the reverse in a remarkably short time.

He regretted that Germany lost World War 2, an act for which he blamed the United States of America and, by sublimed extrapolation, all other democracies. Including that one into which he was born, a democracy that embraced his German born father when, at the age of five, he emigrated in 1950 with Erwin's grandparents, to Australia.

As a result of the skill of his grandfather and his father, who between them built a successful engineering business, Erwin the only heir had inherited a substantial portfolio of shares and property. The magnitude of his inherited wealth was Erwin's security blanket. His income enabled him to avoid working for a living and to indulge in travel. The greatest expenditure of his wealth was to the top lawyer Lenny, who consistently prevailed at Erwin's Court appearances.

His latest exoneration for murder and rape cemented his belief in the oft quoted adage, that a jury is a panel of twelve persons too stupid to avoid jury duty, gathered together to decide who has the best lawyer.

Obviously you get what you pay for and his freedom to walk, freedom to recall details of his latest sexual exploit, the murder rape of a young boy and freedom to contemplate his next adventure, put Erwin in a contented state of mind.

So content was he that never noticed an elderly couple amidst the angry throngs outside the Court, a pair of distraught grandparents shedding tears at their profound belief that a blatant miscarriage of justice allowed a murdering rapist to strut around with a self satisfied smirk. And if Erwin had noticed them he would have dismissed them without any regret for their grief. Erwin could not have guessed he would be the victim of the grandfather's vengeance. If someone had pointed out Ian, the grieving grandfather, to Erwin and told him "That man will cause your death", Erwin would have exploded with derisive laughter and asked "How could that old bald bastard, double my age, half my weight and barely as high as my shoulder, harm me?" For Erwin the entire assemblage of grieving relatives and observers was something he treated with contempt.

Erwin's only other thought as he followed Lenny his lanky lawyer back to Lenny's chambers for a celebratory drop of 15 year old deluxe Scotch whisky, was that if he ever became dictator of the State of Victoria he would arrange summary executions for all people who fed pigeons.

CHAPTER TWO

UNNOTICED BY ERWIN AS HE strode through the crowd outside the Court were an elderly couple clinging to each other in a forlorn effort to achieve mutual comfort. Ian and Julie Ross, the couple, were the maternal grandparents of the eight year old boy who was so brutally murdered. Inconsolable since the cruel death their burden of grief became enormously heavier when they heard the foreman of the jury advise the judge that they, the jury, determined Erwin Dormunt to be not guilty.

The sight of the smirking Erwin following his tall, ugly lawyer through the crowd caused both Ian and Julie to release tears built up during the trial of the person they were certain slaughtered their innocent grandson.

Ian and Julie watched Erwin follow his lawyer across William Street and up the stairs into the building infested entirely with chambers for members of the legal profession. Erwin's exit from the scene caused the seething crowd to disperse. Several sympathetic women friends gave Julie a kiss on her tear dampened cheeks. Several men gave her a hug and shook Ian's hand in an attempt to express their sorrow. Most expressed contempt for the legal system that they felt to be so slanted towards procedures and protocols that a murderer walked free because of the ability of his lawyer to bamboozle a jury.

After several minutes of mutual commiserations Ian and Julie also crossed William Street and walked in silence to the Flagstaff underground railway station to catch a train. Julie's thoughts during the 20 minute train ride were incoherent. In anticipation of a verdict from the jury, Julie had been unable to sleep for many nights and unable to eat at all that day so her mental processes, disarranged by devastating grief, were further dislocated by lack of sleep and nourishment.

By contrast, the thought process of Ian was crystal clear. Ian's apprehension as to the outcome of the murder trial began when he attended an earlier Court hearing to extradite Erwin from the State of New South Wales, where he had been apprehended over a year earlier. Ian thought that the extradition evidence was weak. He was mildly surprised when the New South Wales Magistrate granted the extradition warrant to the Victoria Police. Ian's fears about the feebleness of the prosecution evidence deepened at each subsequent hearing, firstly the arraignment and then the bail application.

The proceedings kept appearing in his mind like flashbacks in a TV movie. Ian recalled how Erwin's lawyer, Lenny, repeatedly returned to any insignificant slip in police evidence like continual picking at a scab to make a slight paper cut into an enormous inoperable ulcer. Another tactic used by the aggressive defense and not properly addressed by the judge in Ian's opinion, was what Ian labelled the "telephone directory attack". An inordinate amount of the murder trial time was taken by the defense lawyer denigrating the police by implying that police deliberately and with malice failed to investigate other possible offenders.

The defense grilled every police witness as to why they did not investigate some person who could have been at the scene of the crime. So many names were mentioned that an unbiased observer might rightly have formed the view that half of the people in the Melbourne telephone directory could have committed the crime. The sheer repetition of the names of possible perpetrators appeared to indicate that police idleness and complacency, since they arrested Erwin, led to perversion of the justice system to malignantly convict Erwin for the heinous murder.

Ian remembered how clearly the defense lawyer built up a case to show that the police hated Erwin. The previous history of charges and convictions of an accused is seldom allowed to be mentioned in court to a jury lest they be wrongly influenced. Each case must be tried entirely upon the evidence adduced as relevant. No previous history is usually allowed, even if the accused had performed previous crimes using a modus operandi identical to that being trialled. Evidence of past propensity is allowed to be introduced by the prosecution only under stringent conditions.

Erwin's money was properly spent in the engagement of Lenny as his defense lawyer. Lenny amazed everyone when he deliberately reversed the conventional practice and volunteered to the jury details of Erwin's previous confrontations. Lenny twisted every police encounter to Erwin's advantage. Admission of previous charges as an element of a defense is rare and risky.

Ian recalled how the long, lean lawyer built up a case to show that the police had constantly persecuted Erwin in the past. In truth, Erwin had been arrested for possession of a small quantity of cannabis by police at a sea side summer holiday resort. Usually such an arrest on a summary charge did not lead to police taking fingerprints. But Erwin's abuse of the arresting officers and boasting of having escaped detection for previous crimes aroused suspicion of the Sergeant in charge who exercised his lawful discretion to request Erwin to provide fingerprints.

Erwin refused. Belligerent behaviour and obscene language was his answer. The Sergeant exercised his lawfully given right to obtain fingerprints by force. In the course of the process Erwin was bruised, as were two police officers. But in the practised presentation of this piece of Erwin's history, Erwin's lawyer convinced the jury that this was one example of flagrant police brutality towards his client. His arrest for the murder of the eight year old boy was tendered as further evidence of malignant police persecution.

His mind focused on the trial, Ian sat beside his distraught wife in the train oblivious of his surroundings. To Ian, the prosecutor seemed to have rushed the case to court without proper preparation. He concluded that the jury were swayed to their findings of Erwin being "not guilty" by dubious contentions and procedural lapses

If those really were the explanation for Erwin being found "Not Guilty", then it confirmed another old adage that "bullshit baffles brains". On the subject of bullshit, Ian was not alone in holding the opinion that the police were required to strictly comply with excessive red tape. That excess offered too much latitude for the defenders of crooks to get acquittals on unimportant technicalities. In the days when far less red tape existed, a Solicitor General named Blackstone wrote "…..it is better if ten guilty men go free than one innocent man be convicted". For the last two hundred and fifty years that writing has been an axiom of the British system of law. Ian had believed in it until now. The weight of evidence, despite some flaws, made Erwin guilty yet he was not convicted. The prospect of Erwin roaming free to rape and murder children was hard to square with the notion that the Law existed to protect the public.

By the time the grieving husband and wife reached Glenhuntly railway station, Ian had resolved to seek revenge. As he and Julie walked slowly to their home Ian's mind was already beginning to focus on what should be the magnitude of the revenge he sought to achieve and how to achieve it. At age 66, Ian was mature enough to realise that intense planning would be necessary, each element of his revenge required meticulous testing to avoid further grief to his wife Julie and their hospitalised daughter, the mother of their murdered grandson.

A "Confucius says" sentence sprang into his mind. "Beware the vengeance of the patient man". Ian resolved to be patient and also implacably unremitting in ensuring justifiable vengeance. Ian had discovered in his research of Erwin's crime that the technical term for a crime involving hideous torture and murderous sexual abuse is erotophonophilia. The very sight of the word made him feel sick. He wanted Erwin dead. Could he kill Erwin? Would it be possible for a sexagenarian to kill a younger, fitter muscular monster? And could he get away with it?

Realising the obstacles to obtaining vengeance, Ian resolved to be cautious, as he had been taught. He knew that to achieve his aim he could not treat any person or process with contempt.

CHAPTER THREE

ON THE BALCONY OF HIS luxurious Docklands apartment block, thirty two year old Bryn Hamley read the morning newspaper over his customary health food breakfast. He paid scant attention to the story of Erwin Dormunt's surprise exoneration for the brutal sex murder of a young boy. Miscarriages of justice, murder and blood were items that Bryn accepted as normal in his line of business. Bryn enjoyed being Melbourne's most prestigious, undiscovered, professional criminal.

Bryn's parents were of Welsh extraction, as evidenced by his first name. Being moderately prosperous in the legal field, Bryn's father had enrolled him in a Celtic orientated prestigious College for a sound education. Persistent rather than brilliant was how Bryn's masters summed him up and awarded to him grades that put him, academically, consistently close to the top 10% but never actually in it.

Bryn's sporting ability put him slightly higher than that and he was always picked in the school teams for football, cricket and swimming earning a reputation as being a reliable performer. Pleased with Bryn's academic and sporting achievements, his father proved not ungenerous in praise and pocket money. Consequently Bryn never ceased to reflect with pleasure on his school days in rare moments of introspection.

Bryn learned a lot at school, but the interpretation he put on the facts would have surprised most of the schoolmasters. Having plenty of pocket money, the sixteen year old Bryn could afford to buy expensive magazines packed with pictures of nude females. He had a copy of "Playboy" in his hand when the school tennis captain mentioned the name of a new boy to the school and asked Bryn to introduce him to tennis team members and show him around the club house. So he would not forget the new boy's name, Bryn wrote it on the nearest available piece of paper, the cover of the Playboy magazine which, after he completed the introduction of the new boy, he secreted in the bottom of his locker.

Later that day his class was told that a valuable piece of school property had been stolen and that normal class would be suspended while all boys stood beside their lockers for a search by the House Masters. On his way to the locker corridor, Bryn recalled that he had a prohibited item, Playboy, in his locker. His brain moved into top gear to work out how to avoid being caught and penalised for possession of a prohibited publication within school precincts.

About fifty teenaged students lined the corridor and for each to stand beside his locker was easier said than done because the tall grey metal lockers were narrower than the taller strapping young men to whom they were assigned. Consequently some pushing and shoving eventuated as it does whenever a group of healthy young men with the healthy competitive spirit are crowded together.

Taking advantage of the commotion Bryn surreptitiously removed the Playboy magazine and slithered it into a nearby rubbish bin, before joining the pushing pack of pupils, with the revitalised enthusiasm of a clear conscience. Eventually the Masters completed their search of the lockers and the cacophony of clangs of the locker doors being slammed shut and relocked had barely dissipated when a Master decided to check the rubbish bin. He discovered the discarded copy of Playboy. With a look of horror on his face and in a tone of voice of fitting an affronted Presbyterian zealot, the Master demanded that the degenerate of the college who desecrated the school by bringing into it the Playboy magazine step forward and confess.

Bryn though the Master's demand was stupid because anyone degenerate enough to have a copy of Playboy was degenerate enough to disobey the demand that would lead to punishment. He kept his mouth shut. And Bryn's opinion of the Master rose as the Master ranted on about the filthy contents with special reference to the centrefold. How did the Master know in such detail of the Playboy magazine's explicit centrefold without having prior knowledge?

The Master's studious inspection of the unclothed anatomy of the young female on the front page shifted and, after a swift refocus, saw the name written on the front cover. Almost as a reflex from years of calling the roll in class, the Master spoke the name. Like a lamb to the slaughter, the new boy stepped forward, also in reflex action and said "Yes Sir". Master, new boy and Playboy headed for the office of the College Principal leaving Bryn in a temporarily relieved state. He was not convinced that he had escaped the peril to which he had inadvertently consigned the new boy. Bryn's reading of detective stories caused his developing analytical mind to be concerned about the possibility that his handwriting may be recognised, or if fingerprints would be taken. If he were to be fingerprinted then he could be embarrassed about the position of many of his prints on the centrefold. And the proximity of his locker to the rubbish bin could be used as further evidence against him.

But Bryn was despondent in vain; evidently the College authorities neglected to read the same detective novels as he and the angelic faced new boy was convicted upon the false evidence of ownership simply because his name was written thereon. Justifiably, the parents of the new boy defended their son and being of a rather difficult disposition told the College Principal where to stick the Playboy and his College and departed with their son, never to set foot again in that august educational establishment.

News of the abruptly terminated tenure of the new boy spread and afforded Bryn one of the most momentous lessons he would learn from the College – if your name is on it you cop the blame. After some more thought Bryn arrived at one of his self imposed lifetime commandments; never put your correct name on anything.

The second of Bryn's life guides emanated from an observation on the College football field when his team's full forward was dealt an unfair knock by an opposition player. The full forward fell heavily and was awarded a free kick but when hauled to his feet by his team mates was too unsteady to put boot to ball and Bryn, being the team member closest to the full forward when the illegal knock was delivered, was given the ball.

At close range Bryn easily kicked the goal and as the team had a robustly healthily winning margin and with only a short time before the final siren, the coach ordered Bryn to remain at full forward. As frequently happens in Australian Rules Football, when one team has an unbeatable winning margin, the losing team turns violent. And as Bryn was a medium sized young man seemingly surrounded by older, meaner boys of the other team, his team coach sent the big resting ruck man to Bryn's area with instructions to protect Bryn.

Upon hearing he had a sizable protector Bryn took comfort. He was far from being a coward but the idea of a protector settled in the sediment of his cerebellum and eventually emerged as Bryn's second self-discovered commandment. Always be protected. He puzzled over what protection he would need and how best to get it.

CHAPTER FOUR

HALF WAY THROUGH HIS FINAL High School year Erwin decided that he had better things to do than listen to school teachers, all of whom he regarded as pathological scum. The deaths of his grandparents and parents during the past year had affected him emotionally very little. Indeed the prospects of acquiring considerable inherited wealth free from even the slightest vestige of parental restraint expunged his brief and shallow grief with remarkable rapidity.

Erwin was not mentally deficient by any standard of measurement; he was just mentally tainted from restricted social access resulting from his propensity to indulge in violence, when thwarted, as a first response rather than as a final resort. Social isolation allowed him the time to focus on literature of one type and his unquestioning absorption of clever but warped political ideas fomented into a pus-like perception of reality. He soon became sated with run-of-the-mill pornography and his new financial status allowed him to buy under-the-counter publications featuring extreme perversions.

His recently acquired driving licence and the purchase of an expensive sports car allowed greater mobility to attend functions advertised on websites of radical political and pornographic groups. Driving home to his newly acquired apartment, at the rear of his former family home, his recapitulation of the inspirational speeches of several ultra right-wing visionaries lessened his attention to the speed limit on the road. A patrol car with flashing red and blue lights drew level with him and the police passenger waved him over to the curb.

Reluctantly he complied and when he noted that the police representative was female, his desire to dominate refused to remain suppressed. He offended the female senior constable with a crude invitation to join him in a sexual act. He only cooperated with the request for a sample of breath in the breathalyser when the driver of the patrol car, a sizable, pistol armed male, approached to lend assistance to his smaller blue uniformed colleague. When asked why he had exceeded the speed limit, Erwin denied it and when told he was over the permitted alcohol consumption limit for a Provisional Licensed driver, zero, he raised his voice to a level entirely out of proportion to the event and abused the constables in language both profane and obscene.

During his tirade of abuse Erwin's large hands clenched into fists and his waving arms and posture were interpreted by the police as a prelude to an attack. He was genuinely surprised to find himself thrown to the ground and to feel the cold metal of handcuffs on the wrists twisted behind his back. The volume of his voice increased and he began to struggle. In attempting to rise, his feet slipped in the roadside stone chips and he fell with his shoulder taking some of the impact but his cheek was grazed in the gravel.

Responding to a radio call a police divisional van equipped with a prisoner cage arrived with two constables. Erwin saw the female police officer looking through his new prestige sports car and his rage increased so that it took the combined efforts of all three male policemen to put the abusive, kicking Erwin into the cage. His disposition was not improved when the police woman read him "his rights" and told him that, in addition to the charges of exceeding the speed limit and driving under the influence of alcohol, another charge of resisting arrest would be added.

Thoughts as murderously dark as wind driven thunder clouds suffused Erwin's brain as he sat on the hard bunk bed in the cell at the police station. He had been offered antiseptic cream for his gravel rashed face but rejected it by telling the custody constable where to shove it.

His only consolation lay in his telephone contact with the lawyer who had handled the legalities of the estate of his deceased parents. The family lawyer had promised to make immediate contact with another lawyer specialising in defending persons charged with offenses relating to traffic transgressions and police brutality. Erwin was cautioned that the services of the specialist were costly but worth every cent. Erwin had concurred with the engagement. The family lawyer further cautioned him to exercise his right to remain silent in relation to any question asked about the events leading to the charges against him. In fact Erwin had refused to answer any questions except in relation to the offer of food.

He did not feel hungry but demanded a hamburger and chips for the nuisance value. After eating two chips and swallowing one bit of hamburger, he had loudly cursed the coppers and thrown the food through the grill in the door to splatter tomato sauce, greasy meat and chips over the floor of the corridor. The sound of a cursing constable cleaning up the mess gave him satisfaction.

Later that night be began to feel hungry and yelled at full volume, kicked the door repeatedly and threatened to sue the police unless he was provided with something suitable to eat. The duty constable appeared surprisingly considerate and told Erwin that the only food available was from an all night milk bar and that all that could be obtained was a chocolate ice cream sundae. Erwin thought that his antics had somehow cowed the young custody constable and with a show of reluctance he deigned to accept the offered chocolate ice cream sundae. The custody constable and his colleagues in the front were laughing their heads off because the chocolate coating so enjoyed by Erwin consisted of six squares of a popular chocolate laxative, shredded over the two scoops of ice cream.

CHAPTER FIVE

BRYN'S DECISION TO EMBRACE THE occupation of crime as a means of life self actualisation and fulfilment was something he resolved to avoid making public. His instinct argued that the general public was insufficiently enlightened to appreciate his election.

His parents were a trifle disappointed that he chose to follow the college vocational advisor's advice to become an accountant rather than follow his father into the legal profession; however Bryn's College graduation results provided entry to the Commerce course at Melbourne University and the prestige of that educational institution soon mitigated their slight disappointment.

During the summer holidays Bryn spent time with school friends whose parents owned power boats and were generous in teaching boating skills to their son's friends. With dedicated landlubber parents, Bryn had never experienced the rapture of sailing and it became an obsessive occupation. He learned safety procedures, rules of navigation and how to read charts. He preferred to have sex whilst sailing, much to the delight of several daughters of owners of the larger motor cruisers.

Bryn's willingness to perform the menial maintenance tasks necessary to keep the big boats in pristine condition, his meticulous cleaning of bright work, his enthusiastic ability to work as a waiter at the larger boat-board parties and his reliability as a sober helmsman ensured that he had plenty of opportunity to pursue his newly acquired seafaring hobby.

Boat parties provided Bryn with masses of knowledge to assist in his criminal career. He had but to listen to the alcohol loosened tongues of the wealthy celebrities. Somehow the guests felt that away from land, inhibitions became void. Peers of the legal, commercial, political and theatrical worlds vied to outdo each other in sharing confidential tidbits of scurrilous events and unpublicised scandals that occurred in their own spheres. Salacious stories that would create outrage if obtained by any newspaper reporter with sufficient guts and insurance cover to protect against defamation, were commonplace around the afterdeck bar.

Bryn learned how an accountant was made a Member of the Order of Australia for philanthropy to a particular religious order. But in fact the large cash sums were not donations to the church instead they were payments made by his mother and other family members to purchase retirement units at a church operated retirement village. The accountant's mistress worked in the office of the church charity and assisted with the Order nomination by inserting into a cash receipt book a piece of cardboard between the original of the receipt and its duplicate. The original showed the apartment price as a "donation" whilst the duplicate contained the correct details for the auditors.

The accountant prevailed upon several clients for whom he prepared distinctly dodgy tax returns, to act as referees. Along with copies of the original receipts showing substantial donations the referees avowed that the accountant had rendered meritorious service to other charities. Some 18 months later the accountant was invested as a Member of the Order of Australia and his accounting practice flourished because his letterhead now had the post nominal AM after his name. The investiture conferred prestige and prestige has positive pulling power in business as it implied verisimilitude. As the accountant completed relating the method of fraudulently obtaining an award, his fellow bibulous boating companions roared with laughter.

After a score of such enlightening trips Bryn made a mental adjustment of his previously held view of the ethics of captains of industry. It confirmed that his resolution to be a criminal was an elevation in morality when compared with that of some of the pillars of society.

The long, warm, wonderful summer of seafaring and sex ended when Bryn arrived at Melbourne University, on a green and yellow electric tram, to commence his studies which the University expected would conclude three years later with the student obtaining a degree as a Bachelor of Commerce. Bryn's view of his future at the University diverged from that of the academic and administrative staff, but he declined to tell them that.

From the University's prospectus Bryn knew that the subjects taught as a part of the Commerce course included Accounting, Commercial Law, Company Formation and Income Tax. One year of study to learn the basics was Bryn's conclusion. After that he intended to pursue his career as Australia's richest criminal.

As a preliminary step on the road to attainment of his aim, Bryn had persuaded his parents that his commercial studies should be practically exercised by allowing him to manage his own finances. Delighted at this display of developing maturity, Bryn's parents encouraged him to open his own bank account into which they deposited a very generous sum calculated as sufficient to cover Bryn's University fees, transport and incidental expenses for the first year.

At the end of the first term Bryn achieved excellent grades from lecturers and tutors in each subject except Economic History. Bryn believed that he needed to comprehend the commercial subjects but what happened four hundred years ago was of little interest to him. He read the history text books but his thoughts too often strayed away from the economic imperatives of various wars. Bryn concluded that war was a waste and that confrontation was counterproductive.

One interesting sideline was a short, after hours course on memory training, initiated by the Student Union. Bryn decided that an improved memory was an essential asset for a career in which he intended to commit to written and / or electronic record the bare minimum. Bryn attended with the added comfort that he was getting something useful for the Student Union fees that were arbitrarily and compulsorily foisted upon him. Until the memory course was offered, Bryn was hostile to the Student Union, which seemed to spend the compulsory fees on ratbag political protests.

A second minor diversion was the University Choir for which he was actively recruited by a divinely constructed female Sociology student. Her full first name was Virginia. They called her Virgin for short, but not for long. When she learned of his Welsh ancestry she presumed that his vocal talents would be superior. But it was not his vocal talents he exercised with the young choral enthusiast. However the combination of him having an inability to sing in tune and the propensity of his partner to share her favours with baritones and tenors with an astonishing lack of embarrassment, caused that diversion to be short lived.

Bryn opined to himself that a sophisticated criminal should strive for exclusivity of his partner's sexual favours rather than simply be one of the choristers. He considered it safer, a practical conclusion, rather than a commitment to monogamy.

As part of the University philosophy of a sound mind in a healthy body, Bryn trained hard at football and played a serviceable game. He quickly learned which team members had fathers who owned yachts and power cruisers and inevitably he passed the football, by punch and kick, more into the arms of those players than other non-boat related players. The coach never complained or twigged the connection. Thus Bryn remained true to his private agenda to aim at being a seafaring, sophisticated criminal. He believed he would attain his aim, the major question that remained unanswered was "How does one start?"

CHAPTER SIX

THE TOILET SEAT HAD BEEN torn away by a previous occupant of the suburban police station cell. So from early morning Erwin had to sit on the suspiciously damp, cold, porcelain bowl rim to evacuate his inexplicably traumatised bowel. The cold porcelain made him almost as miserable as the repetitive contractions of his colon. He attributed his alimentary canal corruption to the seafood volauvents consumed with an unnamed alcohol dispensed from an unlabelled old fashioned flagon at last night's meeting of a white supremacy group.

By the time his referred criminal lawyer arrived mid morning, Erwin's facial appearance was distinctly unhealthy. The problem ameliorated as his alimentary system had by then evacuated most of its contents and so his meeting with the lawyer was only interrupted twice by swift, noisy visits to the unwelcome porcelain receptacle.

The physical appearance of Erwin's criminal lawyer produced almost no reaction from the debilitated Erwin. His name was "Leonard", he said, as he introduced himself. Erwin thought he was still suffering alcoholic withdrawal because Leonard looked like a combination of Lurch and Uncle Fester from the TV show "The Addams Family".

Erwin's washed out physical state, lack of sleep and concern lest he suffer another evacuation of watery residue too swift for him to reach the repugnant porcelain, made him feel so depressed that he actually told the truth to Leonard. He was travelling too fast, had too much to drink and became too aggressive.

The lanky lawyer was horrified at Erwin's confession. He interpreted it as proof that police pressure bewilders innocents to enable police to attain the numbers of arrests demanded of them by a quota set by their superiors. The lanky lawyer, tall, cadaverously thin, 40 years old with a nervous disposition that kept his eyes ceaselessly skittering horizontally beneath luxuriant Groucho Marx styled eyebrows, perceived that he had to embark on considerable character reorientation to properly represent the large, pallid prisoner.

To begin, he sought to establish rapport by introducing himself for a second time as Leonard and asked Erwin a few easy personal questions. Leonard soon realised that he had a long hard road to travel to achieve the status of a confidant. Erwin's physical indisposition and natural truculence made Leonard the lawyer feel as if he were wading upstream, neck deep in a river of cold treacle.

With only an outline of Erwin's charges as a start point, Leonard had ferreted out certain facts and with those as a basis, he began Erwin's re-education of the events of the previous evening. Leonard told Erwin that the two police constables in the police sedan who signalled him to stop, had made no other arrests that night. That the male policeman was in the process of a divorce and that the female police constable had broken with her long time partner several months ago. Of the Divisional Van constables, one had previously been accused of using unnecessary force. The allegation was not proven but never-the-less the allegation existed. So Leonard told Erwin he intended to use it to reshape the events of the previous evening. Leonard asked Erwin to confirm that the red Mercedes Benz two door sports coupe parked in the police compound adjoining the station was Erwin's.

Leonard was pleased to receive Erwin's confirmation as it ensured that Erwin's financial status would be adequate to meet the sizeable account for services rendered that in due course Leonard would submit. Leonard started Erwin's re-education of the events by leaning close and whispering. But when Erwin grunted a reply, the gust of evil odured breath nearly choked him so he sat further along the unyielding mattress on the bunk bed and spoke with a voice lifted nearer to normal conversational volume.

Erwin was told that he was not speeding at all. Truly his driving was impeccable. In fact two bored constables, both with personal problems, saw a beautiful red Mercedes sports coupe being driven well within the speed limit by a respectable young man. They were immediately assailed by envy and decided to abuse their positions of power to harass the innocent, respectable, citizen. Leonard pointed out that the police constables must have been bored because they were located in the one position for several hours without any other interceptions. And both constables could reasonably by assumed to be stringent financially, following wife / partner dissolutions. It was natural that Erwin's expensive car generated asset envy.

Furthermore, as one constable was inspecting his beautiful car with the futile objective of finding a fault, the initial breath testing was administered and observed by only the female constable who held the breathalyser apparatus. It was not observed by the other. Leonard contended that it was reasonable to assume that Erwin was unable to observe the test reading so it was not beyond the bounds to propose that the excessive alcohol reading was blown by the bored, drunken police constable to spitefully disadvantage Erwin.

At the police station Erwin had refused to provide another breath or blood sample. That was completely explainable by Erwin's inability to comprehend the request for him to do so after having been maliciously assaulted by four envious police constables, one of whom had been the subject of a previous allegation of violence. As evidence of police brutality Leonard would cite Erwin's lacerated face and traumatised alimentary canal, undoubtedly caused by low punches. In Leonard's point of view, Erwin was the innocent victim of a collusive quartet of socially maladjusted, bored and envious police who had no reasonable grounds to intercept him. Having done so they set out to frame him for their own corrupt amusement.

As explained by Leonard, Erwin had adequate grounds to sue for false arrest, false imprisonment and gratuitous violence. On hearing this, Erwin's physical indisposition took an immediate step on the road to recovery. The realisation that someone was prepared to fight for him in a forum of which he had no experience, really impressed Erwin. Leonard's disconcertingly perpetual eyeball pupil rhythm somehow lost its irritation aspect.

Over the next few weeks, the vigorously defended case progressed through the Magistrates Court to the next higher level, the County

Court. The four constables, each in the witness box were bombarded with allegations that were largely imaginary but contained an element of exaggerated fact, and having their integrity questioned in the media, the police prosecutor deemed it unproductive to proceed.

An arrangement between the prosecutor and Erwin's lawyer, the lanky Leonard, was struck. All charges of exceeding the speed limit and drunken driving were withdrawn in consideration of Erwin abandoning all proceedings for compensation. Leonard's carefully crafted press releases, along the lines of the under dog prevailing over obdurate bureaucracy, painted Erwin as a naïve young person striving to come to terms with the recent deaths of his beloved parents. Leonard ensured that studio retouched photographs of Erwin were released to the press so the photographs printed in the newspapers depicted a vulnerable, disconsolate youth, thus earning universal sympathy of thousands of readers. When the media reports hinted that Erwin had a sizeable inheritance he received scores of letters offering marriage. Most of the letters were from females.

Erwin enjoyed the limelight as the valiant victim so much that he signed the cheque to pay Leonard's colossal fees without compunction. Leonard arranged an express clearance of the cheque and breathed a sigh of satisfaction when his bank manager phoned to advise that the cheque had cleared without problem. Leonard had no contempt for caution.

CHAPTER SEVEN

BY THE MID POINT OF the second term at the University, Bryn had been formally taught basic accounting, the principles of commercial law and company formation, a modicum of memory training and so much of economic history as he chose to entrust to his newly improved memory. Informally, he learned more dodgy business practices from listening to the well lubricated guests on the large power cruisers on which he acted as a weekend voluntary helper; serving drinks, baiting hooks, helping on the helm, satisfying sexually starved daughters and wives below decks and generally being a nice guy. From personal experience he learned that females in the Arts facility were about 90% more likely to enter into ardent, casual, short term, sexual encounters than, say, females majoring in various sectors of physics, chemistry or mathematics.

But his major educational achievement, he felt, was his realisation that a life of satisfactory, seafaring, sophisticated crime required start up capital. Not capital from ordinary sources that could lead to tiresome complications with the Australian Taxation Office, but tax free, unattributable and untraceable dollars. Doubtlessly assisted by his crash course in memory training, Bryn's brain began to synthesize tidbits of knowledge gained on his boat trips and stored in his cerebellum. He came up with the beginnings of a plan. Bryn enjoyed planning, not short term one off projects but long term patient planning. A critical component of which was protection.

Firstly he needed names, addresses and a bank account. He solved that problem by enlisting the aid of a willing and wanton woman on the board of management of the Student Union who allowed him access to private areas, one of which happened to be the inorganic records of members.

Bryn used "stolen" names of students to obtain two street address suites with mail boxes and another three names with requisite details to register a Propriety Limited company with two directors and a Public Officer / Company Secretary, a company he named United Reinstatements Pty Ltd. The persons upon whom he had conferred the status of company director and secretary remained blissfully unaware of their commercial elevation. Payments for company and mail box addresses were made in cash.

From overheard conversations of his parents Bryn knew of an elderly woman known erroneously but affectionately as Auntie. She lived in a neighbouring suburb and owned a collection of well insured Meissen China figurines that his mother guessed to be worth $20,000. The septuagenarian Auntie regularly visited another old relative at whose house she stayed overnight. Bryn planned to use Auntie to raise start up capital.

He consulted his university sporting calendar and selected a date that a half marathon was scheduled to be run on a date that coincided with the absence of the old Auntie on a visit. Bryn scrutinised the notice board write-on list of runners and selected a person he believed might be approachable. Bryn offered the runner $20 to participate using Bryn's name, so that a certificate of attendance would issue in Bryn's name, not the name of the runner.

The reason for the subterfuge, Bryn explained, was to allow him to enjoy a rendezvous with a sexually active and beautifully built Arts student. He needed a "cover" lest his parsimonious parents found out and restricted his income. The certificate of participation in the marathon would deflect any awkward enquires. Put to him that way, the substitute runner willingly agreed provided only that in addition to the $20, an introduction to the horizontally athletic 19 year old female would be made at some time in the not too distant future. The runner crossed his own name off the list and Bryn's name was added.

On the due day Bryn appeared in running gear wearing the University singlet with the allocated number. With a camera borrowed from his father, Bryn had others take several photographs of him so attired. He returned to the changing room, swapped numbers with his substitute, changed quickly into a dark track suit, baseball cap and sneakers then set off in his car.

On arrival near a railway station close to the home of his intended victim, Bryn parked the car out of CCTV range, took a sports bag containing paper and bubble wrap and walked to Auntie's house. Without hesitation, despite a palpitating heart, Bryn pushed open the metal framed front gate with his elbow and entered the front garden. Shaded by a hedge and trees, Bryn slipped on a pair of rubber dishwashing gloves and used a concrete garden lawn edge piece to smash one pane of glass in the ornamental glass front door near the old style lock. Reaching through the gap he flicked up the lock latch lever, opened the door, went inside and quietly shut the door.

His heart was still pounding; his fingers were twitching as he listened intently in case there was an alarm of which he was not aware. After a minute that seemed a lot longer, no noise smashed the silence. Nor was there any evidence in the cornices of the room of a burglar alarm motion detector, such as those installed in the home of his parents.

Reassured, Bryn opened the first show case containing the collection of expensive china figurines and began wrapping each piece carefully in bubble wrap and paper. He methodically packed each into the sports bag.

Careful packing took over an hour and Bryn's hands beneath the rubber of the gloves were swimming in sweat and his mouth was distressingly dry. It took an effort of mental discipline to control his breathing. Bryn achieved the required mental equilibrium to appear nonchalant prior to picking up the now heavy sports bag, closing the door and walking to the front gate. Peeling off the rubber gloves he pushed them into the track suit pockets.

Taking more deep breaths he pushed open the gate with his arm then stepped onto the footpath. Desperately trying to have his body language appear normal he walked towards his car. From brief glances stolen as he walked, Bryn became convinced that he was unobserved, but continued past his parked car to a seat in a sheltered area near a playground. He took off the black track suit top and black cap. The yellow tee shirt beneath the track suit changed his appearance sufficiently for him to return to his car with confidence that no one had recognised him.

He drove carefully to the St Kilda Marina where the lockers for several owners of motor cruisers were located in a large shed. As he had been given the number to several of the combination locks by boat owners he had no trouble as he opened one locker and placed the sports bag containing the stolen china figurines well to the rear. He covered it with discarded canvas from a wind ripped cockpit awning.

Among so many others at the Marina, Bryn's presence was unremarkable and he was back in his car and on his way to the University within minutes. After changing to his running gear he disposed of the rubber gloves, baseball cap, track suit and sneakers separately into several dumpsters located behind the canteen, the sports complex and the science departments before the marathon runners began to trickle past the finish line.

Bryn's co-conspirator arrived with a bunch of other contestants to register as number 41, a rather credible performance for a fun jogger against many more rigorously trained and motivated athletes in the field of nearly 300. The substitute collected his official placement certificate then met Bryn, as arranged, and handed over the certificate and running number with a lewd smirk. He received from Bryn in exchange, a $20 note and a piece of paper with the first name of a female and telephone number printed on it.

Bryn pinned the running number to his light blue singlet and produced his father's camera for a cooperative passer-by to take two photos of him, with his running number visible and the completion certificate held in both hands triumphantly above his heard. Bryn used up the remainder of the film taking photos of other runners at a nearby pub where he listened carefully and absorbed detail of events that occurred during the running of the marathon.

His parents were agreeably surprised to find him home for dinner on a Saturday and ordered his favourite meal delivered from their customary Chinese restaurant. Bryn told them he was tired after running the marathon and delighted his parents by showing them his certificate. He made quite a big thing out of dedication to studies and told them that he intended to swat that night on commercial aspects of insurance. He lamented that the University course was so theoretical. To really understand the insurance subjects he needed "hands on" experience with actual cases, he told his parents. But none ever seemed to happen within his circle to allow him to exercise his newly learned skills. He did not overdo it, he felt, but his parents did learn that their son's education would be enhanced if he could obtain practical experience to reinforce his theoretical studies. Bryn's father promised to speak with a partner at his law firm to see if anything of educational interest may be available within the legal practice.

The following Monday, Bryn returned home from the Uni to find his mother positively bursting to tell him her news. "It was terrible" she said, then explained that "old Auntie's" house had been burgled over the weekend. Auntie arrived home late Sunday afternoon to find her magnificent collection of china figurines had been stolen. Auntie was distraught to such an extent she barely had the energy to call the Police. Not a lot was achieved that night but on Monday, a special Police squad detective arrived because the figurines that Auntie told her were worth about $20,000 some time ago, were actually insured for $60,000.

It appeared that the initial Police theory attributed the theft to another collector, given the unsaleability of the well know miniature hand sculptured and painted figurines, the fact that nothing else was stolen, the simple but professional removal (bits of bubble wrap were detected) and lack of fingerprints. A door knock of the neighbours and scan of the CCTV monitors in the nearby main shopping area and railway station disclosed noting of interest.

"But darling" gushed his exuberant mother, "guess what?" Bryn made a feeble guess to please. His mother told him that when Auntie telephoned with the awful news she seemed so distressed that Bryn's mother volunteered Bryn's services to assist with completing the complex business of making the insurance claim. His mother interpreted Bryn's big grin as a tribute to her acumen in obtaining a real life insurance experience to assist her son in his university studies. But Bryn was grinning because he knew that another part of his plan had worked.

The conception, the planning, the execution all seemed to have gone well, so far. There were still obstacles but the hardest part of any journey was the first step, according to his father. Bryn's first step had caused a real adrenalin surge, but it was a step best left undescribed to his father.

Instead, he thanked his mother with a hug and a kiss and further delighted her by showing her the recently developed photos taken at the Saturday half marathon at the University. There stood Bryn, in his sports gear with running number prominent, at the start, in several photos. And again Bryn featured holding up, in triumph, his completion certificate. His mother was so proud of her son that no one could have convinced her that the photos really evidenced Bryn's protection against detection for his first positive step to be a seafaring, sophisticated, billionaire criminal.

Was success so far really attributable to his planning and audacity or was it just beginner's luck? The next stage in his plan was crucial.

CHAPTER EIGHT

WHEN ERWIN NEXT FELL FOUL of the police he was sitting on the arm of a threadbare sofa with an unopened slab of beer cans in his lap. There were nineteen other men crowded into the sleazy, cigarette smoke contaminated lounge room of a house in the outer Melbourne suburb of Cricklewood. Each had their eyes glued to the extra large television screen. Showing in exceptionally clear colour was a movie of extreme perversion.

Four slim young men of Asian appearance were involved in sexual acts with two young children, possibly ten years of age. One was a girl and one a boy. Both were screaming and bleeding at the violations of their bodies by the naked, rampant men and the leather, metal and plastic appliances they applied to the helpless children. So absorbed was the drooling crowd in the room that the presence of the police went unnoticed until each of two doors was fully pushed in and a voice yelled "Police – don't move" twice in rapid succession.

Erwin shot to his feet. He raised his muscular arms and adopted a position from which to throw the heavy slab of plastic wrapped beer cans at the intruders. Police or civilians Erwin did not care; they had interrupted his entertainment and therefore deserved to be punished. However as he raised the slab higher above his head, his eyes made contact with the eyes of a policeman. The police eyes were looking at Erwin from the other end of the barrel of a revolver. Erwin's instant assessment of the relative damage that his slab and the police revolver could inflict made him freeze.

He did not realise at that time that the slab of beer cans would later be part of his salvation. Under the explicit threat of the revolver pointed at the centre of his muscled chest, Erwin slowly lowered the slab of beer cans to the cigarette butt littered brown carpet. Other police shepherded him into a passage way where a senior constable stood with a clipboard and pen, recording names and addresses of all at the violent porno video show.

When the name was given and senior constable was certain that the person understood English, he issued the standard caution about the right to remain silent, etc in a monotonous droning voice. The senior constable had a duty to deliver the caution but felt no obligation to render it in any way that provided aural enjoyment to the sleazebags he was helping to arrest. He guessed that some of the names given to him were false. At this stage, it didn't matter. He would check their identities later. If a false name and address was found to have been given, the police would have an additional charge against the smart arse.

Erwin listened to the policeman who asked for his name and address in the sing song catechism that usually occurs when a person is required to recite the same information repetitiously. Erwin was told by the senior constable that he was required to give his correct name and address because the arresting officer believed, on reasonable grounds, that he, Erwin, had committed an offence under Section 70 of the Crimes Act, namely, possession of child pornography.

Erwin recalled some extremely useful information given to him by Leonard the lawyer after his first arrest. Leonard's advice, to be certain to antagonise the arresting officer, caused Erwin to respond by turning his head and cupping his ear. The policeman repeated the required request for his name and address and the reason for the request. This time the policeman added that any refusal to comply was an offence.

Erwin again cupped his ear, screwed up his face in concentration, uttered the sound of "Ay?" in a quizzical tone and seemed to look dazed as the policeman began his recital in a louder voice for the third time. Behind Erwin other alleged porno perverts awaited processing. They were pushing and shoving amongst themselves at the apparent delay, a strange manifestation of impatience, and the police officers were obviously irritated at the time being taken to process Erwin.

When the policeman was halfway through the third recital and eyeing Erwin doubtfully, Erwin pushed his face forward and shouted, "You stupid bastard, I heard you the first two times" then Erwin began loud brays of laughter. He had turned so that his fellow arrestees could appreciate his defiance and join him in laughing. Their laughter was a bit forced but it inspired them to more robust jostling of the police. The pushing and shoving in the narrow corridor increased as the mob confidence returned.

Erwin was turned away from the senior constable with the clipboard so he did not see the swift knee in dark blue trousers that connected viciously with his testicles. He immediately grabbed his traumatised scrotum and pitched himself forward to lay on the floor screaming at the intensity of the pain partly attributable to the excited stage of his gonads caused by watching the half hour or so of the pornographic video. Some of the other porno perverts began yelling at the police claiming brutality. Erwin had turned a relatively orderly arrest into an affray.

He felt his hands being twisted away from his throbbing testicles and handcuffed behind his back. Because of his somewhat higher than normal capacity to absorb pain, Erwin was able to recall further gems of advice from Leonard. He shouted that his arrest was a mistake and that he would willingly give his name and address to the police at the police station. And as he was dragged to his feet he again shouted that he would give his name and address but he had the right to know the name, rank and police station of the policeman making the demand of him.

By now the porn perverts who had previously been compliant realised that they outnumbered the police. Erwin's act of defiance infected them to the extent that, they too, became more unruly. The police had missed a person when rounding up the porno perverts. Someone turned off the house lights at the fuse box and pandemonium broke out. Guessing that the police would not use firearms in the dark, the porn perverts lashed out. Several of the police were assaulted, at least one sustaining an injury requiring hospital treatment. Erwin scored several kicks on shins despite his prone position, before a shot into the ceiling from a police pistol brought some order. The lights were turned back on and most of those arrested were roughly pushed into divisional vans.

Of the nineteen men assembled to watch the porno video, only twelve were conveyed to the police station. Others escaped because the police were too busy trying to restrain the struggling dozen to coordinate any pursuit. On arrival at the police station, Erwin's demeanour became different, not because of fear but simply to carry into effect Leonard's advice to cause confusion.

He asked politely to be separated from the other persons arrested so he could give his name and address without his right to privacy being violated. He did not want the other persons present to know his personal details. He had to make the polite request several times before the woman police constable wrote down his request. Separated from the pack of perverts, Erwin readily provided his name and address and confirmed the details by showing his driver's licence. The woman police constable was very wary because her colleagues had told her of Erwin's belligerent behaviour at the porno video house. She also appeared anxious to maintain space between them because she considered men who attended child porno video shows as likely to be bearers of a contagious disease.

However Erwin's almost excessively respectful and polite behaviour to her did earn him some concession in that he was able to quickly get a phone call to his lawyer. He told Leonard of his current location and the police brutality to which he had been subjected and of the police charges. Leonard promised to be there, with Polaroid camera, early the next morning.

Erwin detested the fellow inmates of the cell block who were rowdy and full of complaints because he hoped to get some sleep as the pain in his private parts receded. He knew he had nothing to worry about so far as the police charges were concerned. His trustees had recently informed him that his inherited investment portfolio was robustly healthy and with the surety that he could pay the bill for the services of Leonard, Erwin stretched out on the hard bunk bed to sleep.

To aid his efforts to sink into slumber Erwin turned his thoughts towards pleasurable activities and imagined himself dismembering thousands of fruit packers who persisted in sticking little labels that he found difficult to remove on apples and oranges. He was motivated by the mental image of filthy, grotesque, gap-tooth harridans slobbering on the adhesive labels to dampen the glue before sticking the labels on the clean fruit. He soon sank into a deep, restorative, sleep.

CHAPTER NINE

BRYN TELEPHONED AUNTIE AND OFFERED his assistance with making a compensation claim with the insurance company. He said that his help would expedite her search for replacements for her much loved figurines. Auntie was so upset with the intrusion into her house and the theft of her beloved figurines that Bryn had difficulty in properly communicating. But eventually Bryn became sure that he had an appointment with her for next Thursday at 10am.

He went by train. As he approached Auntie's house, Bryn noticed a Holden Commodore parked outside. Instinct told him it was a police vehicle and his hand went to the top pocket of his reefer jacket to check that he had one of his father's business cards there. As he stretched a hand to twist the old fashioned door bell, the door was opened by a fit looking man wearing clothes similar to his own, except for the colour of the tie. The same height as Bryn, 183 cm, but heavier. The man looked him in the eye with the direct stare of a man who is accustomed to asking questions and receiving answers.

In response to a demand as to his name and business, Bryn took his father's business card from his pocket and proffered it to the obvious policeman, saying that he had an appointment with the householder to discuss insurance on recently stolen items.

The policeman told him to wait and turned back into the house, returning a few minutes later to hold open the door and introduce himself as a police detective. "OK" he said, "The old girl is expecting a solicitor". The business card evidently led the detective to conclude that Bryn worked for his father's legal firm. Bryn took no pains to disabuse him. Bryn was conducted down a passage to the kitchen where Auntie sat at a table covered with the impedimenta of tea brewing. Auntie looked every one of her 78 years and more. Her voice had the tremble of uncertainly as she acknowledged Bryn's presence.

The detective was openly inspecting Bryn and asked him if he had ever visited the house before. Auntie seemed to have recovered somewhat because she told the detective that Bryn had never visited her, so all Bryn had to do was nod his head in confirmation. The next question directed at Bryn by the detective was how long had his legal firm represented Auntie. Again she precluded his answer by answering "Over thirty years" to which Bryn again nodded.

As a final statement, the detective said that Bryn appeared a bit young to be a solicitor handling a case. Bryn readily agreed saying that he was still at the University but helped out his father's law firm with simple matters such as this insurance claim. Seemingly satisfied that Bryn was not a suspect and out of earshot of Auntie, the detective confided to Bryn that the police could find no witnesses, no fingerprints or other forensic evidence save the shreds of bubble pack. The detective told him that the chance of recovery of the stolen figurines was infinitesimal. These shreds led the detective to conclude that the burglary was a professional job, probably undertaken by a career criminal on behalf of a rival figurine collector. The prognosis of the detective was that the figurines would not surface until well after the death of the old lady.

After making his customary statement of comfort to the distressed victim, the detective shaped to depart. His final advice to Bryn was that the old lady should either have a security system installed or she should consider moving to a retirement village to ensure that she would be cared for in a secure environment. He walked out of the door casting an approving glance at the repaired glass panel in the front door.

Bryn spent the next hour alternatively consoling Auntie and deliberately deceiving her by making the insurance claim procedure appear frightfully complicated. Several times Auntie became incoherent as grief at the loss of her "children", her figurines, reduced her to tears and caused wracking convulsive movements of her small aged body. Eventually Bryn was asked by the distressed lady to take over the entire job of making the insurance claim. Untroubled by any twinge of conscience, he smiled as he reassured Auntie that he would do his best. Bryn telephoned the insurance company and made arrangements to meet an insurance assessor at the site of the robbery later that afternoon.

The assessor arrived, as arranged, and was a male, about 30 years of age, looking primly business like in a light grey suit. He had a copy of the preliminary Victoria Police report and had been briefed by more experienced insurance supervisors who reached a conclusion much the same as the police, ie, that a professional collector had targeted Auntie's collection of figurines and had them stolen by a professional thief. The assessor was quietly sympathic to Auntie and he and Bryn worked together to complete the detailed claim form. For both it was an easy task because Auntie's lever arch file contained details of each purchase and photographs of every figurine. Although the photos were a bit amateurish they were more than adequate for detailed identification. The insurance assessor had perceptive instincts. In a conversational way he asked Auntie about Bryn. Had he been a regular visitor to the house? "No" replied Auntie, "Until her solicitor sent him to the house after the burglary, he had never visited the house until this morning. I already told that to the police". Auntie's reply assured Bryn's credibility.

The nearest Auntie came to a smile that day occurred when the assessor slipped in an innocent question a little later. "Was Bryn a fellow collector of china figurines?" Auntie's lips widened when she told him that Bryn looked at the photographs with total uninterest of the age, style, maker and value of her beloved "babies". Any vestige of suspicion the insurance assessor may have had about Bryn evaporated when Auntie said that a dedicated collector recognises the gleam in the eye of another devotee when shown a photo of an illustrious piece. But, she added, "To Bryn, the only reaction to the photos was that of total incomprehension as to why anyone would want to collect such boring items". Thus Bryn's genuine disinterest in the artistic merit of the figurines acted in his favour and as fatigue and emotion began to reduce Auntie's ability to understand the comments of the assessor, he addressed himself increasingly to Bryn.

The "waiting period", the time before a claim could be settled by financial compensation, would be 30 days as per the fine print in the insurance policy. During that time, the assessor told Bryn, the insurance company's investigators would be making enquires among collectors and antique dealers in the hope that Auntie's collection or pieces thereof may appear. But he expressed little hope of recovery, suggesting that individual pieces could be taken out of the county relatively easily and sold into the specialist markets in Europe and America.

When eventually the assessor rose to depart, Bryn was becoming convinced that his first entry into the realm of criminality appeared promising. It was just as well that the assessor could not see Bryn's face as they walked down the dimly lit corridor, passed the front room crime scene and out to the verandah, because the assessor's penultimate comment was that the insurance policy was based upon replacement value. That would be around $60,000 and a cheque would be issued after the 30 days expired.

Confirmation of his mother's earlier advice of insurance of $60,000 caused an incontrollable grin to briefly light up Bryn's face until he regained control and thanked the assessor. As the assessor drove off Bryn allowed the grin to return to his young face, briefly. He composed himself and returned to Auntie, who was washing up the afternoon tea dishes. Expressing counterfeit concern Bryn asked Auntie about her living arrangements and promised to call again to help if needed. Auntie's "thank you" and expressions of appreciation followed him as he left the house and walked to the railway station to catch a train home. He considered that a day off from his University studies would do him no harm and that he had achieved far more to advance his career than by application to study.

Over the next two weeks Bryn visited Auntie three times, each visiting lasting about an hour. One visit was less tedious that the other two because he persuaded his mother to accompany him to listen to old Auntie's reminiscences. Nearing the end of the 30 day waiting period Bryn telephoned the insurance assessor. He said that he wasn't pushing but would like to know when the insurance cheque may be sent to Auntie. The enquiry, he said, was on behalf of his father's law firm who had advised Auntie to apply the insurance claim towards a deposit on a unit in a retirement village.

Bryn emphasised that Auntie would be more secure in an environment where she would receive more care and the assessor concurred. The assessor agreed that a retirement village would be a good move. He told Bryn that the $60,000 could be credited direct to Auntie's bank account or posted and Bryn suggested that Auntie being of the "old school" would feel better to receive a cheque. So it was arranged that the cheque would be posted to arrive on a Tuesday and when the cheque was banked, "That", said the assessor, "Would be the end so far as the insurance company was concerned".

Bryn visited Auntie to tell her the good news. But he never mentioned $60,000. Instead he told her of the good news that her entire collection of figurines had been recovered by the insurance company, completely intact and he would arrange for the delivery of them to her on Tuesday. Auntie was extremely appreciative and apologised for breaking down and crying and Bryn was appropriately commiserative. He told Auntie several times that it would be unwise to tell people about the return of her stolen collection to avoid another theft. Auntie agreed.

Tuesday morning Bryn recovered the sports bag from the locker at the Marina and delivered the figurines to Auntie. She was overwhelmed with gratitude as Bryn helped her carefully unpack each figurine from the plastic bubble wrap. It took some time for her to lovingly wipe down each one as if the thief had contaminated them. Auntie sat on a padded footstool while Bryn sat on the floor beside her as she told him of the history and provenance of each. He nearly fell asleep with boredom.

During the unwrapping process, the mailman arrived and deposited one letter in the letterbox. Bryn brought it in to Auntie, explaining that the insurance company had sent the cheque almost simultaneously with the recovery of her figurines. So, at Bryn's recommendation, Auntie signed her name on the back of the cheque then on a sheet of her lilac notepaper wrote a short letter of appreciation to the insurance company for Bryn to deliver on her behalf. As Bryn left, Auntie insisted on giving him $100 in appreciation of his help during her time of oppressive grief and his help in the alleviation of that grief. Bryn gave her a kiss on the cheek to show affection then headed for home.

In the privacy of his room, Bryn snapped on a pair of rubber gloves, took out a briefcase containing the details of his fake company, United Reinstatements Pty Ltd and a self inking stamp bearing the company name. Testing the stamp on a scrap of paper a couple of times. He carefully imprinted the stamp above Auntie's signature on the back of the insurance company's $60,000 cheque. He wrote the word "Pay" above that, using the same pen he had loaned to Auntie to affix her signature. The briefcase also held a bank deposit book; one deposit slip he tore out, completed then placed it in a "quick deposit" envelope with the endorsed cheque.

The test stamping paper was torn and flushed down the toilet. The rubber gloves he returned to the briefcase and handling the quick deposit envelope only with a handkerchief put on a floppy sun hat. Bryn drove for about 20 minutes then dropped the envelope through the slot of the quick deposit box at a branch of the bank several suburbs away from the bank at which he had established the account of United Reinstatements Pty Ltd.

Bryn reckoned that if the insurance company ever decided to check on the presentation of the cheque sent to Auntie, his explanation to the assessor about Auntie's purchase of a retirement unit would explain the assignment of the cheque. Whether they did verify the deposit of the cheque or not, Bryn never found out, because the matter was never raised again. After depositing the cheque, Bryn drove on to the University just in time to attend the last class of the afternoon. Academically it was a waste of time because he absorbed nothing. Rather he rigorously reviewed the events of the last five weeks to test his precautions. True there were a couple of small gaps. But time would eliminate those as the memory of people would attenuate with time making his risk level diminish to an eventual vanishing point. The uneventful clearance of the $60,000 cheque would vindicate his scheme. Maybe, just maybe, his precautions were a bit too extreme but he took comfort from those precautions.

Bryn held that if everything goes according to plan then precautions appear superfluous. But seldom does everything go to plan; had he experienced "beginner's luck" this time? If, for some unaccountable reason, an impediment had occurred, the precautions he had taken would be totally justified. Even if the police found out about Auntie's figurines being returned, Bryn had in place sufficient of the attribute he first heard of in relation to the disgraced former President of the USA, Richard Nixon – that attribute was called "Credible deniability". Bryn was a zealot when it came protection; Bryn had no contempt for caution.

After depositing Auntie's $60,000 insurance cheque into the bank account of "his" dodgy company United Reinstatements Pty Ltd, Bryn continued his caution, for example, when a month later he went to the business suite where the mail box for his company's address was located, he spent over half an hour observing the approaches to the doorway. He entered the premises wearing his floppy hat and requested photocopies of some magazine articles from the only person present, a young woman at the counter. While she was making the copies on the copying machine he scanned the ceiling and cornices for evidence of the installation of any CCTV since his last visit.

Only when satisfied that all was clear and after paying for the photocopying did he insert his key into the mail box and extract the half a dozen letters inside. Closing the box and extracting the key he looked at the female shop assistant to detect any unusual interest, but she had her back to him and seemed completely absorbed in other work at her computer. Still, to be sure, Bryn walked smartly from the business suite and continued along the footpath to a nearby park where he sat in a secluded hedged area for another half an hour of heart thumping apparent idleness. With no interest being shown in him, except for a few hopeful pigeons, he opened the first letter with fingers made nervous by his adrenalin rush.

One envelope contained an invoice from the business suite mail shop advising that the three month rental of United Reinstatements Pty Ltd would soon expire. The second letter contained a bank statement showing that the $60,000 cheque had cleared, whilst two of the remaining letters contained adverts and another was from an alleged doctor in Nigeria, addressed to the Chairman of the Bryn's bogus company. In stilted English the doctor sought an urgent and confidential business relationship re the transfer of US $18 million into the account of United Reinstatements Pty Ltd for which service Bryn's dodgy company would obtain 25%. The letter explained at length a situation that resulted for the transition from the previous military regime to a western style democracy and massive unaccounted for funds in a Petroleum Trust Fund that was now forgotten.

The Nigerian simply requested that Bryn's company telex the name, address, bank account number plus other details for the deal to be done. Bryn's pent up tension relaxed when he read the obvious conman's letter. Bryn had a nephew who collected stamps and thought that the stamp may please the boy so he went to tear it off when he realised it was a useless printed forgery. All irrelevant correspondence was torn into pieces and bits placed in rubbish tins in the park and in the next street.

Next day, to test again the safety of the company's bank account, Bryn took the company's credit card and went to a shop that sold up – market office supplies. He ordered a leather, gold-rimmed embossed, financial year diary and requested that the initials AFH be printed in gold on the front cover. Bryn paid for the diary and gold leaf printing with the credit card of United Reinstatements Pty Ltd. He accepted the receipt and told the salesman to hold the luxury diary for collection.

Bryn's testing procedure was based on the fact that the person who he had registered as chairman of the company was a fellow Uni student, a despicable, boozy bastard with no interest in sport but active in promoting his own version of anarchy. Bryn had an aversion to anyone wanting to change a system that he believed held opportunities for wealth. So Bryn had used the student record details to appoint the man with the initials AFH as chairman of the company that he planned to use as a front for his profitable and illegal business.

In assessing how to register United Reinstatements, Bryn had considered using entirely faked names and addresses but on further reflection decided to use the names of actual people to introduce uncertainty should any investigations lead to the company. The only minor changes he made to the names were the displacements of a letter in a surname, for example the boozy anarchist bastard he despised was named Hilliard. Bryn spelt it Hillard on the registration form with all other information, date of birth and place of birth being correct.

As anarchists vehemently oppose all organisations and institutions, Bryn figured that no one would check to see if Hilliard was a company director. And if they did make the connection the natural assumption would be that the declared anti-social anarchist had deliberately misspelt the name as part of his protest. Any counter action by Hilliard would confuse the issue of company ownership even more. Bryn was satisfied that he had selected an impeccably credentialed scapegoat. If something went wrong and United Reinstatements was to be subjected to an investigation, who would believe an anarchist who was on record many times as stating that any lie was justified in advancement of the anarchist cause?

A week later Bryn made another visit to the up-market shop where he collected the impressive diary and walked to the business suite where he paid a twelve month rental for the mail box, using the credit card for a second time. The same young lady shop attendant slipped the credit card through the machine in a practiced routine with no hesitation and Bryn signed a reasonable facsimile of Mr AFH's name on the receipt.

Later that day Bryn used a Student Union computer to print a brief note to AFH from an anonymous admirer and ardent supporter of the anarchist movement. He attached the luxury diary and left it on the Union office counter where he was certain it would be delivered to AFH by one of his misguided minions. Bryn had many inward laughs after that as he saw his selected scapegoat striding around the Uni with the expensive diary ostentatiously displayed. It was a bit like a monk from an order that espoused poverty being seen wearing an Armani suit.

Certain now that his first criminal escapade was undetected Bryn began a regular withdrawal system from the United Reinstatements bank account using the credit card several times each week, at different locations to withdraw modest amounts averaging $500 each time. His floppy hat and sunglasses were put on shortly before approaching the Automatic Teller Machine to render his appearance on the bank CCTV less precise.

In between his nefarious activities Bryn found time to do some serious study as part of his long term plan depended upon him passing his first year with respectable marks. He was assisted in finding time for his studies when the Uni football team failed to make the September finals thus dramatically reducing his commitment to training and allowing him extra time to study.

As well as serious application to Uni assignments, Bryn spent time in mastering seafaring techniques. Skippers of sail and power boats seem naturally inclined towards sharing their knowledge with persons they perceive as truly dedicated to learning. Bryn's obvious love of the sea meant he had many willing mentors. The diversity of advice created no confusion, rather advice from one skipper reinforced that of another. The opportunity to practice skills under expert tutelage was priceless, especially the deep water, off shore, power boat cruiser when Bryn materially assisted in every item on the pre-departure check list.

Fuel and oil for twin diesels, spare fully charged batteries, fresh water, navigation charts on which to pre-plan the journey with waypoints to be checked against GPS readings, VHF radio, SSB radio and a back-up set permanently turned to the weather frequency, EPIRB – Emergency Position Indicator Radio Beacon, tide tables, depth sounder, radar, PFD's – sufficient personal floating devices (offshore quality) for crew and passengers; all the essentials for safe power cruiser trips were Bryn's domain once he won the confidence of his skippers.

He became a familiar figure around the Marina, on first name terms with the security guards who policed the main gate on a roster during peak season. And he walked without attracting any undue attention around various slips, cleaning areas and storage locker rooms. Because it was known that he crewed for several skippers, Bryn's presence in any area was unremarkable.

On trips to the ocean beyond the entrance to Port Phillip Bay, the purpose was blue water fishing with skilled, dedicated and totally thorough skippers. Bryn learned seamanship. However on power cruiser trips within Port Phillip Bay, the purpose of the trip was that of a social gathering spiced with titillating tales of transgressions of business colleagues with some fishing as a side line to the drinking and discussion of business deals. Bryn learned more of the lurks and loopholes in the legal, commercial and medical systems. He stored the information way in his trained memory bank, "on-hold" until after the year one Uni exams. Skippers of the in-Bay "social boats" were considerably less skilled than their deep water fellow seamen, so they appreciated Bryn's capabilities and left more and more duties to him for which they rewarded him with substantial tips.

These tips allowed Bryn to equip himself with the best polarised sunglasses and a personal kit including all the necessaries for comfort on the water. Sunscreen, insect repellent, a top PFD, a GPS Personal Locator Beacon and binoculars, all of which he stored in a locker he hired at the Marina under a contrived name. Year end Uni results were published and Bryn achieved excellent grades in Accounting and Commercial Law with adequate passes in other subjects. His parents were delighted with the result but had they known that Bryn considered his formal education finished, they may have been extremely disturbed. However Bryn had no intention of communicating his intentions to them or indeed to anyone else.

During the Uni summer recess, a permanent recess so far as Bryn was concerned, he advanced his road to riches using the knowledge gained from the Uni and the "social event" motor cruise parties. He believed that his first criminal enterprise that yielded $60,000 was as good an omen as a pragmatist who didn't believe in omens could expect. It had succeeded because of his correct appreciation of the factors involved.

His main concern was for the build up of cash that he was regularly withdrawing from the United Reinstatements company's bank account. He needed another source of reliable income and also a less clumsy method of moving money. And with around $60,000 to finance his undertaking he was, as the Accounting lecturer often emphasised, adequately capitalised. An essential element in whatever scheme that he evolved was protection from prosecution. Bryn had no contempt for caution. Bryn was prepared to expend whatever time it took to plan a watertight scheme to exploit the business system. But fate complies with the plans of no mortal.

CHAPTER TEN

BRYN'S THOUGHTS INCREASINGLY FOCUSSED ON the weaknesses of the insurance industry as his route to riches. His seed capital originated from the successful defrauding of an insurance company. As Bryn was only nineteen and impressionable, he was inevitably influenced by adages. The adage he had heard wafting on waves of alcoholics' breaths in the aft entertainment area of motor cruisers was "know your enemy". This he resolved to do by reading every book and magazine he could acquire on the subject. One of the best magazines for his purposes was a monthly magazine published in the USA by the insurance loss industry. He discovered a copy of it in a technical book and magazine shop. It not only described bogus claims for staged motor vehicle accidents in detail, but also provided blueprints of how investigators were uncovering crimes against the insurance and other related industries.

Over the summer Uni holidays Bryn spent hundreds of hours on the water. The alcoholic social events in the bay provided innumerable tips as to the identities of lawyers with malleable ethics, doctors with an immunity to ethical dilemmas and accountants with imaginative methods of presenting company accounts to the Australian Taxation Office.

Inspirational voyages of another nature were those he crewed with dedicated skippers of sail and power craft on the open ocean. One trip from Melbourne to Sydney increased his mastery of radio, navigation and weather estimation. He learned helm responses to cragged topped waves in a mild storm. The experience emotionally transformed him, temporarily, from all thought of anything except the sun, sea, sky and sailing.

The return trip, Sydney to Melbourne, tested the skipper and crew as the weather failed to behave as predicted by the Weather Bureau and the wind reached six on the Beaufort Scale. Faced with an adverse wind, white capped waves and a malfunctioning bilge pump, the craft was forced to seek shelter in the port of Eden for 24 hours. Bryn entertained few fears during the sleepless event and relished the opportunity to gain experience under the tutelage of the skilful skipper.

Not all of his time was spent out of bed. As a personable, physically fit young man with thick dark blonde hair and a clean, suntanned complexion, he shared time in bed with willing wanton women from the Uni Faculty of Arts. There seemed to be an unending supply and he did his best to cope with the demand but without ever confusing physical attraction with emotional commitment. He formed no relationship that he could not terminate, abruptly and unfeelingly if necessary, after a few weeks. He feared lest propinquity may lead to propagation.

Apart from a few household tasks to keep his Mum and Dad happy, Bryn used his time and planned then planned again, tested the plans, improved as necessary and incorporated a degree of flexibility to deal with unexpected situations that could occur. Each plan involved patience and protection.

Several of the Uni "drop outs" with whom Bryn maintained contact were recruited as "runners" or "cut outs", to conceal his true identity from all other than his inner coterie. Bryn now referred to himself as John in dealing with them and insisted they use that name exclusively when dealing with him. The "drop outs" had either obtained jobs which they needed to accept as indicators of their intellectual "pecking order" level or were still in the soul testing process of looking for a remunerative occupation commensurate with their proven limited ability, though it be less than their heart's desire. Judicicious distribution of $50 notes was all it took for Bryn to divert their attention from their existing impecunious living conditions towards his promise of a lucrative lifestyle. Of the eight informal interviews he conducted, two young men were selected as his first recruits.

The primary purpose of each "runner" was to establish a barrier between Bryn and other members of what would become a mini multitude. The multitude only ever heard of a "Mr Big" by the name "John" or "Johnny". On the rare occasions that Bryn was forced, by the complexity of the circumstances, to meet face to face with a member of the multitude, the meeting took place without any runner or other observers and in noisy discos or dimly lit areas.

A second task of each runner was to recruit suitable, slightly crooked males and females as members of the multitude. Bryn ensured that runners never met each other to lessen the chance of collusion to cheat him and to avoid any ambitious runner gaining sufficient information of his entire operation as to become a competitor, or worse, trying to become a hostile partner.

Throughout the next decade, the recruiting of suitable new runners was Bryn's most onerous task. The runners were Bryn's prime protective barrier and as such were essential. Bryn's empire began small but blossomed magnificently. As expected, there were a few interesting moments but Bryn's respect of the precautions caused only scratches not any maiming injuries, and the business of systematically defrauding insurance companies became his principal occupation.

By the time of his twenty first birthday, he had perfected "staged accidents" to the degree that it became an art form. At a carefully selected venue such as sporting club or a hotel, a member of the multitude, "a spotter" would identify an emerging expensive new car with a lone driver. The spotter signalled the driver of the older car, "a wreck" containing three passengers. At a pre selected stretch of road, the older car screeched away from the curb, abruptly cut in front of the new car, slammed on its brakes and the lone driver of the new car inevitably crashed into the rear of the old wreck.

The driver of the old wreck would stagger out and loudly and belligerently accuse the lone driver of the expensive car of negligent driving. The passengers in the old wreck would tumble out and collapse, crying and screaming at the pain of the concocted injuries. The indignant driver of the expensive vehicle would react by trying to deny any fault, but one or two "independent" witnesses providentially appeared and firmly stated that they saw the entire event and the lone driver was solely, and perhaps even criminally, at fault.

Police and ambulance were called. At one of every three staged accidents the breathalyser results showed the driver of the old wreck to be totally free of alcohol but the lone driver of the expensive car was recorded as having a blood alcohol reading. Even if the blood alcohol reading was below the legal limit, the fact that any alcohol reading registered put the lone driver in disadvantageous position. Exacerbating that were the "independent" witness statements and the lone driver's situation, so far as defending himself or herself in the following insurance claims, was hopelessly eroded. The common understanding in traffic accidents is that you are at fault if you smash into the rear end of another car. And it was deemed a gift from the gods to Bryn's team if the police breathalyser reading showed the lone driver to have an alcohol reading in excess of the legal limit.

The driver of the old wreck, his passengers and the so called independent witness were all members of Bryn's, or as the multitude knew him, "Johnny's", accident victim crews. The same group took it in turns to be the driver, passenger and independent witnesses, changing names and utilising the addresses of unsuspecting acquaintances to make detection more difficult. So well were the accidents staged that the accident victim crew seldom sustained any injury at all. And on the rare occasion when a nose or a finger was broken, it was pragmatically accepted as an occupational hazard.

After each "accident" the driver and his three injured passengers first called at a medical clinic with which "Johnny" had an "arrangement". Each of the four was diagnosed with numerous injuries that would require lengthy treatment from a range of practioners including chiropractors, massage therapists and sometimes psychiatrists. One of "Johnny's" lawyers was the second stop for the injured parties where extravagant claims against the lone driver of the expensive car were made. Given the independent witness statements, police reports and the exaggerated medical reports, the lawyers had a relatively easy task in obtaining a satisfactory level of compensation from the insurance company of the lone driver.

Rarely did a "sucker" driver resolve to fight the accusations levelled against his driving in the light of the apparently overwhelming weight of independent evidence. However whenever really determined opposition was encountered, Johnny's instruction to the lawyers was to back off. Nothing must be done that may have any propensity to attract the attention of law enforcement authorities. Bryn recalled a quotation from the American motivator, Norman Vincent Peale "Part of the happiness of life is not in fighting battles but in avoiding them. A masterly retreat is in itself a victory".

Bryn's scheme grossed his team of doctors $50,000 for each patient / accident victim. In as much as the patient / victim made only one, five minute, visit to the Clinic to sign the Medicare claim forms, the doctors prospered. Bryn received half of that gross from which his expenses to his runners and via them to the "victim" amounted to $5,000 leaving him $20,000. With a car load consisting of a driver and three passengers that totalled $80,000 per accident. At 30 accidents per year Bryn received $2.4 million in tax free cash during his first full twelve months in operation. Some of his best "passenger / accident victims" and "independent witness" were ordinary housewives.

Australia's six States allowed him to instruct his runners to move teams of the best accident / victim actors throughout the country to avoid establishing a pattern with too frequent a repetition of the same scenario in any one State. Several interstate "business" visits per year by star actors in his multitude of players proved more expensive but still disgracefully profitable to the mystical person that his players increasingly began to refer affectionately to as "Mr Johnny". For "Mr Johnny" the slightly lesser amount of remuneration from interstate operations was offset by the protection offered by diversification. Diversification was as theme frequently emphasised by his Economics Lecturer at the Uni. Additionally, staff amenities were negligible in the insurance fraud racket so the crews appeared happy with the holiday-like atmosphere associated with interstate jobs.

Arrangements with flexibly minded lawyers and medical providers who interpreted the Hippocratic Oath with more pliancy than compliance were easy to locate via Bryn's established network. A working relationship was maintained with like minded entrepreneurs for a bit of unofficial referral remuneration. Motor vehicle staged accidents were central to Bryn's business empire, but were only a fraction of what he developed into an enormously diverse, complex web of profitability over a ten year period.

Apart from participating in the proceeds of Medicare payments for medical treatment services never rendered, Bryn obtained the lion's share of special compensation payments made to his accident victims. Not every one of the "accident" victims received huge sums, indeed only six times in five years was Bryn able to substitute a person who was already a paraplegic for a regular crew member, moving the ringer by stealth interstate. But the multi million dollar compensation payouts the imposter paraplegics generated was certainly worth the effort. Via a financial planner with adaptable morals, a large proportion of the capital sum compensation payments were channelled into investments in one of Bryn's newly formed companies. With unsuspecting directors, each dodgy company closed down during the financial year in which it was formed, after being drained of its assets. Bryn picked up close to eight million dollars from those enterprises.

However whilst the big buck bangs were rewarding for the cash and allowed justifiable self congratulations on the exquisite planning, the bread and butter cases were sweet too.

The big bucks cases were always subject to scrutiny from several sources beyond the influence of Bryn to control hence the inordinate amount of meticulous planning to ensure each resulted not only in a success, but that no suspicions were aroused that could lead to further investigation. Smaller compensation claims for "accidents" attracted far less scrutiny. It could safely be accepted that the various insurance agencies viewed claims below $50,000 as a nuisance and pushed the paperwork into a system where, provided each box in the questionnaire had a cross in the right square, a payment spewed out the other end as a matter of routine. Particularly was this so when a motor vehicle registered in one State was involved in an "accident" in another State.

Assuming the avenue to affluence to be an art form, Bryn's masterpiece was a van load of elderly citizens rammed in the rear by the driver of a brand new Mercedes Benz S500 who, unfortunately for his insurance company, was breathalysed at double the legal alcohol limit. Bryn netted close to six million dollars from the staggeringly large variety of complex medical treatments and compensation payments that resulted.

Pursuant to the principles of business taught to him in his first year at the Uni, Bryn embraced both vertical and lateral integration and received regular remuneration from motor vehicle repair shops for the amount of business he shunted their way. Many of the motor vehicles used in staged accidents were supplied from these enterprising businessmen and a significant number of written off wrecks were rebirthed. Some employees of repair shops and even one business owner himself were regular "players" as were several tow truck drivers. Their technical advice was used to add to the verisimilitude of the accidents. A Holden Commodore car had more resurrections that a football team composed of biblical men named Lasuras. After twenty accidents under twenty different registration number plates, the long service Commodore was eventually consigned to a smelter, thereby permanently dissolving any evidence.

It was ironic that Bryn's business banged up passenger conveyances on the one hand whilst on the other he used several companies purporting to be travel agencies as part of his money laundering procedure for the $600,000 per year in cash received as commissions from motor vehicle repair shops.

Not wishing to let easy money go to waste, quite a few of Bryn's ephemeral companies were owners of recently purchased "rebirthed' motor vehicles that were subsequently reported stolen, then found as burnt out wrecks, for which Bryn's bodgy companies in each State received insurance payments. Half a million dollars a year was a regular addition to Bryn's treasury with the advantage that the cheque payments helped the recipient business to appear more legitimate after so much inflow of cash payments.

As a natural progression of horizontal integration a regular regime of remuneration emanated from the tow truck companies who genuinely and generously appreciated being informed in advance of an accident.

Insurance Brokers referred by players via the runners were another source of cash. At least once a year in each State a dodgy company of Bryn's was sued by a "phantom" employee for wrongful dismissal or sexual harassment. This resulted in a claim, via the accommodating broker, against the Directors and Officers policy recently taken out by the dodgy company. After three financially successful years, changes by State governments to the Occupational Health and Safety Acts made the fraudulent practice less remunerative and higher in risk. Bryn was philosophic and rather than fight a government, a costly business, he recalled the Norman Vincent Peale quote and remained thankful for the tax free one million dollars obtained with so little effort.

Another mediocre business abandoned after a few years was his kick back business from medical equipment suppliers, run in tandem with the staged accidents. There was insufficient market volume for his victim / players to require the "phantom" hire of wheelchairs, commodes, and walking frames but it enabled Bryn to obtain an insight into the structure and character of the business and he formed several companies, having titles that inferred they were hiring out medical equipment. Using directors with the names of blissfully ignorant residents of an institution whose personal details were published in full in a government gazette when they were declared protected persons, Bryn maintained his protective barrier.

Drugs acquired by ethically challenged hospital administrators using the identities of patients in palliative care was a profitable enterprise for several years.

Competition from DIY "back yard" manufacturers of amphetamines using drugs purchased over the counter at chemist shops and supermarkets was not acute, at first. But the tightening of State laws and the withdrawal from shelves of chemist shops of easily obtainable raw material caused the DIY manufacturers to intrude on Bryn's quiet scam of the Pharmaceutical Benefits Scheme (PBS).

Consequently the Australian Federal Police stepped up surveillance of the PBS. Greater publicity too, inspired medical professionals to monitor more closely prescriptions issued in hospitals. The increase in risk and decrease in reward motivated Bryn to vacate and destroy all evidence of his involvement, except in one Sydney hospital where to close down the well entrenched, modest operation may have risked unacceptable exposure to Bryn's established operator. He did however curtail the magnitude of the operation to minimise risk and although it then became barely viable Bryn looked on it as a long term venture that could give him access to more exotic drugs should he ever have need in the future. It had scope for resurrection if circumstances changed at a later date.

Generally, Bryn steered clear of illegal activities involving the Australian Federal Police because of the remit of the AFP over the entire continent. Bryn realised from listening to high priced lawyers boasting on the motor cruisers that loopholes in jurisdictions existed between the States, especially between the maverick state of Western Australia, the Wild West, and its counterparts. Loopholes were loveable in Bryn's eyes so where possible his fraudulent ventures were perpetrated in one State and managed in another.

For the same reason as he abandoned the drugs, increased attention by the Australian Federal Police, Bryn abandoned another scheme involving selected hospital administrators who stored copies of the provider numbers of every doctor, present and past, who had been associated with the hospital in any capacity. Using that stored data bank at night, Bryn's player in the hospital clerical division would log in to the medical electronic claim system to bill and direct payments to Bryn's bodgy companies for non existent services. For several years he received payment for dead patients and made claims using names of adult married persons who were still listed as children on the Medicare card of their parents.

On guesswork, for he maintained only cryptic records on flimsy paper near an indoor hygienic waste disposal incinerator, Bryn thought close to two million dollars was his take from this scam for each of the five years it operated at full exploitation level.

Rumours from within the hospital that irate doctors were making enquiries about false claims in their names emanating from the hospital had Bryn of the verge of retreat. Then a major operator in the private hospital business made an offer to Bryn's representative of five hundred thousand dollars cash. The offer was made on behalf of a consortium of doctors and lawyers who were apparently operating a more sophisticated and larger scheme. Bryn's less well protected project was threatening to put into jeopardy their "inside scam". Bryn immediately accepted the cash and vacated the business to remain consistent to his self imposed discipline to avoid attracting the attention of the AFP. The consortium must have avoided adverse scrutiny because no publicity relating to any massive provider fraud ever surfaced so far as Bryn was aware. With over 150 medical personages directly involved, any discovery of the gigantic scam would have made front page news.

Another of Bryn's short lived but profitable ventures involved recycling previously occupied coffins but again the display of massive muscle power by some long established mortuary industry moguls induced a tactical withdrawal with a briefcase full of $50 notes and without scars.

But scars were inflicted during Bryn's years of undetected crime. He had just celebrated his twenty sixth birthday and was congratulating himself on accumulating his first fifty million dollars. One runner entertained aspirations beyond his ability and attempted to blackmail "Johnny" into allotting him a share of the staged accident business. In response to the impudent runner's demand for a sizeable chunk of cash, Bryn exhibited a carefully controlled visage that he hoped conveyed an element of fear. He agreed to meet the runner at the St Kilda Marina where the latest example of his passion for the sea, a seven metre motor cruiser was moored.

Several hours of preparation had preceded Bryn's counterfeit capitulation to the runner, a heavily muscled Samoan who, at 193 centimetres in his thongs towered over Bryn's 183 centimetres of more modestly constructed frame. Bryn factored into his plan the reality that he was significantly out weighed and out heightened and that his exhibition of fear would induce a degree of confidence in the runner as regards his ability to extract from Bryn a chunk of cash. At the Marina, Bryn adopted a subservient demeanour to accentuate their relative positions.

He led the massive runner into the cavernous corrugated iron roofed shed that housed lockers for boat owners to store spare gear, work tables for repairs, coin operated drink machines, an air compressor and high pressure hoses to wash the concrete floors. The entire shed was deserted and this seemed to diminish the confidence of the runner rather than engender assurance of privacy. The big Samoan pulled a knife from a fancy leather sheath that was concealed by his preposterously coloured Hawaiian styled loose shirt.

Confronted by a large, agitated man swishing a knife with a shiny 15 centimetre blade, Bryn felt some of his confidence fade and he backed up, with palms held in a placating gesture, along a path flanked by work tables covered with odd pieces of torn sails, plastic sheet and broken nylon cords. With a jerk of his head to indicate the direction, Bryn told the runner the $50,000 he wanted was in a wooden box on top of the last bank of lockers near the loading bay. Bryn kept moving slowly towards the rear of the shed to maintain a reasonable distance between his stomach and the tip of the sharp nickel plated knife blade.

Bryn had previously parked the wooden box on the top of the locker and then packed it with discarded engine parts found in rubbish bins around the loading bay. He did not tell that to his intimidator, instead he said that the money was in the bottom of the box protruding a little from the top of a bank of grey painted, lightly rusted, steel lockers. Despite his height, the box was too high for the runner to reach so he used his sizable foot to hook a bench closer to him. He gestured with the knife blade for Bryn to "back off", a command with which he obligingly complied.

Positioning the bench closer to the padlock festooned locker bank, the runner stood on it and reached for the wooden box. Even with his massive hands and muscles the box was too heavy to be budged with one hand so the runner again showed Bryn the knife point to indicate that a further back off was required. The knife was swiftly returned to the decorated sheath and the runner, standing tip toed on the bench, stretched upwards with both hands to collect the box.

Standing side on to Bryn he presented a massive but vulnerable target. From the work bench Bryn flipped aside a piece of black plastic sheet, pulled out a spear gun, aimed briefly and fired at this target from a range of five metres. The stainless steel spear, unimpeded by a recovery line, sped straight into the body of the runner precisely eight centimetres below his left armpit and buried itself deep into the massive thorax.

The runner toppled backwards and hit the bare concrete with his 160 kilogram body in a sickening fleshy slap thud that seemed to echo through the confines of the shed. Frothy pink bubbles spewed from the nose and mouth of the toppled Goliath. A few snorting noises and heaving of the chest were the final movements of the would-be extortionist.

Extracting the spear was an experience that Bryn would recall for many years. The barb prevented withdrawal though the entry wound and with the prospect of discovery increasing with every second of delay, Bryn tried several other ways of extraction before taking a hammer and with a dozen hits on the rear end, drove the spear tip and barb several centimetres out through the ribs on the other side of the body of the bleeding inert runner. Bryn seized the barbed spear tip with a large pair of pliers and pulled the spear clear through the exit hole he had smashed.

With a high pressure hose Bryn cleaned most of the blood off the concrete floor before rolling the corpse onto the lip of the loading bay, beneath which was a supermarket trolley, the universal mode of movement of heavy objects for the Marina's members.

Bryn spread a blue plastic tarpaulin over the trolley, judged the position carefully, chocked a wheel with a brick then hoisted himself up onto the loading bay. Using his feet, Bryn pushed the heavy corpse off the loading bay into the trolley. The noise again seemed to reverberate throughout the shed and Bryn had a brief horrified feeling that the trolley had collapsed. But it held and Bryn descended again to cover it with a second tarpaulin that he expertly tied with nylon cord.

Pushing the grossly overloaded trolley to his motor cruiser over the timbers of the gangways was difficult and Bryn cursed the runner every centimetre of the two hundred metre trip. Dumping the tarpaulin covered body into the aft well of his boat created another, to Bryn, horrifying noise but the few other sailors were far enough away and appeared so totally rapt in the own activities that no one even looked in his direction.

After dumping the body Bryn fairly raced with the empty trolley back to the shed where he got soaked to the skin from the water that splashed from the high pressure hose he used to clean the trolley and the entire area of the crime scene of darkly congealing blood. Assured that the area was clean, he wrapped the washed spear gun, spear, hammer and pliers in a piece of disused sail cloth. He also recovered two other fully loaded but unused spear guns he had earlier secreted in the shed in case he required additional penetration power. These he rapidly unloaded and relocated.

He barely glanced a the bulky blue tarpaulin bundle as he cast off and headed his six year old, well maintained motor cruiser on the pre planned route through the entrance of Port Phillip Bay to Lady Julia Percy Island.

CHAPTER ELEVEN

ERWIN WAS IRRITATED BECAUSE THE cells in the fifty year old police station were designed to incarcerate six prisoners. And as several drunks had been locked up before the arrest of the perverted porno show watchers the over crowding caused an unacceptable intrusion into Erwin's personal space. He was resentful enough at being taken into custody without having to bear the self piteous bleating of his fellow prisoners.

His irritation level was only bearable because of the confidence Erwin had in Lenny the lanky lawyer. He recalled Lenny's emphatic and explicit instructions and that helped him to curtail his natural inclinations to punch up his crepuscular cell mates. And because he had given Lenny the entry code to his apartment, he knew that Lenny would be bringing him a change of clean clothes before fronting the local Magistrate later that day. But even with these positive thoughts, the strain of curtailing his natural inclinations increased Erwin's irritation to almost breaking point. He was about to erupt when he heard the sound of Lenny's voice addressing with acidic derision the police custody constable.

Erwin welcomed Lenny with a yell to signify his appreciation of the scholarly insults heaped upon the police. Lenny responded to Erwin's enthusiastic welcome with a facial expression that his few friends recognized as being a smile. Other acquaintances who had observed Lenny's smile were known to have tried hard to copy it to frighten unruly adolescents, but Lenny had a monopoly on visual terrorism.

As usual, Lenny wasted little time in friendly formalities and Erwin was soon stripped to his very brief purple, pink and black Laura Ashley patterned floral underpants and long yellow socks. Lenny took Polaroid flash photographs of the numerous marks on Erwin's body. Erwin sensed that Lenny would prefer not to be sidetracked with insignificant irrelevancies. So he abstained from mentioning that the greyish yellow bruises and bright pink contusions on his back were caused when his fellow porno watchers stampeded out of the darkened house and trampled on him. Consequently Lenny's photographic endeavours, when later referred to in Court, were entirely attributed to policemen and women with violent urges.

When his innocent client was reclothed, in a respectable suit, Lenny told of his early morning activities and as a result, the interpretation he intended to place before the court about the events of the previous evening that resulted in Erwin's unjustified incarceration by vindictive members of Victoria Police. Erwin activated that part of his conscious mind with the greatest receptive propensity to absorb Lenny's version. As Lenny's sandpaper sounding voice related the version of the events of the police porno raid, Erwin found himself becoming justifiably indignant at the gross breach of his civil liberties by members of the very same government organisation that should have been diligently protecting his rights.

Lenny surprised Erwin by placing two fingers into the elasticised top of the long yellow sock on Erwin's left leg. From it he appeared to extract a credit card sized piece of paper upon which was written a house number, street name and suburb and a street directory page and numeric / alpha grid reference. Lenny asked Erwin to read the writing several times as a way to memorise it. Erwin realised that the street number, 24, was the same as the house that was the venue of last night's porno movie show. After Erwin had read and handled the paper enough to have fingerprints on it, Lenny recovered it and placed it into Erwin's suit coat pocket.

Lenny's re-education of Erwin now began in earnest. The consultation at one end of the overcrowded custody block lasted nearly forty minutes before Erwin was escorted back to his cell. Lenny went to speak with the police person who would be putting the police case to the Magistrate later that morning. Lenny used some clever legal arguments to unsettle the senior constable who he found out would be presenting the preliminary prosecution case and obtained the concession he sought, namely that Erwin would be called first on the hearing list. With one win under his belt Lenny scored a second win when he was able to have Erwin use an electric razor to shave.

When the court opened at 10am the police custody constable herded those arrested into the "dock" area. Amongst the ill dressed, unshaven, sullen porno perverts, Erwin stood out like a beacon of cleanliness in his dark grey suit, white shirt, polished Oxford brogues and conservative dark blue tie. Fortunately his trousers concealed the bright yellow socks. Actually the tie was Lenny's contribution to Erwin's sartorial splendour because the only neck ties the Lenny found in Erwin's place were so awful as to almost guarantee a conviction on the grounds of visual pollution. Following Lenny's instructions, Erwin kept his head high and tried not to look aggressive.

When Erwin's name was called he stepped confidently forward. He was not required to say anything because Lenny languidly uncoiled his lanky body from a long wooden bench. In a voice that projected clearly throughout the entire courtroom, he advised the Magistrate that he represented the innocent Erwin whom he assured the bench, had no case to answer because of a mistaken arrest by an incompetent and over zealous group of police.

The Magistrate's disposition took an immediate lift. He had resigned himself to a dull morning listening again, as he so often did, to the lies of the accused and the exaggerations of the constabulary. He knew for certain that most accused would plead mitigation due to what they claimed was an unhappy childhood and he was bored beyond belief when that inevitably occurred. And the list before him had all the appearance of a monotonous morning. Suddenly he had a tall, very thin, top shelf lawyer staring at him through slatted eyelids and protesting the innocence of a well dressed man, who except for his wardrobe had all the hallmarks of a vicious thug.

In the expectation of learning something different by way of argument, the Magistrate adjusted his half-lens glasses, leaned back in the high back chair and gestured with his hand for Lenny to proceed, Lenny used a similar hand gesture towards Erwin in a manner designed to highlight that his clean shaven well tailored client was clearly of superior status to the dismal throng in the holding area.

Lenny asked questions that resulted in Erwin extracting from his pocket a piece of credit card sized paper with an address on it and this was duly passed to the Magistrate. Leonard contended that Erwin had been in possession of that paper at the time of his arrest. The Magistrate read the street number and the street name before offering it to the police prosecutor who made a note of the details and passed it back to Lenny. The senior constable prosecutor indicated that there would be no contest as to Erwin's prior possession of it but appeared mystified as to its relevance.

"Had not Erwin claimed his arrest was a mistake?" asked Lenny in Churchillian tone of the prosecutor who was reluctantly forced to agree that those words were recorded in the report of the arresting officers. To try to remove any evidential value of the agreement, the prosecutor said "They all say that" referring to the community of caught criminals. The Magistrate involuntarily nodded in agreement.

Lenny dispersed the mystery of the address when he stated that Erwin was to have delivered a slab of beer cans to that address but navigated one street too far West, which meant that he mistakenly entered the house of the same street number but the wrong street. And having entered the house and realised his mistake he was about to leave when the police raided and he was physically brutally assaulted, subsequently verbally humiliated and unlawfully incarcerated. The Magistrate exhibited considerable mental discipline and only smiled instead of laughing his head off. The prosecutor, as predicted, rose in highly indignant defense of the police service but that was his only positive move because from there onwards he was overwhelmed by the significantly superior experience of Lenny.

The Magistrate, like a good field umpire in a football game, allowed both contenders considerable latitude and even the spectators and other accused in the holding area warmed to the spectacle of a police prosecutor being demolished. When the prosecutor attempted to dismiss the claim of police brutality, Lenny produced Polaroid photographs of Erwin's bruises, which the Magistrate perused then passed to the prosecutor. Lenny offered to have an independent doctor testify as to the freshness of the wounds but the prosecutor accepted that the bruises were recent.

When the prosecutor read from the arresting officer's statement that Erwin refused to state his name and address as per sub section one of Section 456 of the Crimes Act, Lenny refuted that charge by claiming that

Erwin did not refuse, he only asked that he give his details without others listening, as was his right under the Privacy Act. Erwin had loudly stated that he would be pleased to give his details at the police station. In the holding area several of the accused porno perverts spontaneously nodded in agreement and that instinctive response was not unnoticed by the Magistrate.

To intensify the unease of the prosecutor, Leonard requested that, as the prosecutor had raised the issue of Section 456 of the Crimes Act, then he, Lenny, be allowed to read aloud the short sub sections 4 and 5 of Section 456. Upon receiving the nod from the inarticulate Magistrate, Lenny reminded all present that the Crimes Act referred to the police as "members" then he read, somewhat theatrically that: -

4. A person who is requested by a member under sub-section (1) to state his or her name and address may request the member to state orally or in writing, his or her name, rank and place of duty.

5. A member of the police force who, in response to a request under sub-section (4) –
   a) Refuses or fails to comply with the request: or
   b) States a name or rank that is false in a material particular; or
   c) States as his or her place of duty an address other than the name of the police station which is the member's ordinary place of duty; or
   d) Refuses to comply with the request in writing if requested to do so is guilty of a summary offense punishable on conviction by a level 11 fine. (5 penalty units maximum).

Lenny's voice became more menacing as he asserted that Erwin had requested details of the arresting policeman in accordance with sub section 4 and that request had been rudely refused thereby rendering the policeman guilty of a summary offence, under sub section 5 (a). That assertion stopped the prosecutor in his tracks.

While he was temporally speechless Lenny pressed home his advantage by quoting from the report of the arresting officer in which it was stated that Erwin was holding a slab of beer cans. The prosecutor consulted his notes and reluctantly conceded that point. Lenny told the Magistrate that Erwin's possession of the cans was direct proof of the erroneous delivery to a house of the same number but the wrong street. Lenny said that the intended recipient of the cans, the occupant of the house of the same numbers in the adjoining street was outside and could be called to verify Erwin's innocence. The highly respected home owner was awaiting his beer, which Lenny fervently hoped, had survived unscathed a night in police custody.

Lenny also noted that written statements by other police present at the raid made no positive identification of the arrival sequence of attendees at the porno house and that the time log of arrivals had not been properly signed and several times of the arrivals of persons were omitted. Lenny asserted that these faults made the time log unreliable and therefore inadmissible. The prosecutor recovered somewhat and began to show some fight by claiming that the approaches to the house were dark and that the occupants of the house created confusion when the lights went out, fists were flung, so that the battered police were distracted and perhaps a little remiss in attending to the paperwork.

Lenny quickly turned those statements against him by claiming that Erwin only arrived in the wrong house one minute before the police raid began and nothing in the police records proved otherwise. Whilst the prosecutor was trying to find something in the arresting officer's statement by way of rebuttal, Lenny again pressed home his advantage. Did Erwin cause any trouble at the police station? – No! "That", said Lenny "proves that any adverse behaviour of Erwin, a fine upstanding citizen, was a manifestation of his fright at being confronted by armed police who brutalized him without justification". Lenny attempted to pass around the Polaroid photos again but the Magistrate shuddered and quickly held up a hand to prevent it.

The final nail in the prosecutor's case was Lenny's recital of section 70 of the Crimes Act relating to Sexual Offences and the possession of pornography. Paid viewing constitutes possession. In order to be guilty of possession, proof that money changed hands to view the pornography was required. Attendance at the scene of a pornographic viewing was insufficient. No proof existed that Erwin had paid to attend the viewing hence Erwin had no case to answer.

Lenny's theatrical performance and logical argument impressed the Magistrate. It was bullshit, but cleverly contrived bullshit, so cleverly contrived as to suspend disbelief. Lenny also impressed the prosecutor who also knew it was bullshit, but dangerous bullshit. The refusal by a police officer to comply with sub sections 4 & 5 of Section 456 could, if pressed, lead to an officer being convicted. Erwin was impressed and wondered how Lenny knew that the person to whom he had paid his $100 viewing fee escaped when the lights went out.

Lenny was certain he had prevailed because of his encyclopedic knowledge of the Crimes Act. He was aware of the section in the Act relating to "Perverting the course of justice" but that awareness was subdued into irrelevance as he calculated the size of the fee he would obtain from a suitably grateful Erwin.

The prosecutor wilted and asked the Magistrate for a few minutes to consult with the arresting officer and returned shortly to inform him that the case against Erwin Dormunt would be withdrawn. The Magistrate found sufficient voice to warn the prosecutor that once withdrawn any chances of a renewal of charges were forfeit and the prosecutor most reluctantly acknowledged his concurrence with that advice.

The Magistrate did not have to say anything to Lenny, he simply gestured, in continuance of his Marcel Marceau mime and Lenny nodded likewise then beckoned Erwin to follow him from the court. Erwin was free with his reputation spotless.

CHAPTER TWELVE

LADY JULIA PERCY ISLAND IS a flat topped volcanic island with steep fifty metre cliffs projecting above a tempestuous sea. The island is home to a colony of Australian fur seals. Located in the Southern Ocean, the four square kilometre rock is ten kilometres off Victoria's South coast and twenty kilometres West of the fishing port and holiday destination named Port Fairy. The bleak island was known to the mainland aboriginal tribe, the Gunditjmara, as Dean Maar, the site at which the creator left the world. The modern name of the inhospitable molar shaped volcanic remnant was conferred in the year 1800 as a tribute to a member of the family of the Duke of Northumberland; Percy being the family name. Nautical charts rigorously warn that the island should only ever be approached by experienced fisherman in dead calm weather.

The island's claim to world wide fame rests upon the fact that per cubic kilometre of ocean, compared to any other cubic kilometre of ocean on the planet, Lady Julia Percy's surrounding seas contain infinitely more members of the species Carcharodon Carcharis, of the family Isurudae. Otherwise known commonly as the Great White Shark. Renowned for its voracious appetite, the Great White has killed and maimed more human beings in Southern Australian waters that any twenty other species of sharks put together. The Great White cruises twenty metres below the surface and specimens 6.5 metres long weighing over three tonnes are not uncommon.

A normal adult has tremendously powerful jaws containing up to 3000 teeth.

Generally, other shark species such as the Grey Nurse, Tiger shark and Hammerhead, circle their prey before launching an attack. But the characteristic of the Great White that makes it terrifying to humans is that it never offers an escape by declaring its presence. Once a Great White senses food it attacks directly from below with terrible speed. It has no hesitation because it fears nothing in the watery kingdom.

Lady Julia Percy Island was Bryn's destination. His recently deceased massive slab of humanity was destined to be Great White fodder. As the twin Evinrude engines of the seven metre cabin cruiser propelled the boat smoothly towards the "Rip", the entrance to Melbourne's Port Phillip Bay, Bryn was busy lining up his transit marks with the Bay chart, checking for other sea traffic and cleaning the rear deck with bleach cleaner and paper towels.

Despite plastic bags and tarpaulins, some blood, other bodily fluids and solids were seeping onto the plastic sheeting with which Bryn had previously covered the deck. The considerable quantity of dirty paper towels were disposed of overboard, to seaward, where they would become food for fish that would be caught and finish up in Melbourne restaurants.

After twenty minutes the mess was cleaned and he began removing the clothes he had worn when he executed his ungrateful runner. The training shoes were soaked in dried blood from his spear removing activities, as were his tracksuit pants. All went into a plastic bag. Slowly, one item at a time, Bryn took off every item of clothing he had worn, washed himself in sea water, using special sea water soap, and dressed in tee shirt and shorts.

He had completed the washing and clothing change as he approached the channel to take his boat into the open ocean. For the next half hour his concentration was entirely upon the seamanship required to safely navigate and avoid being washed off course by the wash of the line of giant container ships entering the bay though the narrow heads. Dominated to the East by tea tree covered hills near the town of Portsea and on the West by the impressive, but outdated 19th Century fort at Queenscliff and the Point Lonsdale beacon, the entrance always demanded complete concentration. The locals called the three kilometre wide entrance to Port Phillip "The Rip" because of surges of unpredictable turbulence.

The relatively sedate quality of the water movement within the bay changed as Bryn's boat cleared the Rip and he steered South, South, West in a more powerful swell. His ears became more attuned to the regular weather reports on the Single Side Band radio. The VHF radio hummed but was otherwise inactive whilst occasional calls on the HF radio he deemed innocuous and not appertaining to him. Bryn was definitely not out to attract attention by radio or visual contact and at least five times in the first hour he deliberately altered course to steer well away from other craft.

What with keeping an eye on the weather and particularly the wind strength and direction, checking the lashings on the extra fuel drums stowed in the cabin, and using old fashioned navigational techniques for pure pleasure, an Admiralty chart, dividers and clackers to check against his GPS electronic navigation, it was later afternoon before Bryn realised that the vague uneasy feeling of which he was becoming more aware, was hunger. His concentration had been so complete. To take his relatively small boat into the Southern Ocean on a seven hundred kilometre round trip was a challenge to which he had responded with total effort.

From the cabin he brought a bag of sandwiches and a warmish can of soft drink. He had tuned off the small refrigerator the day before because he was worried about the possibility of electric sparks with the stowage of the extra fuel drums in the cabin. The result was dry bread on the sandwiches and a warm can of drink. But being at sea, totally self reliant, induced a euphoria that surpassed any feelings of dissatisfaction with his cuisine.

Cape Otway is the most southerly part of the Victorian coast West of Port Phillip Bay and afforded a reasonable amount of shelter from the prevailing South Westerly wind. On sailing past the Cape, dominated by the lighthouse, Bryn's boat began sloughing into a stronger Westerly wind that dispersed the sense of comfortable sailing enjoyed until then.

Fuel consumption increased as the throttles needed to be opened to arrive on the seaward side of Lady Julia Percy Island with sufficient light to enable the Great White Shark food to be offloaded, and to enable Bryn to reach the sheltered harbour of Port Fairy for an overnight mooring. With greater fuel consumption, Bryn had to tackle the refueling in seas rougher that he had previously experienced whilst alone. It took a lot more time and a couple of bruised fingers, but was achieved without compromising safety. He noted that his calculations on consumption were a little out but he still had an adequate reserve.

Information from the charts indicated that the sea current took a due South curve five kilometres beyond the Twelve Apostles, a series of rock formations near the town of Port Campbell. Bryn accepted the loss of time and discomfort from a beam wind to head several degrees South for an hour to dispose of his blood stained clothes, trainers, spear gun and spear and other items one piece at a time, including a mobile telephone, that could provide forensic evidence should it ever fall into police hands.

At 5pm that afternoon Bryn reached the seaward side of Lady Julia Percy Island and as far as he could see through his binoculars no other vessel was in a position to observe him. He moved the throttle to neutral.

One hundred and sixty kilograms of dead weight took a lot of heaving overboard but finally the blood stained body slipped head first into the heavy swell and disappeared with barely a bubble. Perhaps it was his imagination but as Bryn advanced the throttle and moved the boat forward, he caught a glimpse of a swift streamlined streak near the spot that was the watery grave of the Samoan. With a freshening wind and consequently heavier seas, Bryn turned shorewards, steering towards the harbour of Port Fairy for his overnight mooring.

He reflected briefly on the chances of the runner being missed and any investigation that may follow. He felt that the odds were substantially in his favour. The Samoan runner was an illegal immigrant, having entered Australia on a temporary visa via New Zealand. Bryn's information was that he was not registered as a taxpayer, employee, or social services recipient nor for Medicare. If the deceased was registered, then it could not have been in his own name. A fact that would confuse any search. Additionally, the runner had not known Bryn's name or address. Bryn had been "Johnny" to everyone in the staged accidents scam and his cautious guarding of his private details was extraordinary thorough. Security had not been breached. Johnny and the Samoan had met face to face only twice. Once in dim light when the extortion demand was made and the second time when Bryn skewered him. All other contact had been by pre paid mobile telephone and that telephone was now in the Southern Ocean about ten kilometres distant from the person to whom it had primarily responded. Bryn had left no fingerprints, no DNA, no money trail. No one had observed the meeting between Bryn and the runner. So any investigation by law enforcement authorities was extremely unlikely. If any danger loomed it may come from within the Samoan ethnic group living in Melbourne. Bryn reminded himself to terminate all contact with the group.

As for discovery of the body of the runner, or portions of it, Bryn recalled a story he read in one of the weekend newspapers about the discovery in 1935 of a human arm when a captured Tiger Shark regurgitated contents of its stomach. To the arm was attached a piece of rope and the arm was tattooed with the figures of two men boxing. Police, fingerprint experts and forensic examiners identified the arm as that of a known criminal and a police surgeon declared that the arm had been severed from the body with a knife, thus eliminating the theory that the main died from a shark attack.

As the law stood then, the coroner ruled that there could be no inquest without a complete body. Two men were tried in court as a test case, but with no conclusive evidence they were acquitted. Since 1935 the law had changed but without a cadaver and no positive link between Bryn and the shark bait, he felt safe. Also, he recalled reading that the three metre Tiger Shark had been distressed at being caught in the bay and put in an aquarium, hence its regurgitation. Bryn thought that nobody could be mad enough to try to catch a six metre Great White in the open ocean to put in an aquarium.

With that comforting thought Bryn motored up the estuary, past Battery Hill, an old fort and signal station and moored at the Port Fairy pier. In the failing light he used the last drum to refuel the tanks, allowed the cabin to ventilate, and seeing an incinerator blazing behind the fishing cooperative, Bryn took the remaining pieces of plastic sheeting from the deck and burnt them. He scrubbed the deck, gunwales and transom for a second time in a strong solution of bleach, dried it all off and with an old towel, changed into another tracksuit then burnt the towel.

By then it was dark so he double checked his mooring lines, locked the engines and cabin and walked to the shopping centre where he bought a bottle of cold Riesling that he took to a BYO Chinese restaurant. On return to the boat he slept all night on a bunk seat. Breakfast he made on items from the local bakery before heading back to Cape Otway and turning to head North East to pass through the Rip, into the bay for a refuelling stop at Geelong. He went shopping at a couple of Op Shops in Geelong city for more clothing to replace those items expended, in case he had to eliminate any other competitor.

As the setting sun turned the barely rippling water of the Bay to an eye aching reflective apricot / gold, Bryn guided his boat into its reserved slip at the St Kilda Marina. Using one of his numerous telephone cards in a public telephone near the wharf, Bryn called a girl friend to confirm a date then attended to the maintenance of his boat for an hour. So far as he could ascertain in casual conversation, his absence from the Marina was unremarkable. But in case some curious fellow boat owner were to enquire, he let it be know that he had cruised around the bay and spent the night at Portsea in company with a lady whose name it was not gentlemanly to reveal.

Bryn felt it did no harm to spread a little disinformation to give him some cover against any future enquiry. He felt that it was a cautious act. He had no contempt for caution.

CHAPTER THIRTEEN

BRYN'S FIRST VISIT TO FEED the Great White Shark inhabitants of seas adjacent to Lady Julia Percy Island was an adventure. Subsequent visits lost the novelty of originality and became routine. But routine did not entail any lack of attention to precautions, rather to a greater elevation of the procedure into the realm of professionalism.

Appalled at the bloody mess caused by his first execution using a spear gun, Bryn thought out the human disposal situation and built up a supply of drugs, in a cleverly crafted acquisition program that left no trail to the man he had prudently maintained at a Sydney hospital. Using Rohypnol, the so called "date rape drug". Any person who sought to advantage himself in a manner that could become a danger to Bryn was rendered temporarily incapable, loaded aboard Bryn's motor cruiser and fed to the sharks in a semi sommulent state.

Bryn's rationale, not justification, for the second disposal revolved upon the victim's propensity towards alcoholism as a result of unaccustomed prosperity. Several of Bryn's staged accident players were members of superannuation funds. Bryn's scheme was to milk the motor vehicle compensation system first. Only then, with updated medical certificates, would an application be made to the superannuation fund of a player for a pension based on the player's continued health deterioration. Bryn appreciated that a successful claim for compensation for a motor vehicle injury would offer to superannuation fund trustees such highly persuasive evidence of genuine disability as to make superannuation settlement certain.

This current candidate for shark food had disobeyed the instructions delivered by Bryn's runner. Greed led to him making a premature disability application to his superannuation fund. Without adequate time in which to confirm permanent rather that temporary disability and without the imprimatur of a Government insurance department's acceptance of disability that virtually precluded refusal by a private sector superannuation fund, an investigation of the incomplete or faulty claim would be certain.

And this is, in fact, what happened. The superannuation fund manager considered the application had the characteristics of fraud. He called in Ian Ross, a licenced private investigator who specialised in superannuation fraud. Like all PI's, Ian worked to a budget agreed with the client at time of engagement. The budget was directly proportional to the element of savings anticipated by the superannuation fund.

Ian Ross had to plan to cover his costs and show a profit. He began with two approaches. First, he sought confirmation from several of the doctors that the medical certificates were genuine. Second, he planned surveillance of the "subject" to determine whether the activities of the subject were consistent with the alleged injuries sustained in the motor vehicle accident. Substitution was Ian's initial theory, that is, somewhere there existed a person with genuine injuries consistent with those described in the medical certificates of the subject. Ian suspected that a genuinely disabled person had attended medical exams in lieu of the healthy superannuation fund contributor.

Ian Ross did not immediately suspect the doctors of collusion because of the number involved but even his low key enquires alarmed the doctors who reported, via their runner contacts, to Bryn that an unwelcome enquiry was made. After one full day of surveillance Ian realised that the claimant, "his subject", was close to being inebriated by early afternoon and it appeared to be a regular habit. It became evident that the subject exhibited none of the limitations expected of a person with permanently incapacitating spinal injuries. Beyond alcoholism the subject had no physical disabilities whatsoever.

Surveillance was began by 10am each morning when the subject emerged from his rental house in the inner Melbourne suburb of Albert

Park and walked to a nearby hotel. At 1.30pm he staggered back home carrying bottles of liquid oblivion. Ian began to speculate whether the subject would qualify for disability on the grounds of alcoholic poisoning.

On day two of Ian's surveillance, the subject left home as usual. One hundred yards from his home, on the direct walking route to the customary hotel, a three year old white Holden Commodore was parked. As the subject drew level with it, the front passenger door was pushed open and the subject bent towards the driver in conversation before getting in. Ian had not spotted the Holden car or driver until the door opened. In anticipation of the Holden driving off, Bryn started the engine of his non descript four year old Mitsubishi. After several minutes on idle, Ian switched off the ignition and reached into the passenger side foot well for the shopping bag in which he kept a video camera.

Carrying the bag Ian got out of his car, crossed the road and moved opposite the Holden. Both occupants were gesticulating and their rapidly opening mouths indicated that a vehement argument was progressing. With practiced dexterity Ian slipped the video camera from the bag, and then dropped the bag "accidently". As he bent to pick it up he placed the video camera on the bonnet of a car, directly opposite the Holden. He aligned the lens, took a quick look through the viewfinder, focused the zoom to get a good image of the driver and allowed the camera to run. He walked to a house and appeared to put something into the letterbox before turning around. He noted the registration number of the Holden as he returned to retrieve the video camera.

As certain as he could be that this activities went entirely unnoticed by the subject and the driver of the Holden, Ian returned to his Mitsubishi. He put the camera back into the bag and took out an old light blue cloth hat. He scrunched it up and put it in his pocket. Crossing the road again he walked 30 metres ahead of the Holden then recrossed the road, unfolded and put on the hat and walked back towards the front of the Holden, apparently unconcerned with anything except the flowers growing in house gardens. He checked the Holden's registration number again and observed that the argument between the two men in the front seat was still going on at maximum volume.

Barely three steps beyond the Holden, Ian heard the door open and his subject emerged. "You can tell Johnny to take his orders and stuff them up his arse" Ian heard him shout. Then the obviously angry subject moved towards his favourite drinking hole at a rate of knots that Ian have never seen him achieve before. Clearly he had no disability to be able to maintain that pace.

Arriving back at his car, Ian looked towards the driver of the Holden who seemed to be talking on a mobile phone. Ian realised that he had heard significant information. The name "Johnny" and the word "orders". He could always locate his subject but not the Holden driver so he acted with investigator's instinct and followed the white Holden. Ian was astounded that the Holden driver appeared to the totally unaware of any need to shuck off a tail. He drove about five kilometres to a bayside tourist spot named Point Ormond. The driver parked, walked up a small hill "the point" and sat on the grass. Ian judged him to be about 175 centimetres tall, average build, dark hair receding and forty five years old. To approach the Holden driver unseen was almost impossible given the great open space, so from another of his shopping bags he extracted a brown paper bag containing sandwiches and a can of diet coke. Ian walked a few steps and sat on a bench two hundred metres distant from the unknown driver.

Sitting there so innocently eating, he blended into the scenery. Ian was into the second cheese and lettuce sandwich portion when he saw a well built man probably in his mid twenties, about 185 centimetres in height. Ian saw him walk towards the Point, pause to look around several times then walk to the driver of the Holden and sit beside him. A conversation of about 10 minutes took place. The driver gesticulated whilst the young man seemed calm and composed and eventually made a few placating hand movements before rising, brushing grass off the seat of his trousers and walking unhurriedly down the slope. Cover was sparse so Ian could not follow the young man who appeared more vigilant than the Holden driver.

The unknown young man stopped on the footpath to seemingly adjust a shoe and sent concentrated glances to each side of the footpath. Ian realised that the young man was obviously alert to ensure he was not followed. Ian found that to be most interesting. Would someone involved in legitimate business be so sensitive to surveillance? The Holden driver walked straight back to his car and drove off. Ian speculated as to the identity of the young man still visible in the distance. Could he be the "Johnny" up whose arse orders were supposed to be stuffed? Too early to say with certainty but stick with the tag for the time being.   With no apparent haste, Ian walked to his own car and drove from the car park towards the young man.   In light traffic heading North on the dual roadway of Marine Parade, Ian saw "Johnny" look back down the footpath before he walked through the St Kilda Marina entrance.

Unable to turn around immediately, Ian drove to a traffic light exit near Melbourne's amusement area named Luna Park. He waited for the green light then headed back South looking for a place to park. At Dickens Street he turned left and found a space some eighty metres from Marine Parade. From his anti surveillance kit he selected and put on a dark blue spray jacket and a white floppy sun hat then crossed Marine Parade in a traffic lull and walked into the Marina. He estimated that over one hundred people were working on sail and motor boats and established that there were two entrances / exits – one via the gate through which he had entered into the car park and the other via the sea.

He selected a place in the shade to sit and appeared engrossed in the scenery. It was a two hour wait. His backside was getting numb but he had hesitated to move because his observation spot offered maximum observation of the Marina entrances. The young man he had tentatively labelled "Johnny" walked out of the cavernous maintenance shed. Ian recognised his walk, the athletic gait, head high stance and the dark blonde hair. Johnny had changed into a track suit and carried a nylon sports bag that appeared very light. Johnny walked to an old faded blue Ford Falcon sedan. Ian quickly moved amongst the boat trailers to read the registration plate. He kept on moving towards the Marina office knowing that he had no hope of getting back to his own car to follow Johnny. The Ford was driven out through the exit gate and merged with the traffic.

At the Marina office Ian tried a time tested ploy of telling the attendant he was supposed to meet a boat owner with a piece of equipment but was unable to locate him – perhaps he had the wrong name? Ian told the attendant that he thought his intended client had just driven out in a blue Ford Falcon and asked for the name of the driver but the attendant said he was newly appointed to the job and couldn't help. You win some, you lose some.

Ian drove the short distance to his own office in the suburb of South Yarra and telephoned the numbers of the blue Ford Falcon and white

Holden Commodore to his contact at the Motor Vehicle Registration Department. The style of his request was illegal. He used the ID number and police station of a non existent person. Both Ian and the Motor Vehicle Registration employee knew it. After dark that evening he drove to a street in Springvale, parked, and walked around a corner to a house that had a brick in the front garden near the water meter just inside the gate. He found a plastic coin envelope of a type used by banks. He placed the envelope in his pocket, leaving two $20 notes under the brick.

When well clear of the area Ian found in the envelope details of the registered owners of the blue Ford Falcon and the white Holden Commodore written on a sheet of paper. The Ford was owned by a proprietary limited company. Ian searched the company records on the Australian Securities and Investment Commission internet site. He wondered why a mail order company, apparently owned by two elderly residents of the provincial city of Ballarat, would want with a ten year old Ford sedan car that had not been cleaned for a long time. Puzzling too was that the company was only recently incorporated. The white Holden Commodore was owned by an elderly lady in the Melbourne suburb of Seddon. Neither the name of the company nor that of the elderly lady appeared in any telephone directory.

Ian had planned to follow up both leads but pressing work for another client took up two days. He was about to reapply his efforts to the Ballarat company and the Seddon elderly lady, when he received a telephone call from the client superannuation fund to cancel further investigations. The superannuation fund manager told Ian that the contributor who had lodged the suspicious application for total and permanent disability benefits had withdrawn the claim. Instead, the contributor advised of his resignation from the employer and the superannuation fund and directed that all entitlements be paid direct to a nominated bank account. So far as the superannuation fund was concerned, the matter was finished. Ian was asked to submit his report and his account for services.

Ian sent off a brief report and his bill, as directed, however his curiosity was aroused. On his own initiative he visited the address in Seddon where the white Holden Commodore was supposed to be garaged. It was a single fronted house in a street that paralleled the railway line and Ian began enquires two houses to one side. Introducing himself in an ambiguous manner that could have conveyed the impression that he was a traffic engineer with the local Council, Ian found out from neighbours that the little old lady who used to reside at the Holden's address was partially blind, never held a driving licence, had no relatives and was relocated by the Social Services Department to a supported accommodation hostel nearly a year ago. The couple now living in the house spoke little English and appeared terrified of someone who appeared to represent authority. Ian's enquiry was a dead end, unless he chose to dig deeper.

Just as he was considering ways to break through the dead end, another superannuation fund contacted Ian regarding a massive fraud, the ramifications of which covered four States of Australia.

Ian dropped his unpaid speculative enquiry and homed in on an investigation likely to provide sufficient profit to pay for his next overseas holiday. Money in the bank was always advantageous and provided a cushion again the uncertainties of a precarious occupation. It was caution to have a cushion and Ian had no contempt for caution.

Johnny, or Bryn did not know that a tiny chink had been chiseled in his protective screen. He would have been worried had he known, but he didn't. Instead he was at helm of his motor cruiser with the drunken, rohypnol drugged body of a disobedient superannuation contributor beneath a cheap blue plastic tarpaulin. Bryn steered through the Rip on his way to Lady Julia Percy Island.

CHAPTER FOURTEEN

ON RETURN FROM HIS SECOND shark feeding expedition the usual exhilaration engendered by sun, sea, spray and successful problem solving was so subdued as to be non existent. Bryn was perplexed. He had a sky of cerulean blue with his view of infinity interrupted only by a few fluffy white clouds. A light South Westerly stern wind added a couple of knots to his journey towards the entrance of Port Phillip Bay.

The disposal of the body of the in retrospect, ill recruited drunk, aroused no more emotional trauma than the squashing beneath his heel of a cockroach. So the dispatch and disposal were not the cause of any mental unease. Bryn could not discern the cause of his irritating mental disequilibrium and while remaining nautically alert in the beautiful environment, he allowed himself a rare time of reminiscence as a possible pathway to self revelation. His first two years in business were tough. So tough he almost modified his aspiration of becoming a billionaire criminal. Deception of his parents was not too difficult. His father still provided regular financial assistance for Bryn's University studies, but Bryn deliberately withheld the fact that he had dropped out after the first year. His daily journey was not to the University but to a rented serviced office in Grattan Street, Carlton, a couple of hundred metres from the Swanston Street entrance to the Uni. It was convenient because he had unrestricted use of the campus.

From that small office he staged-managed the automotive accidents. From the office he could easily walk to the Uni to collect information about students that he needed to feed to his recruitment runners. His lady friend in Student Records had become heavily romantically involved with another man and no longer shared Bryn's bed, but she readily continued to provide information. It was a relationship that remained stable because both recognised that they had power to inflict serious damage on each other if the activity were to be brought to the attention of the Uni administration. Besides that, the young lady became accustomed to the regular $1000 payment at the end of each term.

The Uni was a marvellous field of resources for him to access. When Bryn heard that virtually undetectable forged student passes were available from a forger within the Uni print shop, he bought a forged student pass in the name of another student. On it was a barely recognizable photograph of himself. Bryn truly resented a disgruntled purchaser's dobbing in Rodney, one of the talented forgers. Bryn maintained contact, and an occasional cash contribution via a runner, during Rodney's brief involuntary incarceration. That generous action of Bryn eventually became a mutually satisfactory long term business arrangement.

Bryn's motivation in clandestinely assisting was founded on the premise that a short term guest of the government in a "soft" white collar prison equated with a post graduate Uni course in crime. That proved to be the case and the goodwill Bryn bought ensured such a degree of loyalty that on several subsequent vacations within prison walls, Rodney the forger, made no mention of his connection with Bryn and no incriminating documents linking to Bryn were discovered in police raids.

Debt proved to be Bryn's ladder to covert financial success. From attentative, selective eavesdropping on various motor cruiser conversations, Bryn learned early that any sudden unexplained increase of wealth attracted the attention of the various Federal financial enforcers. The acquisition of liabilities was barely vetted, by comparison. So to become wealthy Bryn reasoned that wealth in the form of solid assets should seem to be submerged in debt to show little tangible net equity.

Buying his first motor cruiser was Bryn's solution to the problem. Bryn registered a company using the names of Uni students as starters, then notified the Australian Securities and Investment Commission (ASIC) of the appointment of additional directors with names and addresses in the Philippines. He also changed the nondescript name chosen for the company start up, to a name indicating that the company was engaged in hiring boats for fishing and pleasure cruises.

Opening a Bank account was easy. With a copy of the ASIC registration certificate Bryn's most trusted runner, Ray, made application for a cheque account, placing $20,000 in cash on the counter as an opening deposit. It was the sight of cash that swung the deal. Procedures that Ray found oppressive were overlooked by the Accountant of the suburban branch of the major Bank. Ray ordered the largest sized books and in due course the deposit book and cheque book arrived at the serviced office. From the stash of cash generated by Bryn's scams, Bank deposits averaging $4000 a week were made until the balance was $40,000. At this point Bryn phoned the bank Accountant posing as the charter boat company's manager to discuss the purchase of a new boat to add to the company's fleet.

Using fake accounts to project a flourishing charter boat business and still depositing respectable cash sums, Bryn was able to obtain a $120,000 loan to purchase a second hand seven metre cruising trailer boat with outboard engines and loads of navigation and radio gear in the cruising cabin.

Debt having been established, Bryn's cash payments were easily concealed. His bank account balance never increased, it was only that his debt decreased. The activities of his company never attracted attention. Should any comment about the amount of cash and the lack of cheques paid in be raised, as once it was by a relieving bank manager, Bryn explained it away as it being customary for fishing parties to pay in cash. After 12 months, the boat loan was repaid, the Bank account closed and the company deregistered. Another apparently genuine company acquired the motor cruiser which it promptly traded-in for a superior, ten metre inboard engine craft costing $250,000 (after trade in) financed by another Bank eager to lend to a company with such a steady cash flow.

With reports that the Federal Government was about to legislate to make compulsory the reporting of cash transactions above $10,000, Bryn changed some of his revenue practices so that his staged accident crew purchased Money Orders at Australian Post Offices for remittances to him. It was as easy to pay runners and players in Money Orders, as it was to use cash. The $1000 Post Office limit per Money Order was easily circumvented by lodging the Money Orders at selected Post Offices for credit to a Giro account, then obtaining larger, "bank cheques" via Giro accounts to pay off loans obtained for boats.

Bryn's forger friend, Rodney, was amenable to being paid in $1000 Money Orders for the forged driving licences and passports produced to facilitate opening of Bank accounts when the Cash Transactions Reporting Act came into effect – an event that caused administrative inconvenience but otherwise did not curtail Bryn's business empire from expanding. The main venue of money laundering became the trust accounts of tractable lawyers. The general population is required by the Cash Transactions Reporting Act to report to the authorities any transaction involving substantial sums of cash that seemed suspicious.

That left the public, particularly employees of financial institutions such as Banks, Credit Unions, etc with a considerable element of discretion. The Australian reluctance to dob in someone, combined with the complexity of the original reporting form plus the prospect of retaliation if the reporter's identity was discovered by the reportee, tended to restrict the actual reports of sums below $10,000 to cases containing an element of spite, malice or envy. For sums in excess of $10,000 however, the exercise of discretion was denied. A person observing a $10,000 or more cash transaction was obligated to report to the authorities on pain of a severe penalty, if the omission were discovered. Given that incentive, the authorities initially received a steady stream of notifications of $10,000 plus, cash transactions.

An important exemption from the obligation to report was the legal profession. Lawyers could deal in large cash sums without the tedious requirement to report.

With his list of amenable legal practioners, Bryn had no difficulty in directing Ray to a particular lawyer with a bag containing up to $100,000 in notes. He instructed that lawyer to represent his employer company in a property conveyance. The lawyer would deposit the cash into the law firm's trust account, usually as part of a deposit with several cheques to make the cash less conspicuous. Ray would augment the original deposit until the trust account held sufficient for a bank cheque to be drawn against it. That was used as a significant deposit for purchase of a property. Using Bryn's system, a loan from a finance source such as a Bank or Credit Union would pay the remainder of the purchase price. Bryn's nefarious activities would swiftly pay off the loan from the finance source in a mixture of cash, Money Orders and trust account cheques from lawyers. Naturally the fee payable to the lawyer would be in two parts. The visible charge for services such as conveyancing and the invisible fee comprised almost entirely of used $100, $50 and $20 notes in a brown paper bag.

Reminiscence of these past achievements did not bring to Bryn the hoped for settlement of an uneasy mind. Although the unease was vague it was not within Bryn's character to allow it to remain unresolved. As he approached Point Lonsdale, the Western point of entry to Port Phillip Bay, the transition from coastal waters to the enclosed waters of the Bay, Bryn was compelled to abandon introspection to concentrate on negotiating the hazards of strong tides, currents and a wind that became increasingly contrary.

Admittedly the task of entering Port Phillip Bat was far less dangerous than that of his first trip to Lady Julia Percy Island in a smaller boat, because after four now deregistered companies and paid off bank loans, the $550,000 craft of which he was the properly licensed operator was a Riviera 4000 Platinum. The 1999 model was powered by twin 430 h.p. Volvo EDC engines. The fully enclosed glass hardtop was equipped with a Raytheon electronic package including GPS and fish finder. The cockpit floor was teak inlay and a generator powered reverse cycle air conditioning.

To other boat owners and admirers, Bryn was conscientious in emphasising that the prestigious cruiser was owned by a wealthy overseas gentleman and that he, Bryn was employed to maintain it. The overseas ownership bit was true, at least on paper. The company that owned the magnificent exhibit of seafaring engineering was registered in Vanuatu. Had any competent enquiry been made the directors would had appeared extremely odd. One was an imbecile confined to an elderly citizens support services retirement village in Tapanui in New Zealand's South Island. The other director that the company purported to have exercising control was a twenty six year old Papuan with an address in Port Moresby, who had not been contactable since a tribal fight in dense jungle two years earlier.

The overseas ownership of the company that owned the luxurious Riviera 4000 presented no problems to authorities because the profit and loss accounts showed a marginal loss each year and authorities seem only interested in profitable entities that can be taxed.

Notwithstanding the profile of the company and of its uncontactable directors, there existed a totally watertight, superbly drawn, Universal Power of Attorney for each director in favour of a person named Benny. To the Power of Attorney was attached a similarly watertight Will appointing Benny, as sole executor for each director or, in the event of Benny's death, then Benny's executor became the person upon whom the director's share in the company shall devolve. The sole executor of Benny's Will was Bryn Hamely's lawyer with Bryn being the ultimate, hidden, sole beneficiary.

Alone at sea, but never lonely, Bryn spent hours thinking about the wonders of the universe. He was particularly keen on scientific programs. At night, in good weather, the undulations of the ocean swell released all ordinary day to day inhibitions and his thoughts roamed widely. Scientific paradoxes intrigued him. If nothing existed but a pin point of matter that exploded into the universe as we know it, and if the universe is expanding, what is it expanding into? Mathematics put satellites into orbit, landed men on the Moon and sent a probe to land, with precision, on Mars. But those same mathematics when applied to sub-atomic particles, became a nonsense. Does that confirm that other dimensions exist?

Bacteria exist in millions of billions; strains still mutating and evolving since before the advent of the dinosaurs. By comparison humans are very much latecomers and insignificant in numbers. Was man bred by bacteria to be a food source? Say; entrée, a shark; main course, an elephant; dessert, a human. Bryn declined to go too far down that path of imagination, although under a starlit sky no thought was disallowed.

Bryn's eyes were constantly absorbing the changing conditions. He felt completely comfortable wearing his fitted Personal Floatation device, a top quality life jacket designed for coastal waters to which was attached an RFD-GPS Personal Locator Beacon. Whether it came to protecting his financial interests or to protecting his personal safety, Bryn had no contempt for caution. But he could not eradicate the uninvited, invasive but indefinable feeling that all was not as it should be in his life.

CHAPTER FIFTEEN

BRYN HAD NO COMPUNCTION ABOUT killing Freddie. Two years had elapsed since his last disposal of a runner and time had only matured the icy disdain affected by Bryn as a shield to prevent any evolution of a troublesome conscience. Freddie was easy prey because he too was a boatie, a boatie and a heavy user of amphetamines. His prosperity as part of Bryn's business plan had overwhelmed him. Freddie intended to adhere to Bryn's strictures about methods to conceal his wealth but somehow the delights of brothels and drugs always diverted his good intentions.

Freddie was a key player in the conversion of dirty money into respectably clean property assets. Freddie was a former office administrator of an Australia wide Real Estate chain of franchises. He dressed respectably, spoke the real estate jargon immaculately but Bryn has recognised the leaning towards larceny when he first met Freddie in the course of making a routine enquiry about a residential property.

In essence, Freddie earned his clandestine cash from Bryn for services rendered in two areas. First, through his contacts, he was able to advise Bryn of undervalued "renovator's specials", seriously deteriorated houses in the suburbs that Bryn had chosen as likely to see improvement in property prices. Freddie's contacts advised of sales by distressed families where a price could be bargained down substantially for quick settlements to pay funeral expenses, divorce arrangements or dangerously pressing debtors. The aim was to buy the worst house in the best street via one of Bryn's companies, then wreck and rebuild using illicit cash to repay the loan raised to finance the building.

It was in the second service that Freddie betrayed Bryn and earned himself a death sentence. The service was as a front man for home loans from superannuation funds. To vary his money laundering Bryn needed to avoid establishing a pattern that may lead to close scrutiny. So he used Banks, Credit Unions, trust accounts of Solicitors, and more recently, superannuation funds that had entered the field of residential mortgage lenders to contributing members of their fund.

Bryn established a dozen companies of a type that had cash inflows such as charter fishing boats, mail order services, sign writing, shop window cleaners, courier services and car washing. A couple were actually genuine just for the novelty. Bryn's methodology was to use one of those companies to buy a small established business using loan funds and pump illegally obtained cash into it. Then pay out the loan and sell the evidently prosperous company at an inflated price. Proceeds of the sale were distributed via bank accounts and phantom people using genuine tax file numbers of unsuspecting dupes. He never kept a money laundering company more than two years.

The residential property companies that Bryn acquired were an exception. In the course of setting up the respectable "anchor" companies Bryn had need of at least one employee. So Freddie was shown, under a slightly mutated name, as an employee of a company. That made him eligible for membership of a superannuation fund to which both he and his employer company made contributions of the amount prescribed under the Federal Government Superannuation Guarantee Levy legislation.

After six months, the usual qualifying term, Freddie's persona applied for a loan of $300,000 from the superannuation fund. With a little assistance from Rodney, Bryn's forger, Freddie's loan documents looked genuine and he appeared to have the capacity to service the loan. One stipulation that Freddie required in the loan agreement was that, in addition to the regular payment of interest and principal by way of direct deduction from his salary, he had the right at any time to make additional payments.

The Superannuation fund readily agreed and deposit books were issued to facilitate repayments. Bryn's scheme was for Freddie to repay the $300,000 loan not in 30 years but in 30 months. He used cash to make monthly payments of slightly less than $10,000, augmented from time to time by sizeable bank cheques from one or another of Bryn's companies of pliable lawyers.

Freddie had assisted Bryn to acquire four houses, all fully paid, within a three year period. House number five had been selected and a superannuation fund loan approved when Freddie's addiction to amphetamines began to affect his judgment and he became fatally over ambitious. He approached Bryn in an injudicious manner whilst high on some combination of drugs that he probably couldn't identify.

The over confidence meant that his previously rehearsed reasonable request for a greater percentage of profits, was delivered as a belligerent demand. Furthermore, when the drugs had worn off and he was assailed with the case hardened post drug depression; he could not remember the belligerent part of the confrontation with Bryn. Freddie's threat to expose Bryn, known to him as Johnny, unless he got more money was forgotten. An endearing attribute of Bryn was his patience. Bryn waited a couple of days. During that time he frequently consulted the weather forecasts and spent time on maintenance and provisioning of his latest motor cruiser. While only half high, Freddie accepted Bryn's invitation to spend an afternoon fishing and at the appointed hour on the due day waited at the Mordialloc pier less than ten minutes before Bryn's boat arrived and Freddie was invited aboard the palatial motor cruiser.

Pleased with the warmth of Bryn's invitation, which Freddie interpreted as an opportunity to press his demand for a greater share in the property acquisition enterprise, he accepted unhesitatingly the offer by Bryn of a whisky, not knowing that the entire bottle of scotch from which the drink was poured was loaded with rohypnol. The first drink he downed quite quickly and answered Bryn's friendly enquiries as to whether or not he had any car parking difficulty. Freddie helped himself to a second drink to assist him to determine the appropriate words with which to persuade Bryn to acquiesce to an increased share. The thought became hard to hold as a sudden, inexplicable lethargy rapidly transmitted into shatteringly soft temporary oblivion that would mercifully persist until becoming a comprehensibly permanent state aided by several voracious Great White sharks.

The outward trip with the comatose Freddie stretched on a cheap plastic tarpaulin had been remarkably unremarkable. Practically no other sea traffic, a docile wind in both strength and direction made progress through the enclosed waters of the bay so easy that Bryn could lock the helm while he searched Freddie's pockets and travel bag for house and car keys and any other item that might be useful or become an embarrassment. Several kilometres through "the Rip" into the permanent strong swell of the coastal waters, Bryn systematically searched the sea-lanes to ensure he was unobserved before disposing of unwanted items of Freddie's impedimenta. In the vast ocean just South of Julia Percy Island, Bryn disposed of Freddie with the same lack of mental perturbation.

On the return trip next morning, departing from his overnight mooring at the Port of Warrnambool, Bryn had little time for reflection due to an unpredicted freshening and direction of the wind that agitated the sea surface well beyond the comfort zone of the design of his otherwise excellent motor cruiser. No respite was afforded to Bryn by the weather on the return even after passing through the hazardous Rip into the relatively less turbulence of the bay. Bryn's mind was occupied in steering, as by comparison with the empty coastal waters, the enclosed waters seemed to have attracted thousands of amateur yachties. Colourful sails crisscrossed his planned course considerably reducing his forward speed as he throttled back and made numerous helm corrections.

Upon mooring he spent some time in refuelling, restocking and maintenance checks before sleeping aboard for several hours. Dressed in his customary crime clean up clothing, cheap sunglasses, trainers, tracksuit and baseball cap, all Op Shop purchases, and with supermarket purchased rubber gloves in his pocket, Bryn walked from the Marina and spent an hour and a half by tram and train travelling to beachside Mordialloc. He located the near new Subaru Station Wagon of the late Freddie in the car park near the pier.

Using Freddie's keys he opened the car, put on the gloves, and searched every place for any evidence linking him with Freddie and found none. Bryn drove the Subaru to a street near Freddie's house in the eastern suburb of Glen Waverley. Keys on the ring that held the Subaru keys had the appearance of being house keys and being unaware of Freddie's most recent domestic arrangement he approached the house on foot with all senses alert. He planned to ring the door bell posing as an odd job man looking for work should someone respond to his call.

Luck is something he never counted upon, preferring careful planning to eliminate any adverse occurrence. When luck came his way though, he never despised it. On this occasion it was with him for as he drew closer to Freddie's house the front door opened. It was then aggressively pulled shut by a short, slightly built woman with hair of a chemical colour that could be described as orange or purple. She carried two heavily loaded sports bags to an ancient Holden Camira car parked in the driveway.

Bryn continued walking at a steady rate and heard, then saw, the car go past him driven by the chemically coiffeured vertically challenged female. Bryn did an about turn and in a short walk, during which he gloved up again, he was at the front door of Freddie's. His first guess as to which key would open the front door proved correct. Alert and ready to tell lies should the house not be empty, Bryn pushed open the door and called "Hello, anyone home" several times but his call died in the gloom of the room.

He took all of 30 minutes to search the house and an outside aluminum sheet garden shed. The search uncovered several notebooks, filled with Freddie's handwritten diary entries, a loose leaf lever arch file, four bank books and several computer discs. Bryn disconnected the computer and put it and all items of interest into a suitcase. He left in place Freddie's three plastic envelopes of white powder plus a container that once held film but now held pills which he did not recognise. Bryn took a half filled can of motor mower fuel from the garden shed.

Outside again, he carried the suitcase, computer and motor fuel to Freddie's Subaru and drove to the park in Coburg where he knew there were public barbeques. Everything that would burn he tore and placed in the bluestone fireplace. On the iron bars of the barbeque he placed the computer and the discs then splashed motor mower fuel over all. He lit the papers and watched as the flames roared upwards and destroyed several years of Freddie's record keeping. A few people looked as the flames caused a short lived dense black smoke cloud to rise from the burning discs and the computer, however their attention was only fleeting. Bryn drove off when he was satisfied that destruction of all incriminating evidence was complete.

With doors unlocked and the key in the ignition, Bryn left the Subaru near a school in Footscray. He reckoned it would result in the car disappearing forever. He disposed of the gloves and baseball cap in dumpsters near a food market and put the track suit top into a charity collection bin before catching a train home. Next morning he put into motion the procedure necessary to recover and conceal the fact that Freddie was no longer alive.

And it was this procedure that reacquainted the Licenced Private Investigator, Ian Ross with the mysterious entrepreneur that Ian made notes about two years earlier. The notes were filed in his computer under the file name "Johnny".

Bryn had experienced propitious luck several times that day. The fact that Freddie's female houseguest had driven off at an auspicious moment, the fact that she had driven off in a direction that precluded her from seeing Freddie's Subaru, the fact that she had not returned during Bryn's search, the fact that the drugs stashed in the house mitigated against police being notified of a missing computer and discs. And the risk that all drivers take on the road that no accident occurred to involve Bryn in having to explain his presence in the car of person he was not supposed to know, wearing rubber gloves.

If you want to make the Gods laugh, tell them your plans. Bryn had heard the saying but treated it lightly. He was not to know that his short term luck would hold but his long term allocation of the commodity was about to unravel, with the curiosity of Ian Ross, the superannuation specialist Private Investigator as the unraveller.

CHAPTER SIXTEEN

BRYN'S "RECOVERY AND CONCEAL" OPERATION for property of Freddie's that Bryn thought belonged to him, was set in motion the day after Freddie joined the marine food chain. One of Bryn's complaisant lawyers wrote a letter to the superannuation fund that held a mortgage over Freddie's Glen Waverley residence advising that the property had been purchased by a private company. Copies of the contract of sale, a bank cheque mortgage balance payment and supporting documentation were enclosed. All looked genuine. The property transfer proceeded like clockwork.

Freddie's superannuation entitlements including the "preserved portion" ie the amount to be set aside, untouched, until retirement age, was transferred in accordance to documents allegedly signed by Freddy, to an approved superannuation fund in Papua and New Guinea, to which country Freddie asserted he was going to live. In fact, the PNG superannuation fund was one of Bryn's frauds. In a short space of time the superannuation money passed through Bryn's bodgy superannuation fund via electronic transfer to a bank on Queensland's Gold Coast. The bank account was depleted by ATM withdrawals and reached Bryn, less commissions to runners, as cash and Post Office Money Orders, via a car wash company that existed only in a serviced office in Albert Road, South Melbourne.

An anomaly led Ian to Bryn. The auditor of Freddie's former superannuation fund discovered that Freddie's payment contained an error and Management sought to correct it with an adjustment cheque. However the superannuation fund in PNG had changed its address to Fiji and efforts to make the corrective payment were defeated because the letters were consistently returned by the Australian Post Office. Ian happened to be in the office of the superannuation fund manager for a celebratory drink following a successful investigation unrelated to Bryn.

In the Australian system of law enforcement, the sworn officers of the law, Federal and State, have powers to apprehend any person subject to certain conditions. By contrast, the licence of a Private Investigator conferred upon the holder no more privileges than that of any ordinary citizen. Indeed in many ways it constrained a PI from undertaking acts for which an unlicensed private citizen would be forgiven but could attract severe penalties to a PI. With no authority to apprehend suspected persons and, frankly, no inclination to pursue drunks, drug addicts and the diseased, Ian's specialty became restitution ie getting back stolen superannuation money, rather than retribution, which was an avenue he left entirely to sworn officers of law.

That being so, Ian was meticulous in gathering information in a transparent form to ensure that every item he reported would be admissible evidence in Court. He was particularly aware of the Federal Government Privacy Act, which he and many others held as one of the greatest pieces of legislation given to criminals, and criminal lawyers (are there any other kind?) to escape just consequences.

Ian was extremely bitter about a case that involved obtaining financial advantages by deception. Two low life predators turned four middle class financially comfortable widows into paupers. The two conmen escaped to a wealthy retirement when the defense was successful in having accepted a spurious accusation that the prosecution had violated the civil liberties of the two accused when compiling the State's case. Accordingly incontrovertible evidence of guilt of the thieves was ruled inadmissible in Court. Laughing all the way to the Bank, the acquitted redeemed themselves a little in Ian's estimation, by paying their preening lawyers with cheques that were dishonoured. In Ian's eyes, the lawyers might have attained some acclaim in asserting that Criminal Law be subservient to the newly introduced Privacy

Act. But the lawyers neglected the paramount principle when defending conmen; always get paid up front in cash.

The successful investigation that Ian was being complimented upon involved a 28 year old superannuation clerical officer who made fraudulent payments, disguised as genuine fund expenses, to a service company for services never performed.

On Ian's recommendation the clerical officer was denied access to the company's information technology system. All access codes were changed by an independent professional computer specialist to protect against the officer or any associate corrupting the system. It also permitted more detailed examination of the confirmed corrupt payment process employed by the crooked clerical officer.

Wider ranging investigation of other segments of the system was conducted overnight using independent specialists hired for the job. This revealed that the fraud had been regularly perpetrated within the fund's payroll and postal systems. The total embezzled over 21 months was $800,000. Ian overtly obtained sufficient information to confront the clerical officer and, in the presence of witnesses, and on consensually recorded audio tape, arranged to terminate the officer's employment without creating a situation that may later have provided a feral lawyer with grounds for launching an unfair dismissal claim.

Ian, in conjunction with the superannuation fund lawyers and embarrassed auditors, made application to the Victorian Supreme Court to issue a Mareva Injunction against the former clerical officer. The Injunction was granted. That restrained the clerical officer from dealing with any assets that may be the subject of a claim by his former employer. The defendant was legally prevented from disposing of assets such as his residence, motor vehicle, money in the bank, (save day to day expenses), investments, etc. The "freezing" restriction was important to prevent dispersal of assets and maybe conversion of assets to cash to assist in flight of the defendant. Only after Ian was satisfied of the security of the assets was the defendant reported to the police. The report was accompanied by such a substantial raft of supporting documents that the defendant pleaded guilty to numerous charges of theft, obtaining money by deception, etc and was later handed a total prison sentence of four years with a non parole period of 26 months.

The Mareva effectively froze the defendant's assets and subsequently allowed the superannuation fund to obtain ownership of items as part restitution to the cash value of close to $800,000, the amount stolen. Ian's primary concern was to protect the superannuation fund so far as possible. Hence his determination to launch the civil, Mareva, action in priority to the subsequent criminal report. Ian's reputation for making the client's interest predominate over law enforcement kept him in regular employment as a PI. Hence his motto and continuing commitment thereto, "restitution prevails over retribution".

Having toasted that motto in a fine drop of Tullamore Dew Irish whiskey with the trustees and manager of the superannuation fund, conversation turned, as it does under liberal lubrication, to peculiar and out of the ordinary happenings. It was in that context that the manager mentioned his inability to contact a person to correct a payment error. Mention was made of several unusual features connected with the person, and the Chairman of Trustees being in an expansive mood and grateful to Ian, decided to given Ian the sinecure job of making sure the cheque was properly cleared. This would avoid the unnecessary inconvenience of reporting of unpaid cheques as required under Accounting Regulations. Ian accepted the challenge, although he though it somewhat denigrated his talents, in the generous spirit in which it was offered and promised to call the following day to commence his task.

Next morning Ian spent writing reports about minor matters and dispatching them to clients so it was late afternoon before he reached the premises of the superannuation fund to find a large envelope of papers, photocopies of the entire file of the elusive former contributor, and the replacement cheque in the sum of $1,109.60. He had expected to receive only that cheque, a name, address and telephone number but the manager had been in a hurry to leave to attend a seminar and his normally explicit instructions to his Personal Assistant were deficient to the extent that the PA decided to err on the grounds on commission rather than omission and photocopied the entire file on the person who had the first name of Frederick. Happy to have accomplished the boring duty of locating, then photocopying every extant document about Frederick, she gleefully handled the filled envelope to Ian, a person known to be well and favourably acquainted with her boss and those Gods of the superannuation industry – the Trustees.

That night, after the evening meal, Ian left his wife to attend to preparations for her Ladies Club meeting and went to his study with the intention of spending ten minutes looking at the superannuation fund file of Frederick. One hour later he was reading the file for a second time, totally absorbed and with every instinct telling him he was looking at a fraud. What disturbed Ian was a gut feeling of déjà vu he could not immediately pinpoint. The superannuation fund file given to Ian was the first time all information of Frederick, or Freddie for short, had been gathered in one folder. Prior to that, to comply with the Privacy Act, each section of the fund had retained only sufficient detail necessary to meet procedural or legal requirements of their own specialised section. Ian had properly collated the information to a form that permitted analysis.

In its final form, Freddie's history commenced when his employer made application to enroll Freddie in the superannuation fund. Freddie's gross annual salary, as shown on the enrolment form was $20,00 and the employer was obliged under the Superannuation Guarantee Levy to contribute 9% of that to an approved fund. Freddie volunteered to have 5% deducted from his gross salary making the total annual superannuation contribution $2,800, to be paid in quarterly sums.

After six months and with $1,400 in his account, Freddie applied to the fund for a loan of $300,000 secured on a house in Glen Waverley. A valuation of $400,000 on letterhead of a well known real estate firm was attached to his application. Freddie claimed to have agreed to purchase the property for $385,000 and to have other resources sufficient to service the loan. As the applicant fitted the fund's loan criteria the loan was granted. A bank cheque for $300,000 was paid by the fund to the lawyers for the vendor. The fund registered a first mortgage on the property at time of title transfer. Every aspect of the property purchase was genuine and strictly in accordance with Real Estate law. The details were fed into the superannuation fund computer which accurately but uncritically recorded loan repayments by direct credit as well as those remitted by the employer as deductions from Freddie's salary.

The magnitude of the direct credit supplementary payments surprised Ian. The computer records showed that Freddie paid an average of $22,000 per month off the loan, in addition the regular deductions from salary. Ian's interest was piqued as the computer print out showed that $22,000 per month was made up of several regular payments averaging $3,000 per payment, always in cash plus two bank cheques of $5,000. In eight months Freddie repaid over $176,000. And this from an employee whose loan application stated his gross annual income at $20,000 pa.

Next in the file was a solicitor's letter endorsed by Freddie stating that he had sold the Glen Waverley house. More correspondence from a lawyer representing the purchaser of Freddie's house and internal memos, settlement records and copies of the final discharge of mortgage documents. Concurrent with the house sale was Freddie's resignation and notification by his employer of the termination of contribution. The penultimate piece of paper was a properly filled out and signed fund form directing Freddie's benefits to a PNG superannuation fund.

The final group of documents stapled together included an internal audit memo indicating under payment of $1,109.60 regarding the property settlement and the explanatory letter and others and copy of the cheque sent to Freddie's address in PNG. Handwritten notes made by fund members, told the story of the return of several letters and failure to contact Freddie by other means. The lawyers involved in the house purchase denied having any address for Freddie. The unpresented cheque, returned by Australia Post, was crumpled and so was cancelled and a replacement issued.

Ian was intrigued to discover from ASIC records that Freddie's employer was a car wash company with its registered office in Albert Road South Melbourne. Originally the single director company, as the records showed, was a 72 year old lady with an address in the country city of Shepparton. The directorship changed shortly thereafter to a 68 year old male in another country town, Tallangatta, in Victoria's North. A directory search showed no telephone number for either person. The following morning Ian telephoned the Tallangatta Post Office seeking an address and was told that the man had left the district and they had no forwarding address. Neither could Ian locate business premises of the car wash company that employed Freddie, only a telephone number operated as part of a suite of serviced offices.

Ian decided that a personal call to the car wash company was warranted. He prepared for his visit to those serviced offices by writing on a "with compliments" slip the words "Urgent re your unpaid money – phone", and here placed the number of one of his untraceable mobile phones. He signed with the name of a person he knew to be a new employee of the superannuation fund. Ian was getting close to retirement age. That fact did not indicate senility to him. Rather it meant experience and his experience gave him the distinct feeling that something was very wrong. He resorted to guile.

He put the slip into a large shocking pink coloured envelope, with a copy of the superannuation fund's interim report booklet. He addressed it to Freddie c/- of the employer, drove to the address of the car wash company and parked where he could view the entrance. On arrival at the floor in the building of the serviced offices, he was politely advised that the occupant of the office was not in but a message could be left. He handed over the bright envelope stressing the urgency of its delivery to the car wash company proprietor. Notwithstanding all of his charm and asking carefully worded questions, he got no useful information beyond the opinion of the receptionist that an officer of the company called in every few days but on which day and at what time she had no information.

Ian went back to his parked car and checked the tyres for a marking that indicated a parking meter inspector had been by. Finding none, he put more coins into the meter to give him a full two hours. There was little he could now do except plan his next steps as he waited for a response to his note by way of a call on his mobile phone. Or, if luck came his way, to identify in some way the person who operated the car wash company that had no premises – but could afford to pay a $20,000 salary to an apparently itinerant person. A person with a surprising access to wads of cash with which to repay the balance of a mortgage. To Ian, Freddie was definitely a person of interest.

Bryn was of the opinion that all tracks connecting him to Freddie had been obliterated. The purchase of Freddie's house and payment of the superannuation mortgage through one of his "shelf" companies had been accomplished with no impediment or hint of scrutiny. All went smoothly according to the lawyer.

Through a recently recruited runner, Johnny offered to the runner's cousin, who owned a truck, the entire contents of the house that once appeared to belong to Freddie. For free, no charge. The only condition being that the premises and garden be left in a clean condition. The cousin acted with commendable celerity and cleared out the TV, VCR, DVD, remaining computer items, refrigerator, washing machine, furniture, bedding, clothing and even the mini aquarium containing four dead goldfish. Before leaving, the cousin used the almost new electric start lawn mower, found in the shed to cut the grass. He trimmed the lawn edges and even swept up the cuttings in a practical display of gratitude. The plastic bags of white powder disappeared.

Bryn's shelf company, now the unencumbered proprietor of the property had placed leasing the Glen Waverley house with a local real estate agent. A married couple with two children moved in as tenants within a week. In Bryn's mind the service of Freddie was now totally terminated and all traces of him totally eliminated.

So when Bryn's long serving runner, Ray, called on the dedicated mobile to say that someone was enquiring about Freddie in the office of the car wash company, Bryn's first reaction to the news was one of petulant annoyance. But he suppressed that emotion and told Ray to meet him near the restaurant located on the Albert Park Lake, only a short distance from the building that accommodated the car wash company's serviced office.

Bryn located the gates providing vehicular access to the Albert Park Lake, drove through and parked his two tone grey Mazda 626. He walked around the edge of the lake being careful to avoid stepping in the droppings of numerous ducks. Ray was seated near the restaurant. He rose and Bryn saw a large fluorescent coloured pink envelope in his hand.

After a perfunctory exchange of greetings, they began to walk along the lakeside path as Ray explained that someone from Freddie's superannuation fund was making enquiries. Ray opened the pink envelope to show Bryn a copy of the fund's interim report booklet with a "with compliments" slip attached on which was hand written the message "please phone me about the receipt – Ralph Wilson," with a mobile phone number following. Bryn exhibited exasperation at being called to a meeting for what appeared to a routine enquiry and told Ray to make the call right now. Ray held up his mobile, punched the numbers, pressed the call button and after a few burps a voice answered, "Yes".

Ray asked for Ralph Wilson and the voice stated that he was Ralph Wilson and asked if it was Freddie on the line. Ray answered "Yes, what do you want" and the Ralph Wilson voice gushed that he was a recently employed member of staff of Freddie's former superannuation fund and that he had incorrectly processed a superannuation procedure. He wanted to send Freddie a cheque and required a separate receipt for the payment that he, Ralph, had forgotten to include with the final paperwork. Ralph was apologetic to "Freddie" but being a new a new boy in the fund he was embarrassed about the oversight and did not want his supervisor to find out about his lapse. Throwing himself upon Freddie's mercy, the voice asked if Freddie would sign and return a receipt if Ralph mailed the cheque to him.

Ray and Bryn had their heads together listening to the dilemma of Ralph Wilson. Bryn raised his hand with a thumb down and Ray, impersonating Freddie, told Ralph that he was travelling and unable to collect correspondence for some time so it was tough luck, he would be unable to sign anything. Ray pressed the call termination button on the mobile phone with a feeling of sadistic satisfaction.

Bryn and Ray talked for another few minutes before Ray tore the lurid coloured envelope and contents into small pieces and desecrated the surface of the lake with the litter. Ray walked back to the building in Albert Road where his car was parked in the basement. Bryn waited until Ray had cleared the scene. Bryn enjoyed all things that floated and spent several stress relieving minutes watching the endeavours of unskilled rowers in hired boats and children's legs pumping pedals of the floating pedal boats. During that intermission his eyes has quartered the area around the path that Ray had taken but detected nothing untoward as he walked back to the car park. He could see no evidence of any unusual activity there either, so he entered his car and drove to the St Kilda Marina where his magnificent new multi million dollar motor cruiser floated in its berth.

In the park fronting Marine Parade, the road to the Marina, Bryn saw children flying kites. One kite was fluorescent pink in colour and a question flashed through his mind "Why would a superannuation fund be using fluorescent pink envelopes" and a brief vision of the Trojan Horse invaded his mind. An idiot driver several cars ahead caused another to swerve and others to brake. Bryn's fleeting thought vanished as he concentrated on traffic matters.

Later that day Bryn thought that there was something he had missed, some inconsistency, but he never retrieved the thought that may have led to a warning. Bryn went to his beloved motor cruiser to prepare for a visit from a female with nymphomaniac tendencies without realising that a fluorescent pink envelope warranted more thought. Had Bryn's cogitations been less focused on pink female flesh and more on a curious bright pink envelope then it could have re-awakened his earlier premonition based on a Trojan Horse. The Trojans believed they were winners, became over confident and lowered their defenses. Disaster followed. But Bryn was only human and a male at that. So like most males anticipating an evening of sexual shenanigans, his primal urges diminished any consideration of caution.

CHAPTER SEVENTEEN

CONTRADICTIONS AND INCONGRUITIES ARE A largely unacknowledged part of Australia. The national song, "Waltzing Matilda" commemorates a suicidal sheep thief. The national hero to many is a murderer, horse thief, bank robber, and would be train derailer. Harold Holt, an Australian Prime Minister disappeared, presumed drowned or taken by a shark, and a swimming pool was named after him.

Given those examples of national ethos it seemed not inappropriate that Erwin drove an expensive sports car but chose lodgement on his travels at the cheapest most tawdry back packer hotels. He chose to reside with the effluent class rather than the affluent class. With a group of fellow back packers drinking beer to excess, the subject of sex was raised as it inevitably does and one humorous member of the group, when asked about sexual relations, confessed that he had some, "Two cousins who are nymphomaniacs" and was immediately bombarded with requests for introductions.

Erwin noted that one member of the group declined to join those requesting introductions to the nymphomaniac females and as the evening devolved into more raucous behaviour fuelled by alcohol, Erwin edged closer to that man. A conversation developed and masked by the surrounding noise Erwin and his new found acquaintance moved cautiously toward the subject of more deviant forms of sexual gratification. This culminated in Erwin being given the torn off top of a cigarette packet on which his new acquaintance had written an address. He told Erwin to show the packet top at the address where he might find something more suited to his sexual preferences. Erwin was told it was expensive but worth it.

Given the amount of alcohol imbibed, nothing further developed that night but a little after sundown the next night Erwin stood at the front gate of the house at the given address. He had arrived by taxi at the cross road at the head of the street. He walked past the house, suspiciously checking all parked cars because he had no wish to be picked up again by the police. He still recalled the uncomfortable incarceration in the overcrowded police cells when he was arrested during a porno video showing. With some anxiety he walked around the entire block passing the Holy Blood of Mary convent in his walk.

Erwin's warped mind read the convent name several times and decided that it reinforced his opinion that Catholics are a repugnantly earthly lot for commemorating the menstruation of a Jewish mother in the name of a convent and then by stacking the convent full of females with the same biological propensity. He looked carefully down the lane at the rear of the convent but could see no police vehicles. At the church adjacent to the convent he walked twenty metres down one side laneway searching for evidence of a police presence but beyond noting the Phillip Adams commemorative chapel at the rear of the church he detected nothing of an unusual nature.

His anxiety allayed, he opened the gate of the innocuous appearing suburban house and walked to the front door where he pressed the bell push. Almost immediately, as if someone was watching and waiting, a voice from behind the opaque metal screen security door asked "Can I help you?" Erwin had not thought what he should say to the occupant of that house when he arrived because he had concentrated more upon ensuring that the property was not under police observation. He was trying to formulate an appropriate response when the voice asked to see what Erwin was holding. The security door opened to the maximum permitted by a keeper chain and two fingers appeared between which Erwin placed the cigarette packet top before the door closed.

It reopened fully and Erwin realised that the packet top was an entry pass. The hallway lights were covered in red cellophane so everything had the ambiance of the interior of the conning tower of a submarine that featured in a video Erwin had watched recently. He noticed that background only briefly because the person who admitted him absorbed his entire attention thereafter.

The red light emphasized the deep blackness of the head of hair poised below his chin. With a straight fringe and side locks that curved forward over the cheekbones, the hair had the appearance of a Roman soldier's helmet. Beneath the fringe and looking out from a flawless golden skin were two large, deep set dark eyes that assessed him boldly. Exceptionally long eyelashes, parabolic eyebrows, a small well shaped nose and a slightly pouting, scarlett mouth completed the above the necklace picture.

The amber necklace circled a delicate neck. Narrow shoulders covered by a clingy black silk kimono that flowed curvaceously to a tiny fraction below crotch level and what Erwin could see of the legs in the dim red light left him unsure of the gender of his sexy voiced companion. The small hand on his bicep that gently guided him down the hallway was androgynous.

The hallway ended at a wall into which a metal grilled ticket window had been installed. On each side was an obviously reinforced door. A figure appeared in the ticket window and Erwin saw what appeared to be a twin of the person now standing beside him. The same helmet of jet black hair, same type silk kimono and same delicate hands. In the same sexy voice he or she asked Erwin his name and he replied "Bill" without hesitation. The vision behind the window informed "Bill" that the all inclusive fee was $500. That covered an opening half hour with the partner of his choice, all refreshments, attendance at the two special exhibitions then unrestricted access to all partners at the unrestrained free for all. "Unrestrained but not violent" he / she stated twice and added that Bill's $500 would see him through the early session which closed at midnight.

Ever practical, Erwin looked at his watch to see it was almost 7pm so he figured that $500 for five hours sounded value for money. He had withdrawn $1,000 in cash, the daily maximum from an ATM and he extracted his wallet from his hip pocket, counted out $500 and placed the money on the shelf beneath the window.

The wad of $50 notes rapidly disappeared behind the window and his companion opened a door to his right. The sexy voice told him to have a shower, put on one of the silk robes hanging from the rack then come back to the main meeting room which he / she indicated was through the door on his left. Erwin's imagination was roiling in anticipation and he interpreted the "meeting room" to be more along the lines of a "meating" room.

The room he entered was once a standard bedroom, he presumed, but now held two fiberglass shower stalls, a toilet cubicle, a long bench with stacks of towels and a rack stretching along two walls. One wall rack had twenty double hooks for hanging clothes and eight sets of men's clothing hung from some of them above eight pairs of shoes. The other rack held black silk dressing gowns or kimonos.

Before he undressed he considered the safety of his wallet then saw that the kimonos had pockets on each side. Further observation of the row of kimonos revealed that they were of different length, which indicated that the longest was the largest size. To test that observation Erwin took the longest one on the end hook and tried it on, over his clothes. It was a reasonable fit and as he began to take it off, prior to shedding his clothes he could hear the intensity of the noise in the other part of the house increase.

His highly salacious thoughts, triggered by the noise, were beginning to cause a physical manifestation when the door was swiftly swung open and the flash of a camera assaulted his eyes. As his eyes adjusted again to the dim light he raised his formidable fists to fight, he knew not what, but it was an interruption that fractured his mood of sexual anticipation and was, therefore, a legitimate target for punishment.

But Erwin was denied retribution as those words that he vehemently abhorred assaulted his ears, as the camera flash assaulted his eyes a fraction of a second earlier, "Police, stay right where you are". The words were metallically repeated three times through a loud hailer. Erwin looked around for a way out but one shower stall blocked exit through the only window and he could see that two uniformed constables blocked the only door.

Erwin was told to put down his fists and sit on the bench. Although the doorway was partly obscured by a large police constable, Erwin could see other uniforms and plain clothes police in the hallway and assessed his chances of an escape by forcing his way through the door as being nil. He heard one of the police constables speaking to someone he assumed to be a superior saying that "The big bloke in here was the last one in and he has all his clothes on". The overheard response was "OK keep him there, I'll see him last".

Erwin tried to compose his mind and to focus on the advice given by Lenny the lanky lawyer after Erwin's last contretemps with the constabulary. His clear recollection was that he should only give his name and other details to the police at a police station and he was to demand, in writing, the details of why he was being arrested and the name, rank and station of the police person requesting his details. He was to be a proper bastard at the place of his arrest but refrain from assaulting the police if the assault could be observed. He must loudly and repeatedly claim that he was arrested by mistake and protest that police had bashed him without any provocation on his part. He must yell frequently that the police had stolen his money. The performance must be maintained until he was transported to a police station whereupon his behaviour must change instantaneously to one of respectful obedience to all police orders. Confusion and contradiction was the aim.

The exception to obedience at the police station was that, apart from giving his personal details, he must not make any other statement whatsoever. He must repeatedly demand that he be allowed to contact his lawyer. Once contact was made, Erwin must sit and silently await the arrival of the cavalry in the form of Lenny the lanky lawyer in his large Lexus.

Erwin began to put the advice into practice by shouting but the police ignored him and eventually shut the door and locked it. When he kicked the door Erwin learned that this old house had very solid doors. After twenty kicks and no response he gave away his protests. It was alright to perform when an appreciative audience was present but he felt a right idiot when the only observer was his own image in a full length wall mirror. So he kicked the mirror to pieces and sat down feeling a bit better.

His thoughts turned to Lenny and a strange, unusual emotional phenomenon crept upon him. It took some time for him to appreciate that the emotion was that of embarrassment. Here he was caught again by the police in an attempt to obtain sexual delectation and again he had failed. The only person whose opinion he valued was Lenny. Erwin did not want Lenny to perceive him as a failure. Fair enough it he was caught bollock naked in a menagerie of frolicking flesh; Lenny would understand that every young man was entitled to some form of sexual satisfaction. But for Erwin to be caught for a second time still some distance short of his winning post was embarrassing. Erwin looked at his watch and was surprised to realise that he had sat in contemplative solitude for almost an hour. His contemplation of how to avoid Lenny's scorn was long and deep and curtailed only by the noise of the key being turned in the lock on the solid door.

CHAPTER EIGHTEEN

IAN SAT IN HIS ANGLED parked car eighty metres on the opposite side of the road to the twelve story building that housed scores of serviced offices. He had topped up the parking meter once and was shortly due to do it again. He had used one of the oldest tricks in the book, even though he never knew what that meant, by leaving the bright pink envelope, addressed to Freddie at the registered office of the remarkable car wash company. Remarkable because it had no premises other than a four metre by three point five metre serviced office. In over two hours of observation of the front door, no one had walked out with the pink envelope. True, one of the scores of people who had gone in and out could have the envelope out of sight in a bag or brief case or left the building by another entrance. Earlier he had established that there existed four entrances and he could only watch the two main ones. The pedestrian and the vehicle.

Time was not wasted because he had re-read Freddie's file. It exhibited every hallmark of a sizeable money laundering operation, even though the superannuation fund did not appear to be the target of a fraud, simply a convenient conduit of dirty cash in, clean cash out. The mortgage loan scheme was unnoticeable debt redemption in a form unreportable in the extensive mandatory reportable financial system. Freddie and his employer company both smelled of corruption.

Ian's self justification for maintaining observation with, at best, a 50/50 success rate, stemmed from experience that if corrupt organisations knew sufficient about any business entity to manipulate its system, then the step from money laundering to other forms of criminality would not be far away. For several decades Ian had made a high standard of living from the superannuation industry by providing high standard service. He respected most of the people who administered and invested the retirement money for millions of Australian workers. He instinctively wanted to shield them and the industry he admired. If his investigation could help achieve that, then he was prepared to spend a few non-billable hours to acquire protective evidence.

Several spaces away a car pulled out and Ian quickly drove into the vacant space. The short trip would rub out the crayon mark of the parking inspector, who had recently passed. Ian used some of his considerable supply of coin to top up the parking meter. The last coin slid into the slot when a man that Ian recognised from an earlier investigation emerged from the building carrying a bright pink envelope, Ian's colurful equivalent to the Trojan Horse. The unexpected recognition gave him a momentary shock.

Ian's memory cells were in top gear but nothing was meshing to provide an identity only a vague feeling of an association with a white car lingered. The "envelope" man stood outside the building where a mess of cigarette butts indicated that this was the congestion spot for the slow suiciders. Pink envelope man was talking on his mobile phone and a couple of times gestured with the pink envelope as if the person on the other end of the call could see it. Envelope man was on the mobile phone less than a minute before walking to a nearby coffee shop. He bought a coffee and a muffin. The envelope was on the table and the envelope man read one of the complimentary magazines provided by the coffee shop as he munched the muffin and drank from his cup. He looked at his watch several times then picked up the envelope and began to walk in a direction that would have him pass close to Ian.

While envelope man consumed his morning tea, Ian put binoculars, a camera and a few items of clothing into a backpack. Many of the items were guesswork because he had no way to anticipate the moves of envelope man. So he put in everything he could think of that may be useful. The man completed the road crossing and turned away, walking along a path towards a large yellow tent seemingly perpetually inhabited by people protesting about the Grand Prix being raced every year around the lake. Ian allowed a two hundred and fifty metre start before pulling on the backpack, a knitted woollen cap, sunglasses and following.

Envelope man stayed on the sunlit footpath. Ian walked in shadow beneath the trees about twenty metres into the parkland from the path. Ian was certain that he had encountered this man before. The angle of the head and the short swing of the arms were familiar. Then it occurred to Ian that he could not attach a name to the man because he had never uncovered his true name. The envelope man once drove a Holden Commodore car registered to an extant but non compos person. The envelope man as associated with "Johnny", someone that Ian has tipped as being a "boss" conman.

People were picnicking around the area of the park where envelope man seemed to be heading. Ian stepped up his pace and closed the distance to one hundred metres. When his target stopped near the restaurant, Ian moved behind a large tree, removed his woollen cap and replaced it with white cloth tennis hat from the backpack. He stood looking into the window of a shop selling light marine gear of the type used by the small yachts on the lake. His target continually consulted his watch. It became obvious to Ian that a meeting was due. This motivated him to seek a spot offering greater concealment but also allowing him to visually scour the area to identify the expected contact.

From behind a galvanized metal dumpster, Ian saw a two toned grey Mazda 626 drive into the car parking area and the action that attracted Ian was the head of driver continually swivelling as if worried about being observed. The Mazda pulled into a bay, an athletic young man emerged, he looked around again, did not see Ian who had retreated behind some lattices, then made his way toward the restaurant where he greeted the man with the pink envelope. The body language testified that the younger man was dealing with a subordinate.

Ian watched the two men looking at the contents of the pink envelope. "Johnny", for Ian felt he had sufficient circumstantial evidence to label him as such, gesticulated and Ian saw envelope man dialing a mobile phone. Despite a realisation of what was about to happen, Ian still jumped a bit when the second of the three mobile phones he carried chirruped into the orchestral rendition of the Radetzki March.

Ian answered, "Yes" and in response to the caller's question agreed that he was Ralph Wilson of the superannuation fund and Ian responded by asking if he were talking to Freddie. On being told that he was indeed speaking with Freddie, Ian, alias Ralph Wilson, prattled on about needing a receipt to cover his omission as a new boy. He said he wanted to send a cheque for which he required a receipt. Would Freddie send it back to him? The reply was uncooperative and terse. Freddie said he was travelling and could not give an address, so no cheque, no receipt, tough luck. The call was disconnected.

Ian knew that the "Freddie" to whom he was speaking on the phone could not be the superannuation fund contributor named Frederick Urquhart because the date of birth of the genuine, if anything could be considered genuine, Freddie, made him at least ten years younger that the man with the mobile phone. Ian smiled at the thought that two impostors were talking to each other on a mobile phone hook up and that he now had captured on his mobile phone the number of envelope man's mobile.

Reasoning that as the envelope man was not the boss, and Ian always aimed for the top target, he opted to risk a trace to establish the identity of the mysterious boss. Ian quickly walked across the car park. With practiced eyes searching to ensure that he was not under observation, Ian placed a magnetic based electronic tracking device inside the rear wheel arch of the Mazda. This enabled him to more reliably tail the car of the person who, if not the boss, was at least one rung further up the ladder of crime than envelope man. Ian began a quick walk towards his own car. Hoping his target was still within the 1.2 kilometre tracker range, Ian opened his car and switched on his tracking console, installed in his car's glove box. He saw the white blip on the flat green screen was beginning to move.

Although not given to intemperate language, Ian swore filthily as the previously clear road experienced traffic build up in front of him. It impeded his progress towards the direction indicted by the blip and its accompanying audio buzzing noise. He busted several traffic laws and annoyed a few motorists before gaining sufficient ground to ensure a good signal. He estimated that six cars separated him from his unseen target in the grey Mazda.

In his effort to get a strong signal, Ian had noted the traffic conditions but not absorbed the area or direction of traffic until the target, after several turns probably made routinely to shake or identity any follower, turned into Marine Parade. At that time Ian had at least nine cars and a van shielding him from observation in the rear view mirror of the Mazda. It was then that Ian confirmed his growing suspicion that the target's destination was the St Kilda Marina. Was the young man the elusive "Johnny", tentatively identified two years earlier in relation to a suspected fraudulent disability claim?

A minor traffic delay bunched up the cars on Marine Parade and Ian saw Johnny drive into the Marina car park. Ian continued further along the road angling into the centre lane and turning, again as he recalled, at the traffic lights near the Luna Park amusement complex. Ian drove along the other side of the dual roadway until turning left into a side street and parking.

Ian took the backpack, crossed Marine Parade and walked into the Marina car park, eyes searching everywhere for Johnny. Near the grey Mazda, Ian seemingly stumbled, dropped the backpack and put his hand on the Mazda to assist him to stand. In so doing he retrieved his electronic tracking device from the rear wheel arch and continued towards the Marina's large maintenance shed. The undetected retrieval of the tracker transmitter relieved Ian enormously. Seldom did he use the device because the Surveillance Devices Act prohibited the installation, use or maintenance of any tracking device to determine the location, of inter alia, a vehicle, without the express or implied consent of the person in lawful control of the vehicle. Even sworn law enforcement officers were prohibited from using a tracking device without a warrant. Ian used the device rarely.

Ian saw Johnny on the aft deck of a magnificent motor cruiser. As he got closer he saw it was named Panygyric and reminded himself to look up the word in a dictionary. He changed direction to walk to the Marina office. The attendant on duty was a tanned fit looking young man in trainers, shorts and tee shirt who was assembling, or dissembling something in a box with the words "sacrificial anode" printed on it. Another marine mystery to Ian, a confirmed landlubber.

Ian held up his backpack and told the attendant that he was to deliver it to someone named Johnny in a boat named "Panny-something" and could he please be given directions. The amiable attendant, eager to help, read out the names of three vessels with names starting with "Pan" but said that none were owned or crewed by a person named Johnny. Ian pointed through the window to the Panygyric and said "What about that one". He got an answer, "No, that's Bryn Hamley one of our best skippers, he looks after the cruiser for an overseas owner. His first name is Bryn – B.R.Y.N, its Welsh or something". Ian's brain instantly cemented in that information then he feigned a look at a tag on the backpack and apologized to the attendant saying that he was sorry and felt like a fool because the bag was to be delivered to the Brighton Marina not the St Kilda Marina.

The attendant smiled and returned to doing whatever a sacrificial anode expects to have done to it, with Ian's admission erasing his visit from the mind of the attendant. An enquiry followed by an admission of error more often than not erased the event so the likelihood of the enquiry ever being mentioned to the newly identified Bryn was negligible. That erasure was part of Ian's technique based on expertise acquired with experience. He did not want to stir up vigilance by his target. Ian was always cautious; he had no contempt for caution.

With a name and the registered number of a motor vehicle, Ian felt he had done enough for one day but then prodded himself into making a cryptic phone call. Later that evening he drove to a suburban house in Springvale, placed $25 under a brick and took a piece of paper with name of the company that owned the two toned grey Mazda being driven by the probable 'Johnny'. The company, he discovered when he read the paper a short time later, was registered with ASIC, as a single director company owned by a 74 year old man in the Victorian city of Warrnambool.

That 74 year old man had no record of ever having been a director of any company involved with a Bryn Hamley. The telephone directory on Ian's computer had no record of a phone number of the 74 year old putative company director alleged to be a resident of Warrnambool, a provincial city 265 kilometres from Melbourne. The same telephone directory showed 25 Hamley's in the Melbourne CBD, of which four had the first name beginning with the letter B.

Enough for one day thought Ian; tomorrow he would visit the former residence of Freddie and ask the neighbours some questions. After that, perhaps a visit to the Electoral Office might provide him with more information to enable a more positive identification of the elusive Johnny.

CHAPTER NINETEEN

ERWIN SPRANG TO HIS FEET and adopted an aggressive stance when a medium sized man wearing a police badge on the pocket of his blue pin striped suit entered. Erwin tagged him as a medium man because the policeman was of medium height, medium weight and a face that seemed not too old, not topped by too much hair nor too little and the hair was a medium mix of mid brown and grey hairs. His medium facial expression did not alter one iota at Erwin's posture. He was unimpressed. He was unimpressionable. Even the smashed mirror fragments on the floor warranted only a passing glance as his shoes crunched over the broken bits. He crossed the room and casually sat on the bench.

In a medium voice he introduced himself as Sergeant Jarvis of the Vice Squad. With a hand gesture he invited Erwin to take a seat on the bench. His medium modulated voice asked Erwin to explain why he was on the premises and to surrender his wallet. He told Erwin that the choice between the hard way and the easy way to resolve the police interest in the matter depended on Erwin's response. Erwin blustered that he had rights and intended to insist upon them. Erwin told Sergeant Jarvis that his legal advisor was Lenny in an attempt to intimidate the Sergeant with a name that was known throughout legal and police circles for aggressive defense.

Jarvis was truly impressed but did not let it show. Jarvis was unconcerned with the aggressive defense proclivities of Lenny, rather he reassessed Erwin's financial status. If Erwin could afford Lenny's exorbitant fees then Erwin was a pigeon with feathers for Jarvis to pluck. Jarvis took the Polaroid photo of Erwin from his pocket and patted the bench beside him as an invitation for Erwin to sit more closely. Unused to such casual indifference to his physical threats and verbal fulminations, Erwin was confused and obediently shifted beside the Sergeant.

Jarvis held out his hand and said "Wallet" and Erwin extracted it from his back pocket and handed it to Jarvis. Without a word Jarvis fingered through the cash, credit cards, Medicare card, and other bits of clutter until he found Erwin's drivers licence. He extracted an expensive gold plated ball point pen from the inside pocket of his suit coat and with it wrote on the back of Polaroid photo the relevant details from Erwin's licence. The licence was replaced and as Jarvis was about to hand the wallet back to Erwin, a black silk kimono on the bench was accidently knocked to the floor. Erwin reached down to retrieve it and placed it on the bench between himself and Jarvis. Erwin was surprised when Jarvis handed back his wallet. When Erwin had put the wallet back into his hip pocket, Jarvis gestured at the Polaroid photograph. Even the hand gesture was so controlled that Erwin rated it as medium.

Jarvis told Erwin that he could walk away right now without any charge being laid in exchange for $5,000. Erwin took a little time to assess that offer. Part of the brief time was expended in recovering from shock at the cool delivery of the blatant bribe demand. He reasoned that it would cost him at least twice that to pay Lenny and it would avoid the embarrassment of having to contact Lenny to confess another failure.

Erwin's mind rehashed the precautions he had taken by way of a reconnaissance to detect police surveillance around the deviant services brothel. He concluded that if this Sergeant Jarvis was smart enough to deploy his police resources in such a way as to be undetectable by customers, then he was smart enough to extricate Erwin from his current predicament. And a predicament it was because Erwin was certain the premises were unlicensed for sexual purposes and strongly suspected that under age sex workers were on the premises.

Erwin nodded in agreement and Jarvis said that the Polaroid photo, the prime evidence of Erwin's complicity, would be destroyed in Erwin's presence when the $5,000 changed hands. Jarvis picked up a disused soap wrapper from the floor, handed Erwin the ball point pen and told him to write the words "Central Park Malvern, corner of Burke and Wattletree Roads, conservatory, 2.30pm". Taking back the gold pen Jarvis told Erwin he wanted half of the $5,000 in used $100 notes and half in used $50 notes. Again Erwin nodded in agreement.

Jarvis rose, opened the door and spoke to someone. Erwin did not hear all of the conversation but thought he heard the word "informant". Jarvis waved Erwin to follow him and Erwin saw that several uniformed police had their backs turned as Jarvis escorted Erwin through several doors into the backyard of the house. A gate in a fence led to a dark lane way and Jarvis pointed in the direction he wanted Erwin to walk, then closed the gate.

As Erwin walked along the cobblestoned "night soil" lane common in many inner suburbs of Melbourne, his eyes adjusted to darkness. Arriving at a major road allowed him to obtain his bearings and he turned right and set off in a confident stride towards the light of a suburban shopping strip. During the walk his feeling was one of relief. The $5,000 that he would have to draw from his bank was of relatively small consequence compared to a Court case. But his sexual frustration was mounting and he considered how to best obtain relief.

Beneath the light from the verandah of a shop front, Erwin extracted his wallet to pay for a taxi home to collect his car and drive to the suburb of St Kilda where he figured he stood the best chance of picking up a rent boy. His expectations disintegrated when he found that the wallet was empty of cash. He recalled an ATM withdrawal of $1,000 and paying $500 to the unlicensed brothel. Where had the other $500 gone?

Erwin recalled that the only time the wallet was out of his sight was for a few seconds when he bent to pick up a black kimono accidently knocked to the floor by the Vice Squad Sergeant. Like the advent of a bright dawn the realisation came that the kimono drop was not an accident but a distraction. Jarvis had obviously taken the $500. With only coins in his pocket and the daily ATM maximum already drawn on his credit card, Erwin had no chance of withdrawing more money before midnight. The coins were sufficient to buy him a ticket to the nearest railway station to his home and his frustration burned every metre of the journey. At home he decided to have one whisky to settle his pent up privations then to drive to an ATM after midnight when his credit card will allow further cash withdrawal. But one drink became two and two became more so that he spent the night on a sofa in an alcohol infused sleep.

Erwin woke because the noise made by the early morning garbage collectors woke everything living within a kilometre. In fact if something organic did not wake up at the garbage cacophony, rumour had it that the State automatically issued a death certificate. And Erwin felt that he almost qualified for a certificate because his hang over was monumental. His anguished head was matched only by the almost crippling torment emanating from unrequieted testicles. He staggered to the bathroom and tried to drink cold water from the tap but the effort to turn his head sideways added to the excruciating conflict that appeared to be at full pitch somewhere behind his eyes. It was fully an hour before cold water and pain killing medication brought the world back into focus.

Reaching into the pocket of his pants for a handkerchief, his fingers encountered a disused soap wrapper and he stared blearily at it in complete bewilderment for a full minute. Only when his shaky fingers dropped it on the table did his eyes focus on the written message. The message prompted the recollection of the previous night's debacle. The memory caused further agonising. Serrated waves of pain tramped between his ears. Many minutes later the realisation that he needed $5,000 to prevent prosecution caused him to look at a clock. On the second attempt he read the time as being 11.30am and a further gust of nausea, this time in his stomach and bowels temporarily incapacitated him.

It was after midday before he found his cheque book and departed, in slow steps to his local bank. He cashed a cheque for $6,000 half in $100's and half in $50's. He stood before the bullet proof screen covering most of the bank teller's cubicle trying to remember something that was vaguely disturbing him and only remembered that he needed used notes not new notes in sequential numbers. However he was forestalled in his request because the notes being counted were obviously used not new. He moved to a less crowded area of the bank and counted $1,000 in notes that he put in his wallet. The remaining $5,000, held by a rubber band, he placed deep into a side pocket and wedged the wad with a well used handkerchief.

His general level of perambulation made him realise that driving was out of the question so he ambled slowly towards a tram stop. Whenever the tram stopped the squeal of its metal wheels on the metal lines as the brakes were applied made his head feel like a moon rocket at launch. After a half hour ride that added to his nausea, he staggered off the tram at the terminus right opposite the Malvern Central Park. His eyes felt that sand and glue had been liberally introduced beneath the eyelids. Erwin consulted his watch, with difficulty, and calculated with greater difficultly that he was on time for his rendezvous with the Vice Squad Sergeant. Slowly he set off around a sporting oval towards the conservatory. His rotten physical condition probably prevented his resentment at the pay off to the policeman from flaring.

Thirty metres from the conservatory Erwin was surprised to hear his name called and turned sharply, a manoeuvre he regretted. Standing in the shelter of several bushes he saw Sergeant Jarvis, with a hand outstretched. Erwin handed over the $5,000 with unaccustomed restraint. Jarvis rippled the notes with a thumb as if to assess the thickness of the wad and from that judge whether or not Erwin had kept his part of the bargain.

Erwin did not notice that Jarvis was a little edgy. He had been anxious lest Erwin had reneged on their deal. Jarvis had observed Erwin's approach to ensure that no member of the Police Internal Affairs was using him as a decoy. Another catalyst to Jarvis's anxious disposition was the thought that Erwin might turn nasty and Jarvis doubted his unaided ability to cope with an angry Erwin. This time he was alone with Erwin. Help from fellow police officers was not at hand. Jarvis had no contempt for caution. He had been careful to take the money with his left hand and make only a token attempt to check that the wad really was $5,000. His right hand, concealed behind his open coat flap, was be-ringed by a set of solid brass knuckles.

But Erwin resembled a zombie more than an oversized belligerent bully so Jarvis relaxed, put away the brass knuckleduster and produced the Polaroid photo for Erwin to inspect. Erwin gazed at the photo with only partial comprehension before Jarvis took out a disposable cigarette lighter and set the photo on fire. He held it by a corner then he dropped it onto the graveled path. The corner burned out quickly and Jarvis used the heel of his shoe to crush and spread the photo ashes. Erwin gazed at the burning through blood shot eyes. Jarvis told Erwin to stay where he was for five minutes. Jarvis turned and left. Erwin did not even look to see which way he went.

Dimly, through a brain that was slowly returning to normal, Erwin heard the sounds of children's voices. He stood unmoving for some time. Then, as if responding to a remote control, took one slow step at a time into the shrubs and trees near the rear of the conservatory.

He paused while still obscured from anyone not in his immediate vicinity. Fifty metres in front of him was a playground full of children. With some effort he focused on them. He disregarded the girls and concentrated on the young boys. From his hidden place his rapidly clearing ability to concentrate was only upon the young, clear skinned, bare legged boys.

Jarvis need not have worried about Erwin staying behind for five minutes so he could clear the area without a tail. Erwin remained in the bushes as a hidden watcher of the young boys for over an hour. And during the hour Erwin's alcohol affected brain began thinking. And all of the thoughts were what normal people would call terrifyingly dark, demonic and incredibly evil.

CHAPTER TWENTY

IAN WAS SATISFIED WITH HIS investigation procedure but still uncertain how his acquired information about the two men and suspect car registrations could be applied. He drove towards his home, taking several precautions en route to ensure that he was not followed. He saw no profit in successfully following a target only to be hoist on his own petard. He refueled at his regular Shell service station, taking a full minute to run his hand held scanner around areas where a tracker transmitter may have been attached whilst his car was unattended. Finding none, he paid for the petrol and drove home.

Next morning Ian's bright mood was in contrast to Melbourne's grey overcast weather. He drove to the street in Glen Waverley where Freddie once occupied a house and began the routine foot wearing procedure of making enquires of Freddie's former neighbours. In response to his first call a raspy voice, presumably female, indicated that he should have sex using only two words. The first word was "Get".

The occupants of other houses were absent or unable to offer any useful answers to his questions about Freddie. Ian was disappointed until he called in at the corner shop, bought a packet of Lifesavers and talked to the teenaged shop assistant. The girl remembered Freddie and said she was surprised when he left so suddenly. She supposed it was because of his split with Kathy, the young woman with whom he had been living for about six months. Kathy, he was told, was about 23 years old, light brunette actually but often lightened up to a multi coloured orangish / purple, drove a red Camira car and worked as a shoe shop assistant on the second level at Southland. That comprehensive dossier exhausted the teenager's knowledge about Kathy and with other customers to be served Ian felt he could not impose further on the strength of the purchase of one packet of peppermint Lifesavers. He smiled a "thank you" and walked back to his car.

The only information he could use was about this "Kathy". It wasn't much, but Ian had achieved success starting with less in the past. He decided to try to locate her.

Southland is a large shopping complex located in the Melbourne suburb of Cheltenham. As the crow flies the distance from Ian's current location in Glen Waverley to the shopping complex was fifteen kilometres. In light traffic along wide, well signed roads, Ian was locking his car in the Southland car park twenty five minutes later. He rode an escalator to level two and saw a twenty something year old young lady with garish coloured hair standing expectantly in the shoe shop. Ian approached behind the disarming shield of his smile to ask about Freddie.

Kathy's reaction, although far from warm, was not uncooperative. She seemed to be bored because of slow business and welcomed an opportunity to chatter. Reading between Kathy's lines took no effort and the distilled essence of her monologue was that Freddie and Kathy had been an item for around six months. Freddie had no regular occupation but worked for a boss known as "Ray", a man in his late 40's she guessed, for whom he arranged things. Exactly what kind of things Freddie arranged, Kathy was vague.

The arrangements of things entailed interstate trips every few weeks of several days duration. Kathy dropped one gem of information. She said that Freddie had once told her that "Ray was the block and Johnny the butcher" from which she implied that Ray conveyed orders from Johnny. Freddie's hours of work were flexible and remunerative, seemingly all income being by way of cash or Money Orders because Ray joked about not bothering the Taxation Department that occupied a lot of floor space at a building in Spring Street Melbourne he called Vampire House.

Kathy thought that Freddie was involved in something just a little bit, you know, illegal but, horror, never something like drugs. Several weeks ago Kathy went to a hen's party for a girlfriend. She left the party early with disastrous results because on the way to the home she shared with Freddie, she spied him with another young woman, imprudently sitting near the front of a coffee lounge. They were indulging in mutual manual manipulation of each other's anatomy in a manner that clearly raised the question "If they go this far in public what do they do in private"? Not liking the answer she gave to herself, and she emphasized, being deathly afraid of HIV diseases, Kathy went home that night to Mother. Next day she used her key to clear out her possessions and departed Freddie's house for good.

Peeved beyond belief was the tone conveyed in her voice when she told Ian that Freddie had never even bothered to call her to find out why she had left, despite the fact that he had ample access to telecommunications because he always carried at least three mobile phones. Nor had he offered to refund to her the rent contribution she made and which she could really use now.

Ian was pleased with her information. Despite the colour of her hair, Ian liked her. He decided to kill two birds with one stone in stretching the truth just a teeny weenie bit by saying that he a cheque of Freddie's that really and truly should be hers if he owed her money. She brightened at being told that and in her lunch break Kathy accompanied Ian to her bank on another floor in the shopping complex. Ian had seen Freddie's signature sufficient times for his trained mind to produce a reasonable facsimile and he did this on the superannuation fund cheque of $1,109.60 endorsing it for payment to the account of Kathy Webb and staying with her until she paid it into her account via an over the counter deposit. Ian had his PI licence and the superannuation fund's appointment letter and was prepared to bluff if the bank teller has asked questions about the endorsement of the cheque of another payee, but the deposit process proceeded unimpeded.

Kathy had some compensation and so was happier and the superannuation fund accountant would be pleased not to have to account for an unpresented cheque of such a small amount. On his next visit to the superannuation fund, it was Ian's intention to check that the presentation of the cheque was processed without question. He was as certain as he could be that no member of the superannuation fund staff would trouble to verify what purported to be Freddie's signature. So far as the fund was concerned, the cheque presentation would totally close the Freddie file. So

Ian's obligation to the fund was finished. Ian decided he would not render an account for having the cheque presented.

What did the facts he has discovered amount to? He felt they were relevant to something in the superannuation industry, but what? Ian recalled that a few years earlier he investigated a claim by a contributor for total and permanent disability benefits on the basis of incapacitating injuries. Ian's surveillance established that the contributor was not incapacitated by any illness or accident but appeared to be heading towards incapacity due to alcoholism. The contributor was accosted by a male, dark hair, mid 40's, average build who drove a white Holden Commodore. A violent argument ensured and he heard the name "Johnny" and word "orders". In the context that the name Johnny was spoken it was obvious that the driver was not Johnny, so maybe the driver was the person mentioned by Kathy. Could he be "Ray"? The age group seemed right. Ian felt it was reasonable to assume it was Ray as a working hypothesis in the absence of other evidence.

Subsequently, Ian had followed the Holden driver Ray, to a meeting with another male, 183 centimetres, or 6 feet tall in the old scale, light brown hair, mid 20's, athletic build, who seemed to have a superior aura when talking to the older Ray. On the basis of this, his second observation, he felt it to be a safer basis upon which to begin a hypothesis to explain the events witnessed.

Ian confirmed the tentatively assigned name "Johnny" to the young man with the air of authority, whom he had earlier tailed to the St Kilda Marina where Johnny was at that time observed to drive a blue Ford Falcon. Further investigation proved that both the cars were registered to "dead ends" – the Ford to a mail order company in Ballarat with elderly company directors and the Holden to a partially blind non-driver woman of nearly 90 years living in "God's Waiting Room" type accommodation.

No further details were uncovered because the investigation was halted when the contributor withdrew the disability application, resigned from employment and was contactable only via the office of a firm of uncommunicative lawyers. Here ended what Ian now thought of as "episode one".

Episode two had all the hallmarks of having commenced and simultaneously ended with the relatively small job of tracking down an errant contributor to another superannuation fund who appeared to be involved in a money laundering operation based on residential mortgages. Like the first contributor, Freddie became uncontactable. A firm of lawyers was involved and up pop two men he identified from the earlier investigation still exhibiting the same employee / employer relationship with a motor vehicle registered in the name of a dead end as was also the fake car wash company that employed the abruptly emigrated Freddie.

The habitual use of the names of elderly persons none of whom had any educational degrees that may reasonably be expected in a company set up, apparently residents of large population centres a considerable distance from Melbourne for company and motor vehicle registrations, outruled coincidence. And Kathy's corroboration of Ian's intuitive allocation of the name Johnny to the younger more authoritative man helped Ian's hypothesis by building a firmer base and added weight to the identification of Johnny's messenger as Ray.

The mobile phone conversation when Ray impersonated Freddie was highly suspicious, but as Ian was impersonating another person also, that event came clearly under the classification of inadmissible evidence anywhere. Ian was almost certain that Johnny was the pseudonym for Bryn Hamley; as for Ray, that too many prove a pseudonym that only testing would confirm. Ian was pleased with his recollections. Further investigation of Bryn Hamley was warranted.

Sometimes the elicitation of information to confirm a hypothesis engendered mild euphoria in less experienced investigators. But Ian was too old and battle scarred to fall into that trap. Two men involved with both superannuation and with Johnny and Ray appeared to have disappeared. Were there others of which Ian was unaware? Ian resolved to maintain a low profile in his efforts to find out more about his target, Hamley, to avoid the situation being reversed; perhaps fatally reversed.

Ian proceeded with all due care. He sought not to be part of a trifecta. He had no contempt for caution.

CHAPTER TWENTY-ONE

SUNLIGHT SIEVED BY LEAVES FROM overhead trees added to the mottled appearance of Erwin's face and provided camouflage. While he remained immobile he was invisible to the dozen young mothers watching their children playing on the colourful equipment in the tan bark carpeted playground.

Most of the mothers had one or two children playing and some had a third in an expensive high tech pram or pusher. A few were heavily pregnant with another child and watched with a protective and jealously assessing eye the integration of their first progeny with contemporaries. A couple of grandmothers kept watch on a slightly older group of children playing more competitive type ball games nearer to Erwin's hidden location.

In the benign springtime sunshine the picture was that of a group of healthy, innocent young children playing happily under the watchful eyes of happy, healthy, wealthy, well groomed, well dressed, doting young mothers. The poison in the picture was Erwin lurking in the bushes looking for an opportunity to abduct a young innocent to satisfy his own barely suppressed hideous urges. Since his meeting to hand over the bribe to Sergeant Jarvis, Erwin had returned to the area of the Central Park children's playground on each successive day. He was fascinated by the young bodies playing guilessly in the sunshine.

For many years, Erwin spent hours at night reading books about the German Nazi party and its leader Adolf Hitler. One chapter in one book now pervaded his dreams. The chapter described the retribution meted out to many of those accused of plotting against Hitler in the failed July 1944 assassination attempt. It became so clear in his dreams he felt he could almost have been an executioner there in a black uniform with shiny leather belt, cross strap and jackboots. Erwin pictured the badly beaten and naked bodies of former high ranking officers of the German Armed Services grotesquely dangling from wire nooses on meat hooks on a metal rail in a dirty white washed brick abattoir. The association of that image converged in his dreams with the suntanned legs of the young children in the playground; dangerously, sickeningly, converged.

If any twinge of conscience flitted briefly through Erwin's brain for the crime he was planning, then Erwin rationalised the blame on Jarvis. Had it not been for Jarvis, Erwin would have salved his throbbing sexual desires in the specialised brothel. But the vice squad raid had stopped Erwin from obtaining satisfaction. Furthermore it was Jarvis who selected this Park as the venue for payment of the bribe. If anything appalling happened to any child in the Park, the blame lay squarely upon Jarvis. Erwin had his absolution worked out in advance.

Erwin realised that he could simply snatch a child and drive him away. But not in his readily recognisable red Mercedes sports car. He needed transport of a more nondescript type to convey his victim from Central Park Malvern, to an abandoned former dairy shed that had what Erwin deemed to be essential prerequisites, a metal beam with metal hooks and white washed brick interior walls.

Erwin recalled leaving the Oakleigh Football Ground some months ago when the motor traffic along Warrigal Road was so heavy that he was forced to stand in the crowd and look at business premises on the other side of road. It was some time before he crossed to where his car was parked. He recalled that one business was a car hire company with "Rent-a-Wreck" type vehicles. The added attraction of the car rental place was that he could easily travel to it by train. His own car would not appear in the area to provide a link to his identity, should something go wrong.

To further his plan, Erwin spent his evenings in some of Melbourne's less salubrious pubs, being generous in buying drinks. He found a man whom he judged to be roughly compatible in looks and got him drunk. Under the pretext of assisting the inebriated new friend, Erwin lifted his wallet and stole his driving licence. Erwin put $100 in notes into the wallet, not with any thought of compensation but solely on the premise that when the drunk partially recovered and found the bonanza of unexpected cash, then a further drinking binge would follow. And that would, most probably, delay any discovery of the absence of the licence and certainly confuse any recollection of the circumstances surrounding the loss.

When Erwin selected an old, white Fold Falcon sedan to rent from Oakleigh Rent-a-Wreck, he used the stolen driving licence. There was no problem because the office clerk was more interested in transcribing the correct licence number onto the car hire document to check the photo clearly.

The traffic was relatively light as Erwin drove the rented car from Oakleigh to the Park at Malvern. He stopped on the way in a quite street and lined the boot with plastic sheet. He parked the car in the shade beneath the trees in Central Park Road. His heartbeat and his breathing rate both accelerated as he scanned the children's playground. He pulled on a shapeless beret and arranged a pair of wrap around sunglasses on the bridge of his nose then headed for the bushes beneath the trees where he could observe the playground area without being seen. He regarded this observation post as "his", a place of solitude where he could observe young boys and to plunge into daydreams of hideous, unspeakable, sexual acts.

There were plenty of youngsters all around his hiding place and on three occasions young boys chasing footballs came close enough for Erwin's mouth to grow dry in anticipation of the snatch, subjugation and abduction that occupied the forefront of Erwin's diseased imagination. But each time the presence of other adolescents or adult joggers on the nearby oval ruled out any possibility of an undetected grab. Erwin experienced frustration at each near miss and the frustration fuelled the increasing violence that was making his muscles involuntarily ripple.

As noon approached, many mothers called their progeny and set off for a midday meal. Erwin noticed, with mounting inner rage, that the number of children playing had been reduced. He was debating whether or not to go away and return after the lunch time break. Then he heard a noise and with surprise turned to find a young boy clad in shorts, tee shirt and sneakers entering the gloom of the bushes in pursuit of a yellow football. With the speed that made him a formidable opponent in the boxing ring,

Erwin sprang. It was a sexually frustrated action because he dispensed with every element of caution. He had not looked to see whether anyone was close who could have intervened or called an alarm. But the luck of the useless that wrecks the lives of the useful was in his favour.

The young boy never saw Erwin. From bright sunlight into the shade of the bushes the eyes of the boy saw only the yellow shape of the football his errant kick had propelled into the shrubbery. Erwin's big strong, left hand, blue veins visible through the thin latex gloves, clamped over the boy's face covering eyes, nose and mouth. Erwin's right arm picked up the boy with ease and Erwin's legs moved with a muscled quick march to the rear of the rented car. The boy had struggled with arms, legs and body thrashing but with restricted access to air, the struggles were becoming less and Erwin had no trouble holding the boy while he extracted the car key from his pocket and opened the lid of the previously prepared boot.

Erwin's action in flinging the boy into the boot of the car resembled in some way the death roll of a salt water crocodile. And it had a similar effect as the boy was knocked semi conscious when his head struck the plastic covering the carpeted board above the spare wheel recess. Erwin's elevated adrenalin level assisted him to speedily attach cable ties to the wrists and ankles of the boy. Erwin's preparation included a roll of surgical tape and he tore strips to rapidly cover the mouth and eyes of the boy who now barely twisted on the plastic sheet.

Erwin slammed shut the boot lid, almost pulled the driver's door off its hinges in his desperate attempt to get away as fast as possible. He cursed loudly as his fingers dropped the car ignition key between the pedals. He broke a finger nail on the ribbed rubber floor mat as he scrambled to retrieve the key. With adrenalin surging, Erwin needed the support of his left hand, awkwardly pushed through the steering wheel, to control the shaking of his right hand sufficiently for the key to be slid into the ignition lock.

Although the engine of the car started promptly, to Erwin it seemed that the starter churned for an inordinate amount of time before the engine fired and then roared because Erwin's big foot was planted on the accelerator with a pressure beyond that recommended by the vehicle manufacturer. Fortunately no other vehicle was travelling closely along Central Park Road when Erwin directed the Rent-a-Wreck vehicle away from the kerb and onto the road. If the rented vehicle had not already been called a "wreck" before Erwin became its driver then it would surely have qualified for that description after he almost demolished its transmissions system.

Erwin was unaware that such aggressive driving could attract attention because he was so carried away with the need to escape from the area. He spent not a second in thinking of the bound boy in the boot, he thought totally of himself and his urgent need not to be caught. Only when he was a kilometre away and certain that he was not being pursued, did Erwin's thoughts return to the boy. Those thoughts were depraved to a deathly degree.

Erwin's plan had worked. His preparations had been adequate. He again had a fellow human being completely at his mercy and mercy was an emotion in very short supply with Erwin. The only fault in Erwin's plan was his panic stricken departure. He had not appreciated the extent of this panic that the abduction induced. He was not stricken by panic when he snatched young boys in the past. The Ford's tyres had shrieked as he took off and his driving for the first few kilometres was erratic. Erwin vaguely comprehended his undisciplined action but as he had got away he dismissed any contemplation of it as irrelevant. His might proved him right.

With despicable desires in control of his actions Erwin had no concept for caution.

CHAPTER TWENTY-TWO

IAN HAD CRACKED BRYN'S SHIELD of secrecy – but so what? There was no substantive evidence to prove Bryn guilty of any crime. Ian persisted with the investigation of his preliminary hypothesis purely upon the premise that Bryn was connected with two suspicious events involving superannuation funds. To Ian, that was adequate warning. If two events were uncovered, then more existed that were yet to be discovered.

Later that evening Ian did a drive past of the addresses of each of the B Hamleys listed in the phone book. The last on his list in West Melbourne was productive. Through a barred window in a lane adjoining, Ian spotted the two toned grey Mazda parked in the underground car park of the apartment building listed as the address of B Hamley in the telephone directory. Ian was startled when the metal slotted door gave a click and began rolling up. A car driven by an elderly woman drove up the sloping driveway into the street. During the brief elevation of the door Ian saw the number 15 painted on the floor near the car bay in which the Mazda was parked. So he now not only had the address of Bryn's apartment block, but also the apartment number.

Next morning Ian went to the Property Titles Office and got details of the owner of strata title unit 15 in the West Melbourne apartment block. He was not surprised to find it owned by a company with an address in Victoria's third largest provincial city, Bendigo.

Although he could have searched the records of the Australian Securities and Investment Commission (ASIC) by himself to obtain records of the companies that had awakened his interest, to do so would require him to provide details that may have revealed his interest. Ian reasoned that his inquiries to date had led to the theory that he had uncovered the tip of a sizeable criminal enterprise. He assumed that any criminal entity would routinely check to see whether anyone had searched their company records. And if so, who had sought the search. Thus the hunter could become the hunted. Ian had no wish to be the object of the attention of any criminal. True, Ian could seek the company details from ASIC using a false identity. However if a criminal checked and found false information, that could serve as a warning.

Ian decided to hire one of the Information Services of which the telephone directory lists around 80, to further preserve his anonymity. Service companies regularly make enquires for Real Estate Agents, Market Survey firms and the like. Their enquiry would not be suspicious.

Ian was conscious of a section of the Private Agents Act that prohibited delegation of functions of a private inquiry agent to an unlicensed person. He salved any tweak of conscience with the fact that he was not employed by anyone in the conduct of his enquiries into Bryn. So his role of inquiry agent was temporarily inapplicable and he was not in breach of the Act when he had his wife telephone the two information services from a public telephone in the foyer of a public hospital. Nor was his wife acting in an improper fashion when she gave an assumed name and arranged to collect the details of each company from the office of the Information Service providers. She was not involved in any criminal activity and so could assume any name she pleased.

Naturally she paid in cash when collecting the company details. On examination of those details, compared to information he already held, Ian could not help being struck by the numerous similarities of each of the companies. Each had the minimal number of directors and share capital. Each had directors aged 75 years or more. Each director lived in a provincial city or country town. Most of the companies existed for less that two years and were voluntarily deregistered with no charges or debts. And not one of the directors had ever held any company directorship before starting the company and none had held any directorship since. Each of the ephemeral companies had a registered office in properties that Ian recognised as housing serviced offices. Not one had an operating address for the type of business that they purported to operate; car washing, mail order, car detailing, medical equipment hire, boat hiring, etc. An hour's search through business directories and phone enquiries to trade organisations produced no evidence of their existence. Every one was phoney.

Beyond a few lines of print on ASIC company reports it would appear that the companies never existed, but Ian had evidence that they were at one time registered as the owners of various motor vehicles, a white Holden Commodore, a blue Ford Falcon, and a grey Mazda. Other suspect companies owned the house that Freddie once occupied and the unit in which lived Bryn, in the West Melbourne apartment block. Ian concluded that the weight of evidence clearly indicated criminal activity and that Johnny and Ray were most definitely involved.

At a shopping arcade not too far from his office, Ian ordered a cappuccino and a custard tart at the Coffee Palace. In the promenade where the chairs and tables were arranged, a pedestal mounted public coin / card telephone meant Ian had only to move the café chair and table a little to enable him to comfortably make calls whilst enjoying a refreshment break. After the waitress placed his order on the table, Ian slipped his prepaid telecard into the slot and dialed the first of his calls. The numbers he called were recorded, in a code of his own, in his "little black book".

Each number dialed connected him with a trusted colleague. Some were members of interstate police forces, others private investigators. Another managed an Australia wide security firm and two were retired members of Victoria Police who had exceptional careers in monitoring the more violent organized crime gangs. The last was a very senior investigator in the insurance industry. Over the next two hours Ian reordered a coffee and custard tart and juggled outgoing calls with responses phoned back by his colleagues to the pre paid mobile phones he retained just for such sensitive calls. He had to scribble furiously in cryptic phrases onto the pages of his clipboard and at the same time keep watch to ensure that he was not under observation.

Once the replies to his questions were collated he summarised them as follows: -

In Queensland, a person suspected of participating in numerous staged automotive accidents was about to be arrested when he abruptly departed by aircraft for Melbourne. He was traced to a cheap hotel near the Victoria Market but the trail ended there. No trace of him has been uncovered and the Queensland Police believe he was murdered. Several accomplices were questioned but released without charges. Of interest were the statements made by two suspects. They said that the missing person was an employee of "Johnny" who was the mastermind of the staged accidents frauds and that Johnny lived in Melbourne.

The insurance investigator was more explicit. He told Ian that a fraud involving staged motor accidents had been smashed and that a mastermind named Johnny was involved. He opined that the Queensland representative of Johnny's organisation fled to Melbourne and was murdered. A similar story emerged regarding a hospital employee who rorted the Medicare and Pharmaceutical Benefits Scheme of several millions, none of which was recovered. He drove to Melbourne, according to a former girlfriend, to see a man named Ray and Ray's boss a man known as Johnny. His car and overnight bag were found abandoned in a Melbourne bayside suburb but no one has seen the hospital employee for more than a year.

The pattern continued. The name "Johnny" was becoming known to specialist insurance investigators through a man involved in several frauds. Under the influence of alcohol he had boasted that his contact was named Ray but the big boss Johnny, was a real brain, who could get him out of what he felt was the closing net of the police. When last heard of, he was departing for a meeting with Johnny. Major crime reports seemed to indicate that a man known as Johnny was a specialist money launderer who had encroached unwittingly into a precinct considered by the big boys to be their exclusive territory. Apparently Johnny backed off with sufficient speed to appease the heavy hitters. But despite his backing off, Johnny was not considered a wimp because rumours indicated he had quietly disposed of several of his own dissidents. That earned him a level of respect and with no territorial conflict, no further action needed to be taken by the larger gang. Live and let live.

Plenty of rumours but so little hard evidence that no law enforcement authority had concentrated on either Ray or Johnny and fledgling investigations that were begun stopped when persons of interest just disappeared.

Ian returned to his office and wrote up a report entitled "Johnny and Ray" on the old computer, unconnected to any telephone line, that he used as a totally secure word processor. A print copy was made together with a disc then the hard drive was wiped. Every so often Ian removed the old hard drive and destroyed it. He purchased a replacement at one of the numerous computer fairs. The disc was later lodged in a safe deposit box in the basement vault of his bank. The print copy he placed in his own special vault. This was a 1936 model, key operated safe made by the Pioneer Safe works in Richmond. It was of solid steel with a 60 centimetre by 40 centimetre door that was 12 centimetres thick. Ian purchased it at a property auction many years ago.

With help from his football toughened 20 year old son, Ian had dug a hole in his concrete garage floor into which was cemented the safe, door upwards. A strip of waterproof tape kept the lock free of water. A wooden cover was made to level the floor and that was covered by a metal oil drip tray. When the family car was driven in, the safe was completely hidden. Access was a bit of a nuisance but access was not frequent and the sense of security outweighed the nuisance quotient.

Within the self made vault, the copy of the speculative file "Johnny and Ray" had the company of two bundles of cash maintained as a reserve and two unregistered pistols, a Colt Python 6 shot, .357 calibre revolver with a 15cm (6 inch) barrel and a Browning 8 shot, 9 millimetre automatic. The pistols and the spare ammunition and magazine were Ian's last line of defense. Ian never sought out danger the way some of the legendary literary or suicidal celluloid "Private Eyes" seemed prone to do with frantic frequency in movies and TV shows.

The pistols he regarded as annihilation protection only in the direst circumstances. He cleaned them occasionally even though their plastic covers ensured they were never really in need of it. And Ian shot several times a year at a pistol club hiring similar pistols to ensure he maintained the right feel. The practice shooting sessions were part of Ian's many precautions. When shooting he concentrated totally but could never completely shut out some of the Simon and Garfunkel song "El Condor Paso" that was popular in the 1960's. The second verse refrain "I'd rather be a hammer than a nail" mixed marvelously well with the smell of cordite. Ian enjoyed his day at target shooting and maintaining of his better than average scores. He hoped never to apply his skills to a human target but, in extremis, he reasoned it was better to be skillful, and remain alive. Ian had no contempt for caution.

CHAPTER TWENTY-THREE

IAN ROSS WAS INVITED TO attend an unofficial meeting of the general managers of a group of large superannuation funds. He was sworn to secrecy, being told only that he was to assist them to resolve issues resulting from persistent but undefined rumours. The manager of the largest of the six funds assured Ian that his fees would be paid but by whom and in what proportion was one of the matters to be settled at the meeting. In view of the long association Ian had with the fund, he had no hesitation or equivocation in accepting the assurance.

At the meeting, with minimum formality, the nebulous issue was condensed and stated as being the existence of rumours that superannuation funds are systematically defrauded by an organised group. The rumours initially emanated several years ago from members of the police forces in several states. The information they passed on was volunteered by criminals seeking favours to persuade the police to charge them with lesser offences than those for which they had been arrested. The names Ray and Johnny were mentioned but beyond that no clues as to identities of fraudsters was forthcoming. Obviously the source of the information was tainted but the information slowly achieved credibility by virtue of its persistence.

Other rumours were conveyed to the managers, in whispered tones, by young lawyers who stumbled upon irregular transactions within the records of law firms by whom they were temporarily employed as articled clerks. Again the names Ray and Johnny were mentioned but that seemed to be the extent of their knowledge as to the identity of the perpetrators.

Yet other rumours came direct from career criminals in the form of sarcastic remarks made to fund managers at social events, such as the Melbourne Cup racing festival, when moneyed criminals rubbed shoulders with financial movers and shakers. If the nouveaux riche criminal thought that a more conservatively tailored silver tail cast a denigrating glance in his direction, he responded with a deliberately deflating, liquor slurred remark, the import of which was to the effect that "You super men are really shit stupid because Johnny's has been ripping you off for years". The names "Johnny" and "Ray" were the only consistent elements within the persistent rumours. No hint of the method of the fraud was given.

Initially the rumours were ignored but the longevity of them motivated superannuation fund managers to encourage their internal auditors to increase vigilance. But to no avail. Nor had exhortations to the large accounting firms who managed the external audit procedures uncovered anything save a few odd cases of petty theft. Spasmodically but relentlessly the rumours persisted. It eventually wore down any resistance of those managers who previously disregarded them.

Over some months the managers, who were normally highly competitive rivals, spoke to each other in veiled language that only someone privy to the rip off rumours would comprehend. And as if by osmosis the unease permeated among managers resulting in the unofficial meeting to which Ian was invited. Even the trustees of each fund were denied access. Having laid out the fears of the funds, the spokesman of the group of managers invited Ian to comment.

Ian surprised himself with the enthusiasm of his response. "Yes" he told the assembly; he had a lead on criminals who masqueraded behind the pseudonyms of "Johnny and Ray". "Yes", Ian had proven that both had connections with superannuation in the past, probably using the industry as a money laundering conduit. Ian withheld further comment because he sensed the mood of the meeting had changed. A collective sigh of relief echoed through the room as the managers realised that they were not entertaining groundless fears.

Indecisive when confronted with unsubstantiated rumours, but now faced with the prospect of a tangible target, the mangers acted with commendable cooperation. They decided to form an unofficial investigative syndicate to which each manager would persuade his trustees to contribute to cover the fees of Ian, plus any experts Ian may need to engage. Each manager pledged to allow Ian unfettered access to their records, to persuade the external auditor to cooperate and order their internal auditors to provide total disclosure. Each manager also pledged full support of their legal advisor. They were surprised when Ian strongly urged that they hold pledges of cooperation in abeyance until Ian had a better understanding of the methods of possible frauds being perpetrated. Ian was wary of lawyers.

Ian emphasised and re-emphasised that the fewer people who knew of the investigation the better its chance of success. As a clincher, to secure the confidentiality he deemed paramount, he stressed that the media would crucify the industry if any substantial losses were publicised. Ian asked that the meeting select two managers with power to work with Ian and they were duly elected. Ian asked how long since the managers first became aware of the rumours and the consensus answer was between three and four years.

Aware that even the most intelligent people love a little intrigue, Ian suggested that the meeting decide upon a code word to be used only by Ian when talking to the managers, or the managers between themselves, to conceal the assembly of data regarding the prospective fraud. Those with a mathematical bent prevailed as the code word chosen was "Pythagoras". Subject to no urgent matter arising, another meeting was scheduled at the same time and venue in four weeks time and the meeting was closed.

Most managers drifted away leaving Ian with the two managers elected as a sub committee. The three conferred for an hour to list Ian's information requirements which they agreed to quietly pass to the other managers, directing all hard copy to Ian's secure Post Office box. They exchanged direct hard line phone and mobile phone numbers and agreed that Ian's club, the Naval & Military Club in Little Collins Street Melbourne would be their meeting place to exchange information.

Ian had another investigation under way involving a 27 year old female shop assistant who lodged an application for total and permanent disability pension benefits from a superannuation fund. The supporting medical evidence of spinal injury appeared accurate but infra red light showed that the typing of the female's name on all medical certificates was out of kilter with the other lines of letters. Substitution was suspected.

To confirm that suspicion, using information gathered, Ian arranged for a fellow female private investigator, Marian, to attend the same female only gymnasium where the suspect was alleged to have registered under a false name. Marian had a video camera concealed in a sports bag. Ian met with Marian and viewed video tape that showed the allegedly bedridden disabled shop assistant quite clearly working out vigorously without impediment on several pieces of gymnasium equipment.

The video may not necessarily be admissible as evidence in a court of law but it could be screened to a Tribunal if the allegedly disabled female chose to fight and claim unfair dismissal. It was adequate as a defense when delivered with affidavits as to time place, etc, from other iron pushers in the gym. Ian wrote up his report and lodged it, with the video, into the safe hands of the superannuation fund manager.

With that part of the job over, Ian went home and extracted the Johnny and Ray file from his home made vault. He noted that almost a year had elapsed since it had been locked away and therefore it was necessary to check the pertinent items. From the most recent edition of the telephone listing he noted that a B Hamley was still registered at the West Melbourne apartment block and he detoured on the drive to that address to visit the Electoral Office in Lonsdale Street Melbourne to verify that information. The task took only a few minutes and he was quickly back at his car.

On arrival in West Melbourne he briefly doubled parked and got out to peer through the barred window in the laneway searching for a car in bay number 15, but the bay was empty. The brief double park did not earn him the ire of any parking inspector and he was quickly off in the direction of the St Kilda Marina. With shirtsleeves rolled up he walked around the Marina but the berth where Bryn had previously moored his cabin cruiser was vacant.

The Marina attendant was hosing down the hulls of a trailer mounted catamaran when Ian asked if Bryn Hamley was around. In reply, Ian was told that Bryn had sailed out a few days ago and was expected back sometime within the next few days. In response to Bryn's query about the craft Bryn now sailed in, the attendant became impassioned when describing the beautiful 12 metre Majesty 66 motor cruiser with its sleet sporting design and characteristic upper works. Panygyric III. Obviously the attendant was well acquainted with Bryn. Ian refrained from further questions lest his visit became memorable and on his way back to his car he cudgeled his memory neurones until they recollected that Ian had earlier consulted a dictionary to find out that Panygyric was "to be laudatory or speak in praise of". Ian was thinking that nothing was worthy of praise as matters stood at present.

Just as he was about to unlock his car he paused; if Bryn's car was not parked in the basement car park of his residence and if Bryn was away for a few days, where was his car? There were only seven cars in the bays within the Marina reserved for long term parking. Ian walked around the group of seven, writing in his notebook a brief description of each that included the registration number. Ian had made the notes, in a circumspect manner as a matter of course, even though the attendant was too busy with other tasks to take any notice.

With the sniff of sea air, Ian's thoughts turned to the possible fate of the numerous acquaintances of Bryn who had disappeared without trace. Ian made a connection between a motor cruiser that was away for days at a time and missing persons. Had they taken a one way journey to become fish bait? Or was he allowing his intuition too much latitude and deceiving himself in attributing homicidal traits to a young seafarer whom he hardly knew?

Next day Ian returned to the asphalt public parking area adjacent to the Marina as the first sunrays of the morning transformed the sky from black to apricot then bright blue. Through binoculars he first searched the berth at the Marina then quartered Port Phillip Bay for any sign of Bryn's motor cruiser. He ate breakfast from the seal top plastic boxes provided by his wife and washed it down with hot coffee from a thermos before reverting to another fruitless search of the horizon of the bay.

The essence of Ian's concentration was to formulate a plan that would allow him undiscovered access to Bryn's criminal activities. Sufficient circumstantial evidence existed for Ian to be certain that Bryn was involved in iniquity even though none of Ian's evidence, at this stage, would stand up in a court of law. Indeed the evidence was so circumstantial that the police would be unlikely to set aside time from the multitude of other investigations to even give it consideration.

Ian's first problem was to identify Bryn's associates, Ray and others, to establish a file of basic data. Obviously the best method was to trail Bryn to identify his contacts. But a 24 hour surveillance, if it is to be certain of remaining undetected by the subject of the surveillance, requires a trained team of around twelve men and women plus six to eight motor vehicles, maybe a motorcycle, and a radio network. Altogether an expensive exercise. He could not justify such an expense based on existing evidence. He needed more facts. He resolved to continue his efforts assisted by specialist support if needed.

The morning dragged towards lunchtime. Ian took several short leg stretching walks then phoned a photographic studio in the suburb of Caulfield where he spoke to one of the proprietors. The studio was owned by a husband and wife team who both worked with sections of the media, particularly local press. Ian had availed himself of their photographic expertise, especially telephoto shots, on other assignments. So when he exchanged greetings he had little explanation to give when he asked if one of the partners could be on standby to surreptitiously take photos. He answered the technical questions about daylight or dark photography, distance, singles or group, moving or still as best he could. He received consent for one of them to respond ASP to any call he made.

Ian made that call just before 4pm after an excruciatingly boring day. His only mental activity involved spotting boats on the horizon and timing the journey to the Marina. At last Ian identified the unique flying bridge configuration for the type of cruiser described by the Marina attendant. Ian's high powered binoculars gave sufficient magnification for Ian to positively identify Bryn. Ian phoned his photographer.

The cruiser glided over the small white crested waves stirred by a strengthening north westerly wind but the helmsman showed skill in steering and reverse thrusting of the engine to cause the cruiser to kiss the pier with barely a bump. After attaching mooring lines, Bryn began a routine by retrieving a trolley and loading on to it several polystyrene insulated boxes before disappearing below deck.

It was while Bryn was below deck that Ian received a call on his mobile from Brenda, the female half of the photographic team, who told him that she was parked in the Marina and asked for more instructions. Ian gave explicit instructions and Brenda strolled towards the moored boat wearing a floppy hat and carrying a beach bag. Ian saw her select a spot from where she could take photos of the aft section of Bryn's boat. She placed two cameras in a concealed position beside a bollard as she sat with legs dangling over the walkway looking like a lady waiting for her sailor.

But for all her lackadaisical appearance, Brenda struck like a serpent when she speedily aligned, first one then the other of her two cameras to take a dozen photographs when Bryn reappeared on deck. Using the skill of a stalker, Brenda shifted to a position near the Marina office and took more photos of Bryn. Responding to hand signals from Ian in the car park on the other side of the cyclone mesh fence, Brenda moved towards the group of cars and took more photos of the unsuspecting Bryn as he loaded the insulated containers into a current model Toyota station wagon. Brenda was walking back to her car, out of Bryn's hearing, when Ian contacted her by mobile, thanked her for the job and received her assurance that the photos would be ready for collection at 8.30am next morning.

Ian drove to the West Melbourne apartment building. He did not have to follow Bryn too closely because he knew the general direction. Ian observed Bryn drive into the basement car park of the converted former printing factory. To be absolutely certain, Ian parked nearby then walked to the lane where the barred window allowed a view of the Toyota station wagon parked in bay number 15. On the basis that if Bryn had been away for three or four days, then he might go out for a meal or entertainment, Ian remained in the area, moving his car and eating food from a take away shop. By 10.30pm he decided to call it a day. Bryn had not left the apartment block either by the front pedestrian entrance or by car and the lights on the fifteen level went off at that time. Ian reflected that being a private investigator could, at times, be one of the most boring jobs on earth. Doing very little can, paradoxically, be tiring and Ian slept well that night.

Precisely at 8.30am the next morning Ian entered the photographer's shop to be greeted by Brenda. The peculiar half smile on her face was her way of saying to herself that she won the bet. When she told Ian the photos would be ready at 8.30am she had a bet with her partner that Ian, "Mr Reliable", would be there right on 8.30am and he was. Brenda's photos of Bryn were excellent, comprising clearly focused full length, half length plus head and shoulder shots that looked as if they had been taken in a studio rather than through a telephoto lens. Brenda had included photos of Bryn's motor cruiser from different angles, including its name and registration number, and shots of Bryn getting in his Toyota, that included the number plate. Brenda was a photographer with an investigator's brain.

From the portfolio of photos Ian took six that he considered best for identification purposes and ordered ten prints of each of the full length, half length and head and shoulders photos to be printed in post card size. Brenda promised them for 3.30pm that afternoon.

At a supermarket Ian used a phone card to make a cryptic call to his contact at the Motor Registration branch giving the registration number of Bryn's Toyota then drove to the Post Office to empty his business mail box. The box was stacked full of envelopes with yellow and red Express Post symbols. Arriving at his office at 9.30am, Ian opened the envelopes and was almost repelled by the size and complexity of the computer print outs. He had asked for specific information and it was provided in such detail that undertaking comparisons looked like a very long job.

Back in his office, he applied himself to the task of comparative analysis of the immense amount of superannuation information with such intensity that the clock had clicked well beyond 3.30pm before he remembered that he had photos to collect. He needed a break from the eyestrain of paperwork and was grateful for the drive to and from the photographers to collect the extra prints. Brenda lost her bet with her partner this time.

Ian was home late for his evening meal. He took extra care to lock the mass of superannuation statistical sheets in his office security cabinet and to check his alarm systems were switched on before leaving. After dark, he drove to Springvale, parked, walked around the corner to the home with a brick from beneath which he extracted a plastic envelope and replaced it with $25. Back in his car he drove towards home and whilst stationary at a traffic light read the name of the company that owned the Toyota driven by Bryn. Ian was unsurprised that the company had an address at a serviced office in Melbourne.

Next morning he was at his office desk before 7am concentrating on solving the answer to one question; what pay-out does a superannuation fund make that could be subject to fraud? He grouped the payments of each fund and made percentage comparisons to see if any were abnormal, but all payments as between funds fell within a narrow percentage range – nothing astray there, at first sight.

Ian reasoned that superannuation funds would have adequate internal cross checks plus two levels of audit; internal and external; plus scrutiny by Government taxation and compliance authorities to obviate any systemic fraud centered on investments. Similarly he doubted whether administration expenses could be ripped off regularly of sufficient money to spark rumours over several years. The same logic caused him to place payments to service providers temporarily on the back burner. In both instances when Bryn was suspected by Ian of being involved in unsavoury activity, the target was patently not the superannuation fund per se. It was as used simply as the conduit to launder money.

Ian realised that no matter how good was his scrutiny of the current statistics of the group of superannuation funds, he needed to review the figures over the time since the appearance of the rumours. On best available evidence the rumours of fraud dated back between three and four years. Allowing that it probably took two years for a rumour to foment and spill around, Ian considered that six years, or to allow an overlap in financial year reporting, seven years time frame should be his target start point.

In order not to disaccommodate the managers too much, Ian had decided what information was strictly relevant. Ian did not want to concentrate exclusively on the suspect area lest in recovering only the suspect information he alerted any employee confederate of Bryn. Ian phoned his manager contact, using the agreed code word "Pythagoras", to request seven year information summaries for each fund on their pension payments, missing person payments and resignation benefit payments. There was no hesitation by the manager who promised a response within three days. Computers make information extraction easy.

Ian returned to routine work and checked the alleged owner of the company that owned Bryn's Toyota. The sole director was an octogenarian gentleman in the country town of Mooroopna. There was no one of that name listed in the telephone directory that covered that locality and Ian's call to the local Post Office revealed only that the gentleman had left the area, current address unknown.

As the address of the serviced offices of the dodgy Toyota car owing company was not too far off the route from Ian's office to his home, he drove there and lucked into a parking space just vacated by another car and lucked into some forty minutes of unexpired time too. He sat for a few minutes to think out a plausible excuse for visiting the serviced office and decided to use a story as close as possible to the truth. He approached the young woman on duty behind the reception desk. He told her he was a private investigator and showed her a photo of Bryn. Ian claimed he was looking for a missing person on behalf of a deserted, pregnant partner. He evidently chose the right ploy because the young lady was clearly supportive but regrettably unable to help with a location for the "louse" in the photo.

While talking to the reception Ian had looked down each of the two corridors at the rear of the reception desk. He counted sixteen offices and noted that about half had fluorescent lights lit. He returned to his car, fed coins into the meter. Ian had a phobia about car parking. Parking costs are tax deductible. Parking fines are not. He was crooked on that Taxation Office ruling. He returned to the front of the building on the assumption that most office workers leave between 5 and 5.30pm.

With the time nearing 5pm he made a quick reconnaissance and took up a position that allowed him a view of people leaving the building by the front steps and also from the car park. Dozens of people walked out and several drove their cars from the car park but Ian was unable to recognise anyone. At 6.15pm he left for home with his thoughts now being directed towards family. With his early start, it had been a long day and he was being reminded by both mind and body that he was getting older.

It was a pity that Ian did not hang around another few minutes because Ray entered the car park shortly thereafter and drove away in a brand new silver BMW535. Sometimes luck is with you, sometimes against. This time it was on the side of Ray.

CHAPTER TWENTY-FOUR

PERSISTENCE PAYS, EVEN THOUGH IT causes sore buttocks. Ian had arrived early to get a car parking spot with a view of the building where the company that owned Bryn's Toyota rented a cubicle office in a suite of serviced offices. Ian was used to using his car as an office and so was not disconcerted by the stop / start regime imposed by having to look at people entering the building while tying to make sense of the mass of superannuation statistics on the papers he had brought.

He had produced a list of major changes in the superannuation industry as a benchmark against which to measure discrepancies. The most momentous change involved the risk shift from employers to employees when benefit promise superannuation schemes declined in favour of accumulation benefit schemes.

Superannuation was once synonymous with a scheme to which employee and employer contributed for a benefit to the employee member of a sum of money payable on retirement or early retirement based upon a formula that included the employee's years of fund membership and near final salary. An insurance against disability of a member was based on a similar formula, as also was the death benefit payable to a dependent upon premature death of a member. In the event that the assets of the scheme, being the investment of the combined employee / employer contributions and the earnings thereon, proved inadequate to provide the promised benefits, then the onus on topping up the deficit fell entirely upon the employer. Traditionally these schemes paid high benefits for disablement and to dependents upon death of a member prior to retirement. Such superannuation schemes are universally titled "benefit promise".

The newly implemented accumulation schemes that largely supplanted benefit promise schemes provide far lower benefit levels; often the payout is based on the total of the employee contribution, the employer contributions plus the accumulated earnings from the investment of both. If interest and / or dividend payments are high the employee is advantaged. However if investment returns are poor then the employee is disadvantaged. The role of the employer as guarantor has gone. The employee bears the risk. The employer's obligation ends with the payment to the superannuation fund of the percentage of the employee's remuneration prescribed by legislation. Employee representatives on the board of the superannuation fund as trustees provide further immunity to the employer against poor fund performances. There are variations to the basic model, such as separately purchased insurance cover or Do It Yourself Superannuation funds that many temperamentally unsuited persons were lured into setting up.

Sometimes superannuation fund managers administered both benefit promise schemes and accumulation schemes on behalf of a multitude of employer companies, some enormous in size. The cohabitation of two schemes is transitional as benefit promise diminishes and accumulation increases. The numbers of employee contributors involved and the vast amount of money in superannuation funds suggested to Ian that a relatively few regular frauds could provide a careful fraudster with many millions of dollars each year.

Sitting in the passenger seat of his car for hours pouring over figures on computer lists whilst looking up whenever his peripheral vision detected an exit or entrance from and to the building opposite was headache inducing. And switching to the drivers seat to move his car to another parking bay as it became vacant was also annoying. After the second car shift to avoid being booked by the parking inspectors, Ian pushed the computer lists beneath the passenger seat and stepped out of his car with the intention of buying a coffee.

A large shiny, new model silver BMW slowed with the indicator lights blinking to signal a turn into the car park of the building. Ian had a clear view of the man he knew as Ray, sitting proudly behind the steering wheel of the luxurious automobile. Ian pretended to reopen his car door, in order to hide his face and kept a keen watch to see Ray drive into a car bay, lock the car with a blip and flash of lights then head for the elevator.

With Ray gone, Ian strolled to the BMW, noted its registration and noted that the rego number was painted on the car park floor. So Ray had a reserved space. Although not as proficient with a camera as Brenda, Ian was not entirely devoid of photographic skills so he strolled back to his car, opened the boot and placed a Cannon 5 zoom digital camera into an airline type tourist bag and returned to the car park. He took photos of the BMW. When certain that he was unobserved, he walked casually around the vehicle as if in admiration. In fact he was looking inside to see if anything interesting was visible.

Ian constrained himself from shouting "Eureka" because a large envelope on the passenger side seat bore a name "Mr Raymond M Woodbury" with an address in the suburb of Knoxfield. So eager was Ian to write down the name and address in his notebook that he almost dropped his bag containing the camera. The ennui induced by a dull morning vanished like a politician's promise.

He went to the café and ordered and paid for a coffee and a custard tart, then sat at a pavement table. It afforded him an unrestricted view of the building entrance. The cup partly obscured his face, for which he was grateful because he was draining the last drop when Ray appeared and took a seat two tables away. Ian slowly swiveled the airline bag around and partially turned down one side, to expose the camera lens. On the pretext of using the table for support as he arose he focused and pressed the trigger button to allow the auto focus and motor drive to take what he hoped would be half a dozen clear full frontal face shots of Ray.

Ian closed the bag and without haste walked away with his back to Ray. When he judged he was out of Ray's direct line of sight, he crossed the road and walked back to his car using other cars, trees and pedestrians to shield him from Ray's peripheral vision. At his car he rested the camera briefly on the roof and using maximum zoom took several more photos of the unsuspecting Ray. After a wait of twenty minutes, Ian noticed Ray chatting with the coffee shop waitress before rising and walking towards his BMW. The familiarly of the chat confirmed Ian's view that Ray was a regular visitor to the area. Ray started the BMW and drove off.

The silver BMW was easy to tail and Ian had no trouble doing that in moderate traffic. Ray drove to the roof top car park of the South Melbourne Market, parked the BMW and seemed to walk away from his beautiful example of superb engineering with regret. In his distinctive, expensive, beige sports jacket over designer jeans and soft leather Cuban heeled brown boots, he was as easy follow on foot as by car. Ian slipped a navy blue spray jacket over his white shirt and followed.

On a main road, at a heritage listed, beautifully restored, grey stone building, Ray stopped, swung open the metal gate in the decorated iron tracery fence, opened the elaborately carved dark wooden door of the house and stepped inside. From his vantage point on the opposite side of the street, Ian waited for ten minutes then obliquely crossed the road and sauntered past the building. He saw the street number in large polished brass letters near the door and read the words "Madame Dolores, Psychic" on an equally gleaming polished brass plaque affixed to the metal gate.

To familiarise himself with the locale, Ian walked around the corner to see that a lane ran parallel to the main road so he turned into it to determine which back yard aligned with the house that was home to Madame Dolores. The yard he identified was partly fenced and partly covered by an angled garage roller door. Through cracks in the grey wooden fence palings, Ian saw a light green Ford Escort hatchback car that he judged to be no more than six months old. He spotted the personalised registration plate.

Fortunately for Ian there were ample food stalls so he could eat, drink, change position, take off his jacket, put in on again and generally try to appear invisible or at least innocuous as he waited for over three hours for Ray to reappear from Chez Dolores and return to his BMW. Ian made another cryptic phone call to his motor vehicle information provider giving the registration numbers of Ray's silver BMW and the green Ford Escort. In congested late afternoon traffic Ian had difficulty following Ray's BMW. He regretted not bringing his tracker. The direction of travel was eastwards, toward the Knoxfield area, so he dropped back a bit further and the journey was more relaxed.

Ian saw the BMW turn into the driveway of the address he had observed on the envelope in the BMW. He drove past in time to see Ray enter the front door of a two storey brick house with a meticulously mown front lawn edged with masses of pink, white, purple and yellow flowers. The property spoke of well kept affluence.

With no place to park in the suburban street that would be inconspicuous, Ian had to make do with the dirt driveway of a vacant block further up the street. Observation by quick peeps through binoculars was unsatisfactory but unavoidable. Any long stares would be sure to be spotted by a curious householder. The public saw so much TV about gangsters that the police certainly would be called. After several slow moving hours, Ian saw a small van drive into Ray's driveway and decided to risk a drive pass. The van turned out to be a pizza deliverer, so Ian continued driving on the grounds that Ray was probably staying home to watch the much advertised football game on TV.

Ian wanted to see the football too and right now he was hungry. However professional discipline prevailed and, after checking that he had $50 in his wallet, he drove to the house of the brick in Springvale and left the $50. He collected a coin bag containing a piece of paper and headed home for a meal. Since picking up the plastic coin bag Ian had kept an eye on his rear vision mirror but discerned no tail. Never the less he employed several stratagems to ensure that he was not being singly or gang tailed. Ian had no contempt for caution.

On arrival at his home all thoughts of business evaporated as he was submerged beneath the arms of several grandchildren all eager to welcome their beloved Grandpa. Later that night, just before going to bed, he satisfied his curiosity by looking into the coin bag. The note confirmed that a Mr Raymond Mervyn Woodbury of Knoxfield was the owner of a BMW, silver in colour. As for the green Ford Escort hatchback, the owner was a company with the title "Madame Dolores Pty Ltd" at the South Melbourne address visited earlier that day by Ray. Ian was somewhat surprised to learn that these cars were owned by persons living at the addresses where the cars were garaged rather than owned by some old geezer up country or some untraceable company.

Ian speculated the Madame Dolores must be a super psychic to have entertained Ray for over three hours. Could she be a fundamentally physical psychic? Is so, Ray would need to be a super man to endure for a full three hours.

With sufficient identification of both Bryn and Ray in his records but with no recent link to superannuation recorded, Ian intuitively speculated that his best avenue towards proof of a superannuation related fraud pointed in the direction of Dolores. At least, he felt, it was worthy of further investigation. He felt a bit stupid in coming to the conclusion because he could not see how a psychic would be connected in any way to superannuation. Given the location of the salon, if that were the correct title of the place of business of the psychic, Ian's assessment of the available cover led to the further conclusion that he would need assistance in surveillance.

He telephoned Marian, a former member of the Victoria Police who had resigned when she and her policeman husband decided to become parents. Three children later, when the last child started school, Marian's aspirations to be involved in investigate work resurfaced and she completed the mandatory course of study. She qualified for her licence as an inquiry agent pursuant to the Victorian Private Agents Act 1966, rather than rejoin the police force with its less flexible roster of duty. Of medium height, weight and moderately attractive at age 38, Marian worked as a freelance, part time, for several inquiry agencies. Her specialty was in trailing on foot.

Marian's ability to use minimum disguise to appear anywhere from 25 to 50 years old was a distinct advantage. A lot of her work involved divorces. She liked doing jobs for Ian because his work in the superannuation industry made a change from photographing lust crazed men and women each cheating on their respective spouse. Marian had introduced Ian to the word "spice" to describe a partner who was bigamously "married" on the grounds that if mice is the plural for mouse then, logically, spice is the plural for spouse. Ian was fortunate that Marian was available. They had worked together before so that little time was lost in detailed explanations as he outlined the job to her on the phone that night.

Next morning they met at the South Melbourne market. Over a coffee he pointed out the premises in which Madame Dolores conducted her psychic business. Ian explained how she and he would work to photograph everyone who entered and exited via the front door and the rear door leading into the back lane. He told Marian about the green Ford Escort hatchback, parked in the back yard.

Mobile phone numbers were locked into their mobiles, hand signals and car shifting arrangements agreed, then Ian took up station almost directly opposite the premises of Madame Dolores, his Cannon camera concealed beneath a copy of the morning newspaper. At 8.20am he focused on the young blonde lady, barely out of her teens wearing extremely tight jeans and an equally tight, well filled, fluffly pink top. She entered via the metal gate, opened the front door with a key and disappeared inside.

Just before 9am a male, sixty years old, above average height, average build, well dressed in a dark grey suit approached, opened the gate and walked to the door that opened when he pushed it. Ian pressed the camera shutter release button twice and hoped for good profile images. Ian had earlier seen the man park a blue car in a bay sixty metres away. He put his camera beneath his jacket and walked unhurriedly in that direction to snap a photo of the car and its registration plate. At 9.25am a female, mid fifties artificially blonde hair, below average height, overweight and walking ponderously, stopped at the gate long enough for Ian to take a profile and full face photo. He phoned Marian to report the arrivals and suggested they swap car spaces. Ian had just pressed the call cancel button when the sixty year old male appeared through the door and walked to his car. Ian took several full frontal photos.

With the parking meter about to expire and a parking inspector seen to be on the prowl, Ian spotted Marian in her car, started his engine then pulled onto the road to allow Marian to take the vacated bay. From then onwards, the visitors to the surveilled premises were regular every half an hour. Males and females mainly over thirty years old arrived and departed with scheduled regularity. Ian and Marian switched car parking spaces every two hours. The only slight break occurred between 12.30 and 1.30pm when no visitors arrived and the young jean clad, jiggly pink topped, blonde female emerged and headed for a nearby fast food lunch shop.

Marian followed Miss Jeans and jiggly, joined her in the shop and started a conversation by saying how busy she had been. Miss Jeans and jiggly responded saying that she too was busy because today was one of Madame's three personal appointment days. Marian was precluded from further questions because the lunch shop assistant asked for orders and other customers pushed forward and separated them. But the information

Marian conveyed to Ian was useful because it explained the regularity of the visitors.

Ian and Marian had recorded thirteen visitors and had photos of nine of their cars, the others had evidently arrived by public transport. At 5.10pm the last person departed. A few minutes after the departure of the final visitor, Miss Jeans and jiggly left and began walking back along the path by which she was seen to arrive in the morning. Ian followed her to a tram stop and waited until she stepped into a tram that headed towards the City before he returned to confer with Marian.

With no more visitors, no signs of Madame Dolores and no easy access they concluded that it was unlikely to be profitable to remain when the crowd was rapidly thinning. They decided that Marian would wait near the tram stop next morning to strike up a conversation with Miss Jeans and jiggly based on an extension of the brief meeting in the lunch shop. The development of the closer bond may yield results as Marian judged Miss Jeans and jiggly to be a friendly and voluble type. Marian headed for home. After a walk down the lane to observe that the green Ford Escort was still garaged in the rear, Ian also left for his home.

Only when he had parked his car and collected his mail did the thought occur to Ian that he had not seen any mail delivery to the address of Madame Dolores. He phoned Marian who said that the mail person had pushed a trolley loaded with letters along the street while she was watching the front, but no mail had been delivered. Ian expressed thanks, said goodbye until tomorrow, then pondered how a psychic's mail would be delivered.

Next morning Marian waited near the tram stop for twenty five minutes before Miss Jeans and jiggly alighted from a tram. Marian, wearing a jacket and carrying a woven raffia bag approached and opened up the conversation with a friendly "Hello, off to work?" and received a similarly friendly affirmative reply. It appeared that Marian was remembered as a fellow lunch shopper and in the walk Marian learnt that the name of Miss Jeans and jiggly was Jodie. She was a receptionist in the salon of Madame Dolores. Marian expressed pleasure at meeting someone with such an interesting job and indicated that she too worked as a receptionist with a company that provided home maintenance services, adding it was pretty dull compared with Jodie's job. Marian was careful to avoid being too inquisitive.

Ian was pleased with Marian's information and decided to change her role from that of a surveillance / photographer to that of a friend of Jodie. Ian was driving his wife's car today and had already parked opposite the salon. He switched cars with Marian, who had her husband's car, but Marian spent most of the morning roaming the market stalls because Ian did all the observation, wearing different hats, sunglasses and jackets.

Ian did not want to risk Jodie spotting Marian watching her employer's premises. Prepared for a lot of photographic work, Ian was surprised that Madame Dolores had no visitors whatsoever in the entire first hour.

Concerned that his surveillance may have been exposed, Ian telephoned Marian to watch the front of the house from a safe observation point and when she called back to report being in place; Ian drove the car out of his watching place and parked around the corner. He waited to hear from Marian that he may have been followed but no call came and he was certain that he was free of a tail. It is easy for the biter to be bitten when concentrating on a target.

Having settled his concerns, Ian walked towards the lane at the rear of the salon of Madame Dolores to see Jodie emerge with a green supermarket carry bag in her hand. He slowed his steps to allow the lead to lengthen. She crossed the road and entered the portico of the South Melbourne Post Office. Ian saw Jodie use a key to open one of the larger private post boxes and load a stack of mail, estimated at close to one hundred letters, into her green bag. Jodie returned to the salon the same way she had left. Ian realised that the use of the lane was simply a short cut rather than an attempt to avoid observation. Sometimes in a surveillance operation the simplest action can be misconstrued. He called Marian, who reported no sign of movement, and told her to relax until nearer lunch time.

The mobile Ian reserved for personal calls burped musically and he noted the call emanated from his home before pressing the receive button. The caller was Ian's wife who told him that she obtained the details he had asked her to collect about the ownership of the company titled Madame Dolores Pty Ltd. It was a $2 shelf company owned by a Ms Dolores Regos who resided in the same building that was now the registered office of the company. She was 32 years old and the company was first registered eight years ago, originally at an address in West Footscray, but changed to South Melbourne five years ago. Ian thanked her for the information that he had asked her to get via an information broker, from the ASIC records. He had based his request on the off chance that Madame Dolores operated an enterprise that would be advantaged by having a corporate structure to afford an element of protection against a vexatious client.

Working on the assumption the Jodie's lunch break would be close to the same time each day, Marian positioned herself to see Jodie leave the salon and head for the lunch shop. Marian ordered a sandwich and was selecting a fruit juice from the glass fronted refrigerator when Jodie walked into the shop. Marian paid for her order and sat at a table near the shop front window smiling and nodding an invitation for Jodie to join her. The invitation was accepted with another smile and the two chatted for nearly forty minutes before Marian said she had to return to her office.

Marian and Ian met shortly afterwards. Marian had heaps of information obtained from Jodie. Madame Dolores was a good employer according to Jodie who had worked with her for almost a year. On Monday, Wednesday and Friday, Dolores gave psychic advice on a personal basis strictly by appointment, at half hourly intervals. Her fee was $100 per half hour and, Jodie enthused, she must be wonderful because she was booked out a month ahead, solid. Jodie knew many of the regular customers, most of whom were very nice and a few of the older men had asked her out for dinner but she had declined because Madame had strict rules about contact with clients.

On Tuesdays and Thursdays, Madame and Jodie attended to written requests for psychic readings, prepared copper love life improving amulets, jade financial enhancement necklets, good luck charms and astrological charts. Jodie would dispatch them by mail. Madame devoted some time to her clairvoyant columns that were printed in several newspapers and magazines. Jodie called Tuesdays and Thursdays, "Office Work" days, lots of typing entering cheques in bank pay-in books and computer data records updates on clients. On some office work days, friends of Madame, both male and female would drop in for a chat. Mostly they went upstairs to Madame's residence. Jodie suspected that a couple of gentlemen friends had more than a conversation with Madame, "You know what I mean", she had said with a wink. Madame often used Tuesday as a day for shopping and regular as clockwork, the accountant lady who tended to Madame's bookkeeping and tax arrived at 2.30pm. The rest of the lunch conversation resolved around Jodie's complex love life.

Ian was complimentary to Marian. He advised her not to meet Jodie the next day but wait until Monday. He munched lunch alone and figured that little was to be gained by surveillance on an "Office Work" day so set off to the Land Titles Office to search for details about the Knoxfield property owned by Ray and the South Melbourne property of Madame Dolores. No record of the person searching the land register was required at the Land Titles Office.

The details of each were different but the pattern was identical. Ray had purchased his house seven years ago and the Certificate of Title recorded a bank as mortgagee. In less than four years the mortgage was discharged. Similarly, Dolores had purchased her property a couple of years after Ray's acquisition and the bank mortgagee recorded on purchase was shown as discharging the mortgage five years later. Both Ray and Dolores held their properties as unencumbered owners.

Ian went to his office, connected to the website of one of the public record providers of real estate sales and elicited the information that Ray's property was worth $550,000 at purchase date and was purchased with a $55,000 deposit. The property of Dolores was a purchase by auction, at $1,112,000 and the deposit was $120,000.

Ray was allegedly unemployed or at best, employed by a $2 company operating out of a miniscule serviced office. Allowing for interest on the house loan that meant that Ray paid off the balance owing on the property at the rate of $145,000 per annum whilst Dolores paid around $280,000 per annum.

Such payments were prodigious given what was known about Ray and guessed about Dolores. Sums of that magnitude confirmed that the fraud, whatever it was, had to be sizeable. If Ray could rake in $145,000 a year just for loan repayments, as an employee of Bryn, it begged the question "What must Bryn be raking in?" Certainly a pattern had emerged and the magnitude warranted Ian escalating his endeavours. The money laundering pattern so far as Ian was concerned, was the pattern designed by Bryn and with the number of missing persons connected to Bryn, it appeared ruthlessly protected by him. But how were superannuation funds being ripped off? The application of the pattern remained obscure.

CHAPTER TWENTY-FIVE

ERWIN'S HOME WAS LOCATED AT the rear of a converted mansion in a tree-lined street in the up-market Melbourne suburb of Kew. Erwin's Trust Fund owned the former family home, a large Victorian, two storey residence fronting the street. When Erwin's parents died, the executor of their estate and trustee of Erwin's significant inheritance exercised some entrepreneurial skill and converted the lovingly preserved semi-mansion home into elegant office suites. Carefully selected businesses occupied the street front premises.

A gravelled driveway around one side led to a building that once housed horses. The stable was converted to servants' quarters in the early 1930's. Erwin's family bought the property in 1960. They renovated the servants' quarters into a well appointed "granny flat". Erwin's very independent grandmother moved into it following the death of her husband. When Granny died, Erwin moved in. Erwin had done nothing to maintain the graceful symmetry of the compact residence. Erwin ignored the tenants of the main house and they were content to return the favour. Indeed they actively ignored him following an aggressive and obscene outburst from Erwin when an office supplier unwittingly parked his delivery van that blocked Erwin from driving out his sports car.

Some months of peace followed, primarily because Erwin had been away on more of his travels. Upon his return the tenants were astounded to hear music from Erwin's habitat. Surprised because Erwin's taste in music, or what pretends to be music at times, had obviously undergone a radical change. In the past, the sounds of heavy metal, funk and grunge rock music shattered the serenity of the afternoon with sudden speed and massive volume impact. The employee of one tenant described it as being like a whack in the ears with a pneumatic road drill.

However, Erwin was now playing orchestral music which they identified as Wagner and Lehar. The tenants were not to know that Erwin's musical conversion resulted from his reading of a biography of Adolf Hitler. The book stated that the two composers most loved by the Nazi Fuhrer were Richard Wagner and Franz Lehar. When Erwin was in residence the previously discordant, savage, ripping of serenity by grunge cacophony now alternated with the orchestral renditions of the Ring Quartet (Die Waikerie, Siegfried, Gotterdammerung and Das Rheingold) and the oom-pa-pa of the Merry Widow Waltz.

Two detectives called at the premises and found Erwin was not at home. On questioning the tenants of the office complex, they learned that Erwin's absences for weeks at a time were normal, his musical tastes had changed about a month ago, that he drove a red Mercedes sports car and had an aggressive attitude. The police already knew about the Mercedes, that was why they were calling. But they had no other information. None of Erwin's previous encounters with the law enforcement authorities was known to them because when Lenny the lanky lawyer won an acquittal for Erwin, no entry appeared on Police files. Only details of convictions are recorded. Indeed the entire Police visit to Erwin was speculative and based on desperation. The two detectives were part of a larger team investigating the disappearance of a young boy.

The total of all information available, to the best knowledge of this team of two, began with the report of an alleged abduction of an eight year old boy from a playground area in Central Park, Malvern. The boy was at the park with his mother and younger sister. He was last seen kicking a yellow football around with several other boys of about the same age. The mother was unaware that other boys were called away by a family member to have lunch and that her son was alone for a few minutes. Attending to the younger sibling distracted the mother for two minutes. Minutes now known to be crucial.

At first the absence of the boy was attributed to his going off with the other boys with whom he played football. When the abandoned football was found in a clump of bushes beneath some trees, the matter escalated in police priorities. Two detectives and two uniformed police were allocated to the task. Information from home owners in the bordering streets, Central Park Road and Kingston Street was collated into an events file and the file expanded infinitesimally as observations from regular park users, shoppers, shop proprietors and a motorist who regularly drove along Central Park Road were added.

By midday of the following day the team had several leads. The boy had not been seen anywhere, no contact of any kind made with relatives. The entire police team became convinced that he was not a disgruntled runaway after interviews with family, friends and neighbours.

A concise summation of the family situation was given by the Grandfather of the boy. The summation had the earmarks of professional composition and that proved to be the case when Ian, the Grandfather, disclosed that he was a Licenced Inquiry Agent. His alibi, plus those of all close family members and neighbours were checked as standard operating procedure. The preliminary police theory shifted to abduction by a person or persons unknown, to quote the standard jargon.

The ground around the abandoned football had been trampled on by a dozen feet. It yielded nothing of value but a passer-by stated that he thought he saw a man in the bushes beneath the trees near the conservatory. Apart from a vague description that the man was large no other useful information was elicited. Acting on the vague titbit, a thorough search was made in two nearby stands of trees and bushes. Over twenty footprints were found in the slightly moist soil of one group of bushes and each proved to be of a size eleven training shoe of a particular brand. A cast was made of several of the shoe prints and sent to forensics for identification. A 30 centimetre square of soil some five centimetres deep was dug, boxed and sent in accompaniment. Tests would yield an approximate weight of the wearer of the shoe.

Another informant mentioned that a Ford Falcon car, either white or cream, screamed along Central Park Road towards Burke Road around the time thought to be that of the abduction. A search of the grassy area where the car was parked revealed several training shoe prints in the moist ground. These prints matched those found in the bushes save that the imprint appeared much deeper, as if made by a heavier person or the same person carrying a load. A soil square was carefully removed from this site also. In a direct line between the trees where the football was found and the car parking space, several more training shoe imprints were found that indicated a heavy person running.

The uniformed constables assigned to the investigation obtained a statement from a shopper that a white Ford Falcon had been parked in the now suspect spot for over an hour on the day of the boy's disappearance. The shopper noted that the car was not occupied when she walked past it but she recalled being amused by a sticker on the back window. With considerable patience the constables refrained from comment whilst the informant struggled to recall the exact wording on the sticker. After a cappuccino and a caramel slice at the coffee shop, the lady shopper, the informant, rather hesitatingly stated that the sticker may have read "Rent-a-Wreck" and that a suburb name may also have been on the sticker. She was unshakeable in her identification of the car as a Ford because her late husband owned a similar make and model about ten years ago.

Based on that tenuous information, the uniformed constables and plain clothed detectives telephoned each "Rent-a-Wreck" franchise in the metropolitan area starting alphabetically with "A". Success was found at "O" when the proprietor of the Oakleigh Rent-a-Wreck stated that he had rented out a ten year old white Ford Falcon on the day in question. The detectives went to Oakleigh and obtained a copy of the rental agreement from the file. The good point was that it carried the number of the renter's driving licence. The bad point was that it was the last of three sheets of carbonless copy block printed agreements and had never been handled by the renter, so no fingerprints. Additionally the signature was an indistinct squiggle, unlikely to have a high value for identification purposes. The credit card imprint held as temporary security, was returned to the renter when the Ford was returned intact, the petrol tank full and the daily rental tariff paid in cash.

The junior of the two detectives busily wrote a précis of the evidence on his event sheet and was about to pass the clipboard to the senior detective for checking when the mobile of the senior constable erupted in an up-tempo version of the Policeman's Chorus from the Gilbert & Sullivan musical, the "Pirates of Penzance". Any comical element to the investigation engendered by the spritely music disappeared as rapidly as the $10 carpets advertised in an eternally reappearing bankrupt company carpet sale. The senior turned to the junior when he flipped closed his mobile and told him that the "kid had been found, sexually abused, tortured and dead". In front of the Rent-a-Wreck operator, the senior did not reveal more.

But what the senior had said and his change of demeanour erased any hesitation that the operator might have considered. The operator regretted that his small business did not have sufficient turn-over to warrant installation of closed circuit television but he did his best to describe the renter of the white Ford Falcon two days earlier. He agreed to assist with the composition of a computer image. The operator raised no objection to the subject vehicle being impounded by the police. He regretted that the vehicle had since been rented to another person and the interior had been wiped over, whilst the outside had been sprayed with detergent and rinsed.

Forensics did not have a very good time with the impounded Ford. The interior yielded only a partial footprint from a size eleven trainer and that was smudged by the much smaller shoes worn by the next renter. Several fingerprints were found in the interior. Several days later, during a "make-sure" search, a fragment of what was thought to be a piece of a fingernail was found. No prints or DNA material on the door and door handles, the handbrake or the boot release. Pieces of adhesive packing tape and remnants of plastic sheet indicated that the boot may have once been partially lined with plastic sheeting of a type readily available in hardware stores throughout the State. It did not help that the subsequent renter had carried several bags of potting mix in the boot and some spillage had occurred. Both the renter and the operator had, as the idiom goes, "cast-iron" alibis and readily agreed to be fingerprinted and DNA'd for the purposes of elimination.

With discovery of the pathetic, mutilated body, the Homicide Squad was given jurisdiction over the entire investigation and immediately absorbed the local Criminal Investigation Unit detectives, who had initiated the lost boy search, into their cohort of investigators. The owner of the driving licence used to rent the Ford was located in a northern suburban police station where he was locked up to sleep off a drunken binge. The drunkard was found wandering too close to a busy motorway. Locating the drunk was the easy part; trying to get him sober enough to answer questions was the hard part. The sun had risen on a new day before the drunkard was sufficiently compos mentis to understand a fair part of the questions being fired at him. The questioning had an underlying aggressive edge because the initial working theory adopted by the questioners was that the drunkard had murdered the boy.

By mid-morning the homicide squad detectives began to doubt their preliminary theorem. The drunkard's shoe size was an eight and his physical condition so poor as to cause him trouble in abducting an arthritic canary let alone a healthy, energetic, eight year old boy. And pieces of information about the drunken binge he had been on for days began trickling throughout the police network. The Salvation Army hostel for homeless men provided information from admittedly unreliable and reluctant fellow hostel frequenters that, when put together, never-the-less built up a credible alibi for the perpetually inebriated suspect.

With regard to his driving licence, the drunkard was vague but attributed its loss to the same time frame, give or take a day or so, to him finding $100 in his wallet. Obviously good fairies did exist, he told the sceptical police investigators. And in the misty period pre his $100 bonanza he had been drinking at a pub near the Victoria Market. Under a lot of pressure he named, or at least gave nicknames, of several of his fellow drinkers. Perhaps because Erwin had bought him several drinks, the drunkard gave a reasonable description of Erwin but could not recall any name.

Later that day the computer image of a possible suspect, prepared with the ready cooperation of the Rent-a-Wreck operator, was shown to the withdrawal symptoms ravaged drunkard. He was almost startled at the likeness of it to the generous drink buyer of a few days, or was it a week, ago? Prints of the composite image were made and shown to the drinking companions of the drunkard. These derelicts had been rounded up from the environs of the Victoria Market. One of them, perhaps smarter than the others or not so brain damaged, told the police that the man in the photo image drove a stunning red car. The promise of a six-pack of full strength beer so resurrected his recollection that he stated with all of the authority he could muster, that the man in the photo image drove a red, almost new, Mercedes Benz sports car. The idea that a drinking mate of this bunch of drunken derelicts drove a late model Mercedes sports car was preposterous. It was so unbelievable that it might just be true. Surely no drunk had the ability to make it up? His brief burst of cooperation was subjected to more questions in an attempt to shake his identification of the vehicle. But he was unshakeable in his answer even though his hands were shaking in anticipation of a six-pack, which was duly provided. From the Motor Registration Branch the police obtained the names and address of eighty-five owners of red Mercedes Benz sports cars registered over the last three years. The lead was tenuous but nothing could be ignored. Every officer involved with the investigation recognised that the chain of evidence was weak. Any deduction made on weak evidence had to be treated with caution. The detectives had no contempt for caution.

CHAPTER TWENTY-SIX

OVER THE NEXT FORTNIGHT IAN continued taking photographs of the clients of Madame Dolores. He was assisted by the photographer Brenda and her husband who were additions to his growing team. Marina was reserved exclusively for expanding the friendship with Jodie, meeting three times a week for lunch. On a couple of days she passed Jodie with hands full of bags of sandwiches and soft drink and smiled, said "Busy day" then rushed around the corner.

There was no office for Marian to rush to, only Ian waiting for nourishment in his parked car. The brief encounter was to avoid overload of acquaintance that may arouse suspicion. Jodie was not the brightest bulb in the chandelier but Ian did not want to spark even the faintest hint of Marian being unearthed as an interrogator.

During the busy fortnight Ian had been "dumpster diving", trade slang for searching rubbish bins. Ian hired a van for this work. The green "wheelie" rubbish bin of Madame Dolores was placed at the end of the rear lane late Wednesday afternoon for an early Thursday morning clearance by the municipal garbage collector. Ian simply drove up near the lane after dark, stopped, opened the van's rear door and tilted then pushed the "wheelie" bin into the cargo space. A few hundred yards away he stopped, climbed into the rear of the van and emptied the contents of the bin into several large black plastic garden refuse bags. He returned to the lane and slid the bin back to its original place. No one noticed. The black bags he took to the yard at the back of his office, connected a portable fluorescent light to a power outlet and by that light he sifted through the smelly rubbish.

Most of the thrown out material was clean; Madame Dolores seemed to eat out a lot. Very little household or food remains were evident, mainly take away cartons. What was evident in abundance were piles of shredded paper and opened envelopes. Like gold nuggets in a washing pan, thirty two envelopes shone through the mullock. Each bore the printed return address of a superannuation fund. Twenty eight were postage paid and four had postage stamps stuck over the postage paid rectangle. After two rubbish bin collections, Ian had sixty suspect envelopes. Madame Dolores seemed to be security conscious enough to shred letters and documents but evidently thought envelopes were innocuous.

One non-client Thursday, Jodie left the house at lunch time with a thirtyish, dark haired, medium height just slightly overdeveloped woman. On instinct Ian, who was on photo duty, snapped several shots then phoned Marian to stay put, rather than meet Jodie, as planned, at the lunch shop. Ian sensed that the woman was Madame Dolores and he wanted to take no risk with Marian being sussed by a woman who must have an above normal perception of people to be able to direct and sustain a thriving business, the bedrock of which was human gullibility. He phoned Brenda, the professional photographer, who was resting in a cafe in the market and guided her to the lunch shop to get more photographs of Madame Dolores from different angles.

The intelligence gathering activity from Marian's increasing friendship with Jodie revealed that Madame Dolores appeared to be operating at two levels. The "legitimate part" of the psychic industry had a degree of high tech. In magazine advertisements it listed the telephone 1900 prefix and credit card and SMS suffix that sent calls direct to a call centre established by Dolores in a low rent outer suburb. By arrangement with a group that cared for physically disabled but mentally alert people, the call centre responded to clients seeking psychic solace by reading from a group of text scripts on a computer screen, the texts allegedly appropriate to the astrological sign of the caller. Madame advertised in several ethnic magazines and had sympathetic people, who spoke the language, available to obliterate curses and deflect the evil eye. For a fee, of course. Again the text provided by Dolores made responses simple. Business was highly profitable and Jodie was full of admiration for the initiative of Dolores in providing employment for the physically handicapped and relieving sufferers from the evil eye which, she said, must be awful.

Similarly Jodie was enthusiastic in her praise of Madame's good luck "jade" necklets, "pure" copper and cobalt life enhancing amulets, talismans and inspirational love bracelets containing "genuine" ionic electrum. Credit card payments were processed only by Madame and Ray. One of Jodie's tasks was the immediate dispatch of the requested charm to those who sent cash in payment. The records of cash payers were kept on discs that Jodie updated with details of the client, noted repeat business with code numbers, and gave the disc to Madame who kept all copies of cash payments in her own private security cabinet. The cabinet had received a special "eyes-on" astrological influence gaze from Madame to confer continuing auspicious auras on cash payers. Jodie though that wonderfully considerate of Madame. As to what happened to the cash, Jodie did not know for sure but Jodie formed the opinion that Madame donated it all to the physically disabled people whom she employed to answer the scores of daily telephone calls. Marian thought pigs might fly.

With cheques, Jodie's task was to computer list them, enter the list in a deposit book and make daily payments to the bank located in a street not far from the rear of the office. The lady accountant who called each Tuesday and Thursday compiled the income and expenditure accounts from Jodie's lists. Charms of various types were dispatched after a delay of a week, when the cheques cleared. Because, Jodie lamented, some people were untrustworthy and about one in twenty cheques bounced. She found such iniquity to be unsettling.

Despite the fact that bounced cheques cost Madame money by way of bank fees, Madame did not invoke adverse powers of celestial potency upon the deceitful; powers that Jodie was convinced Madame had because, after all there was a "dark side", as Jodie knew from watching the entire series of Star Wars on TV. No, Madame was philosophical, a word Madame used frequently. Jodie tried to look it up in the dictionary but could not find it in the "F" alphabetical section. Madame was philosophical because the bank fee was tax deductible. Some mail puzzled Jodie because it came from superannuation funds but Jodie did not have to worry about them; she simply put them in a box and the ever helpful Ray took care of Madame's box.

Jodie regretted that Marian's lunch break did not coincide with hers earlier in the week because she had lunch with Madame in the lunch shop and thought that Marian may have benefitted from an introduction to the marvelous Madame. That statement confirmed to Ian that he had Dolores Regos on film in crystal clear clarity.

Marian's report and Ian's appreciation of the ramifications led him to conclude that a meeting of managers of the superannuation funds was necessary. Ian made a portfolio of photographs and photocopies of envelopes in clear pocket display books. He also drew up an itemized account of expenses to date. Using the "Pythagoras" code word to his principal fund manager contact and injecting a note of urgency into his voice, he suggested a meeting with a group of managers at his Club as the venue and offered several dates / times as alternatives. He received a response in less than two hours and the meeting was confirmed for early next afternoon.

Ian and Marian were watching Madame's salon on Tuesday. Ian in front, Marian in the side street when Marian reported that the Ford Escort was backing into the lane. Ian joined Marian in her observation post, a bus shelter, and confirmed that Dolores was the driver. They saw the Ford drive away but did not follow because their own vehicles could not be reached in time to pursue. Further surveillance was rewarded when a business type woman, auburn hair, average height and build, mid fifties carrying a computer bag and brief case entered the front door of the salon.

Ian had discussed with Marian his intention to grill the "accountant lady" that Jodie had mentioned. Ian said "That's her. Wish me luck, its confrontation time". Marian saw Ian approach the front door and went back to her bus shelter observation post. If she saw Dolores return she would call Ian's mobile. Marian was Ian's back up. If, perchance, Ian ran into trouble and did not phone Marian's mobile every fifteen minutes, then Marian would call the local police station and anonymously report a violent burglary in progress at the salon.

When he entered the salon Ian was greeted with a cheery smile from Jodie who sat at a computer station surrounded by dangling charms, amulets, talismans and astrological figures. Ian had to remind himself that despite his second hand acquaintance, she had never met him. He took the initiative by stating that he had come to see the accountant. Jodie's smile did not diminish and she invited him to walk around the receptionist desk and go through a doorway leading into an office type room. Ian observed an impressive, deep green, velvet covered, brass studded, upholstered door to his left. He presumed this to be Madame's private salon.

Jodie went back to the receptionist desk. Ian had his Private Inquiry Agent ID card in a leather folder and held it up authoritatively for the lady accountant to view at a distance as he introduced himself as an investigator but never offered his name. The lady went to pieces. She shivered, tears filled her eyes and her fingers wound and unwound continually. Ian had never before experienced such disintegration on a simple introduction. The cause of her distress became apparent during his questioning. Ian learned that the accountant held herself out to be fully qualified but in truth, she confessed, she had no qualifications. Ian allayed her fears by promising not to tell her employer.

He began with soothing questions and continued probing for an hour. Every fifteen minutes he phoned Marian and said the agreed word that meant he was OK and not under duress. He learned that the accountant lady never saw or dealt with any cash, but suspected that a considerable amount passed through the business of Madame Dolores. The accountant lady handled cheque and credit card revenue only and recorded outgoings such as Jodie's pay, postage, stationery, etc. Despite pressure, she denied any knowledge of any connection with any superannuation funds.

At the end of an hour Ian had learnt little he did not already know or suspect. The accountant lady was upset to an extreme degree despite Ian's assurance he would not dob her in. Ian departed feeling a trifle sorry for her because if his investigation proceeded as foreshadowed, then Madame Dolores would abruptly cease to be a client. Ian was fully aware that his direct intervention could cause repercussions. In his judgement it was time to inject an element of fear into the criminals.

Dominating the meeting room at Ian's Club was a magnificent mahogany table surrounded by Georgian style, maroon leather upholstered chairs.

From the walls, gold framed portraits of illustrious and be-medalled Generals, Admirals and Air Marshals surveyed the room.

The senior superannuation fund manager took the chairman's position with Ian midway along one side of the massive table from whence, when all were seated, he distributed the display books he had compiled. Ian discussed his preliminary investigation report page by page. Ian described then commented on the implication of each exhibit. Starting with Johnny (he did not reveal the name Bryn) then Ray, Dolores and Jodie, all in colour photos. The following twenty five pages contained four photos per page of clients of Dolores. From the one hundred faces, twelve were definitely recognised as employees or former employees of various superannuation funds with two females that were possibly a wife or partner of a fund employee. The meeting became quite lively with questions addressed to Ian from several directions concurrently, but he pleasantly parried each pending his invitation to turn to the page containing the photocopies of the "wheelie bin" envelopes. The meeting became positively tumultuous. Every manager recognised an envelope with their own fund return address. The entities to which those envelopes were addressed had different names but the South Melbourne Post Office box rented by Madame Dolores was the same for each. Attention was directed to those that were "official" mail compared with those bearing postage stamps that may certainly be designated as "unofficial", ie employer envelopes used for employees personal use, and these stamped envelopes differed from others because they were overtly addressed to Madame Dolores.

Ian now had eight intelligent managers considering the ramifications of envelopes officially addressed to apparently legitimate entities but with the postal address of a psychic. Despite opinions to the contrary, superannuation fund managers are not devoid of humour, even under pressure, and in typical Aussie spirit jokes about clairvoyants circulated. A few managers expressed hopes as to what might eventuate between them and the nubile jiggly Jodie but that type of humour was almost a standard precursor to a communal, intense, period of solid thinking.

Each manager was now both enthused and appalled with the concrete evidence of skullduggery and each wanted to contribute to the discreet exposure of what looked, at best, to the something definitely irregular. Fortunately the irregularity appeared to apply to each fund so no manager could self-righteously abstain from the pursuit of an explanation. After two hours, the competent chairman, with the assistance of Ian, had a common, comprehensive plan of action, the quite implementation of which would throw sunlight on a dark dirty pit of deceit. Each manager was braced to face the prospect of collusion by a member of their trusted staff and each was impressed by the exhortation of the chairman, supported by Ian, of the need for tight lipped security.

Just before the meeting closed, Ian submitted his itemized account. The size of it did not even cause one eyebrow to be raised. The chairman advised that he would obtain authorisation to pay Ian in full and others would reimburse his fund on a pro-rata to membership basis when a better view of the magnitude of the fraud was ascertained.

Ian left the meeting well satisfied and as confident as he could be that the investigation would remain discreet for a short time longer. However he knew that nothing remains secret for long and decided to proceed with utmost practical speed once the various managers responded to the resolutions of the meeting.

CHAPTER TWENTY-SEVEN

DOLORES NEVER KNEW THAT SHE had achieved her most cherished ambition because her drugged brain was only partially reactivated by the physical shock of her naked body hitting the grey-green icy water. Perhaps it was just as well that her brain was inoperative because a great white shark ripped off her right leg. The shock, blood loss and hypothermia combined to send her into unfeeling infinity.

Dolores had arrived in Australia as a five year old migrant and aspired to be a "true-blue" Aussie so it was ironic that she achieved the epitome of Australiana by emulating a former Australian Prime Minister in becoming shark cuisine.

Bryn had no compunction about the murder. In fact the only reaction that Bryn suffered in dumping the body of Dolores into what he regarded as his personal waste disposal area, seaward of Lady Julia Percy Island, was that it caused him to recall the disposal of Ray several minutes earlier.

Ray's committal to the deep had been the first of a triple disposal because Rodney had accompanied him into the marine food chain. Bryn still harboured feelings of deep resentment against Ray. Ray had been one of Bryn's earliest recruits as a "runner" in the staged accident insurance fraud scheme. Ray had graduated to the position of being the nearest to a trusted friend that Bryn ever allowed himself to acquire in his criminal empire.

Ray was Bryn's chief "cut-out", the person who relayed Bryn's orders and shielded Bryn from the scores of other "players" that were employed by the organisation at one time or another. And by always referring to the boss as "Johnny", Ray had created a phantom personality that foiled police efforts when loose lipped recruits tried to trade information in the hope of lesser charges.

Bryn figured that Ray's income far exceeded anything Ray had ever dreamed of when he dropped out of his adult entry University course so many years ago.

In fact it was Ray's inability to conceal his wealth that led to Ray's demise. Without any regular income, Ray had felt it unnecessary to add to the prodigious workload of the Australian Taxation Office by lodging taxation returns. So when a discarded girl friend vindictively told her father of Ray's wealth in the form of an expensive house in the Knoxfield area, the Gold Coast apartments, new car each year, and always stacks of folding money in his wallet, an unfortunate chain of events for Ray was inaugurated. The former girl friend's father was employed by the ATO and he lodged an official dob-in-notice, complete with a fair amount of details.

Eventually the information spiralled up the labyrinthine chain, received the nod of the head noddy and descended again to the peculiarly titled section of the ATO known as the "Betterments" investigators. In essence, if a person has no visible source of income or capital but somehow acquired assets, the ATO assess the "betterments" of a person's financial status between two dates and impose a tax on that value. Ray had forgotten the four month fling with the flighty floozie four years earlier. When the ATO heavies descended, Ray panicked, phoned Bryn on the dedicated mobile phone and at a subsequent meeting exhibited signs of mental deterioration that surprised and alarmed Bryn.

And Ray's timing was most inopportune because Rodney had also become a problem. Dolores, Bryn's clairvoyant access to profitable superannuation fraud, also contacted Ray for assistance in avoiding an investigator. Three problems, each of considerable magnitude, all intertwined, made Bryn feel threatened. And whenever Bryn felt threatened he resolved the threat by eliminating the person or persons who posed it or anyone who could implicate him.

Rodney was Bryn's forger. Like Ray, Bryn considered him part of the team since the early days at the Uni. Bryn had been generous with finances that assisted Rodney out of difficult situations and Rodney reciprocated with reliably forged documents and scrupulous attention to total destruction of anything and everything that may have linked him to Bryn. Rodney had spent three periods behind bars for forgery in relation to some of his own unsuccessful ventures and Rodney had homosexual preferences that led to a decline in his health due to AIDS. This unfortunate condition had progressed slowly but inexorably and Rodney's work quality had declined

A younger group of technocrat forgers, using to advantage the benefits of new computer technology, were getting more of Bryn's business. Rodney, with his declining health condition felt peeved. His first request for financial assistance from Bryn was politely toned and Bryn responded equally politely and generously to what he then perceived, with no knowledge at that time of Rodney's serious medical condition, as temporary assistance. However Rodney had increased the intensity of his financial requirements and his next appeal for finance went to the point of a demand. Bryn's hackles rose, though he disguised his malhumour pending the opportunity to think the problem through.

Dolores was another burden. Of the three she was the most recent of Bryn's associates and was known directly to him, face to face, albeit by his pseudo name Johnny, due to recent mischance caused by Ray's panic. Ray had met Dolores through a mutual friend from whom Dolores had sought advice on how to avoid taxation and police scrutiny on money obtained dubiously. The mutual friend was aware that Ray had shady connections and so the introduction was made and the friend bowed out. Upon learning of the requirements of Dolores, Ray informed Bryn who applied his agile mind towards a satisfactory solution as the first step. Later he would propose an expansion to a degree that Dolores did not forsee, despite her alleged psychic powers.

Dolores was a clairvoyant. She advertised herself without any attempt at modesty as the greatest clairvoyant and psychic in the universe. To around 200,000 people she certainly so appeared. Her family had migrated to Australia and Dolores attended her first school in an outer Melbourne suburb. Both of her elder brothers grew to be tall, athletic, above average height and below average as stand-over merchants. On the day before her

High School graduation both were convicted on eight counts under Section 28 of the Crimes Act, Extortion with threat to destroy property. Dolores and her parents were shamed in the eyes of their migrant community and Dolores felt unable to draw upon the resources of the community to assist her in getting a job. She needed a job because the absence of her two brothers had resulted in a diminution of the income of the family.

She lucked into a job in the office of a magazine publisher and over several years developed expertise that was appreciated by her employer. Perhaps because of the cloud of misery that hung over a family with two sons in prison, Dolores looked for some form of escape and found it by avidly reading the astrological charts and clairvoyant predictions in the magazine her employer published. Dolores absorbed the jargon and was fascinated to talk with several of the authors of the astrological predictions when, on occasion, they called personally to lodge the texts or to pay their advertising accounts. As the introduction of computers meant that the publisher of the magazine required text by email, several of the older charlatans required help and Dolores was pleased to oblige.

When one older woman clairvoyant became ill and unable to submit text for several issues of the magazine, Dolores departed from her comfort zone and composed the text for her. The regular gentleman friend of Dolores, at that time, was employed as a researcher in the office of a stockbroker so Dolores introduced an element of finance into the predictions, based on "pillow talk". The readers of the magazine obviously appreciated the subtle hints, eg "financial favour finds those who invest in the opposite to the abstract" and, sure enough, the following week the share price of a concrete company bounded upwards when a take-over offer was announced. Consequently the response by way of cheques sent to the clairvoyant to pay for individual readings swelled the bank account of the ailing and aging clairvoyant.

A deal was negotiated between the clairvoyant and Dolores. The clairvoyant retired leaving Dolores as the author of future columns and the sole beneficiary of the personal reading payments. For Dolores to have informed her employer seemed superfluous and conducive to her being sacked so Dolores concealed her proprietorship of the clairvoyant's column. She did well. Her columns had a sparkle unseen previously and the subtle financial tips attracted "yuppies". She sold scores of lucky astrological amulets and charms of her own design that netted her a 1000% mark up.

Dolores delighted to receive payments for personal readings and diligently accounted for all cheques in the accounts of the clairvoyant business which she had now incorporated into a single director proprietary limited company. About half of the payments for the $50 personal readings or the $100 intimate and intensive readings were by cheque. The other half consisted of cash in $100, $50, $20 and $10 notes. With little experience in the handling of large quantities of notes, and having bought all the expensive jewellery that her fingers, wrists and neck could reasonably accommodate, Dolores was seeking relief from prodigious demands of the ATO.

A client gave Dolores Ray's mobile phone number. Dolores called Ray and speaking in guarded language, hinted at her problem. Ray was surprised and wary at the contact but agreed to meet Dolores in a café that he knew and liked because of its multiple exits. At that meeting Ray listened to her recital of her cash problem but remained non-committal. Later, after explaining the problem of Dolores to Bryn and receiving advice, Ray met with Dolores again at the same café and outlined the plan to convert "black" notes into "white" collateral using the conduit of the trust account of one of "Johnny's" stable of compliant solicitors. The fee was 20% of the cash.

Dolores felt 20% was too high but without an alternative, resolved to comply as a temporary measure, whilst she sought a less costly but safe, substitute service provider. During a chat with Ray over a coffee, Dolores mentioned that her gullible adherents often wrote to her without reservation about their emotions, sex lives, partnership problems, adjustments to married life, etc. She mentioned that one adherent, a regular $150 per month payer, had written a proposal of marriage. To improve his prospects the proposer mentioned that he held a key position in a major superannuation fund.

Dolores began to follow Johnny's advice as conveyed by Ray. The advice was not only about evading tax but also about marketing. Dolores was astounded at the growth in her business. She resolved to remain with Ray's Johnny because she conceded that the 20% fee was better than the 48% that the ATO would claim. After cooperation with Johnny via Ray for several years, Dolores strolled into the coffee lounge of a hotel in Little Collins

Street Melbourne, the locale of her first meetings with Ray, thinking only of having a coffee. She spied Ray talking with a younger man. Dolores sat down, uninvited, next to Ray, asked about his health then looked with an air of expectation at the good looking younger man in the opposite chair.

Caught off balance, Ray haltingly introduced the man to Dolores, and called him Johnny; Dolores smiled broadly and said how pleased she was to meet the boss at last. Dolores instantly imagined expanding her business relationship to something more hotly and nakedly personal, such as the arrangement she enjoyed with Ray. Johnny appeared distinctly uncomfortable, grumbled a farewell apology and abruptly departed. Dolores was affronted and complained to Ray without affect.

Still unsettled and seething with anger Dolores returned to her salon. Her anger erupted to volcanic proportions when her accountant told her that a private investigator had spent over an hour questioning her about the clairvoyant business. Tearfully, the accountant confessed that she may have been inadvertently indiscreet as a result of the concentrated questioning of the investigator, whose name now escaped her. The thrust of the investigator's questions related to superannuation. Dolores stood paralysed with panic for a full minute then turned about, walked to the outside balcony and dialled Ray on her mobile. When Ray answered, Dolores blurted out that a private investigator had visited her office making enquiries about superannuation. Dolores demanded a face to face meeting with Johnny to manufacture a defense against further enquiries. When Bryn heard this demand he had further questions relayed to Dolores then agreed to the face to face meeting.

The fear of Dolores escalated as throughout the day, eleven of her "faithful" physic adherents called by phone or in person to tell her that superannuation fund investigators had interrogated them about their association with Madame Dolores. Dolores made more panic stricken phone calls to Ray. Ray had just read the demand from the ATO to produce details of his income and assets for the last seven years. Failure to comply could lead to forfeiture of assets or prison. Fear for himself grew within him. The calls from Dolores made him even more frightened for her.

Bryn was thinking furiously all day. He had three dangerous situations, Dolores, Ray and Rodney. With his customary ruthless resolve Bryn determined to kill three birds with one stone, or stoning. He arranged a meeting with all three near the kiosk on the St Kilda pier in an hour. He told each one he could solve all of their problems.

At the pier Johnny invited them to join him on his motor cruiser. He proposed a discussion of mutual problems in the middle of the bay where they would not be uninterrupted. The windless day made the sea surface seem like a mirror and he was surprised at the alacrity with which they stepped aboard. They accepted drinks that they greedily downed unaware of the amount of the drug that Bryn had introduced into the bottles before resealing them. Each was stoned to their eye balls before Bryn untied the springers and guided his prized motor cruiser on the two day return journey to Lady Julia Percy Island. Of the four persons who set out, only one returned.

Bryn further reflected, as Dolores disappeared beneath the waves, that the greatest clairvoyant in the universe did not foresee her own demise otherwise she would have been more cautious. Her lack of caution dented his belief in the fortune telling profession forever.

CHAPTER TWENTY-EIGHT

THE MENTION OF A LATE model red Mercedes sports car by an alcohol ravaged derelict was a frail item on which to base a police search. But fragile though it appeared, it was an avenue of investigation that had to be pursued. The only buttress to credibility lay in the fact that the alcoholic informant had once been an able motor mechanic. It was hoped that experience of motor vehicles was retained by sufficient undamaged brain cells to be reliable. Police teams began to track down owners. Women owners were questioned about persons to whom they may have loaned their Mercedes sports car and all fourteen were virtually eliminated as suspects. Their names were relegated to the lowest part of the priority list. No one ever dropped off the list entirely. Six of the vehicles were listed as write-offs and checks to make sure they had not been rebirthed took some time but they, and their owners, were likewise listed as low priority.

Not all owners were truthful. Some married men gave alibis that were checked and proven false. A hard line of questioning revealed that the stories were concocted to conceal amorous liaisons with ladies other than their current partner. The true version of where they were at the critical time of the boy's death emerged when the police hinted that the untruthful owners were edging towards the top of the list of suspects in the rape/murder of an eight year boy and that police may not be able to stop the media reporting the fact. Shaken, the mendacious owners could not wait to provide police with full details and, with some reluctance, they too were all consigned to the low priority portion of the suspects list.

This process of elimination took time. Eventually the list was reduced to five unlocated owners, one of which was Erwin. At first Erwin was not near the top of the list because his driving licence was nearing expiry and the old photograph on it showed a younger Erwin with a more pleasant facial expression and abundant hair. He did not appear to comply with the description given by the proprietor of the Rent a Wreck car hire premises.

Sergeant Jarvis of the Vice Squad was well into the information loop and as the "persons of interest" list of red Mercedes sports car owners became shorter, he recognised the name of Erwin Dormunt. He pondered for days on what to do. After catching Erwin in a brothel that specialised in extreme sexual perversions, his instinct shouted at him that Erwin must be the prime suspect in the awful murder of the eight year old boy.

Could he make an anonymous phone call to "dob" in Erwin? But what if Erwin tried to wriggle out of an arrest by threatening to expose the extortion activity of Jarvis? With no contempt for caution, Jarvis decided to remain silent as to Erwin's identity. Wherever he could, he insinuated the idea that perpetrator of the horrific crime was likely to be armed and dangerous. Jarvis hoped that his rumour would pervade the police front line investigator team. It could motivate a shoot-out that would leave Erwin a corpse. Jarvis believed in the concept of PYA – protect your arse.

The neck of the net on Erwin began to close when a young, shapely, blonde, off duty police woman emerged from a renowned specialist liquor store in the Jacaranda lined main street of Leura in the Blue Mountains holiday district of New South Wales. Reverse parking a shiny red Mercedes sports car at the kerb was a large framed skin-head. The policewoman paused to examine the label on the bottle of expensive Grange Hermitage wine purchased for consumption with her husband at the celebration dinner for their first wedding anniversary. The pause and label examination were a ploy to allow her a surreptitious examination of the driver as he climbed from the red sports car and walked into the liquor store. The policewoman noted his age, height and build and his black tee shirt, desert storm patterned army trousers and black lace-up parachute boots. He looked entirely out of place as the driver of an expensive sports vehicle. It was this incongruity that caused her to cross the street, rest the bottle on a brick flower box and telephone the police at nearby Katoomba.

She requested information about an APB from Vicpol about a red Mercedes sports car and its driver. In response to her call an unmarked NSW police car arrived within minutes. Two detectives got out, signalled briefly to their off duty blonde colleague that two other police officers had gone around the back. Then a divisional van arrived and parked alongside the red sports car completely blocking it in. Erwin emerged from the wine shop holding a bag containing wine bottles. Instinctively he sensed a threat and raised a fist. Erwin wasn't slow but he could not evade the clutches of the two plain clothes police augmented by the two uniformed men from the divisional van.

Three of the four bottles of expensive German white wine smashed on the footpath during the brief but desperate struggle. Erwin's face made close contact with the footpath, assisted by a polished black shoe pushing the back of his neck. Handcuffs click, click, click, and clicked into full lock. Even with hands locked behind his back Erwin's efforts to avoid incarceration in the back of the divvy van caused the police to exert considerable effort. Erwin's kicking, pushing and attempts to bite became subdued only after he received hard hits on the legs from a baton. On the way to the Katoomba lock-up Erwin's boots pounded the doors, wire covered windows and dividing partition accompanied by uninterrupted verbal obscenities. At the station, after being cautioned and having the reason for his arrest explained, Erwin adopted his, by now, well practiced chameleon like change to that of polite cooperation.

After Erwin made telephone contact with Lenny the lanky lawyer he relaxed as well as he could. The major impediment to his complete relaxation was his inexplicable arrest. He believed that he had obliterated all traces of his encounter with the murdered boy in Melbourne. So began a period of soul searching not tinged with any remorse for the young life he had so brutally extinguished, but centred upon his own prospects for freedom.

Erwin's recapitulation started with the rented Ford Falcon. He remembered driving around several suburbs to add extra kilometres to the odometer and he had stopped several times in deserted streets where kerbside green garbage wheelie bins indicated that a clearance was imminent. Into five bins in different streets he disposed of black plastic garden garbage bags each containing bloodstained underclothes of the victim, condoms, latex gloves, track suit, trainers, cable ties and socks. He saw the light blue collection truck and watched as the mechanical arm picked the wheelie bins and emptied them into the rear. He was certain that all of the disposals were unobserved and all incriminating evidence was totally destroyed.

As for the disused dairy, his chosen depraved entertainment and killing site, he doubted that any evidence remained because he had opened an industrial stop cock and flooded the entire area to a depth over fifteen centimetres with dirty water accumulated in a rusty rain water tank.

Nothing would be left except water and mud. No footprints, no blood, no trace of him. The interior of the rented car he had carefully cleaned with detergent and paper towels before returning it, giving the steering wheel, door, gearshift, and brake handle a further quick wipe on arrival at the car yard.

While engaged in the murderous violation of the young boy Erwin had been totally naked. The track suit he wore to and from the murder scene he had taken off in a sports pavilion four kilometres distant and put on a replacement track suit. Erwin believed that no trace of his activities remained. His precautions were thorough, he thought.

Next day he put a pre packed suitcase into the Mercedes sports car, locked his residence and left on a drive to nowhere. Australia is such an enormous island that people living in the southern part unconsciously head northwards whenever they feel the urge to escape suburban shackles. Erwin just drove automatically northwards because his brain and body were still savouring the savage sexual satisfaction that permeated, it seemed, every cell of his body. When he felt hungry he stopped at a convenient place to eat. When it was dark he pulled into a motel. He paid cash for all travel expenses, including petrol, not for any realisation that credit card purchases could be tracked, but simply because he had a wad of cash stashed away as post-event spending money. The corpses of other boys he had violated and murdered were all well hidden. He had deliberately left the body of his latest victim where it would be found to increase his pleasure by reading the lurid newspaper reports of the crime.

How could police have become aware of his connection with the act of murder? Was it Jarvis? And how much should he tell Lenny when he arrived? He needed a story but without knowledge of what police knew, how could he fabricate a fable with credibility? He deliberately tried to relax by telling himself that imaginative evidence interpretation was the province of Lenny, his lanky lawyer. In the meantime Erwin remembered Lenny's previous advices; insist repeatedly that it was a mistake but never say what "it" was. Make no admission of anything. Better to resist police provocation to talk and later walk free than make any response that the police could twist to frame him.

With an expression of disdain for all law enforcement authorities, Erwin sat silent through each interrogation session by the NSW police detectives. Eventually they gave up and decided to leave the job of information extraction to their Victorian counterparts who were due at the station shortly to complete the documents for extradition of Erwin to Victoria. The charge against Erwin, to justify arrest in New South Wales, was that of assault of a police officer. Continued intense interrogation on that charge could be counterproductive and interpretted by a Magistrate as harassment to a degree such as to result in dismissal of the charge. The NSW police officers were sufficiently experienced to recognise that the pressure they applied must be proportionate to the crime and they did not want Erwin to walk out because of an over zealous attempt to obtain information of a crime allegedly committed in another State. They wanted Erwin safely in custody so the Victoria police could extradite him. The NSW police had no contempt for caution.

At the Katoomba Police Station, a young blonde woman police constable was on her knees tidying the numerous stacks of forms in pigeon holes beneath the counter. She was gently humming to herself because recollections of pleasure of last night's first wedding anniversary celebration were forefront in her thoughts. She recalled the unexpected bonus of finding an intact bottle of expensive German white wine amongst the broken bottles on the footpath after her colleagues had arrested a suspected child rapist and murderer. She had chilled the wine and shared it with her husband. Later they drank the bottle of special red wine she had purchased and they kissed and cuddled and made love several times during the night. Wedded bliss was wonderful and she felt totally happy.

A gentle tap on the counter caused her to look up from her kneeling position. At first she thought that someone was playing a trick on her. From her menial position, with one eye covered by her long, straight, naturally Nordic blonde hair, she thought she was looking at the keyboard of a child's shabby piano surrounded by a stretched, partly inflated, inner tube from a bike tyre. But the inner tube undulated and spoke human words so she sprang up in fright to see an apparition beyond the counter. Horrified by the sight, she quickly retreated two steps. Her hand instinctively reached for the Glock pistol in a holster on her belt. There she paused as it registered that the apparition was a tall cadaverous member of the human race. Just. The blonde had encountered Lenny the lanky lawyer, smiling.

Inwardly, Lenny was pleased to be reassured that he had not lost his ability to inspire instant horripilation. In a voice that had taken him years of practice to develop and which was the envy of all British Broadcasting television newsreaders, Lenny told the blonde that he was the legal advisor to Erwin and respectfully requested that he be given immediate access to his unlawfully detained and completely innocent client. Lenny knew that his description of Erwin as an innocent was wasted on the blonde constable, who was slowly recovering her poise, but Lenny realised that he would have to describe Erwin that way to the press, members of the judiciary and maybe even a jury so he decided to practice it so he could say it without his inner repugnance being evident.

Still with her hand on the butt of the Glock, blondie pressed the buzzer button beneath the counter and a uniformed police sergeant appeared from a side door. Being older and more experienced than the blonde, the sergeant quelled his gun hand's automatic clench towards his holster. Before he could speak, Lenny had another rehearsal about him representing the hapless, helpless, unlawfully detained innocent Erwin. During this spiel his long suntanned fingers extended a business card to the sergeant. The card was read by the sergeant who nodded at a padded bench along a wall. The bench was anchored to the floor and wall with bolted brackets. Lenny was told to wait and arrangements for access to the prisoner would be made as soon as possible.

Contrary to the reaction of the blonde police constable, when Erwin was directed into an interview room he was not repelled by the sight of the unburied cadaver known as Lenny. He rejoiced at the re-acquaintance. For an instant Lenny's eyes seemed about to pop out of the dark bags that surrounded them when it appeared that Erwin may have been about to give him a hug of welcome. But the enthusiasm of even hardened, brutal thugs like Erwin has its limits and Erwin settled for a two handed handshake.

Over the next hour the verbal exchange between Erwin and his lanky legal advisor became heated several times because Erwin wanted out and Lenny wanted in. Eventually Lenny won. In essence, as Lenny told Erwin repeatedly, the charge of assault by the NSW police can be disregarded because Lenny could discredit it as a fabricated holding charge. However the more serious accusation by the Victoria Police required more effort and the most productive method of finding out exactly the strength of the Vicpol case against Erwin was to defend the extradition application. Lenny said that Erwin could not be placed before a Magistrate's Court for an extradition hearing unless he was still in custody; hence Erwin's plea for Lenny to get him out of jail was counterproductive.

Lenny promised to use every effort to assist Vicpol to expedite the extradition application, a course of action he ventured would cause Vicpol a high degree of confusion. Lenny estimated that Erwin would need to spend three or four days in a cell before the extradition hearing. Lenny did not speculate beyond that and Erwin formed the erroneous conclusion that he would walk free following the Magistrate's hearing. To avoid further confrontation Lenny let the matter rest, albeit inconclusively, on that erroneous assumption.

Lenny caught the train back to Sydney, had a late lunch at the University Club then journeyed by taxi to Sydney airport. He congratulated himself on the accuracy of his estimates of travel time as he had only thirty minutes to wait before boarding his plane to Melbourne. Sipping a Johnny Walker black label whisky in the first class section of the aircraft, Lenny relaxed. His method of relaxation was to think about income taxation. Like many other enormously remunerated senior legal counsel, he paid income tax rarely. Between sips he estimated it to be almost time for him to declare bankruptcy again. Perhaps after Erwin's trial, for he had no doubt that a trial would eventuate, the time might be right. He would double check the financial situation of his numerous service company shareholdings and blind trusts with his accountant. When it came to taxation Lenny had no contempt for caution.

With Erwin's arrest in New South Wales, the Victoria Police had no difficulty in obtaining a warrant to enter and search Erwin's residence in Kew. Their prime target for forensic evaluation was a pair of size eleven trainers, or at least a matching imprint. Such a print would be an important link in their chain of evidence. The gravel driveway was unhelpful as was the carpet in the small entrance verandah. They could not know that Erwin never wore those trainers inside the home and so, ever hopeful, the message passed upwards that forensics needed more time but they felt sure that something of value would be found.

Luminol is a substance that emits a bluish glow in the dark when it encounters blood. Expectations of some younger members of the police forensic investigators rose when a sharp fishing knife found in a plastic tackle box showed the characteristic blue glow. The glow is caused by a reaction called chemoluminescene. Older members of the team reserved their anticipation of the detection of a worthwhile clue until the results of a precipitin test were known. Preciptin determines whether or not blood being examined is human. In the laboratory the blood found on the fishing knife failed to produce the confirmatory precipitin line. Later tests confirmed that all of the blood specks were of fish, probably fresh water fish.

One detective with an interest in angling told his colleagues that the fresh water fish blood was consistent with the contents of the tackle box. All of the items indicated that Erwin was a fresh water fisherman rather than a salt water angler. A few days later the knife was returned to Erwin's tackle box. It was never cleaned and so remained covered by a film of luminal liquid.

Easily found in Erwin's residence were two score of pornographic magazines and a dozen books on World War Two with the emphasis on the German Nazi party and war crimes. Also easily found was Erwin's store of canned food. Being unaware that Erwin travelled so constantly the police could not know that Erwin liked to have a stock of canned delicacies always on hand so that when he returned he did not have to go shopping. He detested shopping and went rarely, usually late at night. When he did shop, he purchased a dozen of most items. The well stocked deep freezer and shelves of canned food looked to the police like provisions for a hideout or a siege. A not unreasonable assumption. So a detailed list of the cache of foodstuffs was made. Included in the list was written "ten cans of mushrooms".

When it came to providing for his own comfort it was obvious that Erwin was conscientious.

CHAPTER TWENTY-NINE

INFORMATION FLOODED INTO IAN'S OFFICE from the superannuation fund managers. The official envelopes addressed to the South Melbourne Post Office box rented by Dolores were identified as having once contained quarterly benefit statements to recipients of pensions payable to widows of former superannuation contributors. The largest fund was paying fourteen monthly pensions to widows; other funds were paying lesser numbers of pensions. All correspondence, including quarterly statements and annual taxation information was mailed to the Post Office box of Dolores.

Each widow's pension payment was made by direct bank credit to accounts with names implying financial services for bereaved or elderly persons. ASIC and Consumer Affairs searches revealed that each of the different names were business names of one company. That company had its registered office at a serviced office suite adjoining an industrial park. As Ian anticipated, the sole proprietor of that company was an elderly person supposedly resident in a country town.

For a lowly P.I. to obtain confidential information from a Bank about accounts of clients is often thought to be impossible. So far as evidence admissible in a court of law is concerned that is true. However to obtain inadmissible evidence from an unattributable source, is rare but not unknown.

In response to the considerable pressure that the collective weight of billions of superannuation dollars can apply to a bank, Ian received an anonymous phone call to say that when the pension payments in question were credited to the Bank accounts of the financial entities, an auto transfer whisked the money away into other accounts. The anonymous whisperer named four destinations and terminated the call before Ian could ask any questions. With the anonymous tip and further input from the fund managers, the jigsaw puzzle of the fraud inexorably evolved.

The informal committee of superannuation managers swiftly coalesced into a formal group. Selected trustees were invited to attend to add more credibility to the committee and to contribute advice. Another fifteen superannuation funds that were also being rorted, joined the committee. The information they contributed provided corroboration and defined the magnitude of the fraud.

Ian knew that this expansion of the number of persons privy to the information would totally fracture any security, but he opined that sufficient intelligence was now held to put a stop to the massive fraud. His conjecture proved correct. Details of the suspect South Melbourne Post Office box number were circulated through all staff levels of the superannuation funds.

A curiously consistent story emerged. Over a period of several years, a staff member and sometimes their spouse or partner had received an invitation to a free physic reading from Madame Dolores. The Madame claimed to hold exclusive secrets of their future love, financial, health and career paths. Each letter contained details that were so remarkably accurate as to arouse their curiosity and lure them to accept the free consultation. At that consultation more incredibly accurate information was revealed.

Many had converted the initial free psychic session into regular monthly consultations with Madame, at $100 or $150 a session, mainly paid in cash. Madame had a remarkable insight into aspects of their personal life, career and finances and Madame's insights helped them when they were lonely or misunderstood. Almost as an aside, Madame commented upon investments and being in the superannuation industry put them close to investments, so it was easy to check the ASX listed shares and to follow her advice. Following Madame's financial advice had proven profitable and her fame spread.

When questioned by their manager, the superannuation fund employee clients of Madame were generally quite disturbed at the association of Madame with anything unsavoury and were defensive of her. A few confessed to using office envelopes to send personal cheques to Madame for the purchase of good luck charms, but usage of an odd envelope was a hardly a sackable offence. Most were thanked for their admissions and returned to workstations with a request that they treat the matter as confidential. A few did.

Suspicions fell heavily upon several who had not come forward but who featured in the photographs taken outside the salon of Madame Dolores. Those who made no confessions found that Madame's forecasts of a stellar career in the superannuation industry were way off the mark. All they encountered were obstacles.

Ian arranged for two suspect computer technicians to be summoned to attend a meeting at which several superannuation managers, trustees or senior staff were present. Members of the Victoria Police Fraud Squad also attended the Melbourne meetings. The two computer technicians, who provided maintenance services to many of the funds, refused to make any statement and went straight back to their employer, a nationwide computer company, to demand protection against prosecution. The computer company lawyers appreciated the seriousness of the position of the company due to the allegations of possible criminal activity of their employees and that those offences against the Privacy Act would constitute grounds for the superannuation funds to terminate lucrative contracts. The company's reputation could be ruined.

The lawyers initiated urgent "without prejudice" contact with the lawyers of the major superannuation funds. Within 24 hours a joint agreement was entered into whereby complete cooperation of the computer company would be taken as substantial mitigation for the transgressions of the errant employees. The two technicians, in exchange for limited indemnities, spoke freely about their part in illegally accessing member records and of overheard conversations between Ray and Dolores.

Working as project manager for the superannuation fund investigative committee, Ian collated the information from various sources; auditors, the computer company, and staff members who searched records of Madame's clients. The essence of his draft report, with a few bits here and there to be filled in, was that a massive fraud of six years duration was perpetrated upon twenty five superannuation funds. The scope and sheer audacity of the initiator of the deception roused a reluctant degree of admiration from most managers.

Madame Dolores was the prime instigator of the crimes that started many years ago. An intelligent man with a personality defect became a regular telephone caller to the number appearing in one of the advertisements of Madame Dolores in a popular magazine. Back in her early days as a clairvoyant, Madame answered all calls herself. Sensing an opportunity to improve her income, Madame asked Harold to a private psychic session and spotted his maladjusted social relationship and consequent bleak loneliness. She gulled Harold along in a way that left him feeling invigorated, less lonely, more appreciated, at the end of each session. He never realised the sheer volume of information she extracted, recorded on tape and fed back to him in a modified form that convinced him that Madame Dolores really could read his fortune.

From Madame's part time lover, the Stockbroker's office manager, Madame obtained privileged information that she threaded into her advice to Harold. He was astounded at the number of correct predictions so effortlessly made by Madame. He was an "easy mark" as the con men say, and completely dominated by her will.

Harold provided Madame with a set of computer discs containing details of every member, past and present, of the sizeable superannuation fund of which he was a respected, technically proficient middle level executive. His people relationship ineptitude, not his technical ability, had impeded his promotion to a higher rank. The computer discs were Harold's convoluted way of rewarding the person who so well catered to his emotional yearnings. It also constituted his personal act of revenge on his employer for by-passed promotions.

That data base became a gold mine to Madame, because the company recorded personnel and superannuation details in the one employee file. The files contained intimate details such as full names, dates of birth, addresses, telephone numbers both hard line and mobile, email addresses, previous work experience, names of referees, educational information, promotions, salaries, names of dependants or nominated beneficiaries, medical history, workers compensation claims, tax file numbers, bank account details, medical benefit membership details, attachments to salaries in connection with child maintenance payments, disciplinary actions or absence thereof, to name the main items. In a few cases even minor criminal records. With a plethora of accurate information it was not difficult to access details of bills for municipal rates, electricity, gas and telephone. A hacker client told Dolores how to access library records so she could obtain details of the books people borrowed.

Personalised letters inviting superannuation contributors to discuss the astrological influences to be embraced or avoided to achieve their divinely intended partner, or the roadway to health, resulted in sessions where Madame seemed privy to every aspiration of her client. Sometimes she would tell clients who were leaving a session that their library book was due for return today or that the gas bill needed to be paid tomorrow. A tremendously impressive comment to convert a sceptic to a believer.

Word of mouth advertising convinced early doubters who became praise singing converts. Madame sucked them dry of information, with a subtlety that would have earned her a position with any national intelligence service. All responses were faithfully recorded via the microphone hidden in the carved wooden zodiac wheel centrepiece of the salon table. Superannuation being a somewhat specialised industry, with people transferring employment, some of Madame's adherents moved to other funds and spread the word of her omnipotence. Inevitably this admiration attracted those seeking solace from the slings and arrows of a society in which they found adjustments difficult and just as inevitably Madame exploited the few truly gullible, forlorn souls to obtain details of other funds.

Those details that she did not obtain from staff members she acquired from a computer technician client who serviced several "untapped" superannuation funds. He was later joined by a colleague. Although an element of their own credulity was involved in the recruitment of the technicians, cash contributions from Dolores ensured regular computer updates. Madame's data base became enormous. The cash assisted the technicians to maintain their attachment to recreational drugs. A lot of details of the association between Dolores and Ray came from statements made by the technicians. They testified that Madame Dolores said that the organising genius behind Ray was named Johnny and that Johnny's speciality was hiding cash from the taxman and turning illegally obtained "black" cash into "white".

What the technicians did not know was the earlier history of the fraud. It later transpired that, on the advice of Johnny, Ray and Dolores went premises hunting and located the property in South Melbourne that had suitable elegance for the premises of psychic. The handsome, architect-designed gentleman's townhouse was a little dilapidated but that was all the better because improvements over time, paid in cash, result in higher capital appreciation. Ray made no secret of the fact that he worked for a boss named Johnny and that in advising Dolores, the brain behind the scheme was not his but Johnny's. Dolores applauded Ray's honesty however it was not his mental attributes that attracted him to her. Ray prided himself on his superior sexual endurance and recovery. Dolores was delighted.

One night in bed Dolores mentioned to Ray that a client had not kept an appointment and enquiries revealed that the client had died suddenly. Dolores expressed her sorrow at the sad ending of such a lonely person, a person who had no family. When Ray mentioned the case of a member of a benefit promise scheme dying with no dependents and no family, Johnny acted swiftly. This became the point where Madame Dolores deeply entered the large scale exploitation of the superannuation industry.

Through Ray all details of the deceased were quickly assembled. Through Rodney, his forger, Bryn obtained a forged marriage certificate, birth certificate for a "phantom" wife and forged Will using facsimile signature of the recently deceased extracted from the superannuation contribution application. From one of the pliable solicitors a demand for a pension to the widow or a commuted lump sum in lieu was made. The fund replied that only pensions were payable to legitimate dependents and acting on the documents submitted, commenced pension payments forthwith.

That initial fraudulent claim became the template. Minor variations to suit the circumstances were included from time to time, but the fraud was to cause superannuation funds to pay pensions to "phantom" widows based on forged documents. An element operating in favour of frauds was the practice of superannuation funds to not enquire too intrusively at a time of grief. When the Privacy Act was introduced in 1988 one result was to make the checking of deaths by, say, distant family members extremely difficult, a factor favouring frauds and frequently foiling justifiable convictions. In the view of many, it handed an easy ride for defense counsel of an accused to have common sense information rendered inadmissible in court on a technicality. Bryn took comfort from that concept.

The superannuation funds investigation committee found evidence from benefit promise schemes to prove that a long term fraud was based on timely inside information. The value of the fraud was estimated on the near-final salary of the deceased as being $600 per week with a widow's entitlement averaging 60% of that making it $400 per week or $20,800 per annum. Multiplied by two hundred and ten phantom widows that meant $4.368 million each year at the current rate; but extending backwards the average was calculated, after CPI adjustment, as $3.6 million for each of the six financial years. A total $21.60 million stolen from the reserves of the superannuation industry.

One aspect of the fraud was patience, a rare commodity among criminals. Bryn's criminal genius was his ability to systemize the crime of obtaining money by deception with a long undiscovered time horizon. There never appeared to be any equivocation and the counterfeit paperwork was exemplary. Indeed some managers were non-plussed to learn that several of the fraudulent files were used as benchmarks in the fund's staff training courses.

Shortly after commencement of a pension payment the superannuation fund received a direction to pay the pension proceeds to an entity purporting to provide support services to the bewildered, bereaved, incapacitated or elderly. Ian's earlier information leak via the clandestine phone call from an anonymous banker indicated that the autopay re-directions of the bank accounts of those alleged support service companies sent the money to a group of genuine companies operated as subsidiaries by reputable insurance companies. The trustees were appalled at the size of the fraud, but became even more appalled at the audacity of the perpetrator when the various audit firms followed the trail of the pensions. They were astounded to discover that the pensions had been securitised and sold to annuity providers.

The initial reluctance of the insurance companies to cooperate was overcome by top level approaches from influential trustees resulting in testimony that each insurance company had purchased what they believed to be authentic tax free income streams generated by lease payments on infrastructure owned by tax exempt municipal authorities. The supporting paper work looked genuine and a fair amount of effort was required to show that no such infrastructure leases existed, so good was the quality of the forged documents.

It was the Victoria Police Forensic Laboratory that ended all speculation by certifying that every piece of paper work, Marriage Certificate, Lease Documents, Municipal Authority resolutions, letterhead of lawyers, etc all originated from the same fabrication factory. Analysis of paper, ink jet applicators, ink irregularities, nibs of pens used for signatures in some documents, ball point pens in others, handwriting and fake rubber stamps left no doubt. As a single set of documents, each looked impeccable. But assembled and compared the consistencies removed any doubt of forgery.

A further police contribution came from the Australian Federal Police acting on a request from their Victoria State colleagues. The AFP advised that the payments made by the duped insurance companies to the fraud perpetrators ended up in untraceable Swiss bank accounts via the Cook Islands, Samoa, Vanuatu, Fiji and Nauru, principally as supposed proceeds from betting.

During the sessions of exploration of iniquity, Ian's hired help Marian, Brenda and husband Michael had worked to a heavy schedule of surveillance and photography. Alternating between photographic observations of the establishment of Madame Dolores, they had spent time following Bryn because whilst concrete evidence was available on Ray and Dolores, Bryn was one step removed from provable involvement and they wanted evidence to convict the "Mr Big" not the flunkies.

Included in their portfolios of photographs or video camera cassettes were images of Johnny meeting a visibly agitated Ray, Johnny meeting with an equally agitated unnamed male whose appearance induced an observer to conclude that the male was ambiguous in his sexual orientation, and several images of Ray and Dolores.

Again the Victoria Fraud Squad, that was now leading the investigation, shed light upon the identity of the sexually ambiguous gentleman. They identified him as Rodney, a miscreant who courts had deprived of freedom of movement for fraud. As punishment he was ordered to be confined within an establishment that fed him three healthy meals per day, provided computer access, sporting facilities, free gymnasium, educational enrolment, a complete dental make over, constant free medical supervision, free pharmaceuticals when necessary, television with latest DVD capacity, free legal assistance and other facilities in modern air conditioned accommodation, otherwise known as prison.

Rehabilitation for Rodney was a giggle. He simply advertised his wares as a forger among a receptive community of potential customers. His physical necessities were well catered for too. Rodney's work was excellent but no matter the level of technical precautions, forged documents can be linked to each other by modern forensic methods and this is exactly what the police did. They satisfied themselves that Rodney had forged the documents upon which the massive superannuation fund fraud was founded. The police were confident that their forensic evidence would survive any challenge in court.

Ian's work was over. The rumours that led to his appointment were proven to be well based and the matter was best left to the law enforcement authorities who would seek retribution on behalf of the community. Ian's speciality was restitution and there appeared little hope of that if the money was in Switzerland. In his view the fraud case would provide lucrative employment for many members of the legal profession for the next decade.

Ian's investigation did, however, stop the continuance of the bleeding of the superannuation funds reserves as all funds involved immediately stopped the bogus pension payments. Ian spent two full days drawing up an itemised list of expenses and gave it to his accountant to complete by adding in the adjustments for the General Services Tax, the GST, before submitting it for payment. The coalition of superannuation funds must have appreciated his efforts and confidentiality because payment occurred forthwith and included a highly unexpected bonus. Ian shared part of it with his sub contractors. Goodwill is priceless.

Ian followed the course of the investigation through comments passed on by superannuation managers with whom he had become even friendlier during the course of uncovering the fraud. One told him that the police had obtained warrants to arrest Dolores, Ray and Rodney. In addition they intended to invite Bryn, whose identity, as "Johnny" was now solidly suspected, to assist with their enquiries. The police could only invite not compel Bryn because there existed no evidence against him that would be admissible in a Court without substantial sworn corroboration from Dolores, Ray and Rodney.

But they were unable to serve the warrants or to extend the invitation because all four persons had disappeared.

CHAPTER THIRTY

THE UNEASY FEELING BORDERING ON mild depression that occasionally assailed Bryn on his solitary sailings remained undefined until two deaths created a climate of concentrated consciousness that brought it into clear focus. And the remarkable thing about each of the two deaths was that they were due to what the medical and legal professions call "natural causes". Bryn had no involvement with either. The sharks would have to make do with a diet of fur seals.

Auntie was the first to go, the Auntie who owned the Meissen porcelain figurines used by Bryn years ago to raise his first working capital. Auntie bequeathed to him the self same set of figurines in her Will. Bryn was interstate on business when Auntie died and a letter from the lawyer to Auntie's estate advised Bryn that for Probate purposes a valuation of the figurines had been necessary. That value was $96,000. He could never, in his wildest dreams, have imagined that he would ever be the legitimate owner of the items that he had kidnapped to finance his first foray into felony. With no desire to set eyes on the figurines, Bryn phoned the lawyer who gave him the address of the valuer. Bryn contacted him to arrange a sale of the porcelain inheritance. Bryn was unworried about the prospect of the insurance company learning of the sale. The Limitations of Actions Act time limit had long passed. A prosecution for his fraud was now statute barred. After commission, Bryn received a nice clean cheque for $90,000. The first unsullied income he had received for years.

The second death was that of his much loved father. The death at his desk was quick and painful for only a few minutes, as a massive heart attack killed him. Bryn was amazed at the deep degree of inconsolable loss that hit him. He was steering his motor cruiser almost due East in the open sea near Cape Schanck when the phone call from one of his father's, late father now, business partners caused the grief to crash upon him. He reversed direction, into a head wind now, with an inauspicious increasing swell. He tried to telephone his mother but the phone was answered by a neighbour who told him, in a voice shaky with sadness, that his mother had collapsed. She was now asleep after receiving a tranquilising injection from the family doctor. His mother's physical health had been of concern to both him and his father for some time and he now feared his mother's mental health.

Weather conditions deteriorated and Bryn's experienced brain compensated for them as he steered the cruiser from the upper bridge. The salt water spray mingled with his non-stop salt water tears for most of the jolting, wind whipped journey back to his mooring. Bryn neglected all ship maintenance on return to hurriedly visit his mother who seemed to him to have shrunk in stature and been drained of initiative. When she was not in a drug induced sleep she was in a semi comatose state. Bryn really tried hard to offer as much comfort as he could. His efforts were of some help but the chasm of cataclysmic loss could not readily be closed. Time, everyone said, would help to heal. But Bryn's mother seemed to be beyond the healing process. Her inability to cope before and after the funeral deteriorated to such a degree that her doctor advised that a supportive accommodation care facility be seriously considered.

The legal firm partners of his late father were very good in assisting with arrangements for finances and resettling of Bryn's mother in a residential care unit. She did not have any financial problems because her late husband had provided adequately. She desired that the family home be given to Bryn and the partners arranged the conveyancing of the house expeditiously, foregoing any fee in a practical expression of their genuine sympathy for the family and a mark of respect to Bryn's father. Bryn hardly thought of the increase in his clean assets, his grief persisted beyond his own, unexplored, expectations. With thoughts constantly upon mortality, Bryn recalled that, beyond a few bequests, Auntie's estate went to charity because she had no heirs. And with his father gone and his mother's health showing no signs of improvement, Bryn prepared himself for another loss relatively soon. Bryn would be their only heir.

But he had no heirs. And that brought to the forefront the uneasy feeling that had pervaded his mind especially on long, lonely trips at night on the water. Bryn realised with a rising crescendo of clarity that he wanted heirs. For what good did it do him to have created a clandestine criminal empire only to be the richest unlamented, unrecognised corpse at a sea burial when his time was due? The recognition of the strength of the previously subliminal, visceral sensation generated shock waves that seemed to shake his entire body. The shock waves caused him to look at stars in a different aspect and contemplate the abyss of infinity. He tried valiantly to reason with himself but ultimately concluded that emotion has a logic of its own and he could not wrench free of something so deeply imbedded within.

The process of examination of the recognition and eventual acceptance of the desire for heirs took several months. He had to accept that at age thirty two he was getting older.

Having finally accepted that he wanted heirs and that he needed to make a life altering change of course to achieve emotional contentment, Bryn set about planning the process to achieve his new set of aspirations. His thinking was subject to starts and stops but eventually he perceived he had to make a fresh start with money from an untainted source. And Auntie's legacy again offered him fresh start finance. He knew he must disassociate himself from all connections with his brilliantly successful criminal past, so he cudgelled his brain to recall gossip overheard on boozy cruisers during his more youthful and innocent past. The memory training course that he had long ago quietly castigated himself as an indulgence, now paid a dividend for almost instantly he recalled the name of the legal firm that had often been ridiculed as being straight, by less scrupulous members of the same profession. Bryn was too cautious to be caught up further with any disreputable lawyers and did not want to use the services of his father's old firm.

Bryn located the honest firm in the phone book and asked the receptionist how long each of the partners had been practising with the firm. She was flabbergasted by such an inquiry as nobody had asked such a question in the fifteen years she had worked there. He was told that there were eight partners, four of whom had been with the firm for over a decade. Bryn reasoned that if he sought advice from one of the longer serving partners, his chances of getting an honest lawyer were better. So Bryn asked for those names and elected to seek a consultation with Mr Thomas Llewellyn on the grounds of fugacious recollection of his Welsh heritage.

At the consultation several days later, Bryn instructed Mr Llewellyn to create a residential unit trust company with Bryn as the promoter. An essential element in the unit trust structure must be the capacity to expand so that a listing on the Australian Stock Exchange, the ASX, could eventuate. Formation assets would be the former parental home inherited by Bryn and now registered in his name, cash of up to $100,000 was indicated as being available. Bryn stressed that he wanted to avoid scrutiny by ASIC and the Australian Prudential Regulations Authority because of costly administrative and compliance requirements. In order to achieve exemption from ASIC and APRA supervision, Bryn was adamant that any invitation to invest in units be explicitly restricted and directed only at persons with a minimum of $250,000 to invest. At that financial level, investors were deemed by ASIC and APRA to be professionals who possessed sufficient market savvy to conduct their own due diligence enquiries to protect themselves. Below that $250,000 level both ASIC and APRA considered investors to be mentally retarded and in need of protection which justified the imposition of weighty reporting requirements.

Bryn's knowledge of the intricacies of the unit trust industry impressed Mr Llewellyn. He stated candidly that he doubted that his legal practice had sufficient in-house commercial expertise to fulfil Bryn's requirements. Bryn took that assertion as confirmation that the lawyer was straight and advised Mr Llewellyn that he had no objection to Llewellyn's firm seeking an independent expert opinion from an experienced and highly qualified Senior Counsel. To cement the deal, Bryn handed Mr Llewellyn a bank cheque for $10,000 for which he received a signed receipt, a warm smile and firm handshake. Bryn walked out of the office thinking that he had clearly adopted the correct tactic in proffering a bank cheque. Had he placed on the desk a wad of one hundred dollar notes of the same monetary value, he was certain that the patently honest Mr Llewellyn would have declined to accept instructions.

It was a fortnight later that Bryn received a phone call asking him to return to consult with Mr Llewellyn. The older lawyer seemed pleased with the draft of the constitution of the residential unit trust that resulted from his firm's conference with a prominent commercial Senior Counsel, S.C., and to advices received by the S.C. from the ASX. Mr Llewellyn was further impressed with the concentration applied by Bryn as they jointly scrutinised the draft constitution, clause by clause. Over the next hour and a half Mr Llewellyn telephoned the S.C. twice to seek amplification or elucidation of items in clauses at Bryn's request. When Bryn left, expressing satisfaction with the final draft containing the amendments sought by him, Mr Llewellyn was relieved the intense meeting was concluded. He was even more impressed with Bryn's grasp of commercial law including obscure but important stipulations. However he still harboured some reservations as to whether Bryn had adequate capital.

Bryn was informed three days later that the trust constitution was registered and the trust, now named ECARUT because it operated along the East Coast of Australia as a Residential Unit Trust, was able to legally operate. Bryn opened an account with one of the "big-four" banks. He paid into ECARUT Pty Ltd's account a large proportion of the squeaky clean money left to him by courtesy of Auntie's figurines. In return for the cash injection into the Bank and for the original $10,000 up front money to the lawyers, Bryn issued to his newly created personal family trust, units in ECARUT at par, ie one unit for each dollar of subscription. Similarly he conveyed the former parental home to the ownership of the ECARUT in exchange for more units, to his family trust, paying stamp duty and conveyancing costs from the cash held in the bank account.

Bryn appointed a firm of real estate agents to lease his former family home and remit rent to ECARUT. Using those transfer documents as a template, Bryn began to transfer to ECARUT the scores of other properties he owned via bodgy companies registered in the names of bucolic octogenarians. Units were issued at par, to the putative owners of the bodgy companies. Because each property so transferred had a value in excess of $250,000, Bryn was in no danger of arousing the ire of the relevant financial watchdogs. Bryn then arranged a transfer of the units to his "family" company. Family company was a misnomer because Bryn had no close family. But he was starting to work on that oversight.

No actual cash payments ever took place as consideration for Bryn's acquisition of units in ECARUT from the octogenarians. In the deletion of the name of one unit holder and substitution of that of his family trust, the ECARUT registrar had no legal obligation to sight evidence of any payment. It was sufficient that the appropriate form was correctly completed and that the appropriate State Stamp duty payment was evidenced by Revenue Office impressed stamp or adhesive duty stamps.

Upon completion of the asset transfer, that included large amounts of accumulated rent in some cases, Bryn would apply for voluntary liquidation of each dodgy asset-less company, using the names of unsuspecting "owners". Acting entirely alone to preserve secrecy, Bryn had little time for marine activities over the month it took to arrange the numerous transactions in Victoria and other States.

He consolidated lease management of groups of the properties into the hands of three firms of real estate agents, bargaining a bulk rate discount from each. Because he applied his own valuation to each property, a "Director's Valuation", rather than obtaining a strict market value, the properties entered ECARUT's bookkeeping at a value below market. Hence the rental yields obtained for accounting purposes were in excess of the "going rate".

By the time Bryn had deregistered the last dodgy company, by transferring the units to his family trust, ECARUT owned one hundred and sixteen residential properties in good locations at around 80% of their true market value. With an average issue of units of 500,000 per acquisition, ECARUT had issued 58 million units. Bryn's family trust was the sole owner. Because of Bryn's clever method of substituting tainted cash for units in a clean trust, no authority was alerted and Bryn began to apply the massive cash flow towards further development, often purchasing adjacent properties, demolishing them and erecting town houses for sale or rent.

With the closure of the multitude of dodgy cash concealing companies and his invariable use of pseudonym "Johnny", Bryn was assured of a high degree of insulation from discovery. His true name never appeared anywhere and he believed that no one had any proof of his involvement in crime. Several shyster lawyers had inklings of Bryn's irregular activities but not one of them had sufficient proof of a type admissible in a Court and each had as much, if not more, to lose if those inklings of irregularity became public knowledge. Bryn took care to destroy all company records by shredding and burning. He reasoned that if ASIC ever decided to investigate, the lack of hard evidence would make investigation difficult and that, with time, all putative company owners would be dead due to old age. He considered himself safe. Totally safe.

This metamorphosis profoundly altered Bryn's outlook. He had made millions as an undiscovered criminal in insurance and superannuation fund fraud. Now, like a butterfly emerging from a cocoon, he shed criminality and confronted the world as a brilliant substantial butterfly – a young genius, flattered and entertained by estate agents, builders and bank managers. His mother, only vaguely attached to reality due to Alzheimer's encroachment, said she was proud of him, when she had lucid moments.

For a man still comparatively young who had shunned any limelight, the transformation was so great that he began to believe some of the flattery conferred upon him in the Property media. Furthermore he had abandoned his pursuit of readily available, short term sexual partners and began to search for a woman suitable to be a respectable wife for a respectable property developer. Bryn had a big reputation, as it appeared to the financial fraternity he was a person who performed the impossible; packaging residential properties into a profitable enterprise when previously so many had failed.

Bryn's business circle now provided opportunities for him to meet many more respectable young ladies. When he operated on the fringe of criminality he suspected that the virtue of the females he encountered began at a low benchmark. Bryn now assessed each new female acquaintance by a different set of criteria as he absorbed his new theorem of respectability and community adulation. He realised that future fornication would cease to be entirely recreational and involve an earnest effort at being procreational.

CHAPTER THIRTY-ONE

BRYN WAS DEJECTED AFTER MONTHS of unsuccessful searching for a woman. One who met his exacting requirements for a wife and future mother of his future family. He discovered that his previous theories about the promiscuity of respectable young ladies being lesser than that of those closer to the fringe of criminality was false. The discovery was not an unalloyed disaster as recreational rutting conferred its own rewards. And his own increasing reputation as a whiz kid of residential finance increased his attraction to the opposite sex.

On the business side, to edge his ECARUT nearer to ASX listing, Bryn made a modest revaluation of ECARUT'S properties and issued more units to his family trust on the basis of increased property values in ever rising residential property markets. Bryn found that the estate agents continued to be zealous in recommending opportunities to acquire desirable locations, so he sat high near the top of the information pyramid. To acquire the desirable locations for development, Bryn repatriated to Australia several millions of dollars from his Swiss bank accounts in the guise of loans. This enabled him to restock his Swiss accounts with cash as tax deductible interest payments on those loans.

To ensure that the financial community were aware of ECARUT, Bryn borrowed money from large Australian financial institutions from time to time. He only had one refusal. That occurred when a major bank declined to lend on the construction of a fourteen storey accommodation block for students he intended to erect near Melbourne University. Bryn took umbrage at the refusal and funded it entirely from his Swiss account.

On the day the student accommodation block was opened by the State Government Minister for Education, a public relations firm acting for Bryn, guided the media to emphasise that 100% occupancy of the new block occurred on day one and that a net yield would be above that obtainable from other commercial developments. Bryn ensured that all of the Directors of the Bank that had refused his request for a construction loan were informed of his success. The Loan Manager's promotion prospects dimmed and bank thereafter sought to cultivate Bryn in the hope of offering loans. Banks strive to lend to those who do not need money. Bryn enjoyed that exercise as it allowed him to be a right vindictive bastard under cover of being an intuitive business brain and a benefactor of the burgeoning foreign student element in Australia's education industry.

With over 100 million units in ECARUT registered in the name of his family company and another 100 million in the name of an overseas registered front company for his Swiss interests, Bryn deduced that the time was right to expand into more residential apartments, many of which he leased in bulk to companies specialising in non-hotel accommodation. The increasing trend towards lo doc loans removed a lot of the humbug from the procedure and kept paperwork to a minimum. A lien over a number of units in ECARUT was usually sufficient for him to obtain finance for residential or well located industrial estate developments. He raised millions of dollars at advantageous interest rates from private lenders seduced by the media reports of his superior financial acumen. Often the number of units pledged as a lien exceeded by far the prudential requirements prescribed in the constitution of ECARUT. The deliberate over pledge induced in lenders a sense of complete confidence.

In a booming economic environment with a prosperous property market, few lenders properly performed the due diligence to ensure Bryn's millions of borrowed dollars were capable of timely servicing. The slack and idle lenders came to no harm purely on luck. Bryn recalled the adage that bad loans are made in good times. The size of his operations and his temporary curtailment of investments allowed revenue to stabilize and reduce debt and so avoid over commitment. Bryn's reputation for responsible management spread through the financial community. Other entrepreneurs who borrowed to the limit without prudent stabilization of debt level collapsed, enhancing Bryn's reputation as a brilliant and sound manager.

A curious characteristic of males is that occasionally they marry women with whom they have sex but they almost always marry females who refuse them sex before marriage. It seems the rebuttal is perceived as a barrier and males react to the challenge of surmounting every barrier. It is an instinctive trait inherited over thousands of years of human evolution. However the same evolutionary instinct as motivates men is not unknown to smart members of the opposite sex seeking a partner with the assets essential to ensure a life of luxury. Stephanie was one of those perceptive females.

Stephanie learned early in her high school days that early pregnancy consigned the pregnantee into poverty. Poverty equated to arrant stupidity in Stephanie's lexion. She had been endowed with long blonde hair, eyes of a shade of equidistant in colour between blue and violet and a natural slim figure that benefited from callisthenics and regular swimming. She loved both of those sports because they involved minimum clothing and maximum exposure to the adulation and envy of audiences.

At the University, her education in Arts paralleled her education in life management skills. She observed young, full of life, girlfriends who indulged too frequently in pursuit of sexual pleasure. Some achieved the accolade of class slut with surprising rapidity, a couple of careless girls found it necessary to have clandestine abortions, a couple dropped out to be mothers and one particularly incautious girl succumbed to AIDS. Stephanie planned her life of uninhibited effortless luxury and realised the importance of manipulating men as the method to achievement of her objective. So she was extremely selective in her few sexual partners and projected an image of aloofness to the extent that many of her classmates derogatively referred to her as the "Ice Maiden" or even "Miss Frigidity". She had no objection to the appellations and cultivated them carefully.

With an Arts degree majoring in Impressionist Painters, Stephanie obtained a job at the National Gallery in the nation's capital of Canberra. It was where she met Bryn. Bryn was being conducted through the modern wing of the Gallery by the Head Curator. Along with several other billionaires, Bryn was given a "chosen persons tour" in the hope of a generous (tax deductible) donation. Bryn strolled past the works of the modern masters without being impressed.

At a recently acquired Manet in the Impressionist section Bryn paused. He found that a young blonde was also looking at the exquisite painting, apparently absorbed in admiration. They turned to move to the next exhibit simultaneously and their eyes met. The curious regal chemistry that scientists have been unable to desecrate by rendering it into a common chemical formula reacted within each set of optic nerves. The glance converted to an unembarrassed state generating pheromone secretions in each that neither had experienced to such a shuddering extent in their lives.

Pheromones evaporate common sense in men and Bryn later felt like an idiot when he recalled his first moment. He took a business card from the top pocket of the immaculately tailored Prince Albert patterned suit and handed it to the epitome of his dreams in an open handed gesture favoured by Japanese businessmen. Reluctantly Stephanie broke eye contact with Bryn to accept his card. She responded with a card of her own from the smart crocodile skin card holder taken from the pocket of her equally well tailored blue skirt suit. Both smiled, an invitation to coffee by Bryn was accepted, and with amnesia as far as the world famous Impressionist Exhibition was concerned they walked wordlessly to the Gallery coffee lounge. They stayed there for three hours. To each the time went as if it were three minutes. Events continued, chastely at first, then more intensely over following days.

Bryn had met his angelic, intelligent, respectable, healthy looking and therefore presumably fertile, dream woman. Stephanie had met her perfect match; an enormously rich man with the added attraction of being young, only ten years her senior, reasonably handsome and athletic. He carried no baggage such as a wife or children. They became constant companions, platonic at first but propinquity breeds, as the saying goes, and Stephanie's left ring finger was soon weighed down with a white gold band bearing several carats of diamond.

To further complete his metamorphosis Bryn transferred his West Melbourne apartment into ECARUT in exchange for units based on a properly obtained valuation from a legitimate valuer. One of his Swiss companies purchased a $5 Million sumptuous apartment in Melbourne's newly constructed Docklands. The selection of the apartment was done by Bryn and Stephanie with the thought in both their minds that this would be their breeding ground. Bryn traded his previous watercraft and bought a new, twenty metre, motor cruiser, nearly $4 Million dollars worth on the water, equally, if not more sumptuously furnished, than the Docklands apartment. Stephanie loved the larger cruiser. She believed that size definitely mattered. He changed his mooring to the new state of the art Docklands Marina almost directly opposite the main entrance to his apartment building.

These purchases, the residential relocation and new motor cruiser closed the door on Bryn's criminal career, almost. His grossly obscene salary as chairman of Australia's largest incredibly profitable, privately owned, residential property trust was more than adequate to support himself, wife and future babies in a style of luxury beyond belief to 99% of Australia's population.

Bryn aimed to change ECARUT'S legal status to comply with ASX listing rules, appoint intelligent but malleable and disgustingly respectable directors, revalue the property assets so as to increase his wealth by a further issue of units, then list ECARUT Limited on the ASX. Following what he believed would be an enormously successful float enabling him to raise huge sums by way of respectable capital to expand his empire; Bryn planned his nuptials to Stephanie. It was envisaged as a grand affair with the ceremony to wed the two atheists at the picturesque blue stone Welsh Church. To add colour to the event the minister agreed that the nuptials be conducted in the Welsh language. In anticipation of his forthcoming nuptials, Bryn made the final surrender to respectability by making a Will with Stephanie as his sole beneficiary.

As Bryn and Stephanie had already said "yes" to each other in the most fundamental physical fashion, the planned exotic Gaelic service was little more than an additional element of theatricals. These were designed to ensure maximum respectable publicity via the main multi-coloured magazines that elevate celebrities to mini-royalty status in the interest of maintaining and boosting circulation.

These were his plans and they looked good and unstoppable. Then Bryn's plans began to decompose as the deadly plans of another person commenced.

CHAPTER THIRTY-TWO

ERWIN'S IRRITATION INCREASED AS IT became obvious that Lenny's prediction of the time he had to spend "inside" was way out. Two days after his arrest he complained bitterly that his civil liberties were violated when he was relocated from the Katoomba lock-up to central Sydney Remand Centre without prior consultation.

He was somewhat mollified when he found that the Remand Centre was roomier but he had to share the space. One large but out of condition fellow remandee injudiciously tried to set himself up as the king-pin. Erwin was able to somewhat purge his frustrations in a fight that left the would-be-king-pin semiconscious. The Remand Centre staff turned a blind eye. Erwin was treated with respect thereafter by all the riff raff. He really enjoyed that. Lenny the lanky lawyer phoned Erwin every day, ostensibly to verify information but in reality his calls were more to ensure that Erwin was not talking to any fellow inmate. It is not unknown for police to put an undercover cop into the prison system in the hope of obtaining evidence from a bored or boastful prisoner. Eventually Erwin faced a Magistrate, at an open hearing, with a few visitors in the public gallery outnumbered by media reporters.

Erwin was oblivious of the presence of Ian Ross sitting in the gallery. Lenny was in his element, pushing up to the limit of contest with the Magistrate as to which one of them was in charge of proceedings. From the Vicpol legal representatives, Lenny extracted, like a massive hand squeezing a lemon, every drop and nuance of every drop of information disadvantageous to his client. As a consequence the Magistrate's court was given a concise catalogue of the case against Erwin. By law, the prosecution must reveal to the defense every scrap of evidence it holds, even if that evidence is favourable to the defense. However the defense is not obliged to reveal any incriminating evidence to the prosecution.

Lenny's questions fired off allegedly in opposition to Erwin's extradition but carefully crafted to test the Vicpol case, were recorded by Lenny's tape recorder. Recording in court without permission is very naughty. Lenny's state of the art recorder was disguised as a law book, a present from a previous client. Later, after repeated listening of the tape, Lenny collated the case into two categories of evidence. Human and forensic. Under human, Lenny noted the yet to be tested identification of Erwin by the Rent-a-Wreck proprietor, a female passer-by in Central Park Road and the driver of a passing car. The identification of Erwin's red Mercedes sports car by a perennial drunkard was useless. None of these were problematical in his view.

As to forensic; the training shoe imprints and ramifications, a fingernail fragment found in the Ford Falcon; blood on a paper towel found in a hedge thirty metres from the crime scene, unproved as germane because of lack of DNA identification. The scores of pornographic magazines, books on Nazi Germany, video tapes and DVD's found at Erwin's home, all convinced Lenny that the case against Erwin was distinctly unrobust.

Lenny could have won the case against extradition on strictly legal issues but the Magistrate was annoyed with Lenny's attempted usurpation of this authority. He therefore laid much emphasis upon Erwin being a resident of Victoria and the heinous crime of which Erwin was accused occurred in that State. He granted to Vicpol the right to extradite the corpus of Erwin to Victoria. An order to have Erwin's Mercedes similarly transported to the Victorian Forensic facility was also issued. Lenny raised no objection. At the conclusion Lenny was excessively polite to the Magistrate who was left with the impression that maybe he had been manipulated. The Vicpol representatives looked pleased then departed to arrange transportation of Erwin. Lenny was not displeased. Air travel could be tedious. With Erwin in Melbourne, Lenny would have easier access. Erwin was confused. He had Lenny's assurance that there was nothing to worry about but doubt still lingered. As the handcuffs were re-applied several members of the media called questions to him but Erwin ignored them.

Ian remained seated until the court was empty then rose slowly with an awful gut twisting premonition. Every instinct, honed over four decades as an investigator, shrieked in his brain that Erwin was guilty. He left the court knowing that he had just seen the killer of his grandson, and that the killer would soon walk free. Subsequent events were to vindicate Ian's premonition but not before Erwin was subjected to a series of irritations contributing to a rise in resentment against that amorphous federation known as society.

After extradition to Victoria, Erwin had to endure numerous indignities in which everything seemed to go against him. Following Lenny's hints, Erwin protested his innocence often and loudly and especially to the media. He protested that the police case was based on police incompetence to locate the real murderer so they vented anger on Erwin out of envy.

As if to clinch the matter of his innocence, Erwin told one media reporter about the fate of his Mercedes sports car. The police had pulled it apart and found nothing but a soft porn paperback available on any newsstand, a European history book dealing with the period 1936 to 1945 (others called it a history of Hitler's SS) and some evidence that cocaine may have been on the rear seat. What did that prove? Erwin asked in injured innocence. With the vinyl top down, the car was exposed. Anyone could have sprinkled a small amount of drug into it at any time. That is, if it wasn't done by the police themselves. Nothing about his cherished red sports car linked him to the crime yet the police had maliciously dismantled it and had not put it back together properly. The value of the car was reduced due to police incompetence. More evidence of petulant police envy, Erwin claimed.

Whether society likes it or abhors it, law is the adhesive that binds human society. In the absence of law, society would cease to exist. And always within any society there springs up a vocal minority with hatred for the law. The actions of these supporters of their own warped version of the law were often designed to subvert the law they claim is unjust. Naturally this group avoid any impartial examination of evidence, nor will they allow a proper court to do so. Instead they prefer to loudly and relentlessly advocate that their combined voices should determine guilt or innocence and in this case a near-anarchist group stated unequivocally that Erwin was innocent.

Erwin took great comfort and amusement from their protestations. Ian and his family were appalled. Along with the anti-law pseudo anarchists there were anti-law enforcement proponents, some of who held high profile positions in the press. These journalists used or abused their well remunerated positions of trust to highlight the protestations of the "Release Erwin" protestors and to over emphasise the slow progress of the police.

When Lenny lost the attempt to have Erwin refuse to give DNA, the lanky lawyer was unperturbed because Erwin had consistently denied being anywhere near the Ford Falcon in which a finger nail fragment was allegedly found. Likewise Erwin had constantly denied approaching the scene of crime, the disused dairy building. Only after a court order allowing the use of force to obtain a DNA sample did Erwin confide in Lenny that perhaps he may have been within proximity of both the Ford and the old dairy.

Lenny frequently asserted that his role as a legal defender was the most important in the legal system. He claimed that this was a dual responsibility, one part to his accused client and the other to the Court. Lenny was obliged to accept what his client says as truth and vigorously represent that position no matter how sceptical he may be about the accuracy. He also has the duty of absolute integrity to the Court in the presentation of facts. But when it comes to the crunch it is the client who pays the fee, not the Court. Lenny felt that his suppressed assessment of Erwin's guilt was vindicated, but as Erwin's lawyer and a fierce defender of justice he insisted that it be his duty to keep the police force honest and make them prove their case beyond reasonable doubt. The fact that Lenny was a master of introducing numerous delusive doubts troubled not his conscience.

Lenny knew that if the prosecutor came upon evidence that pointed to the innocence of an accused it must be immediately revealed to the defense, however if the defense came upon evidence that pointed to guilt of the accused there was no obligation to disclose it. So Lenny applied himself to re-examination of every part of the police evidence. He also re-examined his defense plan. Erwin's belated admission raised his suspicions. He must not now let Erwin testify. Upon his return to Erwin's cell Lenny began to ask questions. Lenny could not, heaven forbid, rehearse Erwin in untruths, but after an hour of a certain type of questions Lenny recognised that

Erwin's position on the finger nail fragment was that Erwin recalled a visit to the Rent-a-Wreck car yard.

Erwin now clearly remembered his first sight of the car yard after attending a football match nearby. Erwin recalled the two teams and the final score. He recalled the heavy traffic on the road that delayed him going to his own luxury car and gave him time to look at the car yard. He recalled that he was curious to see how the working class obtained transport. He recalled walking around cars in the car yard and looking into several vehicles. He recalled that he pulled off a piece of cracked fingernail and discarded it on the gravel.

Lenny congratulated Erwin on his recollection, which, Lenny jubilantly declared, solved two riddles. Firstly, the Rent-a-Wreck proprietor must have seen Erwin in the car yard on the day in question and confused him with the person who called later and rented the Ford Falcon using the stolen driving licence. Lenny assured Erwin that his wonderful recollection was entirely adequate to completely nullify any identification of Erwin as the renter of the vehicle under investigation. As for the fingernail fragment, Lenny opined it was obvious that the actual renter of the car must have stood on it; the fragment adhered to the renter's footwear and was conveyed then deposited into the ridged floor mat of the presumed abduction vehicle. If the fragment was not so deposited by the unidentified renter then possibly the proprietor, when wiping out the vehicle or the next visitor to the car yard inadvertently conveyed the fragment into the vehicle.

Lenny told Erwin that he would question the proprietor and subsequent renter about the fingernail fragment at length. He was certain that neither would be able to deny absolutely that they did not deposit the broken fingernail on the Ford's floor. Lenny appreciated that it would be important for the Court to hear those denials. The fingernail fragment was part of circumstantial evidence. Any circumstantial case fails unless it can exclude an innocent hypothesis.

As for the paper towel with the blood smear that police claim to have recovered from the scene of the horrendous crime, Lenny said he would seek "discovery" from the Forensic Laboratory of the DNA matching before visiting Erwin again. He confidently hoped Erwin's memory would again be responsive. Lenny was totally sympathetic to Erwin's inability to recollect all of his movements around the time of the murder.

Without a shadow of doubt on his cadaverous visage nor with any tremor of sanctimonious condescension in his voice, Lenny told Erwin that other clients too had experienced some memory impairment as a result of the being maliciously accused of a terrible crime which any unbiased observer could plainly see they were constitutionally incapable of perpetrating. Lenny did not tell Erwin that many of the innocent persons maliciously accused were exonerated by his, Lenny's, connoisseur quality legal expertise. Nor did he mention the number of those innocents who needed Lenny's expertise on a regular basis.

As Lenny so perspicaciously predicted, Erwin's memory about his visit to the crime scene vicinity returned, albeit a trifle spasmodically. Lenny's secretary phoned to advise Erwin that the DNA of the blood found on a piece of paper towel near the crime scene, matched the sample of DNA so forcibly and unfairly taken from Erwin. Erwin was furious at the news. He clearly recalled carrying the semi conscious boy to the area he thought of as his private slaughterhouse. He dumped the tied-up boy and returned to the Ford Falcon to put on a pair of latex gloves. The gloves were tight on his big hands and Erwin's adrenalin was racing so that his grip slipped as he pulled one glove on and he hit himself in the nose. Concerned about leaving his own blood on the scene, Erwin had torn a square from the roll of paper towel he had brought and used it to wipe his nose. The bleeding was slight and dried quickly, helped by a strong wind. Erwin placed the blood stained paper towel in a black plastic bag, added the latex gloves and put a brick on the bag to prevent it blowing away. Only then did he return again to the Ford and more carefully pull on another pair of latex gloves. Deliberately he had placed the black plastic bag on the floor just inside the door of the dairy under the water outlet pipe and its stop cock.

The next hours of his activity he had relegated to that part of his mind from whence he could regurgitate extraordinarily satisfying experiences. When Erwin's beastical appetite had been quenched and he returned to the bag, he vaguely noticed that the strong wind had blown into the bag despite the weight of the brick. At the time he had assumed that nothing had blown from the bag. He recalled feeling something in the bag and supposed it to be both the paper towel and the discarded original latex gloves. Menacingly, the strip of paper towel now occupied his thoughts and he devised a scenario to try to meet the menace.

Everything else about the clean up had worked well. All stained material went into the plastic bag and the spilt blood, bodily fluids and footprints on the damp soil were eradicated when he opened the stop cock. Water had spurted a metre from the outlet pipe to stir up the mud and the bird droppings. The floor was totally flooded. The best Erwin could devise to innocently account for the paper towel was that a couple of days before he had been walking in a paddock about a kilometre away from the disused dairy hoping to gather mushrooms. On that day Erwin would say he remembered carrying a supermarket plastic bag. He hoped to find some mushrooms to put in the bag. A couple of squares of paper towel were in the bag to protect the fragile mushrooms. After a visit from Lenny, Erwin recalled the event with crystal clarity, the only minor geographical adjustment being that he had been in a paddock about a kilometre on the other side of the disused dairy building. This geographical discrepancy was corrected after Lenny had hinted, during question time of course, that enquiries from the Weather Bureau revealed a consistent westerly wind had blown during the day in question.

At the committal proceedings, Lenny explained to Erwin that the prosecution must convince the Magistrate that at least enough evidence against the accused exists for a prima facie criminal case to be made. This process ensures that the defendant is protected prior to the actual trial and is not unjustly held in custody during the assembly by prosecution and defense of the materials necessary for a trial; sometimes a long process. Lenny the lanky lawyer was positively languorous in his carefully planned and restrained attack on the evidence of the prosecution. He manoeuvred to ensure that evidence which he could easily discredit at a full trial was not attacked. He attacked only the forensics. Some people at the committal hearing thought that Lenny had lost. But Lenny knew he had won the battle of shaping the direction of evidence at trial. And a courtroom trial was the battlefield on which he could win the contest in such a way as to confer immunity from later prosecution of Erwin.

Erwin was committed – just. The Magistrate may have been moved by the heinous nature of the crime and perhaps to a certain extent, by the amount of publicity that such a shocking crime arouses. The Magistrate may also have been influenced by the depositions of the potential witnesses and the expectation of the police of forensic evidence in addition to that outlined to the court in the committal hearing. Erwin's belligerent appearance may also have been detrimental to his case.

When the Magistrate decided that Erwin must go to trial, Lenny registered feigned annoyance. Lenny had some concerns, he told the Magistrate, for Erwin's safety. Erwin was innocent until proven guilty but in a prison environment other convicts had shown a disdain for the law and imposed their own form of misguided justice to alleged murderers of children. Lenny played the "persecution of an innocent" ploy to perfection. The Magistrate made a special protection order applicable to Erwin so that Erwin must be detained in the Programmes Unit, an area reserved for prisoners considered at risk from other prisoners who called child molesters "Rock Spiders".

Lenny knew that the protection order would not only afford Erwin relief from violence but would allow Erwin several privileges denied most others. Erwin was far from happy but was also far from despondent because he believed, without reservation, the promise made by the longitudinally exalted lawyer to have him out and exonerated with the minimum of delay; given the constraints of the overburdened calendar of the court system.

CHAPTER THIRTY-THREE

WITH THE DISCOVERY OF MASSIVE quantities of gold in central Victoria in the 1850's, Melbourne became Australia's financial capital for 140 years. Then Sydney, the capital of Australia's most populous State of New South Wales, surreptitiously slipped the financial capital crown on its own cranium.

Melbourne is still a creditable challenger and the rivalry between Melbourne and Sydney remains. Bryn's inclination towards more open spaces caused him to reconsider the location of ECARUT's head office needs. Technological improvements enabled decentralisation and the virtual mandatory requirement to have an office in Melbourne's long established business district was beginning to fade. After an examination of attractive moorings, Bryn looked to the growing sea side town of Mornington. It was located within Port Phillip Bay, had sheltered anchorage, boat refuelling facilities and a pleasant main street.

He found a two partner Accounting practice located in part of a store fronted former bank in the main street. Bryn contracted with the surprised and delighted partners to handle ECARUT's business records keeping. With the expansion of the retail unit trust, the Mornington Accounting practice expanded. First using the part time services of several retired accountants and bank managers who had chosen Mornington for their retirement residences. Eventually the partners added younger University graduates to maintain increasingly sophisticated technical services to ECARUT.

During three years of rapid growth and profits, the original two partners seldom remembered that they had a three year contract with ECARUT. When the subject was raised, Bryn used his personality and people manipulation skills to distract the partners and resolution of the issue faded. Bryn frequently demonstrated his sincerity and generosity with gifts such as theatre tickets, invitations to the Australian Open Tennis and entertaining cruises on his magnificent boat as distractions.

The partners were horrified when they received in the mail, via Bryn's lawyers, an invitation to tender for the services that they were already providing. They had presumed that Bryn intended them to continue. To meet ECARUT's requirements the partners had forsaken all of the local business. Other Accounting firms had taken over. Furthermore the partners had borrowed heavily to purchase the entire building that was built in the 1850's in classic Colonial design, and for the computer equipment.

The balance sheet of their accounting practice showed only a small excess of liquid assets over liabilities because the practice invested heavily in illiquid assets to accommodate Bryn's business. The prosperity and existence of the firm would be in jeopardy if they lost ECARUT's lucrative business, to which they had become totally committed in reasonable expectation of bounteous future profits. The partners did not realise the Bryn had applied the ancient Chinese tactic of "giving before you take". Bryn fobbed off all entreatments to be reasonable with the excuse that he planned to list ECARUT on the ASX and so every contract must clearly be seen to be transparent and independent.

Bryn began to demand lengthy written explanations about relatively innocuous items that he had dismissed as immaterial in the past. When it came to seizing a dollar, Bryn was an obnoxious bastard. After several weeks of pressure, the two partners found themselves staring at ruin and an impecunious retirement because the specifications of Bryn's tender exceeded even their competent existing capacity to meet. Bryn called on them when his local spy, one of the data input ladies, phoned to say that one partner was in the coronary care section of the local hospital and the other was imbibing copious quantities of alcohol. Bryn considered it a propitious time to exert more pressure.

With no consideration whatsoever for their dedicated past services Bryn made an offer, part cash, part units in ECARUT, to buy out their business and relieve them of their worries. The magnitude of the offer was insultingly meagre. The partner in coronary care managed to bargain up the cash component by around 10% before he expired with a massive heart attack. His bibulous partner signed Bryn's contract, took his cash and units and moved out of the area. He sold his ECARUT units, unknowingly to one of Bryn's nominees, early in the next financial year primarily to be totally disassociated with his former proudly owned company.

Bryn cancelled the unreasonable tender process because he now had ECARUT's Accounting Division located in the beautiful seaside town of Mornington, an enjoyable hour and half's sail from Melbourne in his motor cruiser. He estimated that it cost him less than half of the cost of establishing it himself from scratch. In celebration he approved a minor splurge of ECARUT's massive reserves in tastefully restoring the heritage listed double fronted façade and modernising and expanding the rear of the premises. Another death and a broken life meant little to Bryn when in pursuit of his aims. His aim was now precisely engraved in his mind. He wanted respectability, recognition and heirs. And having the registered office of his company in a prestigious, restored, classic example of Colonial architecture was another step towards that aim. Bryn had risen from a Uni drop-out commerce student to the respectable owner of properties worth several hundreds of millions of dollars. And all in little over a decade. His success was due to his discipline in adhering to his policies of planning, patience and protection.

The book of Ecclesiastes in the old testament of the Bible has a chapter in which it's reputed author, King Solomon the wise, philosophises that there is a proper time for every event on earth. Bryn had absorbed that wisdom and profited by its application to his business strategy. He reasoned that every business has its cycle. He knew that his forte was start up and ride the upward curve to maximum marginal profit level. As the business matured, entrepreneurial abilities became less important and success required more managerial talent. Bryn was taught that principle at the Uni but observation had taught him other principles. One of which was how to deal with dangers unknown to legitimate business men. His solution was the swift, undetected murder and disposal of threats. Bryn knew when to get out and he knew to how get out.

During his career he sold out portions of his criminal enterprise that were approaching maturity but leaving ample avenues for growth so that the purchasers never felt resentment at buying an overpriced or underperforming entity. Yet another lesson learned from the legitimate business world was that success spawns imitators. Competition in legitimate business was sometimes glibly referred to as cut-throat when rivalry became intense. In Bryn's business domain the term cut-throat was apt and actual.

Bryn sold out parts of the multi faceted criminal empire slightly below the "going price" and a happy buyer expanded the business. The criminal owner of the newly acquired business made money and forgot Bryn. No fuss, no threats, no need to extract revenge. The buyer usually contributed to the competition that inevitably eventuated as a consequence of the buyer's undisciplined ostentatious displays of wealth. Buyers of Bryn's bodgy businesses lacked Bryn's discipline and went for the quick buck. Word of their success spread. Competition sprang up, violent turf wars occurred, the police intervened. People went to prison. Governments legislated new laws.

By that time Bryn was so far removed that even if rumours of "Johnny" did emerge they presented no threat to Bryn because the only link to Johnny was through Ray. And Ray was always viewed by Bryn as expendable.

CHAPTER THIRTY-FOUR

LENNY HAD HIS WORK CUT out keeping Erwin from doing anything stupid. The long incarceration was seen by Erwin as punishment of an innocent, for Erwin convinced himself that he was innocent. Lenny's attempts to explain the system of law did little to stem his building volcano of resentment. Lenny tried to make Erwin understand that the special protection order he had argued to obtain was for Erwin's benefit. Lenny did not want Erwin to boast of his exploits because he knew that many prisoners would gladly testify to Erwin's confession to earn a concession from the Parole Board.

When Erwin learned that his trial date would be four months in the future he almost exploded. Had a guard or anyone else but Lenny been with him in the interview room, Erwin would have vented his pent up frustration by beating the shit out of them. To pacify Erwin, Lenny reluctantly agreed to make an application for bail. To date Lenny had been loath to do so on the grounds that an Erwin loose in the community was a danger to himself let alone others. And Lenny wanted to successfully defend Erwin because it was good for business. How else could he otherwise advertise his services amongst the criminal community?

Lenny had that morning received news from his Accountant to the effect that a bankruptcy declaration after being paid for the successful defense of Erwin will be most advantageous to him from a taxation point of view. Not advantageous to the Australian Taxation Office to whom he owed tax for the last four years totalling $550,000. Lenny enjoyed his bankruptcies. He relished the clandestine transfer of assets overseas via betting accounts, payment for fictitious services, investments and repayments of loans to private companies around the world. When his numerous creditors, including the Australian Taxation Office, got too close to instituting legal action for recovery of amounts due, Lenny would file for bankruptcy and foil them all. Having an orderly state of mind he liked to do it on a Friday. This would allow him to have a week's holiday in the sun with the best looking woman money can buy, pre paid in cash before the bankruptcy. Upon return, refreshed from his physical endeavours, he easily coped with the process of re-establishing his legal practice. Ostensibly the re-establishment was financed by loans from friends.

With the protection of his finances occupying part of his brain and protection of his client in another, Lenny was reluctant to apply for bail for Erwin. Nevertheless he proceeded with the bail application and, in the event, the rejection of bail provided Lenny with an opportunity to advantage Erwin. During the unsuccessful bail application the Magistrate asked questions about Erwin's life style. She was unimpressed when told that Erwin had no regular employment since leaving school. Languidly looking through lizard lidded eyes, Lenny detected the Magistrate's displeasure at a young able bodied man with no recorded medical impairment being perpetually unemployed. Lenny reasoned that if the Magistrate was offended then so would a jury. Lenny resolved to redress the shortcomings prior to Erwin's trial. Lenny had no contempt for caution.

After the bail application was rejected, Erwin was furious. Again Lenny was at full stretch to pacify his pugnacious client. Efforts to explain his strategy to exonerate Erwin had no immediate effect so Lenny waited for Erwin to pause in his string of profanities then launched his counter attack. "Erwin", he said, "You must get a job". That stopped Erwin cold. The prospect of actually working opened in Erwin the mental image of a deep dark chasm jammed with contorted images reminiscent of the macabre painting of Hieronymus Bosch. Erwin still had the stunned look on his face when Lenny pressed home his attack. Erwin was told that if he had a job his horizon of acquaintances would expand exponentially and he could be certain that somewhere in that expanded horizon he would meet far more people with interests similar to his own. Lenny also made the point that a jury at a trial would resent an accused having an affluent lifestyle without being employed. That resentment might cause an unexpected "Guilty" verdict.

Thrusting home his attack, Lenny told Erwin that the ideal time to obtain the necessary qualifications was when he had plenty of time with few distractions. Indeed, if Erwin could decide on a future occupation then he could pursue his acquisition of a qualification at State expense. Lenny pointed out the benefits of Erwin's current position. Ample time, quiet conditions, access to a comprehensive library and a computer. Lenny sensed that he had prevailed and before leaving the still stunned Erwin, Lenny promised to send to Erwin a package of short term courses wherein a qualification could be procured by correspondence.

The concept of having to work made Erwin ever more restless. He needed to get out of his confinement. A word that Lenny had mentioned drifted to the forefront of his affronted senses. The word was "library". To visit the library would entail leaving his confined cell. So not without serous reservations about the likelihood of being infected by academia, Erwin demanded of his regular guard that he be allowed to visit the prison library. He was astonished to be told be could do so in 25 minutes.

Not having been convicted and being located in a special protection section of the prison had some advantages. A booklet detailing the prison rules was given to Erwin on his initial incarceration but he had declined to read it. He now retrieved it from the wall recess that served as a wardrobe and on page twelve found the policy statement about library privileges. On three days of each week and between certain times, Erwin had access to the library on request. The prison system management allowed prisoners of various categories to have escorted library access for up to forty minutes. Erwin's demand had been made, fortuitously, just prior to one such privileged time.

Escorted by a guard, Erwin walked the three hundred metres to the library through a maze of brightly lit windowless corridors and barred, electronically operated doors. At the library he stood before a desk behind which sat a low risk trustee prisoner who performed the function of a librarian. Apart from Lenny and guards, Erwin had only spoken to one other person, the prison Chaplin, and then he only said "Bugggger off". So the opportunity to speak with another person relieved the monotony.

The librarian was tall, thin, with sparse grey hair, thick reading glasses and a demeanour that struck Erwin as being that of a professional academic. Erwin later learned that he had, indeed, once been a professor of chemistry. The reason he was now a prison librarian resulted from his concoction of a chemical compound that erased erase-proof ink-jet ink. Using the invention he erased the name of his University employer on several sizable cheques, that were paid into bank accounts from which the money was swiftly withdrawn in cash. Regrettably he lacked the foresight to invent a concoction to both erase his fingerprints and obliterate his image on the CCTV of the ATMs of the banks where he deposited the altered cheques. "Professor" or "Prof" asked Erwin for details necessary for the issue of a library card.

Erwin was incredulous. Why would a prisoner need a library card? Where could overdue books be hidden? Gently the Prof advised that the bar code on the library card was a means of management control. The authorities may want to ascertain what books and DVDs an inmate had access to. Erwin considered such an invasion of his privacy to be a diabolical liberty but grudgingly consented to the arrangement. The "Prof" offered Erwin assistance by explaining the library lay out and during that procedure Erwin told the Prof that he was looking for a short term course that would quality him for congenial employment on the outside. The guard escorting Erwin had to retreat behind a book case for a few moments because he convulsed with laughter when he heard Erwin's request.

The Prof suggested that Erwin may need some experienced advice and introduced him to a small, fat, fortyish, dark, hairy man sitting at another desk. The Prof introduced Erwin to Vincent, very formally, and told Erwin that Vincent was a fully trained and experienced vocational guidance counsellor. Erwin's guard and Vincent's guard sat on nearby chairs and indulged in friendly conversation whilst Vincent interviewed Erwin. In ten minutes Vincent scooted through occupations for which some qualification could be obtained by correspondence within the time frame between now and the date scheduled for Erwin's trial. Vincent's long, luxurious, black sideburns moved unevenly as he recited the educational opportunities available given the restrictions caused by Erwin's low level of formal education.

Aquaculture had some brief appeal to Erwin but as Vincent progressed through the list to Zoology, Erwin became confused. Too many choices. Vincent perceived that Erwin was a bit slow in the mental apparatus but prudently declined to comment as he also perceived that Erwin appeared to have compensation by way of power in his abundant muscular apparatus. Vincent suggested that Erwin consider a Real Estate Representative Course. It would take only six weeks by correspondence so it suited Erwin's time frame. The good side was that Erwin would benefit from the proximity of experienced mentors. Vincent told Erwin that a fully qualified and former licensed Real Estate Agent would make an ideal mentor. "We have plenty of them in here", Vincent proudly told Erwin. The bad side of the course would be if Erwin were to be convicted, because an element of the granting of a graduate Real Estate Representative Certificate includes no criminal convictions. With some pride, Erwin told Vincent that he had avoided a "Crim tag" so far and bragged that Lenny the lanky lawyer would beat the charge the police had maliciously dumped upon him.

Vincent expressed appreciation for Erwin's trust in Lenny and said he regretted not being able to have afforded Lenny's tariff. Lenny would have convinced the jury that Vincent had no knowledge whatsoever of the stolen gold bars, marked with mint identification numbers of the media magnate owner. Vincent never discovered how the bars could have materialised in his refrigerator, he said.

Erwin commiserated with Vincent, thanked him for his advice and accepted the caveat about a conviction negating a Real Estate Representative's Certificate. Erwin asked Vincent to prepare and lodge the appropriate entry documents. Vincent promised to do that. After he consulted a TAFE syllabus, Vincent suggested that Erwin should receive notification of his successful enrolment as a correspondent student within five days. Vincent also undertook, on Erwin's behalf, to complete the requisition form so that the State Government financed, Prison Welfare Scheme would pay all course fees and technical book costs.

Erwin was feeling satisfied with his resolution and when his guard tapped him on the shoulder to say that library time was now over. Erwin made no protest and returned to his cell like a lamb. Erwin had images of being an outstanding success in the Real Estate industry. Erwin pictured himself as an auctioneer. He wondered whether he could squeeze in a

TAFE course in yodelling. About the time the guard checked that Erwin's cell door was locked. Vincent was earning $50.

Ian, the grieving grandfather of the brutally violated and murdered young boy, was calling in past favours. A couple of telephone calls kept Ian up to date with Erwin's location. Vincent's call on a borrowed mobile phone updated Ian's dossier on Erwin.

Allowing time for Erwin's documents to be processed by the correspondence department of the Technical and Further Education (TAFE) institution, Ian set in train his own process to track Erwin's progress. Ian had no direct access to an informant within the TAFE. But through a contact with a comprehensive computer system, Ian was able to locate an employee in TAFE administration closely related to a female who had been a victim of rape. Ian watched that TAFE employee for a few days to assess his prospects of a sympathetic hearing. He observed that employee sitting alone in the TAFE canteen and determined to try his luck. "If you don't ask it's an automatic no" was his philosophy.

Ian sat down slowly and equalled slowly and in a non threatening manner introduced himself and showed his inquiry agent's ID card. The TAFE employee appeared intrigued rather than offended or defensive. Ian took from his briefcase newspaper clippings of the murder of his grandson and the arrest of Erwin. Ian laid his request on the line. Erwin had enrolled at the TAFE correspondence course and Ian wanted to be kept informed of Erwin's progress. He admitted that any information given would be in breach of the TAFE privacy policy but he promised to treat all information given with the utmost discretion.

Before awaiting an answer, Ian changed the discussion to the rape of the TAFE employee's cousin and the ridiculously light sentence imposed on the convicted man. Ian knew straight away that his assessment of the TAFE employee was vindicated from the pained expression brought on by the mention of the lenient penalty. The employee was enormously dissatisfied with the injustice of that sentence and immediately understood Ian's apprehension regarding the alleged murderer of his grandson receiving a sentence inappropriate to the severity of the appalling crime. Privacy Law or no Privacy Law, Ian gained an immediate volunteer who promised to pass on every item of interest regarding Erwin's Real Estate Representative Course.

When law abiding members of the public become disillusioned with the justice system they will become breakers of minor laws themselves, without qualm, if they perceive that in so doing they contribute to a fairer system. And that they are most unlikely to be caught. After working out the mechanics of a safe transmission of information by fax and telephone, Ian rose to leave. He was almost overwhelmed by the thanks given to him by the TAFE employee who now had some method of attenuating his inner frustration at the legal system. The system purports to be just and must be seen to be just. But although society's cohesion depends on the law, an increasingly large proportion of society feel that the legal system is leaning disproportionately towards rehabilitation of criminals. Victims are made to feel like second class citizens as perpertrators' rights appear paramount.

How does a Magistrate or a judge distinguish between the convict's remorse for his crime and subsequent damage to innocents on the one hand, and the self pity of the convict for himself for being caught on the other? Many victims of crime feel that too much emphasis is given in mitigation to remorse, an unassessable, easily counterfeited emotion, and in his perception of the frustration generated by the eager relative of a victim of crime, Ian found a recruiting ground for a willing informer.

Erwin's correspondence course with TAFE was as phoney as a three legged emu. With Vincent as his conduit, Erwin arranged for the most cerebral of the numerous imprisoned, fully qualified Real Estate Agents, to answer all of the correspondence course questions for him. Erwin simply arranged for Lenny's clerk to transfer funds from his bank account, ostensibly as a legal fee pre-payment, direct to the legal office trust account. A cash withdrawal from the trust account bank was made and the $3000 handed over to the girlfriend of the mobility challenged Real Estate Agent.

Erwin graduated as dux of his course with his marks being so high that several Real Estate companies sent invitations, via the TAFE, offering employment. None of the prospective employers associated the name of the brilliant student with that of an accused murderer. Erwin had quite a laugh at each but could not respond because a Police Check was required before he could make application for certificate that would entitle him to practice. Lenny advised him to wait until after the trial, the date of which was drawing closer, before submitting the application.

Ian's spy passed on the astounding news about Erwin's superlative achievement. Ian knew that the exam result was spuriously obtained but refrained from further investigation. It was sufficient for Ian to know that Erwin had passed the qualifying exam at this stage. The information was added to Ian's expanding dossier on Erwin.

One of the employment offers made to Erwin came from the recently appointed Sales Manager of a very large residential real estate trust with a head office located in Mornington. Erwin wondered at the odd name on the letterhead, ECARUT. It looked to him like it was in Latin. And he knew that if something was written in Latin then it had to be a disease. Erwin put the letter of invitation in the file along with the others.

Erwin started to read the book he had borrowed from the library but after the first page he cursed and flung it with fury against the far wall of his cell. He had eagerly grabbed the book from the library shelf when he read the title in red print on the spine, "Penology". Expecting to read salacious stories about the male sex organ he was totally disillusioned to discover that penology was the study of crime and prison management. He realised he should have been more cautious in his selection but except for certain occasions, Erwin had contempt for caution.

CHAPTER THIRTY-FIVE

THE DAY OF THE TRIAL was a distinct disappointment to Erwin. With a respectable hair cut, a quiet, quality suit, white shirt and for the first time in months, a tie, he appeared before the jury looking presentable. After some preliminaries and him replying "Not Guilty" to the question of the judge, the Prosecuting Attorney rose to tell the jury about the crime, for which he confidently asserted, Erwin was clearly guilty. But within a few sentences Lenny was upstanding on his broad, immaculately shod, splayed feet to protest. The judge was acerbic at Lenny's interruption, it being traditional that the principal protagonists be allowed to deliver their opening barrage to the jury without hindrance.

But Lenny was adamant and quoted legal precedents with a turn of speed that would have been the envy of a rabid football supporter screaming abuse at an umpire. The judge visibly wilted then regained sufficient composure to order that the jury adjourn from the court to the jury room.

Erwin was not required to leave the court. He sat in the dock guarded by two muscular officers of the Prisons Department. He listened to Lenny's buzz saw voice directly flailing his opposition counsel and, by inference, the judge. Lenny really stirred matters up to the extent that the judge declared an adjournment to consider Lenny's claims, with the court to reconvene after the luncheon recess. Lenny was obviously happy with the morning's effort because he smiled at Erwin. Lenny's smile was endured by Erwin who had become accustomed to it. Both prison guards were confronted with it for the first time and each took an involuntary step backwards. Upon reconvening, the judge expressed a few remarks to the reconvened jury and the prosecutor re-commenced his opening address. During that address the judge wrote the occasional note in his personal record book. When not writing, the judge directed a baleful glare in the direction of Lenny, ready to combat any attempt by Lenny to further impede the court procedure.

Ian and his family sat in the public gallery balcony looking down into the court. The court gallery was full of spectators, including a group of six wearing highly imaginative styles of dress. These misguided souls were supporters of Erwin who, they claimed, was falsely accused. To any who would listen they would say, through mouths decorated with studded tongues and black lip gloss, that Erwin was the victim of politics. Stunned by the atrocious crime, they claimed, the politicians had pressured the police to make a quick arrest and Erwin was the political scapegoat.

Ian could not discard the thought that the preposterously pierced personages had an element of truth in their contention. Ian listened carefully to the prosecutor's opening address. His concentration gave him a period of relief from the burden of desolation of spirit that had descended upon him at the loss of his cherished grandson. It became sickeningly clear to Ian that the prosecution case was weak but despite that weakness Ian was absolutely certain that Erwin was guilty. Absence of evidence did not necessarily mean evidence of innocence.

It seemed to Ian that the decision to arrest Erwin was hurried and made in anticipation of further supporting forensic evidence that did not eventuate. To a certain extent the euphoria of the police in locating Erwin at the NSW holiday resort, added to by political pressure, resulted in the premature charging of Erwin. Insufficient trails of evidence were established.

As an example, the prosecutor's opening address outlined the charge and the law and details of evidence. One item of evidence was intended to show that Erwin's flight to NSW could be interpretted as an attempt to evade justice. As a link in the chain of evidence against Erwin it could have been seen as significant by a jury. Lenny, however, had destroyed it as a persuader of guilt. His interruption of the prosecutor when the word "flight" was first uttered was intended to do just that. Lenny's lanky frame had sprung to its maximum elevation as he verbally flung precedent after legal precedent at the judge. Every flung precedent had some bearing on the level of admissibility of the implication that a prosecutor may attach to a person of interest to the police who is not apprehended in the immediate proximity of a crime scene.

The fact that Erwin was travelling when apprehended could not be used as evidence against him, Lenny vehemently asserted. Erwin had a ten year history of travel, the judge was told, so Erwin being in NSW was normal not abnormal. Lenny told the judge he was prepared to call twenty witnesses to Erwin's propensity for travel. The prosecutor's attempt to infer that what was norm for an innocent man was in fact incriminating evidence against Erwin equated to a malicious prosecution or persecution, claimed the lanky lawyer. Lenny won the point on the weight of the legal precedents he fired at machine gun speed and volume. The prosecutor, inadequately briefed by the police, agreed to withdraw all references to flight when he resumed his opening address. In the hasty re-write of that address the prosecutor lost some of his aggressive accusative assertions resulting in a dilution of the impact of his opening address on the jury.

From Ian's viewpoint, the prosecutor's lack of facts about Erwin's peripatetic life style was a demonstration of poor preparation. Matters deteriorated thereafter as the prosecutor presented his witnesses. The identification of Erwin by the Rent-a-Wreck proprietor seemed positive at first but became tentative under Lenny's remorseless verbal examination onslaught. Lenny put it to the proprietor that Erwin had been on the Rent-a-Wreck premises on the day before, hence the proprietor's recollection of his face. Lenny asked if the proprietor could categorically deny it. The answer was "NO". That destroyed a main point of human evidence.

The identification of the Ford Falcon at the abduction site was similarly shaken. As for the driver of the passing car, Lenny presented graphs based on relative speeds of motor vehicles and length of time of a glance by a driver in control of a vehicle. He convinced the witness that he had seen someone for less than half a second. Lenny reduced the driver to such a state of confusion as to eliminate his credibility as a witness.

On forensic evidence, starting with the imprint of size eleven trainers, the police forensic expert stood his ground against Lenny so Lenny finished his questioning quickly but did extract the information that thousands of the size and make of trainer had been sold. No one could identity Erwin as a purchaser and no such trainers or imprint of trainers were found at Erwin's house. Another link in the evidence chain destroyed.

Another forensic expert took the stand and gave a clear and understandable explanation of DNA, using several large charts. When Lenny began cross examination he congratulated the expert witness on the presentation before homing in on the essential element of timing. "Assuming that the fingernail fragment you found in the Ford Falcon was that of his innocent client", said Lenny, "Can you tell the court how long the fragment had been in the car?" The court room was hushed in anticipation of the answer of the expert. When the forensic expert said that he could only give an approximate number of days, spectators in the public gallery exhaled held breaths collectively. Lenny asked the expert to repeat his answer and while the answer was being delivered Lenny held out his long tentacle like arms in a theatrical gesture indicating the court clocks as if to emphasise to the jury the worthlessness of the expert evidence in relation to time. On that note, day one closed.

The forensic expert who specialised in blood identification was first witness on day two. Evidence was drawn from him by the prosecutor in the evidence-in-chief. To a large extent his evidence followed his predecessor witness and he used the same charts. In drawing evidence the prosecutor appeared less sure of himself. The question to the fingernail expert by Lenny clearly indicated that no major challenge was forthcoming to the expertise of the forensic experts or to the conclusion they had reached. The prosecutor had anticipated a ferocious attack on the competence of the forensic experts but Lenny appeared to have passed up his main chance. It was uncharacteristic for Lenny to let an opportunity for a display of verbal aggression pass. The prosecutor had half a mind on trying to fathom Lenny's tactics when he questioned the forensic expert on blood in cross-examination. Lenny almost appeared to be conceding that the fingernail and blood both belonged to Erwin. The prosecutor couched each of his re-examination questions with exceptional care until, at last, he felt he had clarified every facet of the identification of the blood found on a soiled portion of paper towel to be Erwin's without any shadow of reasonable doubt.

Lenny allowed the prosecutor ample time to sit and stared with apparent intense concentration at the court's large brass central chandelier for some time. All eyes were upon him. His timing was immaculate. He sprang to his feet a milli second before the judge could chastise him for wasting the time of the court. Lenny softened up the forensic expert by moving close to him and smiling. The expert blanched and recoiled. Languidly but loudly Lenny asked the forensic expert how he had received the paper towel and the reply was that it was given to him in a plastic evidence bag. Lenny pointed at the labelled plastic bag that the prosecutor had earlier admitted as evidence. Lenny asked the court usher to show the bag to the expert who looked at it and replied to Lenny's question by saying that he positively identified it as being the bag that enclosed the paper towel. Lenny asked the expert to look more closely at the side of the bag and to tell the court what he could see. Perplexed, the expert put on a pair of reading glasses and closely examined the plastic evidence bag.

He then told the court that there appeared to be what he presumed was a very thin strip of paper adhesive on the side of the bag other than that side which had the full sized adhesive paper label, used by the forensic laboratory for identification of the paper towel. With deliberate calm Lenny asked the expert to tell the court about evidence handling procedures. Lenny asked slow questions and gestured at the jury as if his questions were suggestions that the jury may consider as being a common sense way to help the jury reach a decision. Every jury member clearly perceived that Lenny was treating him or her as an intelligent, rational person and Lenny's only purpose was to assist in guiding them to a logical conclusion.

At the end of the expert's description Lenny went for the kill. He asked if the expert could deny that the evidence bag showed signs to indicate it had been used before. The expert could not. From a low baritone rising to an alto boy soprano in tone, Lenny asked the expert if he could guarantee to the court that the paper towel with the blood stain had not been contaminated by whatever had previously been contained in the used evidence envelope.

The expert squirmed in the witness box and looked imploringly at the prosecutor for deliverance. The prosecutor however had his own inner turmoil to contend with. He had just seen a major element of his evidence to convict suddenly, shockingly and severely weakened. Lenny made no movement to intimidate the expert witness. Indeed he stepped one long pace backwards, and with lowered head remained silent. It was left to the judge to ask the expert to answer the vital question put to him by counsel for defense.

The expert said "No". The word broke another anticipatory silence that had settled over the court and a rustling sound was evident as visitors in the packed public gallery and jurors in their box shifted arms and legs that had been temporarily frozen pending the answer to the vital question. To be certain that the importance of the reply was fully appreciated the judge paraphrased the question and answer when he put to the expert witness that the reply of "No" meant that he could not assure the court that the evidence now in the evidence bag had not been contaminated. This time the discomforted expert witness answered "Yes".

The prosecutor rose in an attempt to retrieve an unexpected and devastating situation but the judge anticipated the action and told him to sit. He would have another say in re-examination. The judge added a throw away line that he thought that opportunity would occur shortly. His was right. Lenny's final question to the unhappy forensic expert had all the attributes of the final nail in a coffin. Addressing the expert, Lenny asked if contaminated evidence could produce a false DNA result.

The expert spent several minutes advising the Court of the numerous ways it may not perhaps, necessarily, markedly distort the DNA comparison result. But in the end had to conclude that he could not entirely eliminate a false reading due to contamination. Lenny moved closer to the juror's box, pointed at the expert, let his arm drop to his side, made a slow nod of his head that was almost a shallow bow to the jury, then about turned and resumed his seat. Lenny did not want to take the issue further at this stage. His planned tactic was not to discredit scientific evidence but to prove incompetence in evidence handling procedures in his final address to the jury.

The prosecutor spent over twenty minutes in re-examination trying to salvage the situation by putting alternative scenarios to the expert but the damage had been done. Some people in the public gallery whispered that Lenny would, could or should make application to the judge that the trial be aborted due to use of unsafe evidence against Erwin. The judge resolved the speculation by adjourning the court until the next day. He told the court that he appreciated that it was a little earlier that his normal closure time but he felt it to be an appropriate time to adjourn. The judge appreciated that Lenny would make no application for the trial to be aborted. Lenny wanted Erwin to have a completed trial; a trial at which Lenny would have Erwin declared "Not Guilty".

When an accused person is tried for a capital crime and found "Not Guilty", the accused can never be tried again for the same crime. "Double jeopardy", is the term used to describe being tried for the same crime after an accused is found not guilt by a jury of his peers. It is outlawed. Lenny did not want Erwin locked away because with Erwin on the loose there was always the prospect that trouble would occur leading Lenny to be engaged to defend Erwin again. After all he had to protect a reliable source of future income. Exoneration was Lenny's aim. Lenny had no contempt for caution.

The next day seemed like a parade of police. Each was sworn in and the prosecutor obtained testimony from each to prop up the disintegrating prosecution case. Lenny was brilliantly merciless and deliberately repetitious. Each police officer was asked if he was aware of the number of persons on the police sex offenders list. Lenny read out twenty names. "Did you question this person?" asked Lenny and on being told "No", Lenny put the question, more of a statement really, "Is this another example of police incompetence?" "Did you arrest Erwin for revenge? Has Erwin any proven sex deviant history?" The repetition eight times, with "No" answers each time from the seven police officers, had more effect on the jury than some sections of the evidence.

During Lenny's questioning he often stood in profile to the jury. Several members of the jury panel remarked that Lenny bore a strong resemblance to the famous British actor William Pratt. Otherwise known to cinema goers as Boris Karloff. On the subject of the search of Erwin's Mercedes car, a police officer from the police garage read from a list of items that included the CD disc discovered in the built-in CD player. In reply to Lenny's question the puzzled police officer replied that the CD was of the light operetta, "The Merry Widow" by Franz Lehar. A lady member of the jury instantaneously decided that Erwin must be innocent as no one who loved that superb music could possibly be a depraved monster. On that musical note the Court was adjourned for the day. Erwin went to the cells feeling confused. The prosecutor went to his chambers feeling furious. Lenny went to his chambers feeling satisfied. Ian went to his office feeling sick.

CHAPTER THIRTY-SIX

AT THE COURT NEXT MORNING, the foyer serving the public gallery buzzed with partly subdued conversations amongst members of the various groups. An unseen but tangible electric tension tingled in everyone, in anticipation of the climax of the trial. Ian and his family were accorded a modicum of respect with a pace or two of space between them and the throng of inquisitive spectators. At the other end of the gallery a similar space existed around the pro-Erwin anarchist/white supremacist group, however that space did not signify respect. It was a spontaneous demonstration by the public gallery patrons of their deep dislike of the exhibitionist group.

Ushers opened the doors at the ends of the foyer to admit the public, each one of whom was cleared by the security officers operating x-ray and metal detector portals. As a complete irrelevancy Ian wondered how the obnoxious anarchist mob obtained entry given the number of metal body piercing pins they flaunted.

The muted conversations continued as the public gallery filled and the usher ordered all to rise as he announced the entrance of the judge. The judge, sensing the public expectation that this session may be exceptionally interesting, took the unusual step of pounding the gavel several times to demonstrate his authority to command silence.

The prosecutor was a martyr to congenital haemorrhoids. He deeply regretted eating a particularly spicy beef vindaloo the previous evening as it made his swift rise to his feet extraordinarily painful. He manfully subjugated the pain as he caught the eye of the judge and respectfully requested permission to recall the forensic expert in re-examination, with the objective of amplifying the technical evidence presented the day before. As if to emphasise to the jury the panicky posture of the prosecution, Lenny unfolded his lengthy frame without haste or consternation and with voice inflexion full of incredible respect to his honour, registered his absolute opposition to the recall. Experienced observers felt that the judge had already formed the view that the prosecution case was subsiding and he had no need to prolong the inevitable. They were not at all surprised when the judge refused the recall probably on the grounds that the evidence already extracted was as convincing as it was likely to be.

The pile prone prosecutor had spent many hours the previous evening with the forensic expert endeavouring to put together an accurate but simple explanation of the very complex DNA testing procedure. The intent of their deliberations was to try to repair the damage done by Lenny's introduction of the probability of contamination of the DNA evidence. Their efforts were irrelevant because the issue of contamination was not germane. The location of the paper towel and how it arrived at the place it was discovered was Lenny's real issue, as they were about to discover. Refusal of his earlier request was taken badly by the prosecutor who was so distracted as to inadvertently fail to place his painful posterior on the air cushion on his chair. His resultant grunt of excruciating pain brought a look of reprimand from the judge who misinterpreted it as vocal protest against his ruling. After a few inconsequential procedural matters were dealt with, the prosecutor rose with tear-rimmed eyes and advised the judge that the case for the Crown was closed.

Lenny rose with slow dignity that literary personages imagine surrounded the appearance of the magic sword Excalibur from the mystical lake. With eyelids clinking rapidly in the manner of notice boards at airports, Lenny indicated that he was ready to seriously defend.

The first witness for the defense was called and sworn in. He gave his occupation as that of retired railway worker. He testified that he lived in a house 400 metres to the west of the scene of the crime; the old deserted dairy. He was asked to describe the area opposite his house and he did so by describing it as several sports fields maintained by the Municipal Council.

In response to Lenny's question about what other activities took place on the sports fields in daylight hours, the witness told the court that it was well known for its mushrooms. It attracted many mushroom gatherers. In response to a question from Lenny about an event two days before the date of the murder, the retired railway employee recalled a brief, friendly conversation with a mushroom gatherer. The memory of it remained clear in his memory because the mushroom gatherer suffered a blood nose during their friendly conversation. The blood was staunched with a piece of towel taken from a plastic bag in which he saw several freshly picked mushrooms.

Lenny's next question was equally casual in delivery. "Is the friendly mushroom gatherer in this court"? To which the witness unhesitatingly replied "Yes" and with a fully outstretched arm and warm smile pointed a finger directly at Erwin. Having ensured that the jury absorbed the positive identification, Lenny gestured contemptuously to the prosecutor as if granting him permission to attempt to shake the testimony of the witness. And the prosecutor did his best to discredit the timing of the alleged meeting and the identification. The witness clearly associated his meeting, with the person he now knew as Erwin, as being on the day of a visit from relatives and he remained unshaken in his identification. The prosecutor applied pressure to the extent that several jurors began to feel he was offensive.

A second witness, a 40 year old female resident of a house near the sports field, essentially corroborated the testimony of the former witness. She confidently identified Erwin as the mushroom gatherer. She did not observe the nose bleed because she continued walking towards the shops. Agonising physical pains permeating the exit orifice of his alimentary canal combined with an intellectual pain triggered by disbelief of the testimony of Lenny's two witnesses lent vitriol to the prosecutor's questions. He scored a couple of points that weakened the fringe of the story of the female witness but the essence of her story was unshaken. So vitriolic were the pain assailed prosecutor's questions that the judge frowned several times and whatever advantage the prosecutor gained was lost as the sympathy of the jury swung towards the badgered witness.

Traditionally, the accused in a criminal trial is allowed to maintain secrecy as to the line of defense, save only that if an alibi is to be a plank in the defense platform then advance notice must be given to the prosecution so they have sufficient time to test that alibi. Lenny was perfectly aware of that and because he had not given notice to the prosecution, the prosecutor with the agonising anus assumed that an alibi would not be proffered. The prosecutor approached the bench and asked that an issue of law be clarified. Lenny was consulted in hushed tones then the jury were asked by the judge to leave the court.

In the absence of the jury, the prosecutor protested to the judge that the two witnesses called by Lenny were in breach of the convention that an alibi witness called to testify must be made known in sufficient time to allow police to test the alibi. Although not a direct alibi, for the time of the crime, the prosecutor claimed that the witnesses were a one-step removed alibi, if not for Erwin, then for a critical item of evidence. Lenny disputed the alibi claim. The essence of the testimony would directly link the prosecution forensic evidence, he claimed. The judge over ruled the prosecutor and held in favour of Lenny. The prosecutor protested again but the judge was obdurate and over ruled the protest. The only concession granted by the judge was his allowance of the recall of the two defense witnesses should the prosecutor convince the judge that a recall was warranted. The judge was tempted to prompt the prosecutor to pursue those witnesses to establish how they could possibly call "friendly" a brutal bastard like Erwin, but why prolong a lost cause?

The jury were called back and the judge warned the jury not to draw any conclusions from the brief interruption. The trial continued. Erwin, sitting in the dock, marvelled at Lenny's ability to locate witnesses. He could not recall ever having met either.

Nowhere in the deliberations of the prosecution team had they guessed that a senior officer of the Australian Government Weather Bureau would be subpoenaed to attend the court. Surprisingly he was; a gentleman appropriately named Dr Sleet was called. Lenny opened with the customary "pedigree" questions establishing the personal credentials of Dr Sleet. That led to Dr Sleet detailing his impressive list of Australian and International qualifications and included his thirty plus years of experience. Lenny asked the judge to accept Dr Sleet as an expert witness and receiving no objections from a perplexed prosecutor, the judge consented. Dr Sleet had several computer lists and a video cassette in his hands.

Lenny's questions became more deliberate and more clearly enunciated. And to drive home Dr Sleet's answers, Lenny repeated each one while looking directly at the jury. Dr Sleet's testimony finished at the lunch time adjournment and covered the fact, proven by records printed in the computer lists that for three days prior to the murder the prevailing wind had blown from the west at an average velocity of ten kilometres per hour for over fourteen hours per day. From the video that Lenny had arranged to be admitted as evidence and to be shown on the four video screens permanently located in the court, the jury saw Dr Sleet with an anometer, a wind velocity measuring device. He also displayed an electronic equivalent of a wind vane that determined wind direction. Both instruments were connected in such a way as to allow the measurements to be shown on the wall mounted video screen. The figures were similar to data recorded on the days prior to the murder.

Those assembled in the court were treated to pictures of squares of paper towel being dropped in the mushroom gathering area where the retired railway employee testified that Erwin had dropped the blood soiled paper used to stem a nose bleed. Tracking several pieces over several hours, accelerated by time lapse photography, showed every single square ended up within a metre of where the police claimed to have found the stained paper towel on which they placed so much reliance as evidence against Erwin. The jury were saturated with science. At the luncheon recess the spectators vacated the gallery expressing their private opinions that the prosecution ship had been torpedoed. Ian intuitively concurred but remained uncommunicative for fear of exacerbating the grief of his family.

Upon resumption after lunch, the prosecutor picked patiently away at the methods used to produce the video, attempted to dilute evidence regarding wind velocity by unconvincingly arguing about the efforts of turbulence and local variations. He won a couple of points but goals not points were needed and Dr Sleet was finally spared. Lenny had shown the jury a picture and the thousand words of the prosecutor had failed to dim it. The judge called a short recess.

Lenny's next witness was the Detective Senior Constable, named Jason Lyons, who had located the blood stained paper towel. Lenny's tactic in calling the Detective Senior Constable for the defense was many facetted. Lenny learned from Erwin that the relatively inexperienced Detective could be impulsive. When Erwin had repeatedly referred to Lyons as defective Constable Lyons; the detective had responded by hissing threats to Erwin. Detective Lyons looked to be a tough customer who was not intimidated by Erwin. Lenny planned to humiliate Lyons. Lenny's objective was to establish his ability to intimidate any police called as witnesses against his future clients. And in the process Lenny intended to induce the prosecutor to further damage his ailing anus. Lenny was not only lanky but loathsome.

With the judge in place, the gallery settled, the trial resumed. The tall, handsome, impeccably dressed Detective Lyons resembled a model of the type found in male clothing catalogues but without any sexual ambiguity. Lyons was sworn in and was standing with his finger between the pages of his police note book. Lenny was exceptionally polite to Detective Lyons. The excessive politeness worried Lyons who examined his every answer as if he were approaching a verbal ambush. Lenny took Lyons through, step by step, the events leading to the discovery of the blood soiled paper towel. Lyons responded to each question slowly and precisely and Lenny made no effort to speed up his replies to his first questions.

Lenny had learned how long the prosecutor's pain killing suppository would remain effective. As the prosecutor's relief receded Lenny implemented his persecution plan. Lenny quickly asked Detective Lyons about impediments to the paper towel blowing from the mushroom gathering area to the scene of the paper towel discovery, such as fences, bushes, parked vehicles, etc. The question may have been acceptable if put to the witness in another way. But Lenny's lightning delivery alerted the prosecutor to instinctively leap to his feet and object on the grounds that such an answer was too general and required an opinion from the witness, which objection was sustained. Lenny waited for his legal adversary to sit then fired off another question to which the prosecutor was drawn to his feet in another protest claiming the question was "leading". Lenny argued that his question was relevant given that Detective Lyons had a notebook from which such information could be gleaned.

Lenny now rapidly fired off more questions to Lyons. The prosecutor was forced to match the speed with objections to the judge. All were sustained. Usually Lenny supported his argument with quotes of legal precedents. Indeed had he done so, he may have won the right to have the witness answer. Lenny's apparent deliberate omission passed unnoticed.

As he continued to win his objections the prosecutor was lulled into a sense of minor victory. It dawned upon him with a clash of clarity what loathsome Lenny had done when he placed his painful buttocks on his air cushion for the tenth time in as many minutes. The anodyne affect of the suppository introduced at lunch time had worn off due to his recent ups and downs. The pain must have been reflected on his face because the prosecutor looked up and was repelled by the broad knowing smirk on Lenny's lizard like features.

Having achieved part of his aim, Lenny now delivered his verbal kill shot to Detective Lyons. He obtained permission for the video to be screened then put on pause at a scene showing nine crumpled squares of white paper towel lodged in the low green hedge twenty metres east of the crime scene building. He asked an usher, to whom he had earlier given a two metre long pointer, to pass the pointer to Detective Lyons. He then asked the Detective to move to the screen closest to the jury box. When the reluctant Detective complied, Lenny asked him to indicate with the pointer tip precisely where the incriminating paper had been found.

With a profoundly painful effort the prosecutor rose to object. But his objections and pain were in vain. This time Lenny had his legal precedents ready and fired off four in rapid succession, concluding that, as Detective Lyons had his notebook with the record of the precise millimetre of the position of the soiled paper towel, then no opinion or conclusion whatsoever was required of the witness. Simply the indication of a location to help the jury. As Detective Lyons raised the pointer Lenny reminded him that he was under oath and any divergence from previous evidence given about the measurements would be harshly treated by the court. Lyons shot a dirty look at Lenny.

Both the jury and the gallery seemed to hold their collective breaths as the tip of the pointer directed by Detective Lyons stopped right in the middle of the paper towels used by expert weatherman Dr Sleet in his experiments of the effect of prevailing winds. Detective Lyons knew with sickening certainty that Lenny had used him to destroy completely the most damming item of evidence against Erwin. So did the judge, the prosecutor, the jury and Ian. Lenny thanked the Detective and with the resonating tones declared his presentation of evidence closed. The judge consulted his watch. The court session still had over 40 minutes to run but he deemed forty minutes an inadequate time for the prosecutor to deliver his final statement. With a wiggle of his eyebrows at the prosecutor and Lenny both of whom responded with a nod, the judge adjourned the trial until the next morning.

Lenny visited Erwin and said that he would book a table for them at Melbourne's best restaurant for the following evening. Erwin's despondency disappeared and he began taunting the guards again. Lenny interrupted his journey home that evening to call at a supermarket and buy a packet of snowballs. Apart from the fact that he enjoyed eating snowballs, Lenny needed the snowballs as part of his plan to make absolutely certain that Erwin was adjudged "Not Guilty". Lenny was determined not to overlook any avenue for making the "Not Guilty" verdict inevitable. So it was that he bought the snowballs, because Lenny had no contempt for caution.

CHAPTER THIRTY-SEVEN

PILLORIED BY PAINFUL PILES THE perturbed prosecutor never-the-less summarised the Crown case to the jury with considerable skill next morning. His scathing scepticism of the convenient coincidences put forward by the defense stopped a sliver short of accusing Lenny of lying. Heavy emphasis was laid upon the heinous nature of the crime against an innocent young boy. The mildly detached manner in which he recapitulated the horrible crime made it sound even more incredibly hideous. The prosecutor knew that elements of his case were demonstrably weak and that the decision to quickly prosecute had been made under political pressure possibly because of the forthcoming election. So he directed his most strident verbal assault at the reasons why the defense refused to allow Erwin to testify. Erwin had simply read a brief and unsworn statement from the dock and thus could not be cross examined.

The prosecutor did so well that a number of people in the gallery thought there was a fair chance that the jury might have been persuaded to convict. But Ian knew that the final say rested with the defense and he never underestimated Lenny's ability. Having summed up the case for the prosecution, the prosecutor, pain free on a recently inserted suppository, gave a spirited final appeal to the jury to make the community more secure by putting Erwin in prison.

Lenny began the defense case by moving around the court in a manner that was not prohibited but was sufficiently unusual that it earned him several looks of displeasure from the judge. Succinctly, Lenny reviewed the police human evidence and reiterated that every shred of police identification was flawed to such a degree that it was unsafe and should be disregarded. In his perambulations Lenny's proximity to Erwin made Erwin seem less forbidding by comparison.

Lenny stood before the accused as he dissected and damaged the identification evidence of the witnesses around Central Park. Lenny asserted to the jury that his client categorically denied ever having been in Central Park. Lenny theatrically dry washed his hands, a la Pontius Pilate, before moving to stand in front of the witness box. From that position with effective voice inflexions and cadence he discredited the weak evidence of the trainer shoe imprint reiterating the fact that no such trainers had been found that belonged to Erwin and that thousands of the same size and pattern were sold in Melbourne.

As to the blood stained paper towel, Lenny was sincere in expression as he sympathised with the police in assuming that they genuinely believed it to be an authentic clue. Lenny chose not to contest the DNA evidence but did emphasise the incompetent manner of its collection and probable contamination. Lenny's expression became sombre as he related the reasonableness of the presence of the square of paper towel and that the testimony regarding it was unshaken. He paced the court room floor in an attempt to demonstrate distances to the jury to stress parts of the evidence of Dr Sleet, the weather expert.

At one point in his travels he was momentarily standing on the short stretch of white floor tiles leading from the jury box steps to the jury room. Given the height of the judicial bench and the height of the jury box partition, Lenny's hands were out of sight. Lenny's left hand swiftly reached into his pocket, grasped many pieces of coconut shavings that he had salvaged from his previous night's indulgence in snowball quaffing. He sprinkled the coconut pieces on to the tiles. The sprinkling went totally unobserved and raised no suspicion. Lenny's black robe covered the motion entirely. Effectively Lenny had taken a further step towards being a shyster lawyer; a lawyer perverting the cause of justice for personal gain. Resuming his pacing Lenny reminded the jury that, on the evidence of the police themselves, many tins of mushrooms were found in Erwin's residence after police smashed in the door to gain access. So why then did the prosecutor cast doubt on Erwin's mushroom gathering? That activity is entirely innocent; thousands of people do it every year.

Lenny reminded the jury that the police had placed a lot of weight upon the fact there were pornographic magazines in Erwin's residence as also were books, which the prosecutor claimed, were evidence of Erwin's identification with the Nazi party. Lenny asked the rhetorical question as to the provenance of the literature, "Were the magazines permitted to be legally sold"? And "Did not the State Library of Victoria classify the books as European History"? "Why then this condemnation"? Possession of the magazines and books was absolutely lawful. Inferences of homicidal tendencies drawn from the literature came from the imagination of the police and prosecution and were not fact only circumstantial but poor circumstantial evidence at that.

And Lenny's look at the jury convinced him that his dismissal of claims of the prosecutor had scored. As for the opportunity, the other essential element in a crime, half of the criminal population of Melbourne had opportunity. From a list of convicted sex offenders now out of jail, Lenny had earlier asked if the police had checked the alibi of ...and Lenny read out twenty six names. Lenny dwelt upon the list of recorded sex offenders and the lack of police action to check them when, through mistaken identification, they focused in on Erwin as their victim to score favourable publicity by making a quick arrest.

Lenny described the heinous crime to a degree beyond that of the prosecutor but Lenny turned the concept of public concern into the reason why the police had rushed to arrest Erwin, a person with no substantial criminal record, a person studying to be a Real Estate Representative, a person whose residence was broken into, a person whose vehicle had been dismantled without result, a person linked to the crime only by police inferences drawn incorrectly from explainable coincidence.

"Every person accused of a crime had the right of silence", Lenny told the jury. That right is enshrined in law to protect the innocent as its primary purpose. Erwin had been falsely accused and suffered as a result. Lenny asked of the jury "Is it fair that he now voluntarily surrender a right simply to please the prosecutor", he argued that point in different ways for over thirty minutes and told the jury several times that Erwin was not required to prove he was innocent. Lenny's oration was masterly in delivery and masterly in timing. He wanted to allow the judge insufficient time for a summing up prior to the lunch time adjournment. And he wanted to deliver a most telling verbal blow and he did that by referring, at last, to the piece of broken fingernail proven by DNA to be Erwin's.

Lenny cast doubt upon where it had been found. Was it truly found on the driver's side floor of the Ford Falcon or was it actually found in Erwin's residence? The police had admitted that the blood stained paper towel, a square of evidence they regarded as crucial was contaminated. Could they not be mistaken again? Did some police person succumb to pressure? After all, the fingernail fragment was not found until the search warrant on Erwin's house had been executed. "But assuming", said Lenny "that the fingernail fragment was found in the Ford Falcon, there was a completely reasonable explanation. It had been in the sole pattern of a shoe and carried to and left in the rented car".

Lenny said a few more words about reasonable doubt, not emphasised so much for his own speech but rather as a lead in to what he knew the judge would have to tell the jury in his summation. Lenny stood before the jury and again referred to the fingernail fragment. He assured them it was entirely probable not just possible. Lenny invited the jury to inspect the soles of their own footwear at their first available opportunity. Lenny sat down, the judge called for a lunch time adjournment and the jury walked purposely toward the jury room, tramping through the vestiges of coconut from Lenny's snowball feast, to sit in the jury room and examine the soles of their respective footwear. Lenny learned later that most of them did just that. Most found one or two pieces of squashed desiccated coconut. The coconut curiously resembled a fingernail fragment. The practical example was powerfully persuasive.

The trial resumed with the post prandial entry of the judge. He knew that this was the first time when all eyes and ears were his. His was the last real word. His summing up of the case would highly influence the jury and he adopted a mid tone of voice devoid as far as possible of inflexions that might be considered advantageous to one or other of the two verbal gladiators who had performed in the contest. However when he looked at the accused, Erwin, his facial expression betrayed distaste he could not totally suppress.

The judge directed the jury on aspects of the law relevant to the case. He fairly and objectively advised that the onus of proof rested with the prosecution and summed up the major elements of the police investigation making precise distinctions between evidence corroborated and presumed. His Honour instructed the jury that two components essential to safely convict an accused of murder are "Mens Rea" or the intent to kill, and the "Actus Rea" the act of killing. It was the prerogative of the jury to determine whether or not the prosecution had satisfactorily proven both components.

Similarly in measured mien, the judge summed up the defense case and instructed the jury that they must not misconstrue the exercise by Erwin of his legal right not to take the witness stand. The jury were advised that they couldn't impute adverse conclusions on the refusal of the defendant to give evidence. The judge spoke of rules of evidence and that the jury alone determine what is or is not a fact.

After nearly an hour the essence of his influence on the jury was encapsulated in his dissertation on the law in relation to reasonable doubt and how it may be applied to this case. If the jury believed that unreliable evidence or insufficient evidence was present then those deficiencies constituted reasonable doubt. If there be reasonable doubt then the only option for a jury is to deliver a verdict of "Not Guilty". Only if the facts point to guilt beyond reasonable doubt would it be safe to convict. The judge then directed the jury to assemble in the jury room to consider their verdict. He adjourned the trial, rose and retired to his chambers.

One hour and twelve minutes later, that is eighteen minutes before the end of the Court's day, the Court reassembled on being told that the jury had reached a verdict. Gallery visitors flocked back in, print and electronic media people congregated as near as legally possible to the boundary of the Court precinct. All attention was directed at the medium sized, moustachioed, air conditioning installations manager who had been elected by the jury as their foreman. In formal tone the judge asked the jury foreman if a verdict had been reached and received a "Yes" response. The judge addressed the foreman again to ask if all agreed the verdict, and another "Yes" was the response. "Please tell the Court your verdict", said the judge. He was not surprised to be told "Not Guilty".

The decision of a jury to acquit an accused in a criminal trial is sovereign. No appeal is possible save in the most extraordinary circumstances. As

Lenny could not detect any evidence that members of the jury had been bribed or coerced into reaching the "Not Guilty" verdict, then he concluded that his client, Erwin, was free for life of any legal censure for the hideous rape and murder of the young boy.

That did not mean that Erwin was innocent in the eyes of the majority of the public. Nor necessarily innocent in Lenny's estimation. But that was immaterial because Lenny the lanky lawyer had the ability to be selective in his assessment of clients with unfettered ability to pay his fees. Human conscience is notoriously elastic. The suffering of a beloved son and grandson was simply a technicality in the adversarial system of Law, of which Lenny was a proud practitioner.

The judge thanked the jury and formally discharged Erwin. The judge then rose and retired again to his chambers convinced that the rule of the law had been upheld but justice had not resulted. Given the paucity of police evidence and Lenny's demolition of the strongest forensic items any opportunity for the judge to delicately influence the jury was denied. The judge sometimes entertained reservations about Lenny's court room performances. Had he known of the shredded coconut he would have called a mistrial.

Most of the public gallery patrons deplored the decision and indignantly departed. The few with the weird clothes and facial piercings left disappointed too. They had tried to lean over the gallery balustrade to wave to Erwin but by the time they got there he had gone. Notwithstanding that disappointment they took comfort because Erwin's victory seemed to prove their claim that society was disintegrating.

Back in his chambers the prosecutor spoke harsh words to the police about the contaminated evidence, then took his painful piles to his proctologist. The police team accepted the jury's decision badly. The Detective Inspector in charge of the investigation bitterly condemned himself in private for yielding to the political push for an early arrest. He firmly resolved to resist pressure in future, no matter where it came from, if indeed he had a future.

Senior Sergeant Jarvis of the Vice Squad heard of Erwin's exoneration after he had put the finishing touches to his plan to raid an inner city den of drugs and unlicensed prostitution later that night. He knew that Erwin had been at Central Park and he could have proved it. He had not. Now his conscience was beginning to trouble him. Jarvis was considered the best raider in the Vice Squad. He now gave thought to how he could track Erwin to a place he could raid. Almost ten years had passed since a police raid had led to a fatality. It was about time for another in his opinion.

The media were deployed in their benchmark push and shove scrum, shouting predicable questions and hoping that by provoking the winner into a response on the wings of euphoria or the distraught and disappointed family in the abyss of grief, a newsworthy quote may emerge. In both cases they were disappointed.

Lenny led Erwin through the jostling pack. Erwin had strict instructions not to open his mouth. He mainly complied with Lenny's instruction but could not restrain the smile of contempt he had for media who portrayed him as a malicious perverted killer and who had now been proven wrong by a jury. To demonstrate his utter contempt he paused and glared around. The media closed even more tightly around him in anticipation of something, anything reportable to justify their lengthy wait on the courthouse pavement. Erwin did not oblige the media with quotable quotes. But he did enjoy the attention of being notorious. At last he responded to the pressure of Lenny's long fingers squeezing his arm and propelling him towards the traffic lights and thence to Lenny's chambers in the building opposite. Lenny acknowledged the congratulations of legal colleagues on the way.

With every indication that Erwin would remain silent, a small contingent of the media concentrated on the exhibitionist performances of the weirdly dressed, tattooed, abundantly pierced members of Erwin's unofficial fan club. News reports attracted much public condemnation deflecting community outrage towards them and away from Erwin. Lenny's throw away line to the media was that he was a public benefactor for keeping the coppers honest, the cops couldn't get away with framing an innocent man because of their incompetence, let the lazy cops go out and find the real killer who was a danger to society and still at large. "Condemn the cops not my innocent client" was Lenny's last line.

Erwin's flaunting of his freedom and contempt for the crowd did a favour for Ian's family, albeit inadvertently. His behaviour drew the media attention away from Ian's desolate family. They managed to slip away into the underground rail loop station. An intrusion into their silent surround of pain would have been exceptionally unwelcome.

CHAPTER THIRTY-EIGHT

REVENGE. REVENGE, ABSOLUTELY DEVOID OF even a quark of highly strained pity. Revenge teetering on the cusp of obsession assailed Ian in unremitting waves. The hideous crime against his cherished grandson infected his family with a depressive degree of self destruction as certain and deadly as the Black Plague. If it were possible to add another element of distress to the unbearable, then the exoneration of Erwin by the Court imposed that.

Ian held his grey haired head in his hands as he stared at the two files situated between his elbows on the desk in his office. Retrieved from his hidden safe, one file was five centimetres thick and the cover was creased and stained by age and usage. No name adorned the cardboard cover; it would have been superfluous because only Ian knew that it referred to the brilliantly shrewd, cautious yet audacious, merciless, millionaire mass murderer, Bryn Hamley, a.k.a. "Johnny".

The second, newer, file contained less than two centimetres of paper sheets. Most of the information printed on the sheets were notes made by Ian at the appearances by Erwin at hearings such as the extradition, bail application and the flawed trial, that provided future immunity against prosecution to the muscular murderer. Ian's notes included opinions conveyed to him by friends in the force that Erwin was undoubtedly a serial rapist murderer. Although not introduced as evidence in Court, a private psychiatrist engaged by the police had observed Erwin during several sessions of police interrogations and opined that Erwin exhibited a more than normal number of the aberrant behavioural characteristics of a psychopath. All attempts by the police to have Erwin examined in a proper consultation were thwarted by Lenny. The psychiatrist expressed disappointment at Lenny's obstruction and thereafter referred to him, in private, as Lenny the legal leper.

Adding weight to Ian's accumulation of circumstantial evidence about Erwin were five other unsolved rape/mutilation/murders of young boys in other States. Two common factors in these cases matched the atrocities perpetuated on Ian's grandson. One was the horrendous injuries, the other the absence of evidence. Ian appreciated that only luck had led police to Erwin. The planning and precautions taken by the offender to avoid discovery were thorough in most aspects. The precautions confirmed to Ian that Erwin was the multiple murderer and Erwin must be eliminated to protect other young boys from falling victim to the psychotic predator. And for Ian to assuage his seething urge for vengeance.

Ian began another reading of the files looking for a way of conflicting the muscular mass murderer Erwin with the intelligent mass murderer Bryn. Several hours of reading Bryn's file produced no opportunities until the name of Bryn's startlingly successful company, ECARUT seemed to revive a vague memory. Ian had read the name before, many times, and knew it to be part of Bryn's business domain, but where had he seen it in a different place? Importantly, where had he read it in a context close to Erwin?

Pushing aside the unread part of the file on Bryn, Ian opened the slimmer file on Erwin. The first pages were notes of his own observations compiled after following Erwin for several weeks after his release. He knew Erwin's address and phone numbers. He saw Erwin visiting several showrooms of four wheel drive specialists and saw that Erwin traded in his red Mercedes Benz sports car for a massive 4.5 litre turbo four wheel drive off-road vehicle with an exceptionally intimidating bull bar. Ian surmised that Erwin's recent court victory inspired an escalation in belligerence with which a small red sports car was ill matched. The dark green four wheel drive was probably the nearest legal road vehicle to a tank or Nazi panzer that Erwin could obtain. Ian noted the registration number as an automatic action.

Ian had followed Erwin to a Post Office and recorded the number of the post box from which Erwin collected his mail and he had written down the dates and times that Erwin had visited his bank and the office of the trustee administering the substantial legacy, the source of Erwin's bountiful monthly allowance. Ian knew which pubs, take-aways and restaurants Erwin favoured and even where he had his close cropped hair cut. But nowhere in those notes did Ian see the name ECARUT.

Puzzled, but still convinced he had seen ECARUT mentioned somewhere, Ian read through the other information in the Erwin file. Ian's confidence in his recollection was beginning to wane when he found several of the hand written sheets faxed to him by the TAFE employee who had advised of Erwin's progress in the correspondence course for a Real Estate Representatives Certificate. Near the bottom of the fourth page was a memorandum stating that several real estate agencies and property companies had been in touch with TAFE following the publishing on the TAFE web site of the marks attained by students at the final exam. Among the dozen companies that had expressed interest in offering employment to the achievers of high marks was ECARUT.

Ian realised that he had a connection to use to bring together the two killers. From a public telephone Ian contacted the personnel Manager of ECARUT. Purporting to be a TAFE student counsellor he learned that Erwin had not responded to the invitation from ECARUT to attend an interview. The Personnel Manager made the most of his opportunity to establish good relations with an educational institution that produced graduate students who ECARUT may need as its business expanded. In return, Ian extolled the attributes of Erwin and promised to exert influence to have the excellent student reply. Ian persuaded the ebullient Personal Manager to fax a copy of his letter to Erwin at the TAFE.

Ian was assured that the fax would be sent within half an hour and contrived to wait by the TAFE fax machine and obtain the letter. During that half hour, Ian pondered on the perspicacity of the Personal Manager who spoke so intelligently on the telephone about employment prospects but was so dumb that he did not associate the unusual name of Erwin Dormunt with the name that had been front page news for days. Ian inferred from this that his half formed idea about how to juxtapose Erwin and Bryn was well worth the extra effort in the light of the Manager's unenlightenment.

The result was Ian's fake letter. Bearing the name and post office box of Erwin it opened by politely responding to the Personnel Manager's offer of employment. "Erwin's" second paragraph apologised for not replying earlier. It was the final paragraph of the forged letter that Ian judged would precipitate Erwin's destruction. It read "I read that an old friend of my family, Bryn Hamley, is now Chairman of the Board of ECARUT and as character references for me I suggest he may care to initiate a deep conversation with Raymond M Woodbury late of Knoxfield and Ms Dolores Regos late of South Melbourne. Although each has recently left their address I am certain that Mr Hamley will know where they are now and I am looking forward to a very rewarding appointment with your company". The concluding salutation read "Warmest regards until I see you", signed Erwin Dormunt.

To thrive in the private investigation business an operator has to develop a feral cunning. Ian was one of the most successful operators for three decades. His investigation history clearly demonstrated that he had no contempt for caution but he had no hesitation in acting with the speed of a striking mongoose when an unbidden enhancement to "Erwin's letter" flashed through his consciousness. Ian recognised the thought for what it was; a mixture of past experiences and intuitive prescience that Dolores would have treasured. So he checked the telephone directory and keyed onto the heading of "Erwin's letter" the office telephone number of Lenny.

Ian had taken precautions to ensure no fingerprints or other traces of contact material would cause forensic identification with him and he signed Erwin's name with his left hand. To ensure an easily identifiable link between this and other letters that may follow, Ian put a pin hole in the top right hand corner. Using equal care, Ian sealed the letter in a self sealing envelope and posted it to the Personnel Manager of ECARUT. He went to a café for a brain stimulating coffee and another session of serious thinking. Past experience had taught Ian that there were some situations where every single step of an investigation involving people manipulation required to be planned to an incredible degree. Other situations required a charging bull approach to create considerable collateral damage and use the fragments to create a mosaic to better depict the criminal activity.

Ian's experience was not altogether applicable to his present undertaking, an execution by proxy. And his proxy, Bryn was a smart and experienced executioner. But Ian could not be certain that simply posing a threat to Bryn by a letter from Erwin would be enough incitement. Indeed if Bryn were to conduct a conversation with Erwin then Bryn might conclude that Erwin knew nothing of the murderous journey taken by Bryn to establish the ECARUT empire. Should that happen then the unthinkable could eventuate; a collaboration between the two multiple murderers. To avoid that possibility Ian needed to heap more serious threats against Bryn. Threats that clearly emanated from Erwin.

Random observations of Bryn were complimented by Ian's reading of financial media reports of the wonder boy of residential finance. From these he concluded that Bryn had shed his cloak of criminal obscurity and now sought the golden glare of celebrity status. Ian reasoned that Bryn had drowned his pseudo personage of Johnny when he fed to the sharks the people most dangerous to his new life style.

Ian appreciated that he had sufficient persuasive evidence to submit to the Australian Securities and Investments Commission, to at least cause ASIC to open a file. However Ian remained sceptical about any actions that ASIC may take having noted that a flamboyant conman from South Africa allegedly defrauded individuals, banks and financial institutions of up to $30 million and escaped, despite numerous complaints by victims to ASIC over a three year period.

Another debacle that Ian remembered was the massive collapse of a large property company in Western Australia. Rumours of its precarious business methods were circulating around financial circles for years. The property company eventually collapsed owing around $320 million and sections of the property media and financial industry expressed serious dissatisfaction at the lack of ASIC action for so long. So for Ian to submit detailed reports to ASIC in an endeavour to humiliate Bryn to the point of murdering Erwin seemed pointless. It would not be improbable that his submission could rebound and that ASIC's first target might be Ian himself.

Ian reassessed his mission to have Bryn kill Erwin and decided that success required a more spirited attack on Bryn. Without doubt Bryn had acted speedily whenever his business was in jeopardy. But Bryn's emergence as a celebrity presented an opening for an attack that had not existed when Bryn was a nonentity, an obscure, very obscure, businessman. An attack on Bryn's reputation at that time may have caused minor anguish and even an element of injured pride. However Bryn now basked in public adulation prior to his wedding to a beautiful young lady of impeccable social pedigree. Bryn never had to protect this elevated position previously. It was Ian's conclusion that Bryn was vulnerable due to his vanity. Ian decided to strike at that vanity and to make it appear that Erwin was the striker. Ian used the outdated computer he kept solely for word processing purposes on which to prepare "Erwin's" response to ECARUT and on the same computer he now composed a series of letters addressed to persons named in the financial media as prospective directors of ECARUT, prior to the company being listed on the ASX.

As the sender, each letter bore the name and address of a person listed as a director of one of Bryn's bodgy companies, now many years extinct after being absorbed into ECARUT. Each letter alleged that Bryn was a thief, money launderer and taxation evader on such a scale as to bring ECARUT under scrutiny from both ASIC and the Australian Taxation Office. Each letter provided a few verifiable facts about an extinct company used as a front by Bryn.

Ian reasoned that an accusation of fraud would stir the prospective ECARUT directors much more violently than any accusation of murder. Ian mailed letters to Bryn's future ECARUT directors and to the senior staff of ECARUT. Each was pin holed in the top right hand corner and each was prepared so as to offer no clues should it be forensically examined. Ian had no contempt for caution. Ian was sure that many of the recipients of the poison pen letters would give the originals to Bryn. Recipients may not attribute any significance to a pin hole but Ian was certain that Bryn would appreciate that the pin hole on each of the letters signalled, "I've got you".

Timing was Ian's principal problem. How long after sending the "Erwin response" to ECARUT should he wait before posting the poison pen letters as a follow-up? He needed to speculate on how much time should elapse before the Personnel Manager of ECARUT discussed Erwin's response with Bryn and he had no way of accurately assessing that. He considered posing again as a student counsellor and phoning the Personnel Manager but decided against it.

Ian felt it would be better if Bryn was acquainted with Erwin's partially veiled but potentially lethal threats two days before the other letters began to be referred to him. Ian wanted Bryn to seethe at Erwin's threat and then to be moved into a rage of action against Erwin at the impending threat to his reputation and freedom by the other letters. The combined fear and hatred should provoke immediate action fatal to Erwin.

Two days seemed sufficient. In two days Bryn would know all about Erwin. Unlike the ECARUT Personnel Manager, Bryn would know who Erwin was. Ian was certain that Bryn kept up to date with the news. And when Bryn realised the identity of the person who appeared intent upon blackmailing, humiliating and destroying him, Bryn would be forced to kill the child killer without delay. So Ian hoped.

So two days after sending the pin holed punctured letter from Erwin, Ian mailed the other pin holed punctured poison pen letters.

As events transpired, Ian's timing proved to be way off.

CHAPTER THIRTY-NINE

ERWIN'S PRESENTATION OF A SIX figure bank cheque from his trust account payable to Lenny made both of them feel good and in the mood of euphoria, Lenny gave Erwin practical survival advice.

"Watch out for surveillance" Lenny said, several times. "Police can be vindictive bastards when they lose a much publicised case and they may try to get you on trumped up charges, such as shoplifting or road traffic violations". Those were Lenny's words but the hidden meaning was a warning to Erwin not to go looking for out of the ordinary sexual experiences. Lenny knew that frustration caused by abstinence from sexual activity due to several months of incarceration, combined with the over confidence often engendered by an exoneration, made the survivor feel bullet proof. This typical invulnerable reaction could generate contempt for the police and lead to another arrest.

Much and all as Lenny appreciated being promptly paid for Erwin's defense, he did not want any immediate interruptions to his plan for another bankruptcy. Once he had safely transmitted a substantial portion of Erwin's fee to his Swiss Bank and stored the remainder in cash to cover incidental expenses, he had a holiday planned. Lenny doubted that the police really would pursue Erwin so close to the conclusion of the trial because that would be publicly perceived as harassment. But it cost him nothing to give the advice and it could cause Erwin to be cautious. It also made Lenny appear avuncular and thus reinforce with Erwin that Lenny was the lawyer of first choice when he ran foul of the law enforcement authorities next time.

Erwin mumbled something about putting any copper who followed him into a coffin and Lenny had to adopt the role of avuncular counsellor again to convince Erwin that the police sometimes seek to entrap fine upstanding citizens. They provoke a one-on-one confrontation, Lenny told Erwin, but with immediate unseen back-up to justify them inflicting painful and frequently permanent injury. Lenny's larynx worked overtime in an up and down motion as he spoke earnestly to convince Erwin that the smart thing to do, the thing that equated to a two finger salute and was infinitely more insulting, was simply to look the undercover cop in the eyes, smile and shrug and thereafter completely ignore him.

Lenny little realised that Erwin's acceptance of his advice would, over the next weeks cause a score of innocent citizens; male and female, to become the recipients of a glare, contemptuous grin and shrug from a muscular thug. Some were so badly traumatised that they needed a cup of tea, an aspro and a lay down to recover.

One matter Lenny raised again with Erwin was that it would certainly be advantageous for Erwin to have regular employment and Erwin reluctantly agreed. He reminded Lenny of the successful completion of a Real Estate Representatives course while on the inside. Lenny had overlooked that achievement but promised to "see what he could do" to assist Erwin find employment with opportunities suited to Erwin's talents. Privately, Lenny felt that Erwin could be extremely successful in the eviction of recalcitrant tenants. Unpalatable through Lenny's advices were Erwin accepted them. He was out now and did not want any restrictions on his freedom.

All during his "inside" time Erwin had worried about his car. He was told that it was securely locked in a police garage. His worries were exacerbated by comments from other inmates who told him that police mechanics could pull apart anything but when it came to reassembling they were renowned for sloppy work. Erwin presumed that comments of that nature by some prisoners were heavily loaded with envy. Word spread that Erwin owned a near-new Mercedes sports car that was dismantled by the police in a vain search for forensic evidence to support their charge of murder.

Erwin tended to believe some prisoners, particularly when they spoke in terms indicating they had mechanical training. One prisoner told how police deliberately sabotaged a front wheel alignment. He claimed that he had a brother who fell victim to precisely that type of a police scam. He said that his brother's car was pulled apart in a fruitless search for a pistol that police claimed was used in a hold up. The police put the car together again and returned it to him. The police made no mention of the dozen or so washers, nuts and springs that were left over. The day after the brother was released on bail he was stopped by a patrol car and the patrol officer issued an unroadworthy notice on the grounds of mechanical defects. The prisoner told anyone who would listen that it was a set-up designed to harass his innocent brother.

Some prisoners denigrated the police claiming they knew of someone who had a car impounded and experienced difficulties in having it released. When the car was released it had 20,000 more kilometres on the odometer than it did when impounded and the brake pads were dangerously worn down. Stories like these unsettled Erwin especially when he had so much time to brood. Erwin came to believe that his much loved Mercedes was tainted by police hands wandering all over her parts. He made up his mind to trade-in the Mercedes. He weighed up the relative merits of many types of vehicles that featured in motoring magazines he read in the prison library.

Erwin couldn't help noticing that pages listed in the index of the motoring magazines as dealing with locking devices or vehicle security systems were missing. He thought at first that the authorities may have ordered them removed until Vincent told him that library workers tore out those types of pages and arranged for delivery to prisoners with records relating to car theft. Those inmates were keen to ensure that their professional qualifications were not diminished due to any temporary inability to pursue their trade. It was comparable to an Accountant maintaining Continuing Professional Education.

Erwin opened one motoring magazine to reveal a photograph of an SUV four wheel drive vehicle that the magazine reviewer described as "The Beast". The accompanying technical description boasted that the 4.5 litre turbo engine was the biggest non-commercial power plant sold and that the enormous bull bar surrounding the front-mounted winch was the heaviest permitted on the road.

Erwin fell in love instantly. Only two days after reclaiming his Mercedes, Erwin was the proud owner of a dark green "Beast". Sitting behind the wheel at such an elevation gave him a sense of power that he never experienced in the low-slung Mercedes. And the CB radio, a state of the art detector set to signal police radar speed cameras and GPS gave to Erwin the feel of riding in a tank. True the 88 millimetre gun was not poking out in front, but he could imagine it. He wondered if he could obtain even greater satisfaction were he to have the body re-sprayed in panzer mottled grey and the insignia of the Nazi Waffen SS painted on the front doors.

On the road the Beast was a delight to handle. The modified exhaust produced a gut gripping shrieking roar when his foot flattened the accelerator pedal and the entire mass flowed forward with startling velocity. The Beast cowered other drivers. When the massive bull bar appeared in a rear view mirror most drivers promptly peeled over to allow him to pass. Even in dense traffic vehicles found a way to allow him unimpeded progress. Any recalcitrant or inattentive driver who failed to promptly pull aside risked the shattering blast of the super sized carillon of horns.

Erwin felt immortal when riding behind the powered steering wheel of his enormous beast. He felt superior to drivers of the lowly mass of inferior vehicles and was not unaffected by the phallic symbolism of the frightening forward slanting shiny black bull bar. Even the fact that it cost half a wallet of banknotes to fill the gigantic petrol tank did not diminish his imagination of himself as the Kommandant of the incomparable, attention attracting, mechanical monster. To flaunt the Beast in venues where the audience are most appreciative, Erwin returned to meetings of the Neo Nazi white supremacy fanatics. He was accorded the status of a prodigal son by many of the warped brained members of the association and participated with renewed enthusiasm in various activities, with one of which he became infatuated. The subject was that of bomb making.

Erwin's months in prison became his passport for entry to the innermost secret division of the organisation. There was no way he could be an undercover cop. And his release from prison was incorrectly attributed to his own superior circumvention of the law rather that the actions of his shyster lawyer, so his status within the association was further elevated. The manipulative David Koresh replica who held sway over the mass of ignorant, envious, mainly work shy, Neo Nazi members recognised Erwin as easily motivated cannon fodder. At one meeting Erwin was awarded a book as a prize. Receipt of a book disappointed Erwin. Until he thumbed through it to the section containing black and white photographs of Nazi SS Colonel Otto Skorzney and saw that the book was his astounding biography.

Erwin read the biography several times and imperceptibly began to identity himself with the extra-ordinary Austrian commando who daringly freed Mussolini from internment, abducted the Regent of Hungary and carried out sabotage operations in Hitler's last gamble, known as the Battle of the Bulge, in the Ardennes just before Christmas 1944. Like Erwin, Skorzney stood trial for his freedom, accused of being a war criminal. Also like Erwin, Skorzney was acquitted. How Erwin rationalised his own status as a hero for raping and murdering young boys is a mystery that only a team of criminal psychiatrists could unravel. But Erwin identified with Skorzney, a true war hero, with whom he shared Germanic blood.

Erwin's unquestioning absorption and adoption of every anti-social piece of drivel uttered by the Neo Nazi "leader', his "Fuhrer", together with Erwin's regular contribution of one hundred dollar notes elevated him into the inner circles of the Knights of Socialist Australia. Seldom did inner circle numbers exceed ten. Precautions were taken to ensure that KSA members were informed by means not subject to interception of the date, time and venue of each assembly. KSA members were taught techniques to avoid being followed and Erwin dutifully applied these techniques against the horde of undercover cops he imagined constantly on his tail.

Ian followed Erwin once or twice a week. Even using disguises it was inviting discovery for one man to try to trail another, aware person, more often than that. Erwin lost Ian more than once in a direct trail. Ian was reluctant to attach an electronic tracker transmitter because he suspected that one may already be attached. As Ian followed Erwin he saw that someone else was doing a similar job. That made Ian doubly cautious. Brief glimpses of the vehicles and equipment being used convinced Ian that the followers were not Victoria State Police but either Australian Federal Police, the AFP, or the Australian Security and Intelligence Organisation, ASIO. Ian altered his usual trailing technique and kept further away making far more use of his night vision binoculars than he preferred.

It was only after he observed that the shadowy trailers appeared to be alternating surveillance on all of the KSA men that Ian concluded that Erwin was not the exclusive person of interest so Ian persisted in his intermittent trailing efforts. Ian's efforts were made easy by Erwin's habit of driving the Beast at normal speed in a certain direction then veering off at a dangerously high speed, Erwin frequently ignored red traffic lights and even one way street signs. When Ian lost Erwin he consulted his street directory and drove around the area in a grid search. He always found the highly visible Beast parked about three kilometres from Erwin's veering off point. Ian knew that Erwin was a lazy bastard when it came to walking. So Ian would circle on his street map the equivalent of a five minute walk. Somewhere within the circle would be a meeting of the KSA and a quartering of the streets usually enabled him to locate the meeting place.

If Ian saw Erwin load an insulated bottle carrier into the Beast then he knew to look for a garage with lights on. If no bottle carrier then it was odds on the meeting place was a pub. The other "shadows" learned that too, so Ian approached with extra caution and if he spotted a shadow then he abandoned any further attempt to get closer. He checked for tracker transmitters on his car then went home in a way that made sure he was not being followed. Ian wanted no contact with the AFP or ASIO because that would entail compilations. He did not want complications because he was intent on manoeuvring to have Erwin murdered. Complications could lead to conclusions of his complicity in Erwin's death and he wanted no recognition of his involvement that could lead to charges.

Ian's retreats in order to investigate again were no defeat, only sensible tactics. Ian had no contempt for caution.

CHAPTER FORTY

THE PERSONNEL MANAGER OF ECARUT read "Erwin's" letter with increasing concern. He had no way of knowing the implicit threat contained in the references to the referees, but he did clearly appreciate the potential threat to his own power if he hired an employee in a junior position who appeared to have a channel of direct access to the Chairman of the Company. On the other hand, he mused, if he neglected to hire such an evidently brilliant student he could be in trouble if any of the referees mentioned to the Chairman, Bryn Hamley, that Erwin was overlooked for a job that he seemed abundantly qualified to perform.

Procrastination, wrote the great literary alumni Charles Dickens, is the thief of time. Over fifteen hundred years earlier, the New Testament Gospel of St Matthew counselled believers that "sufficient unto the day is the evil thereof". The Personnel Manager elected to adopt the advice of the earlier author. Accordingly, he picked up Erwin's letter and in so doing his fingertip discovered the pin hole perforation in the top right corner of the letter as he filed it with "Pending" material. Ian's scheme to have Bryn advised in advance of the corrosive contents of the communication completely collapsed.

Two days later by a quirk of the Australian Postal system, Ian's anonymous poison pen letters were delivered to ECARUT's address at their headquarters in Mornington, fifty kilometres as the crow flies from

Melbourne's Central Business District, at roughly the same time as the remaining letters were delivered to CBD addresses.

Being drilled in conscientious attention to customer service, the young ladies attending to mail distribution made short work of delivery of letters marked "Confidential" addressed to each of the senior managers of ECARUT. Each manager opened his letter without delay. Each manager was repelled by the accusations against their Chairman, whilst simultaneously being intrigued. Each letter was specific in detailing the name and date of birth of an octogenarian director, the name and registered number of a company, its alleged area of business activity and the date of deregistration. Each letter asked the manager to search ECARUT's historical data base to verify assets improperly transmitted to ECARUT from the person / company mentioned, and determine who was the ultimate beneficiary of the assets. Several chose not to undertake such a search. Others tried but learned only that the databank did not date that far back.

The Manager of ECARUT's Legal and Compliance section called a meeting of other managers in the Board Room when he learned that they had received similar anonymous letters containing details of allegations of wrong doings of the Company Chairman. Although each manager expressed support for Bryn they nevertheless felt an instinctive unease because of the specific detail in each letter.

The Chief Finance Officer, in an act of solidarity, which he hoped may one day stand him in good stead if a vacancy at board level occurred, stood and told the meeting that anonymous allegations were frequently made about prominent people. The allegations were groundless and inspired by envy, he said. Having established his support for the Chairman he proposed that all of the letters be placed in a file and held in safe custody until handed over to the Chairman. Not everyone spontaneously concurred. In particular the Legal and Compliance Manager, the convener of the meeting, counter suggested that the letters be handed to the senior partner of the External Audit firm. He said an independent investigation was warranted to determine the author of the defamatory letters with the intent of taking legal action.

Discussion wavered between the two proposals but eventually it was collectively decided that each manager should retain a photocopy of the letter addressed to him before surrendering the original letter to the

CFO. It would be the Chairman's decision whether or not to take further action. As the managers lined up at the photocopy machine a seemingly insignificant comment about a pin hole in the top corner of the letter caused each manager to further examine his own letter. All agreed that a pin hole existed but only the Personnel Manager guessed that the tiny hole had something to do with Erwin.

The Personnel Manager had received a letter with precise details of dates, company numbers, bank accounts, etc about a car wash company alleged to be bogus and the putative employer of a man named Ray Woodbury who, the letter claimed, had since disappeared without trace. The Personnel Manager realised the name was one he had encountered recently but until the pin hole was mentioned he had not associated it with the letter in his file from a candidate for employment in the property management department. He decided not to mention that letter to the other managers. He would reveal it to the Chairman in private, at a time he deemed most appropriate to enhance his own prospects for advancement. He too had eyes on a position as a director of ECARUT.

He had no objection to the Legal and Compliance Manager telephoning Bryn. Often the monarch tends to hold the delivery of bad news against the messenger and the Personnel Manager did not want to be associated with any dark news. The Personnel Manager preferred to deliver news that offered a monarch a ray of light. But a little while later when the crowd around the photocopy machine had dissipated, he used the machine to make copies of the employment seeking letter signed by Erwin Dormunt.

Every aspiring executive needed to have leverage and spare copies of such a precise list of details may be advantageous in the future. The Personnel Manager had no contempt for caution.

CHAPTER FORTY-ONE

BRYN WAS NOT SCHEDULED TO visit ECARUT's registered office in Mornington that day. Bryn abhorred regular schedules for himself even though he insisted upon them for his ECARUT staff. Bryn set up ECARUT so that he could control operations from his motor cruiser. In the luxurious genuine cedar wood panelled salon on the main desk was a sophisticated, intercept protected, wireless computer that facilitated control.

Alone on the flybridge, Bryn was gliding at mid-throttle due to the wispy patches of fog when he heard the trill-beep-trill signal that indicated receipt of an email on the computer. He remained at the helm for another few minutes until the fog cleared sufficiently for him to confidently vacate the bridge leaving the auto pilot to control the reduced forward speed. The trill-beep-trill began again as he descended to the main deck and approached the computer console to read the screen. The message listed came from a man that Bryn had earnestly cultivated over several months. A man entrenched by birth, inheritance, schooling and consequently social position into the solid centre of the Melbourne establishment and whose name was associated with several blue chip company boards. He liked to be called, deferentially, "Sir Mervyn".

Succinctly, the email asked Bryn to make contact immediately because a distressing communication denigrating Bryn had been received by several associates and himself. Puzzled, Bryn read the other email from the manager of Legal and Compliance at ECARUT that carried a message disturbingly similar to the first. Reasoning that he could more readily deal with the first communication if he were acquainted with details of the second, Bryn reluctantly turned on his mobile phone and pressed the pre call button. His Legal and Compliance manager sounded subduedly panic-stricken and repeated some details twice in his confusion and embarrassment at having to deliver the message about the obnoxious letters.

Bryn listened and his muscular, sun tanned hand, tightened around the mobile phone at such pressure that it tested the quality of construction of the phone casing. His sunny disposition disappeared instantly and his single reply was to order that all letters be held secure until he arrived at Mornington in less than one hour. Bryn then terminated the phone call and moved with intense concentration to the flybridge of the cruiser. He decided to defer calling his blue blood associate, Sir Mervyn, until he had gathered a greater understanding of the accusations in the letters sent to ECARUT.

Flicking off the auto pilot Bryn turned the wheel to port, waited a few seconds for the response to prevent wallowing in a wave trough, then advanced the throttles to fire up the Volvo diesel engines to maximum revs. He made a further minor steering adjustment to take the surging cruiser with its frantically foaming bow wave on a direct course for Mornington. Bryn exceeded the permitted bay limit and wilfully disregarded every tenet of the conduct of vessels in restricted visibility required under the Maritime Safety Act. The beautiful curved bow wave subsided as he eased the throttles and steered the state of the art cruiser to a meeting with the wharf fenders as gently as a kiss to a newborn baby. With athletic agility Bryn set the springers to the wharf bollards, set the intruder alarm, locked the cabin and headed along the grey wooden planks of the wharf to the asphalt ramp leading to the main street and the registered office of his creation. ECARUT.

He attracted quite a few admiring glances from females at sidewalk coffee tables as his tall athletic figure, clothed in a designer label dark blue polo shirt, white fitted trousers and white trainers strode up the slight slope of the street. He angrily pushed aside each of the double doors in the tastefully restored classic façade of an 1860's former bank. Never renowned as an effusive greeter, Bryn maintained that reputation. He stormed stony-faced past the receptionist and several front office staffers without so much as a grunt in response to their cheerfully respectful greetings.

The entrance to the administration area was flanked by a matching set of acarpous miniature lemon trees. The leaves fluttered at the slipstream made by Bryn's enraged stride. He pushed open the door of the office of the manager of Legal and Compliance and walked up to the desk with his hand held out. No greeting, no smile, not even a request but simply an outstretched hand. The manager was awaiting Bryn's arrival and rose from his padded chair behind the large brown laminated topped desk and moved toward a safe in a rear corner. He pushed the numbers of the combination into the keypad before turning the locking lever upwards and swinging the door open. He extracted an A4 manilla envelope and handed it, wordlessly, to Bryn.

Bryn snatched the envelope and quickly withdrew to his own sumptuous office on the other side of the corridor. A few seconds later a dutiful curvaceous young office assistant appeared with a silver tray, a boating race trophy actually, upon which was loaded a silver coffee pot, another of Bryn's boating trophies, filled with Bryn's favourite coffee blend, plus the usual crockery, cutlery and biscuits. But her ambition to impress the boss was thwarted as Bryn curtly waved her away.

While the would-be waitress retreated with an affronted and disappointed expression, Bryn had an intense expression of his own as he read each letter addressed to his senior management team. Bryn was horrified and sickened by the contents of the letters. Names of people, most long dead, names and details of companies now all deregistered, dates that appeared accurate to his well trained memory and statements to the effect that Bryn was a fraud, a money launderer and tax evader on a large scale. Each letter posed the question, "Where is Mr Woodbury now?" or "Miss Regos?" or "Rodney Todd?"

Bryn was plunged into an abyss of depression deeper than the waters surrounding Lady Julia Percy Island. For a full minute his breathing ceased, his face contorted, the tendons around his neck tensed into temporary paralysis and the muscles all over his body hardened to that of a marble statue. The human body has the ability to produce this paroxysm but in the absence of artificial chemicals the inherent survival characteristic of the body over rides the combination of natural hormones produced in reaction to the terrific shock, anger and despair. They are dispersed as the kidneys siphon them off into the bladder. Only when the survival instincts took over did Bryn suck in air and his muscles relaxed leaving painful echoes of the temporary cramp.

Minutes passed as murderous thoughts mingled with suicidal flashes. Bryn contemplated the ruin of his work in life to date; the possible destruction of his reputation, his marriage plans, his financial domain and perhaps even his liberty. And without these accoutrements his ability to be at sea would end. Should he be denied the ability to roam the seaways then life could end for all he cared. Eventually his breathing returned to normal and his heart rate returned from a cataclysmic level that could have killed a man in a lower level of psychical fitness. With the return of his body to more normal operational levels his climactic fury abated and his brain began to operate.

He coughed and swivelled his high backed, leather padded chair around to enable him to open the door of the small refrigerator and take a bottle of mineral water. As Bryn twisted the aluminium cap the pent up gas shushed out and, as if the noise were a signal, a firm knock sounded on the solid decorative panelled door of his office. Bryn was sipping from his bottle when the Personnel Manager eased his way into the office. Bryn's eyes flashed in regenerated fury at the uninvited intrusion and only his still dry throat prevented him roaring to the precocious Personal Manager to get out. The Personnel Manager who had pushed his luck in entering without Bryn's acquiescence, found luck working for him. Acting only on instinct he looked into Bryn's bloodshot eyes and said only eight words. "This is the bloke who wrote the letters". Hearing this, Bryn's vocal chords strangled the roar. The Personnel Manager took several steps forward and laid the file carrying Erwin's letter in the centre of the hand tooled leather desk pad directly in front of Bryn. He took one step backwards, turned and walked out of the office closing the door quietly behind him.

Bryn stared at the file for what seemed to him a long time. The sun tanned hand that he finally extended to open the file was slightly shaking. He slid his chair forward on its castors to better read the letter in the file. He read it several times and with each reading his mind and body returned to normal function. Bryn was not dealing with a supernatural avenger he realised, rather a shake down merchant, and Bryn considered himself the match for any shake down merchant on earth. He now had an aim. To eliminate the tormentor, the blackmailer and destroy the blackmailer's incriminating records. Bryn's emotional equilibrium was slowly restored and he began to plan, an activity at which he was exceptional.

As a priority he realised that ECARUT's senior staff needed reassurance so he pushed buttons on his communication console for a conference call to his senior managers summoning them to a meeting in the Board Room in five minutes. That period gave him time to think and plan his path to the elimination of this Erwin Dormunt. The name rang a bell, as the cliché has it, but which bell evaded him. With his self confidence partly returned, the fact that he could not recall the circumstances with which to immediately associate the name created no self recrimination.

Five minutes later he entered the board room to meet a phalanx of sombre senior managers who were astonished at Bryn's big smile and confident demeanour. With a wave of a now steady hand he invited them to sit. He explained in a tone of total verisimilitude that an extortionist was operating against several emerging companies; all of the targeted companies were on the verge of ASX listing so that the apparently realistic accusations could do damage to them at the particularly sensitive time. No matter about truth, the extortionist's weapon was the threat of retraction of public confidence by starting rumours. If public confidence retreated then the pre-listing float could fail due to the withdrawal of support from the underwriters of the issue. Given the large amount of expenditure necessary to comply with the pre listing ASX requirements, any failure to be listed would have serious consequences on the finances of the company. For undercapitalised companies, a failure would certainly be fatal making them easy prey for the unscrupulous take-over predators.

But for ECARUT, Bryn assured his rapidly relaxing managers, although a listing failure would scratch their capital, it would only be a minor irritation. Bryn exhorted his executives to continue their excellent work and to demonstrate loyalty to ECARUT by helping him squelch the malicious, untrue, unsupported allegations of the extortionist. Bryn told the meeting that all of the allegations contained in the letters they received were spurious. The extortionist had made similar allegations about other companies. Legal action was underway to protect ECARUT and an investigation to identify the culprits was in progress. As he delivered that last line Bryn looked directly into the eyes of his Manager of Personnel. At the time of the glance Bryn was thinking that he would have to give serious consideration to the permanent removal of the Personnel Manager because he knew too much. The Personnel Manager misconstrued the glance as one of appreciation of his efforts in linking Erwin to the malicious letters.

Bryn was so relaxed sitting in the chair of authority at the top of the large polished table that every manager completely accepted every word spoken by Bryn as truth. Bryn invited questions but all seemed so satisfied and reassured that none were posed and the meeting concluded. As the Personnel Manager departed Bryn reached forward and patted him on the arm, a gesture that reinforced the manager's idea that a future promotion was in the offering.

Considering that Bryn had only five minutes to think out his explanation, his performance was brilliant, bordering on genius. The concept he put was logical. Every element contained information that was accepted knowledge in the commercial community. The apparently irrefutable logic dissolved all doubt and re-inspired the managers, such was Bryn's brilliance.

And with his speech as a prototype for explanations to others, Bryn felt more confident. He assumed that all presumptive directors of the soon to be ASX-listed ECARUT would have received a similar scurrilous letter in view of the email sent to his blue blood, colleague, Sir Mervyn. Bryn's next task must be to reassure them. Bryn walked back to Panygyric Five at the Mornington wharf with a hint of a spring in his step. From the mobile phone he called Sir Mervyn and assured him that all of the accusations were lies designed to extract money from Bryn by an extortionist or possible company predator at this sensitive time prior to ASX listing. Bryn suggested that his friend convene a meeting for mid-afternoon next day at which Bryn would report progress on the investigation currently under way to identity and bring to justice the extortionist.

Sir Mervyn appeared mollified but said he still had reservations. Grudgingly he consented to convene the meeting. Bryn resumed his journey back to Melbourne over a sea with subsiding swell under a clearing sky at a speed within the prescribed Port Phillip Bay limit. He allowed his thoughts to drift to his fiancé and the night they planned to spend together. Stephanie had purchased special creams and razors and after a long hot spa they intended to shave all of the hair from each other's lower body.

CHAPTER FORTY-TWO

ERWIN'S INDIGNATION WAS STIMULATED TO fever heat by the KSA leader, an inspirational speaker who made Erwin and his cohorts aware of how this flaccid society deceitfully deprived the Knights. Positive potent people like the Knights of Socialist Australia were deliberately marginalised, they were told by the eloquent orator. Exactly what Australia's democratically elected government had deprived them of was unclear from the convoluted rhetoric of the speaker, but Erwin became convinced that rightful recognition for the essential value of the Knights was cruelly suppressed. He therefore listened with unusual intensity as the next speaker, a less charismatic technician, explained how to make a bomb from readily available materials.

After the bomb making lessons, the inspirational leader resumed. He warned that the reason for teaching them, the chosen elite, how to make a bomb stemmed from their need to defend themselves. It was inevitable, he told them, that the Government would turn the secret police loose on the Knights. At the conclusion of the meeting the technician placed on the table some electrical detonators, each with one red and one black ten centimetre wire protruding, and invited the Knights to take one each for future use. Erwin took three. Walking through a dark lane to the street where he had parked the Beast, Erwin fingered the detonators in his pocket and felt a surge of power. He didn't realise it but if he had fingered the detonators a bit harder anything in the area of his pocket could have been blown away. He also felt the beginnings of an urge to demonstrate his power with another act of murderous sexual depravity but he knew that satisfaction of that desperate desire must remain suppressed until he could be totally certain that he had shaken any police surveillance. His sexual frustration was temporarily appeased. But destructive thoughts towards the manufacture of what the Army of the United States called an I.E.D., an improvised explosive device, arose.

The following morning he awoke reciting the formula for an IED that last night's technical speaker told the Knights was used so effectively in the now infamous Oklahoma outrage. Over breakfast of five Weetbix, toast, sausages, cooked tomato, baked beans, fried mushroom and coffee, Erwin planned his day. Using a street directory, he selected the outer Melbourne suburb of Cranbourne. He knew of a food supermarket close to a large hardware store and the journey of nearly an hour from his home should enable him to identify any followers. Before setting out he carefully examined the underside of the Beast for a tracking device. The KSA regularly warned members about surveillance. At the meeting of the previous evening the Knights leader had expressed the opinion that the Government secret police had them "tagged". Erwin was disappointed at not finding any electronic tag.

He took off in a spin of tyres that showered gravel from the driveway onto garden beds 30 metres away, pushed into traffic with total disregard for the blowing horns of angry motorists and incurred the wrath of the same and other drivers when he braked sharply after a hundred metres and pulled with screeching tyres into a side street where he stopped. Erwin waited to note the details of any vehicles that followed but was disappointed again because no other vehicle entered the side street in pursuit.

Using other side streets memorised from the directory, Erwin drove within the speed limit to a road that allowed entry to the Monash Freeway and slipped into the fast moving traffic without detecting a following vehicle. Spurred on to greater efforts by his intention to buy bomb materials, Erwin took other precautions to be positive he was not being followed. At Dandenong he drove up the freeway off ramp then swung to the other side of the main road and drove down the ramp to continue on the freeway. No vehicle followed. He drove in the centre lane as he approached the Cranbourne turn off, then accelerated across the path of an irate motorist to turn left on the Cranbourne off road.

Again he checked and again saw no pursuit so he decreased speed to that shown on the traffic signs and drove sedately to the supermarket. He bought three, two litre plastic containers of mineral water at the Safeway food store and three nine volt batteries. At the Motor Vehicle supplies store nearby he bought brake fluid, insulation tape and plastic coated copper wire. With these items placed under a towel in the back foot well of the Beast, he walked across the road to the large hardware store and bought a packet of rubber wedges of the type used to stop windows rattling, three mouse traps and a ten kilogram bag of nitrogenous garden fertilizer. Totally satisfied that his purchases were unobserved by anyone likely to remember them, Erwin drove into the town centre for morning tea in the food court of a shopping complex. At that time of the morning young boys were in school so Erwin did not have anything sexually stimulating to look at. After finishing his luke warm coffee he headed back to his house.

He checked his rear view mirrors on the way home more out of habit than expectation of spotting a follower. Had there been a follower then Erwin would surely have seen the vehicle or vehicles in the light traffic but he saw none because there had not been any following by anyone that day. Ian had been too busy doing other things to bring about the demise of the depraved murderer of his grandson to be concerned with trailing the murderer. The Victorian Police did not have the resources available. The Federal anti terrorist squad was on the trail of the manipulative leader of the Knights.

Erwin nearly did to himself what Ian was planning to do as he assembled a bomb based on inadequately memorised assembly instructions. Erwin's certainty that he could not have been identified as the purchaser of the bomb components engendered a degree of confidence unwarranted by such an insignificant non event. And over confidence is a dangerous mood for anyone when assembling a bomb even for an experienced bomb maker, let alone an explosives ignoramus like Erwin. He began by empting the mineral water down the sink without thought to pouring the water on the garden in a city affected by drought. It was the two litre plastic container that Erwin wanted, not the contents. He upended the clear plastic containers on a window ledge where the afternoon sun would quickly dry out the residual water droplets.

Staring at the empty containers he tried hard to recall the sequence of assembly. He recalled the formula for making the explosive compound but realised that he was hazy about some items. As he concentrated, some details returned to his memory and he heated a metal meat skewer over the flame of the gas cooker and pushed the red hot poker into the red screw top on the water container to make two holes. By the time he had completed those punctures the empty container was dry so he took it outside onto grass near a hedge and carefully filled the container with granulated fertilizer.

He measured an amount of brake fluid and poured it slowly over the fertilizer. That caused the fertilizer to change from granular to the consistency of a thick jelly. Erwin poked the pencil thick, silver detonator into the coagulating contents, with the two plastic covered wires protruding. Erwin threaded a wire through each of the holes in the container cap top then pushed the cap down onto the container neck, the force of his push clicking the red cap securely in place by over riding the plastic threads of the screw top. As Erwin recalled the words of the bomb technician he scrambled around his untidy residence looking for items he had forgotten to buy. In the second bottom drawer of a kitchen cabinet he found a couple of stubs of used birthday candles, one of which he lit and used the warm dribbled wax drops to seal around the holes where the two wires protruded from the red cap on the container.

Batteries for power to initiate the detonator were Erwin's next concern. He was absolutely sure that the voltage required was nine volts so he taped a rectangular nine volt battery to the side of the plastic container, a container Erwin now thought of as his bomb. Next came the mousetrap. He prepared it by stripping insulation from a length of copper auto wire and wrapped the bare wire twenty times around the wooden part of the mousetrap so that the spring trap wire slapped down upon that hank of bare copper wires. The other end of that wire he attached to the nine volt battery. Beneath the spring trap wire Erwin inserted a rubber window wedge before tightly winding another length of copper wire several turns to the spring trap wire. In a demonstration of sheer blind stupidity Erwin attached the wire to the other end of the battery then taped the mousetrap to the container. The electrical circuit to the detonator was complete, interrupted only by the rubber window wedge. When that wedge was dislodged the spring trap wire would clamp down on the hank of wire beneath. That contact would complete the electrical circuit, the detonator would discharge and Erwin's bomb would blow. Between Erwin and obliteration was a two cent rubber wedge.

Erwin felt no sense of achievement in having built the bomb. Intellectually, if that term could be sarcastically applied to Erwin, he was convinced that the container on his kitchen table was a bomb but somehow he was unconvinced that it would actually explode. Erwin felt he needed to test it and figured that he had to pull the rubber wedge out from a distance. A not unreasonable assumption. His eyes went darting around and rested on his fishing rod with its reel of fishing line. There appeared to be sufficient line to allow him to reach a safe distance. Erwin decided to drive to a deserted country area, attach the line to the rubber wedge then unreel the fishing line to a safe distance behind a rock or a tree as protection. He would jerk the fishing rod to dislodge the wedge and hope for a big bang. Exactly how big a bang and what damage it would cause he was unable to envisage.

With his mind focused on a test explosion as his next job, Erwin put his bomb into the plastic box he used for fishing tackle. He had to take some items out, a side cast reel, lures, sinkers, spare reels of nylon line and his extra sharp fishing knife to make space. After putting the bomb into the box Erwin had second thoughts and replaced the knife. He noticed a sticky film on the handle of the knife but though no more of it. In fact the film was dried liquid applied by the Victoria Police Forensic Officers some time ago to determine whether or not the fishing knife had been in contact with human blood. The test was negative so the knife had been returned. Daylight was fading as Erwin put the fishing rod and fishing box into the luggage area of the Beast. Erwin decided to leave early the next morning for a sparsely populated area he knew near Anakie, West of Melbourne.

He locked his house and the Beast and walked to a pub that served a good dinner. On the way he passed the Post Office and on reflex took out his key ring and opened his box. Apart from some advertising material which he dropped into the gutter there was only one letter that he opened as he walked. The letter from the property company ECARUT invited Erwin to make phone contact with the Chairman of the company, whose direct mobile phone number was given, to discuss a job. The letter requested that Erwin bring the letter with him to the interview and contained the word "Respectfully" above the indecipherable signature. It was the word "Respectfully" that won Erwin. He could not recall that anyone had ever used it in reference to him. He decided to phone next day before he headed off to Anakie.

CHAPTER FORTY-THREE

THE RETURN TO THE DOCKLANDS berth of the multi million dollar Panygyric Five inflicted on Bryn more ups and downs of mood swings than the waves. He tried to concentrate on the forthcoming night he and Stephanie would share. Usually the thought of a naked Stephanie and what he would do with her precluded any other, but his thoughts were continually interrupted. Temporarily unstoppable brief attacks of furious panic were curtailed only by the imposition of Bryn's iron will. The curtailment proved only temporary as his brain resembled a kaleidoscope constantly changing with dark red and black colours predominating, oscillating, and throbbing, always depicting betrayal.

When he attacked the wealth of others he was full of confidence, audacious and concentrated. But now it was his wealth under attack and his confidence, audacity and concentration were ill accustomed to a defensive role. Unbidden suspicions about friends, business acquaintances and employees intruded. He began analysing each as someone seeking retaliation or vengeance for some past affront, but dismissed each on his mental list. His precautions were watertight. How could this Erwin have acquired the sickeningly accurate information written in the poison pen letters?

For several seconds he entertained the thought that the clairvoyant Dolores, was striking back from her underwater grave in retaliation for his murder of her and her lover, Ray. That thought vanished as spray from a maverick swell swept the foredeck and diverted Bryn's attention to a steering correction. Bryn was a logical personality not given to superstition so that illogical idea about dead Dolores remained as dead as she. The question still lingered, how Erwin Dormunt could have acquired such devasting information? Other thoughts intruded. What if the letters caused an investigation? From overheard comments of well liquored lawyers aboard booze boat cruises, Bryn was aware of the public perception that white collar crimes attracted lighter sentences. Partly this was because a proportion of the generation of judges sitting were as confused as the jury by the evidence about computer crime. Much of the terminology was alien and judges and jury had not yet overcome their fear and mistrust of electronic equipment.

Many white collar criminals were successful in parlaying a lighter sentence, upon conviction, because lawyers convinced the judge that the computer presented the accused with an irresistible temptation. That plea is identical to the process of the lawyer of the accused twisting the interpretation of evidence to "try the victim". Demonise the dead, who cannot respond, to exonerate their murderers. The tactic worked spectacularly well on juries in the past so counsel for the accused present enormously persuasive arguments to a jury to persuade them that the computer is the perpetrator. In the former argument the murder victim was unable to testify in his / her own defense. In the current scheme the computer likewise is unable to speak in its own defense.

Bryn's spinning mind reasoned that only someone close to him could have stumbled upon the incriminating facts, so he turned to a re-examination of the possibilities of betrayal by an employee using the name of Erwin as a cover. One by one he considered possible means of access to details of his past, concealed, business practices. One by one he again eliminated each employee from his list of traitors. His mind then jumped forward to the prospects of him being charged by the police. True, convicted white collar criminals appeared to receive lenient sentences in the past, but Bryn's logical mind caused him to appreciate that the new breed of judges on the bench and the new breed of yuppies summoned for jury service are infinitely more computer literate than a decade ago. The large sum of money stolen by a computer fraud seemed almost irrelevant to the token sentences imposed in the past. Bryn recalled one affable fraud being sentenced to three years for liberating nearly $16 million. A bank robber stealing the same amount would have got twenty three years.

But the world was changing; an inevitability, and Bryn could see that longer sentences for white collar criminals would also inevitably become the norm. This realisation spun Bryn's brain into another paroxysm of fury before it emerged again with a terrible resolve to annihilate the person behind the poison pen letters.

He was almost back to the mooring before he realised, with brain rattling clarity, where he has seen the name Erwin Dormunt. This Erwin was a despicable child rapist and murderer who had beaten conviction because his lawyer was the renowned shyster Lenny. Bryn now recalled some details of the court case. A murderer he himself may be, but he only eliminated adults and then almost painlessly. Bryn's indignation at Erwin's viscious and perverted attack on a child was genuine. Bryn would never be so depraved as to kill a child and he became increasingly horrified as he remembered media reports of the rape and mutilation of an eight year old boy.

Bryn resolutely intended to kill the person who threatened his entire life style but now his resolve to eliminate Erwin took on an element of community retribution. He began to feel like a public benefactor. With one hand on the wheel he pulled Erwin's letter from the folder, read the telephone number and dialled it on his mobile phone. He knew not what to expect and was surprised when an educated female voice advised him that he had contacted the office of Lenny the renowned criminal lawyer. Not that the voice said those exact words. Rather the warmly moist voice announced Lenny's full first and surnames with his post nominal letters "SC" (for Senior Counsel) being emphasised.

Bryn decided not to respond with his own name but asked if he may speak with Erwin. The voice expressed no surprise at Bryn's request and asked if she may have his contact details and the reason for the call. She undertook to ensure that any information given would be passed on to Mr Dormunt. Still reticent about providing identification, Bryn replied by telling the voice that he represented a real estate firm interested in offering employment to Erwin. Bryn curtailed further conversation by saying that he preferred not to leave details, as they were rather involved. Instead, he said, he would write to Mr Dormunt. That way the full information would be better conveyed, then he terminated the phone call. The fact that Erwin Dormunt was using his lawyer's phone number seemed logical. Obviously this Erwin was selective when it came to protecting his privacy.

The remainder of the journey required more concentration from Bryn as he dodged the multitude of yachts, water skis and amateur fishing boats near the entrance to the river on which his prestigious mooring awaited. He kept the docking procedures to the minimum then composed a letter to Erwin on the computer in the salon of the cruiser. The brief letter invited Erwin to phone Bryn's mobile phone to discuss employment in a real estate role consistent with the high marks received in the recent examination for a certificate as a Real Estate Representative. Almost whimsically he concluded the letter with the "Respectfully" rather than the more common "Yours Faithfully" or "Yours Sincerely". Somehow he could not bring himself to address a child murderer with words "faithful" or "sincere" so he wondered afterwards how in hell he chose to write the word "respectfully". Was it the recognition by one successful, unconvicted, killer of another? He was repelled by his own warped rationalisation. No way would he compare himself to a child murderer. But the word was written and he was running short of time to meet the evening mail clearance deadline so he scribbled a sort of signature, printed Erwin's address on an envelope, attached a postage stamp and jogged the one kilometre to a mail box where he deposited the letter into the slot only a minute or so before the mail collecting contractor arrived to clear the box.

Bryn jogged back to the Panygyric Five, spent a further fifteen minutes checking his list of docking procedure duties then walked the short distance to the entrance of the expensive waterfront building on the upper floor of which he owned an elegant apartment. With the letter mailed and the prospect of a contact with the putative blackmailer, Bryn's mood began to lighten. Bryn decided to calm his mental turmoil with a fast four kilometre run around the Docklands. In his apartment he changed into running gear. On return from his run, breathless and sweaty he had still not achieved mental serenity. He burned for action to eliminate a threat, this Erwin, but he also had a rampant urge for sexual fulfilment and knew that an evening with Stephanie would ensure complete satisfaction in that realm. Did the threat of disgrace and prison and his need to eliminate that threat impose upon him a challenge, and did that challenge account for his increased sexual potency? Visualising the evening that his enhanced sexual energy would involve, he was as close to contentment as he had been all that awful day.

When he stepped into the shower he wondered not whether to kill Erwin, but when and how. It must be soon. It must!

CHAPTER FORTY-FOUR

ERWIN HAD INTENDED TO START off early to test his bomb but a few too many drinks the night before resulted in him sleeping in and only the telephone brought him awake. He recognised the plummy voice of the female receptionist at Lenny's chambers. A shiver of fear brought goose pimples to his scalp as he wondered whether the call was to say that the police were after him again.

His fears were dissipated when the cheery "Good Morning" greeting was followed by a message saying that a real estate company would be writing to him. Gently the receptionist chided Erwin for not responding on his answering machine. She expected not much in the way of a reply from him based on past experience and so was not disappointed at Erwin's grunted "OK" before he hung up the receiver. Only then did his hung-over affected eyes register that his answering machine red light was blinking.

Erwin staggered to the toilet where he sat in contemplation of the floor tiles for some time before wobbling into the shower stall. When towelling himself dry he remembered the letter inviting him to telephone someone to a make time to discuss a job in the real estate business. He decided that breakfast would make him feel better and prepared two plates of breakfast cereal followed by three fried eggs, bacon, mushrooms, toast, marmalade and coffee and felt a lot closer to normal. In his pocket he found a letter from ECARUT and in view of the phone call from Lenny's office concluded that Lenny was responsible. Lenny had said he "would see what he could do". That being so he felt bound to follow it up even if only to please Lenny.

It was mid morning when Erwin made contact with Bryn by phone. Erwin was unguarded because of his assumption that the person on the telephone was someone associated with Lenny. Bryn was far too guarded when answering and became confused. The person who identified himself as Erwin seemed so relaxed in the conversation as to make Bryn doubt that he was talking to a blackmailer. There being only one way to find out, Bryn suggested that they meet for lunch. Bryn wanted a meeting so he could assess his opponent face to face.

Still hung over with an image in his brain of the fishing rod and tackle box in the Beast, Erwin sought to postpone the meeting to another day. He mentioned fishing. Bryn was quick on the up take and responded that Erwin should kill two birds with one stone by meeting Bryn at the St Kilda Marina. Bryn used his most persuasive voice on Erwin to say he could fish from his boat and talk at the same time. Bryn extolled the features of his motor cruiser and assured Erwin that the on-board bar held all that could be desired in alcohol.

To Erwin this seemed an excellent and unusual way to attend a job interview. He mentally thanked Lenny for having a Real Estate friend who was not bound with rigid employment conventions. The arrangement sounded good, the Marina an easy drive, free drinks, some fishing and an opportunity to go out on a motor cruiser, something Erwin had never done. So Erwin agreed to meet Bryn at midday and proudly told Bryn, in response to Bryn's question, the type of vehicle in which he would arrive. They concluded the call simultaneously. Erwin to meander slowly around his residence to find some suitable clothes to wear on a luxury cruiser and Bryn to race frantically to the basement garage to obtain the hidden store of rohypnol.

Ian had spent two days of solid investigation to bring up to date his file on Bryn. He had to proceed carefully in order not to be identified and such painstaking care was stressful. The Bryn file had grown fatter but nothing of any direct criminal consequence emerged. What did emerge was reinforcement of Ian's intuitive guesses that Bryn's ascension into elite society via financial brilliance and his forthcoming marriage had enhanced Bryn's public persona to a degree that Bryn would kill to defend it.

As a change from investigating Bryn via ASIC records, newspaper reports and computer research, Ian judged it appropriate to drive to the Docklands where his files recorded Bryn had moved into a luxury apartment. The front entrance of the thirty storey high-rise faced the paved surfaced pier at which Bryn's multi-million dollar motor cruiser Panygyric Five had an exclusive berth.

Ian parked a kilometre from the pier in a public viewing area intended for tourists to gaze enviously at palatial motor cruisers moored in the Yarra River. Ian still thought of the floating toys of millionaires as "cruisers" despite colleagues telling him that the upper crust called their floating palaces "yachts". The word "yachts" always reminded Ian of the hoary old joke about yachts being boats that shags shit on all week and shits shagged on all weekend. Ian still called them cruisers. They seemed big enough and powerful enough for the word to be apt.

In a touristy precinct, peering through binoculars was so normal as not to attract attention. Ian leaned his elbows atop his car to maintain a steady view and fingered the adjustment wheel to sharply focus on Panygyric Five. He almost jumped in surprise when Bryn stepped aboard, pressed numbers on a key pad and disappeared through a panelled wood door. Ian wondered what Bryn was doing aboard the cruiser at 11.30 am. From previous observation Ian knew that Bryn set out at sunrise when cruising for several days or at 9am if loaded up for a business buddies booze cruise on the bay.

By Ian's watch, Bryn was below deck precisely eight minutes before emerging, unlocking a locker at the aft end and taking out a yellow plastic spray jacket that he slipped on before climbing up four chrome railed steps to the upper deck cockpit. Ian saw twin puffs of smoke from the ruffled rear waterline before the noise of starting engines reached him. Lifting the line of his binoculars slightly, Ian could see Bryn slide into the pedestal seat behind the helm, or as Ian thought of it, the steering wheel, and then it seemed to Ian that Bryn was talking into a radio microphone.

Bryn appeared to be satisfied with whatever response he received because he sprang with cat-like jumps to the front then rear of the cruiser removing mooring lines before again almost leaping to the steering wheel in the upper control cockpit. Bryn's head turned several times as if double checking his clearance then Ian could see through his binoculars that Bryn's hand was pushing forward two chrome handles. Water at the rear of the cruiser churned more robustly and the massive piece of marine engineering slowly moved, straightened, then the speed increased as it headed towards the river mouth into Port Phillip Bay.

Ian decided to observe Bryn's cruiser from the shore so far as he could. He slid into his car and drove towards Beaconsfield Parade, Port Melbourne, from which sea front boulevard he would be able to view Bryn's entrance into the bay. He obtained a vantage point near Port Melbourne Lifesaving Club and even before he switched off the ignition he saw Panygyric Five clear the bay beacons. With a white bow wave and stern water churning, the gleaming white cruiser glided along the blue-green bay water in the direction of St Kilda.

Ian swung his car around, impatiently waiting for clearing traffic to allow him to re-enter the boulevard and follow Bryn's cruiser. Ian speculated that Bryn may be heading for his old mooring at the St Kilda Marina so accelerated to overtake Bryn. Ian took a few chances, irritated a few drivers and pulled into the car park of the Marina to see Panygyric Five headed for the Marina's public mooring pier. Ian parked at the rear of the car park in a patch of shade. He slipped binoculars into his trouser pocket, took off his sports coat and tie and tossed them onto the back seat of his car. He walked towards the end of the long, two level boatshed from which, without being conspicuous, he could see Bryn securing mooring lines.

A squeal of tyres torturing bitumen made Ian turn his head to see the cause and involuntarily his grip on the boatshed corner tightened without him realising it. He saw the big green Beast parked smack in the middle of the almost empty car park with wisps of smoke rapidly dispersing from around the oversize tyres. Erwin was standing beside the open driver's side door looking directly at him. Ian wished he had the .357 Colt Python in his pocket rather the Tasco binoculars.

To Ian it appeared as if he was transfixed as he returned Erwin's gaze. A call broke Ian's momentary mental paralysis and Erwin's head turned to look at the man who had called. Ian also turned to look and saw Bryn emerge from the shadow of the far end of the boatshed into the sunlight of the car park. Dressed in a yellow spray jacket and wrap-around sunglasses, Bryn strode confidently towards an uncharacteristically hesitant Erwin.

Within a few paces of the Beast, Ian saw Bryn hold out his hand to Erwin who delayed slightly, as if unaccustomed to being greeted in a friendly manner, before shaking Bryn's extended hand.

A conglomeration of thoughts and emotions raced through Ian's brain commencing with relief that Erwin had not been looking for him. Erwin would not recognise him because Ian knew he had kept well to the background, sunk invisibly into the throng, at each of Erwin's Court attendances, but Erwin's unexpected appearance was a jolt. Ian saw Bryn talking to Erwin and the impression Ian gained was that Bryn was making all the effort in the conversation. Bryn's hand action indicated that he was praising the Beast and Erwin seemed to the responding by indicating features of the massive green SUV. Ian saw Bryn point into the back of the Beast and saw what appeared to be Erwin declining an invitation. Bryn's smile and hand gestures seemed to change Erwin's mind because he took a fishing rod and tackle box from the Beast, locked the vehicle with a flash of orange indicators and carried the fishing gear in the direction of Panygyric Five.

Ian almost choked with relief. He almost cried with elation. Whatever, however, God Almighty, Halleluiah, his plan had worked. He barely restrained himself from falling to his knees and thanking Jesus, Yahweh, Allah, Buddha, Ron Barassi and every other god in the universe for bringing to fruition his plan to put in terminal jeopardy the man who he was convinced horrendously murdered his beloved grandson. Could the old adage be right? Was the pen mightier than the sword? Would his letters result in the death of Erwin? Tears in his eyes reminded Ian that he was getting more emotional as he grew older. He watched Bryn escort the hunk of murderous muscle, Erwin, to the cruiser. Through binoculars Ian could see Erwin's eyes widen in wonder at the exquisite sumptuousness of the fittings of the rear deck-well. Ian saw Bryn indicate to Erwin a fishing rod recess built into the port gunwale and watched as Erwin put his rod into the recess and push the tackle box between two rear seat cushions, presumably to prevent it moving when the cruiser cleared the pier.

A few tears continued to spill from Ian's lower lids and ran down his cheeks. He must be going mad he thought. Bryn's beautiful boat could be Erwin's hearse. He was witnessing the prelude to the funeral of a human being and tears may be an appropriate response at a funeral but unashamedly

Ian knew that the droplets of saline that slipped down his cheeks were tears of retribution, of a diminutive relief of depression, a massive amount of consolation and placation of sheer red hot gut burning revenge.

Immobile in the shadow of the overhang of the boatshed roof, Ian watched as Panygyric Five slid through the choppy water with its bow pointed directly towards the centre of the bay. Bryn was steering with one hand; one buttock perched on the pilot seat as he turned half sideways to talk to Erwin seated in an adjoining pedestal seat.

Ian's immobility was broken when he moved his head as his finger wiped away a tear. As his head moved, Ian's eyes were drawn to a silver Toyota sedan parked on the other side of the car park. The incident that drew his eyes to that particular vehicle was a flash of light from the passenger seat. Curious, Ian remained as still as he could in the boatshed shadow and slowly raised his binoculars. They showed him two men in the front seat. One had a pair of binoculars raised to his eyes and was looking out to sea. The man's mouth was moving and Ian shifted his binoculars slightly to look at the driver. Ian saw the driver speaking into a microphone. It seemed to Ian that the man with the binoculars was commentating on whatever he was observing and the driver was relaying the commentary through the microphone.

Slowly, slowly, so as not to attract attention and keeping well within the noon day shadow, Ian moved around the corner of the boatshed and out of view of the two men in the Toyota. Ian looked out to sea to see what the man with the binoculars was so keenly observing. One object disturbed the bay, apart from the white tops of the waves. That object was Panygyric Five. So the two men were interested in Erwin, Bryn or both.

The identity of the two men and the government organisation they represented, for government authority seemed stamped all over them, was immaterial to Ian. He felt that he had achieved his objective. He did not want to be involved with any law enforcement authority. So he waited in the shadow for some time and only went back to his car when he saw the Toyota leave. As a reflex action he memorised the registration number and later pencilled it into the file on Bryn and also the file on Erwin. But he declined to telephone his informer in the Motor Registration Department because if the car belonged to police, State or Federal, any enquiry about it could lead to his informer being detected. Ian needed to protect his source in order to protect himself. Ian had no contempt for caution.

CHAPTER FORTY-FIVE

THE TWO MEN IN THE silver Toyota Camry Sedan observed by Ian were named Jarvis and Lyon. Both were members of the Victoria Police force. Both men had an intense hatred of Erwin. Detective Sergeant Jarvis because of guilt and practicality. Guilt because he was intuitively certain that the meeting arranged at Central Park Malvern to shake down Erwin for $5,000 led to the abduction and abominable rape/murder of an innocent boy. Knowing Erwin's warped sexual proclivities was adequate evidence for him. Had he gone to the prosecutor and made a sworn deposition that Erwin was familiar with the area of Central Park, an item that Erwin's lawyer had denied in Court, his own involvement would surely have resulted in his dismissal from the force. And any such deposition would have been of such infinitesimal evidential value as to be useless in advancing a conviction of Erwin. So the guilt that troubled Jarvis was lessened by that rationalisation.

Of far more importance to him was the practical consideration that Erwin still had the capacity to cause him serious grief in his vocation as a Police Officer. Erwin, as an insignificant unknown person, posed little threat to a Detective Senior Sergeant with the length of exemplary service of Jarvis. However an Erwin who had achieved newsworthy notoriety and furthermore, had a lawyer of the ilk of Lenny as his communicator, then that Erwin was decidedly a threat to Jarvis. Practicality demanded that

Jarvis neutralise that threat. How to perform an efficient neutralisation occupied much of the thinking time of Detective Senior Sergeant Jarvis.

Similar thoughts occupied the mind of Detective Senior Constable Lyons and had done so since Lenny the leprous lawyer had humiliated him during the course of the farce that the media called the Dormunt trial. Lyons was the driver of the Toyota and Jarvis the passenger and officer-in-charge of the surveillance operation. Chance had brought Jarvis and Lyons together. Shortly after Erwin's legal exoneration, Lyons was transferred from his short assignment at the Homicide Squad to the large inner suburban police station at St Kilda. He felt betrayed by his seniors. The transfer from an elite squad to general duties was demeaning. It made him the scapegoat for a trial that should never have proceeded on the paucity of admissible evidence. On the first acquaintance with the evidence against Erwin, Lyons was sceptical about it being adequate. As the new man in the squad he was reluctant to complain. Only the constant promise of more forensic evidence made him repress his objections. His seniors had pushed for the trial probably having been pushed in turn by their political masters. If the anticipated conviction had occurred then the politicians would have extracted every laudable drop of political mileage from the incarceration of a vicious child rapist and murderer.

Regrettably the botched assembly of insufficient evidence and the flaunting of the weaknesses in the chain of evidence by Lenny resulted in a political embarrassment. To immunise politicians from the stigma of failure, scapegoats were essential to deflect the mandibles of the media. Both Lyons and the haemorrhoids blighted prosecutor had received sideways postings as cosmetic sacrifices. General duties meant that Lyons was available for any of the menial tasks ordered by a superior.

Jarvis was visiting the St Kilda Police Station in response to rumours of an unregistered brothel newly opened in the precinct. He went to the canteen for a coffee. The Station Commander entered and called out to all and sundry in the canteen that he needed two volunteers urgently for surveillance in the area. Neither Jarvis nor Lyons, who was sorting routine paper work nearby, responded. With the telephone held to his ear, the Station Commander added that the request for surveillance came from the Anti-Terrorist Squad who needed short term assistance. Still there was no rush of volunteers from the uniformed and plain clothed officers around the canteen tables.

The Station Commander relayed the incoming information as he heard it over the telephone and in a last ditch effort to get volunteers before he knew he would have to revise the roster and order officers to the mission, he said "The job is to tail Erwin Dormunt the effing rock spider who killed the kid from Central Park. The AT Squad have info he has some bomb detonators and want to know what he's up to". From the back of the canteen a voice expressed the hope that Dormunt would stick the detonators up his fundamental orifice and set them off. That hope received grunted support from many.

Jarvis and Lyons did not join in the chorus of grunts; rather each stepped up to the Station Commander who appeared surprised when Jarvis a visitor, said that he could squeeze in a couple of hours to help the ATS. He was less surprised when Lyons volunteered. For a second the Station Commander seemed about to caution Lyons. He recalled that Dormunt was part of the reason for the re-assignment of Lyons. He knew Lyons from past training courses and judged him to be an intelligent and well balanced officer. The Station Commander had heard the odd rumour about Jarvis but odd rumours were always the norm about anyone who worked in Vice. Other than the odd rumour, Jarvis was highly regarded, so the Station Commander never hesitated in endorsing the station log to show that a Detective Senior Sergeant and a Detective Senior Constable had volunteered to assist the ATS on a short term surveillance task.

Jarvis was introduced to Lyons with the briefest of information. He was handed a faxed mission statement pro forma by the Station Commander. The pro forma contained hand written essential information about the surveillance mission. Jarvis read the start point address, a description of the subject and vehicle, details of reporting procedures and timings. He told Lyons they would use the Vice Squad vehicle Jarvis had parked in the police compound. Lyons nodded, followed Jarvis out and deftly caught the car keys tossed to him. Jarvis had the street directory open to give Lyons directions to Erwin's residence when Lyons said that he knew where the house was in Kew.

Lyons talked about Erwin all the way to the Kew address and the bitter tone in his voice convinced Jarvis that he and his short acquaintance confederate were of one mind in their opinion of Erwin. The ATS information that Erwin was connected with a possible terrorist group surprised them both. Child sex predators are usually solitary personalities. Lyons drove with trained skill and Jarvis felt none of the discomfort that several other police drivers induced. Jarvis pressed the buttons on the communications console and established radio contact with the ATS on the frequency channel written on the mission statement. Names were not mentioned on radio despite its electronic protection from interception. A note at the bottom of the mission statement indicated that Erwin's motor vehicle was referred to by him as the "Beast".

Lyons drove the unmarked police car into the tree lined street. His attention was directed towards finding a parking spot from whence he and Jarvis could observe Erwin's premises. During conversation on the trip from St Kilda Police Station Lyons wondered about this medium sized, quietly spoken, unremarkable Detective Senior Sergeant. What was his interest in Erwin? Jarvis was a good listener but sparing in response. Lyons did not feel he could ask the question outright to a superior officer on such short acquaintance.

Jarvis asked most of the questions, only responding with information directly applicable to the task being performed. On the radio to the ATS Lyons heard him ask short, sharp totally pertinent questions most of which he repeated back, more to allow Lyons to be informed than to ensure correct receipt of the message. Lyons heard that ATS were short on manpower due partly to illness of members and partly because a member of the Knights of Socialist Australia had taken umbrage at being excluded from a top level KSA briefing and turned informer. The informer told of a meeting at which bomb making instructions were given and named people who took the detonators handed out by the instructor,

The ATS churned out the name of Erwin Dormunt and his recent walk from the tentacles of the Victoria Police. Assistance was requested to surveille Erwin and report. ATS members would take over mid-afternoon. The subject was forbidding in appearance and would undoubtedly be violent given an opportunity to use his considerable array of muscles in a secluded place, but violence in public was considered improbable. Erwin may look a bit dumb but his mentor had taught him well about the hazards of publicly punching police. Avoid any confrontation was the essence of the ATS instructions. Observe and report only.

And observe Jarvis did. Lyons had pushed the gear lever forward to reverse the Toyota into a suitable vacant space beneath a big tree when the sharp, scalpel voice of Jarvis said "There he is" and nodded up the street where the Beast bounded onto the road on its oversize off-road tyres and accelerated away from them towards a main road intersection. Lyons responded with effortless ease co-ordinating eye, hand and foot to check the road was clear before smoothly pulling out and following Erwin. Lyons saw Erwin demand road space as he thrust the Beast into the traffic with a right hand turn that would have earned a traffic infringement notice had there been a traffic cop around. Lyons drove the Toyota in an almost sedate manner by comparison, but that appearance was deceptive because the Toyota was skilfully inserted into the relatively light traffic flow without causing impediment. They remained on the tail of the Beast all of the twenty five minute journey to the St Kilda Marina.

Given the density of traffic along the beach front boulevard, Lyons had no option but to follow the Beast into the car park of the Marina albeit at a much more unobtrusive speed. Lyons drove along the rear of the parking area and pulled up at the far end near a slipway entrance. Jarvis had slumped down and sent a radio message to the ATS that it looked as if the Beast was about to make a meet and gave the location. As a matter of routine, both Lyons and Jarvis checked the entire area around their position. Nothing behind, five cars in the park, all unoccupied, get the regos later if needed, no one on either right or left. Someone, a male, probably the attendant, in the Marina office, no other person that they could see. They missed seeing Ian, immobile in the shadow at the end of the boatshed.

Jarvis was about to make a more detailed sweep of the area when he saw Erwin get out of the Beast. He nudged Lyons' elbow and nodded in Erwin's direction. Almost simultaneously as Lyons was moving his elbow to nudge Jarvis a young, suntanned, athletic man walked swiftly towards Erwin. Jarvis was moved to comment that the unknown bore some resemblance to Lyons, similar physique, dark blonde hair and powerful walk. Lyons saw Erwin meet the unknown man. Jarvis was busy setting the camera he had taken from the glove box but was in action clicking away only seconds later. They both saw a fishing rod and a cheap green topped tackle box taken from the Beast then Erwin and the unknown male headed towards the short term public dock.

Lyons told Jarvis he recalled seeing movement near a large motor cruiser when they pulled into their parking spot and Jarvis used his binoculars to read the name of the cruiser, Panygyric Five, aloud. Lyons wrote the name on the mission pro forma. Jarvis radioed the ATS to report the meet then confirmed to ATS the name of the motor cruiser as Erwin and the unknown male stepped aboard. Jarvis kept the ATS informed of the Panygyric Five's leaving, heading towards the centre of Port Phillip Bay, with the unknown male at the helm and Erwin sitting in a seat on the upper part of the ship. When the cruiser was two kilometres away, the ATS radio operator ordered Jarvis and Lyons to cease surveillance, return to St Kilda, write a report, attach the undeveloped photo cassette and a security courier would collect it within an hour.

Jarvis and Lyons speculated on the meaning of the meeting between Erwin and the unknown male without being able to draw any conclusion. The only positive result of the fortuitous meeting between Jarvis and Lyons was that the pair proved to be companionable, leading Jarvis to sound out Lyons upon the prospect of him applying for a transfer to Vice.

At St Kilda Police Station they completed their joint report, and then surrendered it and the photo cassette to the internal courier service collector. They received thanks from the Station Commander before each returned to his regular duties with an unspoken feeling of satisfaction because they had done something of detriment to Erwin no matter how slight. Jarvis phoned Lyons later that day to say that the owner of the motor cruiser was a millionaire property developer named Bryn Hamley. Did Lyons know anything about Hamley? Lyons said he had never heard of Hamley.

CHAPTER FORTY-SIX

BRYN WAS TOTALLY CONFUSED AND confusion was an intellectual condition that he prided himself on rapidly eradicating. Try though he might he could not dispel the confusion. He had dreaded the meeting with Erwin. The image he formed from reading media reports on the Internet was that of an ill-mannered, foul- mouthed, belligerent brute. Certainly the photographs of Erwin leaving the Court after his trial were angled by the photographer to accentuate his size and supercilious glare. Bryn anticipated the meeting with his putative blackmailer to be tense, with a distinct element of physical danger. He expected Erwin to demonstrate the condescending attitude of a blackmailer, that of having complete control of his victim. Bryn had mentally rehearsed his response, a response completely concentrated on his aim to get his enemy, Erwin, aboard the Panygyric Five and have him drink one of the multitude of drinks spiked with rohypnol.

Everything else was subordinate to that aim. He must wrest the position of domination away from his tormentor, Erwin, and to achieve that aim he was prepared to temporarily accept any verbal denigration that may be flung his way. His resolve was boosted by his intuitive appreciation that Erwin was a physical type of person not a dilettante and physical types tended to expect danger in a physical form. Reliance on their superior musculature became the basis of their self confidence. Bryn's tried and tested plan to attack Erwin from an apparently non-violent vector sustained Bryn in steeling himself to submit to Erwin's expected hostility. Yet the Erwin that

Bryn had just met in the car park of the St Kilda Marina exhibited none of the anticipated anti-social tendencies. True he was a solid slab of muscular humanity about the same age as Bryn and true he drove the enormous green SUV with obvious aggression. But when Bryn approached and introduced himself, Erwin smiled, shook hands without crushing his fingers, and in all aspects appeared non-aggressive and relaxed, even respectful.

This response confused Bryn so much he double checked by asking Erwin, with a trifle less tact than usual, if Erwin were looking forward to a new career in Real Estate now that he was clear of the law. Erwin's reply was a barely illuminating "Yeah", I'll give it a go" but it was sufficient to confirm to Bryn that this Erwin was the author of the letter seeking employment with ECARUT.

Bryn suggested that Erwin bring his fishing gear, pointed at Panygyric Five and began to move in that direction. Bryn had chosen the St Kilda Marina as the meeting place because he frequently moored there to collect business colleagues for day trip bay booze cruises and his boat would therefore not attract attention. Notwithstanding that reasoning, Bryn did not want to hang around lest too many should recall his visit. The car park seemed empty of people except for a Toyota sedan parked near the slipway entrance containing two men. That parking spot was often used when the driver was waiting for an incoming vessel so Bryn attached no significance to it being there.

As they stepped aboard the Panygyric Five, Bryn had another sideways glance at Erwin and was reminded of a muscular Samoan appropriately named "Latrina" who had tried a shakedown over a decade ago. Bryn obtained some comfort from his earlier loading and concealing two spear guns. Bryn had no contempt for caution.

Erwin was confused, but he was more tolerant of confusion than Bryn because Erwin had learned to live with unexplained confusion for years. He was not disturbed at the unusual job interview anywhere near the degree of Bryn. Never having been to a job interview before he could only rely on half remembered snippets of conversations overheard at the gymnasium. He found it hard to reconcile the image of a job interview involving a desk, with an inquisitor sitting behind it, with this relaxed meeting with

Bryn. Erwin's mild trepidation stemmed from the prospect of questions about the real estate exam that he was supposed to have completed with marks so high that he was dux of the TAFE school year. He knew that if he were questioned he would be uncovered as an ignoramus and on the one hand that created unease. On the other hand, Erwin reasoned, if Lenny the lanky lawyer had arranged the meeting, as the phone call from Lenny's receptionist seemed to confirm, then he need not worry, Lenny had fixed it. Overall he felt he could relax.

The meeting at the Marina indicated that any interview based on real estate knowledge would be superficial and Erwin was inclined to think that his prospects of employment would rest more upon the assessment by the employer of his personality. Unaware that he was devoid of that attribute, Erwin resolved to be as pleasant as he could to justify the effort put in by the only person he respected, Lenny.

Erwin's eyebrows elevated in surprise when a man of his same age and height approached, asked his name and then reached out a hand for a handshake. Few people wanted to shake hands with Erwin. This friendly stranger could not be the boss of the property company ECARUT Erwin thought, but Bryn's introduction confirmed that he was indeed the Chairman of the Board. Trepidation drained from Erwin as he sized up Bryn and decided that in or out of the ring he could account for Bryn in a fight. Bryn looked fit, flexible and well muscled and Erwin knew that Bryn would be reasonably formidable in a fight before Erwin's power prevailed. Erwin tended to assess other people upon their physical ability. That assessment completed, Erwin relaxed further and so was easily persuaded to bring his fishing gear to the moored motor cruiser indicated by Bryn.

Erwin was astounded by the luxury of the Panygyric Five. He noted the name on the stern and thought it looked like Latin and wondered, briefly, why such a magnificent piece of marine architecture should be named after a disease. It was at least consistent, he thought, with a property company with the odd Latin name of ECARUT. He stored the rod in a special channel made for rods in the side wall of the ship and recalling what was in the tackle box, it wedged between two cushions. Erwin was given a quick glimpse of the main salon. He was told that they would sail to a sheltered part of the bay where they could anchor, Erwin would be given a full tour of the boat, and they could do a bit of fishing, have a meal, have a talk and be back before sunset. That sounded beaut to Erwin. He had never been on a boat trip before and the sumptuous elegance of this floating palace made him round-eyed in envy. Bryn cast off the mooring lines and headed upstairs, calling for Erwin to join him.

Erwin's feet fairly flew up the steps of the metal ladder to join Bryn on what he was told was the flybridge or upper control position and his feet felt a pleasant slight vibration as Bryn pushed forward chrome throttle levers. The massive cruiser effortlessly gained speed seeming to glide above the white capped waves rather than slicing them. Although the cruiser was stable, barely rolling or pitching, Erwin began to feel a bit queasy in the stomach. Briefly he regretted the size of his breakfast. He listened to Bryn making conversation, pointing out marine markers and beacons sliding by outside and describing features of the cruiser inside, the GPS, radar, etc. Bryn indicated a panel near Erwin's left elbow and asked Erwin to push near the top. Erwin was dumbfounded because he had not noticed the panel and it clicked then swung open to reveal a refrigerator stocked with over a dozen bottles and cans of alcoholic beverages.

Erwin was asked to pass to Bryn a half-chilled bottle of Chardonnay and Bryn expertly twisted off the top and swallowed a mouthful. Erwin was told to help himself and hesitated for a moment as the cruiser gently lifted then lowered in a sea swell reminding him of his stomach unease. As Erwin hesitated, Bryn told him that the best drink at sea was still wine rather than gassy beer or Champagne and suggested that a half bottle of not too sweet Riesling was good for settling the stomach. Bryn recommended Erwin try the Riesling in the lower door shelf. Erwin tried to emulate Bryn even though he was not keen on wine, but he could find no other Chardonnay in the refrigerator. Erwin appeared reluctant because Panygyric Five had risen and lowered again a few times but he reached for the Riesling when Bryn delivered his clinch line. Mendaciously telling Erwin that the half bottles cost $50 each. Erwin could not resist a drink of such an expensive tipple and, anyhow, his pride would not allow himself to be beaten by anyone in a drinking contest.

So Erwin twisted open the black aluminium screw cap. It came off easily as if it had been opened before. He felt another stomach lurch as the cruiser precipitously lowered into another trough between the increasingly boisterous seas, then resolutely put the bottle aperture to his lips and swallowed part of the contents. The chill felt good. His stomach accepted the liquid kindly so he poured more into his mouth.

This time it was his head that seemed to lurch rather than his stomach. He saw that Bryn was briefly distracted and quickly leaned over the side. The quick movement made him a bit light headed. He tried to appear unconcerned, indeed his head appeared unconcerned with anything; it appeared to be floating, floating unconnected into a languorous warmly comforting darkness,

Erwin never felt his body falling, rolling completely over the safety rail off the flybridge to land with a reverberating thump on the non-skid rubber matting of the well deck 2.2 metres beneath the deck of the flybridge. Erwin was an inert victim of rohypnol less than ten minutes on his first sea voyage.

Sea safety manuals caution about the hazards of sailing and alcohol but Erwin had never read a sea safety manual.

CHAPTER FORTY-SEVEN

A CLUSTER OF SIX METRE yachts participating in a club sailing contest from the look of their top pennants, precluded Bryn from engaging the auto pilot for nearly ten minutes. However as he steered to give the yachts right of way, he felt no impatience because he realised that the senseless shark bait in the lower deck was his tormentor and his torment would soon conclude permanently. Bryn eased the twin accelerator levers to the rear then slightly forward to achieve the optimum speed, given the strengthening wind, for steady progress before switching to auto. With athletic ease he slid down the marine grade 316 stainless steel handrails to the deck-well near Erwin, opened a locker and extracted a light plastic tarpaulin. With the tarp he covered the comatose Erwin and wedged him near the transom door to the rear swim platform using waterproof cushions from the seats surrounding the deck. Bryn then retraced his steps to the flybridge control position.

His practiced eye covered the instrument panel and all indicators showed satisfactory reading except the fuel gauges. Yesterday's high speed trip to ECARUT's office in Mornington, the return to his docklands berth, the highly satisfactory Olympic standard sexual sessions with Stephanie last night and the unexpected meeting with Erwin had left him little time to refuel the diesel tanks. Bryn checked forecasts again and noted that further deterioration in weather conditions was predicted. He must refuel to be certain of reaching his disposal area and having adequate fuel reserve to return and reach a sheltered harbour. With no alternative he disengaged the autopilot and steered towards Mornington to refuel at the fuel wharf. Bryn resigned himself to a journey of night navigation into a strengthening head wind.

With the fuel hose connected and the wharf attendant overseeing the supply, Bryn slipped into the galley area adjacent to the main salon and raided the well stocked refrigerator to make a quick lunch. Refreshed, he attended to the fuel payment and headed the twenty metre Panygyric Five for Lady Julia Percy Island. The magnificent cruiser would handle any weather with Bryn's skilled hands on the controls. He would never have ventured such a trip in such adverse weather twenty years ago in the far smaller Panygyric One.

Even before the cruiser entered the main shipping lane from Port Phillip Bay into the Southern Ocean the increase in sea swell became apparent. By the time Bryn entered the sea lane approach of the Rip, he was experiencing some slight jarring and thumping. Bryn was unperturbed because of his confidence in his seamanship and the array of navigational control position in the panels set in a semi circle around his control position. Time taken to refuel had delayed his exit from Port Phillip Bay but full tanks reinforced Bryn's confidence and he knew the delay was justified.

In the open sea Bryn steered west, into a sun that was lowering on the horizon. He was glad of the blue glazing on the toughened glass of the cockpit because it considerably reduced the ocean glare. On auto pilot again, Bryn checked Erwin and found him still unconscious. Some spray had left droplets on the tarpaulin causing Bryn no concern because he anticipated Erwin being far wetter within a few hours. After a quick visit to the "head", Bryn made a sandwich and coffee for afternoon tea then threw overboard the twenty drinks from the refrigerator he had spiked with rohypnol.

At the helm for another hour and being certain no other vessels were within visual range, Bryn double checked the radar, scanned the sky to see it clear of aircraft then engaged the auto pilot again. He partly removed the tarpaulin from Erwin, screwing up his face in disgust when he saw that Erwin had expelled a lot of half digested food. Bryn hated cleaning up vomit. He sunk a heft kick in the region of the tarpaulin he hoped covered Erwin's soon to be redundant reproductive equipment. In the deepening twilight, Bryn searched Erwin's clothes taking every item from the shirt and trouser pockets. Bryn noted with some pleasure that one of the items he collected was the letter he had sent to Erwin with the request that it be brought to the meeting. Erwin had, at least, followed Bryn's request. Erwin's compliance reopened Bryn's confusion. In the short time that Erwin had remained conscious, he had exhibited not one characteristic of a tormentor. Yet it had to be Erwin. The pin holes on the poison pen letters and Erwin's application were a puzzling but never-the-less a direct link. Bryn speculated that maybe Erwin had an accomplice but without any evidence, Bryn declined to examine that possibility further. He had Erwin to dispose of and he must concentrate on the immediate task. On the way back he would have time for speculation.

Bryn tore the letter into small bits and the strengthening wind tore the small bits away from Bryn's hands at a velocity that surprised him. The increased motion of Panygyric Five with deeper booming thuds echoing through the hull partly convinced Bryn to abandon the complete stripping of Erwin in preparation for his deep sea dive. The other object that partly contributed to Bryn's reluctance to fully strip Erwin was an abominably putrid smell of the large amount of Erwin's vomit. Bryn pulled off Erwin's shoes and threw each overboard into the darkening swell of the Southern Ocean followed by Erwin's expensive watch and cellphone. Bryn wanted no traces of Erwin ever to be found.

Several more severe jarring wave crashes conveyed to Bryn that the heading of Panygyric Five needed alteration to better cope with the heavier seas so he left Erwin, made his way with some difficulty to the flybridge control position and resumed manual control with a helm adjustment of twelve degrees. Bryn had taken Erwin's wallet and keys with him to the flybridge. He memorised the address on Erwin's driving licence before throwing the wallet and contents into the white capped waves. The keys he put into the pocket of his yellow spray jacket.

Bryn was so busy coping with increasingly inclement weather that he never noticed that one of Erwin's eyes flickered.

To Bryn, it seemed that Erwin had swallowed the entire 375 mil bottle of Riesling. But while Bryn was distracted with shipboard duties, Erwin had spat overboard the second mouthful resulting in the amount of rohypnol actually taken into his system being only half of that estimated by Bryn. Furthermore, shortly after Bryn had covered him with a tarpaulin, the combined effects of the sea motion on Erwin's stomach, loaded with a heavy breakfast, caused an involuntary expulsion of a substantial portion of its contents including some element of the anaesthetic drug. What remained of the rohypnol in Erwin's system was sufficient to render unconscious a young woman victim of a date rape sex offender.

Erwin's bulk, however, was different in size to that of a young woman. Erwin was an athlete used to sustained periods of violent exercise and had a metabolism to match. And every anaesthetic drug is body weight and metabolism related as to the duration of capacity to impose insensibility on the animal to which it is administered. Slowly but inevitably the dominance of the drug was wearing off Erwin. Erwin's first feeling was his frozen feet. The discomfort made him wriggle. He became aware of traumatised testicles, cold wet clothes, a foul taste in his mouth, a smell in his nostrils and infernal bumping and twisting of the platform on which his semi-comatose body law. Initially, brain stupor prevented recognition of his miserable situation. He became aware of a madly meandering white light a long way upwards but all else was black and he slipped back to sleep, too lethargic even to try to move to a position of less discomfort.

Bryn remained on his pedestal seat behind the helm. Weather conditions had deteriorated beyond the forecast predictions and Bryn needed to continually correct the cruiser's heading to preclude some swamping by the heavy dark waves. He was not deeply concerned, indeed he felt a degree of inner pride at his ability to take into account, evaluate and apply all of the elements necessary to ensure that his contribution to the testing of Panygyric Five in these seas matched the expertise of the engineers who designed it. Bryn had no contempt for caution on matters relating to the sea and seamanship. Indeed he was most diligent. Unfortunately for him the concentration required was so intense due to the stormy conditions that he neglected to sufficiently supervise Erwin's condition.

And Erwin had moved again. This time both of his eyes opened.

CHAPTER FORTY-EIGHT

ERWIN DRIFTED ALTERNATIVELY FROM SILENT, blissful oblivion into a rapidly noisy, twisting, bone jolting nightmare surely conjured by his favourite artist, Hieronymus Bosch from the depths of a fit of demonic dementia. In damp darkness a brilliant white light intruded intermittently in frenzied choreography. He desperately wanted to sleep out this maniacal nightmare but each thrust into the nightmare seemed to last a little longer.

Erwin was thankfully about to surrender to a state of feelinglessness again when he was deluged with cold salty water. The shock effect of which destroyed the leaden lethargy that up to then prevented any effort to relieve his acute discomfort. He tried to move his inexplicably unresponsive arms. The beginning of an inner wave of fury forced him to persevere and in his fourth attempt his right arm moved a few centimetres. Another dousing of very cold water prompted further efforts and his left arm moved almost double the distance of that of his right. He was moving both arms simultaneously when the next cold wave of water splashed over the gunwale, nearly choking him and initiating a fit of coughing to clear his mouth and nose.

With eyes mostly closed Erwin endured the demoralizing crazy motion of whatever he was lying on. His fingers now outlined a rough textured cushion that seemed to be wedged between him and a rubber mat. With cognizance returning, his brain made the connection between the sickening motion, salty water and a boat. He was on a boat. He told himself that a dozen times before the questions slowly formed, "Why was he on a boat?" and with that question his brain began sluggishly emerging from rohypnol's mastery. "Why no shoes"? His fingers felt numb. In a clumsy manner he asked himself questions, where was his watch, why am I wet and cold, why am I aching all over, why is it dark, what is the faint green glow, am I dead, am I going to die – others too, questions upon fuzzy questions but no answers.

His lower body felt wrapped in something and Erwin's fumbling fingers pulled the crumpled tarpaulin from his aching hips and legs then the wind seized the tarp pulling it away, slashing Erwin's neck and cheek leaving bleeding gouges from the brass eyelets. Erwin tasted blood before another wave deluged him triggering a reflex response to try to sit up. His first effort failed because the Panygyric Five had completed a highly risky 180 degree turn and threw him backwards. That last large wave was the maximum water intake thanks to Bryn's consummate seamanship and the sheer power of the ship's twin diesel engines.

Erwin was totally unaware that Bryn had successfully navigated his marine masterpiece into the lee of Lady Julia Percy Island. Consequently the wave action generally was decreasing as the squall moved eastwards. Aided by the slightly decreased motion Erwin realised that the crazily dancing white light was not one but two white lights on the back of the boat. Bryn, the seaman, would have called them stern lights.

Erwin was able to vaguely orient himself as being in the back cockpit entertainment area, a flat, rubber floored area surrounded by built-in seats to which cushions were attached by nylon straps and metal press studs. Most of the cushions were in disarray, some were missing, but nearer the entrance to the main saloon where the extensions to the cabin walls provided shelter, Erwin could see a pile of undisturbed cushions. He grunted in recognition of the bright green top of his tackle box showing between two cushions before he fell as a wave thudded against the transom.

Bryn had steered by GPS and radar as close as he considered safe to the leeward of his favourite fatal shore. Constant references to instruments confirmed his location and the powerful twin forward spot lights showed him a sea of smooth black swells. With no signs of the high white flecked breakers, the predominant feature of the unsheltered Southern Ocean, Bryn knew he had reached his chosen spot. If further confirmation were needed, Bryn's feet and ears registered the absence of jarring vibrations and noises. Bryn stared intently at the motion of the long, smooth, black, undulating masses of lethal liquid framed in the illumination of the spot lights. He looked for the right configuration to allow a safe turn of the cruiser. When he saw a long low smooth valley followed by another he spun Panygyric Five using forward propeller from one engine and reverse from the other, supplemented by maximum rudder. His timing, the response of the diesel motors to his demands and the superb hull design of the cruiser made the manoeuvre appear effortless.

In the hands of a less skilful seaman the 180 degree turn could have been disastrous. If turning in mountainous seas, in the dark, with limited light ever became an Olympic Event, then Bryn would have won a gold medallion. But in the lee of the lethal islet in funereal blackness, Bryn's brilliance was unappreciated. Only the brief phosphorescence of a small wave as it smashed over the transom of the cruiser provided light from any natural source. The artificial illuminations were the white spotlights and stern lights, all of which, combined, looked like a Christmas tree from a distance. Bryn allowed himself a small grin of self congratulation at having turned around the cruiser with only minimal intake of water over the aft of the vessel. He swung the spot lights towards the rear of the cruiser to illuminate the huge never ending black ocean swells. He began to balance engine speed and rudder to the optimum for stable slow progress of the cruiser. Having achieved it he engaged the autopilot.

In the reflected illumination of the spot lights Bryn double checked the belt of his PFD, Personal Floatation Device, made a final check of the instrument panel readings then climbed down the stainless steel ladder to the aft cockpit well. Bryn's aim was to tip Erwin overboard. He saw the dark lump on the deck in the strong shadow cast by the spot light. Bryn was aware that the body had moved about a metre and a half from the position near the transom where he had earlier wedged it with cushions. He attributed the move to the motion of the cruiser. Bryn had faith in rohypnol because of its past effectiveness. He did not consider that Erwin could have moved of his own volition.

At the bottom of the ladder, Bryn held on to the rails and focused his attention on the lump in the shadows. He detected no movement beyond that which may be expected from the motion generated by the undulating sea. He maintained his watch for a full minute to be sure that the lump in the dark shadow exhibited no spontaneous motion of his own. Never-the-less Bryn approached cautiously. His eyes were adjusting to the dimness now he had passed through the brightness of the overhead spot light and he saw the outline of Erwin's head against part of a seat in the well deck.

Bryn braced himself for a lift then grabbed Erwin's exposed ankle. Making sure he had a good grip, Bryn coordinated his pull with the subsiding motion of the cruiser to pull Erwin's substantial body a third of a metre rearwards. Two more pulls had Erwin's inert body lined up with the seat. Bryn needed to lift Erwin on to the seat before tipping him over the side where Erwin would become a solid meal for a Great White Shark. Lifting a comatose body can be difficult, lifting a very large framed body even more so. This degree of difficulty increased exponentially when the body was difficult to grip, wet, and the entire environment was moving in an irregular and unpredictable motion. In the shadow of bright white lights surrounded by blackness unrelieved by a vestige of starlight, Bryn battled to bundle Erwin's body into a position from which it could be pushed forward.

Bryn's PFD jacket proved to be an impediment when it came to lifting. Attachments that would undoubtedly be of value to the wearer was he dumped into the ocean, seemed to snag on Erwin's wet shirt and make Bryn's lifting more laborious. Bryn was not consciously counting but when he eventually had Erwin laid out on the seat cushions his brain seemed to say that it had taken ten exhausting lifts to achieve the pre-final push position. A large wave lifted Panygyric Five effortlessly then dumped it into a trough and Bryn turned his ear to the sound of propellers briefly thrashing into air not water as the cruiser's stern was forced upwards. Bryn felt the props grip again but the force of the motion had detached his hold on Erwin and he leaned forward and gripped the gunwale to retain his balance.

As Bryn straightened up he felt his ankle gripped in a painful vice. Straining to see in the shadow cast by his own body and the constrictions of the bulky PFD, Bryn twisted towards the bow. The motion of the cruiser shifted the shadow and he was shocked to see his ankle gripped by Erwin's right hand. Bryn's head jerked upwards just as the deck motion moved his shadow sideways and he was staring directly into the contorted face of Erwin.

Erwin's eyes were opened and focused on Bryn in a terrifying stare. Erwin's large white teeth showed through lips stretched in a grimace that made the head appear skeletal. Bryn only saw Erwin's left fist when it was too late for him to completely dodge. It caught him on the shoulder at full power and with less force skidded to hit him between the eye and ear and knocked him two metres backwards into the door of the main salon. The impetus of Bryn's crash into the door was increased by the pitch of the ship so that the topmost hinge of the door burst from its screws causing Bryn to roll into the luxuriously fitted out interior entertainment area, the main salon.

Erwin was emerging from a brief bout of unconsciousness when Bryn's pulling and lifting speeded his recovery. At first Erwin thought that Bryn was helping him, then memories of his earlier self questioning returned. Erwin realised he had been drugged. Only Bryn could have arranged that. Bryn had encouraged him to drink the wine, the only way he could have been drugged.

Through half closed eyelids Erwin had observed Bryn wearing a fluorescent coloured life jacket, whereas he, Erwin, appeared to have been stripped of much of his clothing. He was freezing cold and wet but Bryn appeared to be lifting him onto the bench as a preliminary to pushing him off the cruiser rather than doing anything to help him. The realisation that Bryn was attempting to murder him by drowning triggered an adrenalin rush that reactivated frozen muscles. Erwin saw the effort in lifting him and the irregular motion of the ship temporarily unbalanced Bryn. Erwin's hand snaked out and grabbed Bryn's trousered ankle in a grip made ferociously tight by outrage. Erwin's other hand clenched into a fist that he flung at Bryn's face. His prone position and the undulations of the cruiser made him miss his intended target, but not by much. He did not immediately feel any impact with his half frozen hand but he did see Bryn knocked backwards so he pulled hard with his right hand and as Bryn disappeared from view Erwin heard a splintering crash above the background noise of sea, wind and intermittent propeller churn.

Erwin staggered to his feet and was flung across the cockpit well by a moving deck. With senses clearing and an anger growing to murderous fury, Erwin rose on hands and knees. He saw a movement through a shattered door in the shadowed salon and began crawling towards his tormentor. Quite clearly Erwin knew what he must do. He had to kill Bryn; with Bryn around he could not get help. Erwin recalled the radio and how Bryn had simply pressed the switch on the microphone to talk to someone to obtain weather details.

Erwin knew he could not handle a ship without help and that the radio was his only hope. He had no hope without the radio. With Bryn, his killer adversary as an impediment, Erwin was certain he would be denied access to the radio. Erwin could not take any chances if he were to survive this nightmare. He had to kill Bryn. On a heaving deck he crawled implacably towards the prone Bryn.

CHAPTER FORTY-NINE

THE MOTION OF PANYGYRIC FIVE subtly changed from that of short choppy buffets to less frequent but larger, longer, smoother rises and falls. The worst squall had moved eastwards and the lee of Lady Julia Percy Island now provided better shelter from the abated wind. Neither of the gladiators aboard the luxury cruiser appreciated the improved maritime conditions. Each knew he had a fight to the death in the colosseum cockpit of the luxury cruiser, but both protagonists were oblivious to the opulent setting.

Bryn's left shoulder was an area of intense pain. The punch from Erwin hurt. It coincided with the jerk in the deck from the cross wave as the sea settled and these combined forces had propelled him with considerable velocity into one of the partly opened doors that separated the aft cockpit from the main salon. The angle at which Bryn struck the door pulled it partly off its hinges and it hung flapping with each motion of the ship on the long swells rolling in from the stern. It was the upper part of the breaking door that axed into his deltoid muscle. Bathed in dim red and green lights reflected through salon windows, Bryn lay in pain on the expensive carpet. Through the flapping broken door, bathed in bright white light against an intensely black background, Bryn saw a crawling animal with ferocious fangs bared in a grimace of deathly hatred. The bright overhead white light left the animal's eyes in dark shadows beneath a large Neanderthal brow that emphasised the size of the gleaming white teeth.

Sight of the apparition generated fear and fright in Bryn. Then his brain overrode the pain as he realised again that the dripping animal approaching him was Erwin. Erwin his tormentor. Erwin who must be destroyed. Why was he not unconscious? Work that out later. He must not only kill to preserve his reputation but kill to survive. The crawling Erwin was a prime example that the most deadly living organism on this planet was man.

Bryn's survival syndrome helped him rise to his feet as the crawling Erwin's hand pushed aside the broken door. Bryn had the advantage of playing on home ground but that thought, as such, never crystallised in his mind. He instinctively reached for a weapon and in the dim red/green lit salon his right hand flipped up the nylon tab that released a red 1.7 kilogram dry powder fire extinguisher from beneath the bank of inbuilt cupboards separating the galley and salon proper.

Sensing the wave motion Bryn half turned to coordinate his movement with the next lift of the deck. He saw the hideous sight of Erwin's face peering past the flapping door. Part of the face was red, part green and the parts changed colour as Erwin's head moved around as his eyes adjusted to the lesser lumination in the dim salon. As the deck began to roll, Bryn struck down with the fire extinguisher at the head of the kneeling Erwin.

The erratic movement of the broken door deflected a lot of power from Bryn's stroke so the fire extinguisher grazed Erwin's head. Even so the blow was severe and Erwin felt the force fling him to the deck before the excruciating pain enveloped the top of his skull. Boxing training is designed to instil reflexes and it was entirely a reflex that made Erwin twist his body and fling himself backwards from the salon doorway into the cockpit. Erwin's reflex saved him from Bryn's second strike; a strike that Bryn instinctively realised had to be made while the target appeared dazed. Without time to adjust the swing of the stroke with the uplift of the deck the stroke missed Erwin's head but struck his left hand and smashed three metacarpal bones serving his pointer, middle and ring fingers. Encouraged by the success of two strikes Bryn moved forward to deliver a third to the body writhing on the deck.

Although in terrible pain from his shattered hand, Erwin saw the dim red/green light obscured and reflexes took over again. He kicked towards the approaching shadow. His bare foot hit Bryn's leg, just above the knee and sent him sprawling backwards to land on his already traumatised shoulder. The fire extinguisher slipped from his grasp and rolled forward out of sight. Had it not been for some cushioning effect from the PFD that he wore, Bryn would have been incapacitated.

Both injured men, one in the red/green dim light of the salon and the other in the shadow of the bright white of the cockpit, struggled as quickly as their respective injuries allowed, to stand upright on the swaying deck. Bryn's brain had no drug impediment. It realised that a weapon was needed and both of the loaded spear-guns were unreachable, being hidden outside. Bryn's eyes swung to the galley. His body followed and the fingers from his uninjured arm curled into the slot of the galley drawer where kitchen implements are stored. A slight jerk upwards freed the drawer runners from the detent that stopped accidental opening due to motion. Bryn pulled the drawer open to the extent allowed by the built-in restraint lip that prevented drawers from sliding out onto the deck. Bryn's experience of all ship board items allowed him to reach into the drawer and take out a black handled, sharp, serrated, fish preparation knife. Steadying himself as well as he could with his sore shoulder, Bryn staggered towards the door to the cockpit with the blade of the knife reflecting the red and green of the navigation lights.

No sound of human voices had added to the noises of the diesel engines, the slap of the sea, the intermittent churn of the propellers and vibrating hum of the wind on the top deck radio aerials. Only grunts and moans of pain had briefly interrupted the dark atmosphere. One noise is recognisable universally and that is the jinkling sound of the cutlery drawer. Since early childhood the sound of the kitchen cutlery drawer being pulled open stimulated the cochlear nerve and was lodged in the memory cells of the brain of most of the world's urban population. So it was with Erwin. As Bryn opened the galley drawer the distinctive sound of the cutlery was recognised by Erwin. He realised that Bryn was arming himself with a knife and that he too needed a knife, especially as his left hand was painful and swollen beyond any injury previously sustained in the boxing ring. Erwin remembered his tackle box and knew that his fishing knife was inside.

Erwin saw his green tackle box top amongst the cushions and staggered near enough to flip open the top. He was in the process of reaching for the knife handle when Bryn burst through the dangling door separating the salon and the cockpit. Bryn had one arm dangling uselessly but the other arm lifted the hand that carried a knife. Erwin's uninjured hand moved sideways. He grabbed the edge of a cushion and flung it with a velocity that tested every fibre of every muscle. His aim was perfect and the heavy waterproof cushion struck Bryn in the chest causing him to fall back into the salon. The brief transition from the dim red/green lit salon to the bright light above the cockpit had left Bryn with a momentary blindness that prevented him seeing the airborne cushion heading in his direction. And with only one functioning arm he could not steady himself. Again several thick nylon layers of the PFD pillowed his fall and he rolled towards the shelter of the galley bench to struggle to his feet. He still held the knife in his right hand and that gave him some confidence despite the surprise knock down.

Erwin's hand returned to its earlier mission, the knife in the tackle box. His fingers closed around the handle. With only one functioning hand he struggled to stand at the same time as he grabbed the knife. The luminal sprayed on the handle by the Victoria Police forensic investigators some months earlier had never been wiped off. The liquid film made the handle slippery to Erwin's salt water dampened fingers and his grip was a slip, pushing the knife towards one end of the box causing the blade to slip between two shallow fitted trays. Erwin grabbed again clamping all four fingers around the handle and locking it into his large palm. He lifted the knife upwards intending to use it against the similarly armed Bryn.

As Erwin lifted the knife the tip of the blade snagged on a two cent rubber wedge jammed under the wire spring of a mouse trap. The wedge dislodged and the spring tension pushed the trap wire onto a coil of copper auto wire wound around the wooden base of the rodent trap. Instantaneously the interrupted electrical circuit was made a complete circuit. Electricity from a nine volt battery triggered the detonator to detonate. That caused Erwin's fertiliser-based bomb to explode. Erwin was blown to pieces before the significance of the slight impediment he felt on the knife blade could register. Along with Erwin went an irregular but roughly triangular shaped five metre piece of the aft hull and cockpit bulwark of Panygyric Five.

Cruisers are constructed to resist compression from the outer force of the sea pushing inwards. Internal forces such as that exerted by internal explosion are less well catered for in the construction. Hence the magnificent Panygyric was vulnerable and a score of hull fractures developed with cracks radiating from each like the lateral supports in a spiders web. The water pressure applied against each fissure by the sheer weight of the cruiser tore the cracks wider. The continued forward hull pressure from the twin propellers further widened the gaps as hull pieces flaked off and water began to squirt into the lower hull. The unchecked deluge mingled with the flood pouring in from the triangular hole that had once been part of the cockpit lounge.

The Emergency Position Indicating Radio Beacon (EPIRB) was attached to a bracket on the bulkhead separating the salon and the cockpit. The explosion destroyed it. With that loss any hope of help from a vessel that might have responded to the distress signal disappeared.

Laying flat on his back in the salon saved Bryn from direct bomb blast damage and wounding from secondary projectiles such as pieces of the hull and metal and timber fittings that sprayed around. Bryn was bewildered by the blast and blundered toward the crazily swinging cockpit door. Erwin was a secondary consideration now that the cruiser was so obviously endangered. Bryn was compelled to save Panygyric Five. With an immobilised left shoulder he struggled to rise and with great effort reached the doorway. The shattered door was swinging madly on its broken hinge in a stream of black inflowing water that had white, red and green flickering facets.

With one arm he heaved his way into the cockpit area. He was horrified to find the entire starboard bulwark missing and a black hissing torrent of water swirled powerfully around the deck. He could not have conceived that the curiously shaped bits of light coloured flotsam were the splattered remains of Erwin. All he knew was that Erwin was no longer there and so was no longer a threat.

Bryn felt in his feet the list to starboard taken by his beloved floating palace. His nautical training motivated him to painfully push his way to the main control position. In his mind the imperative task was to start the pumps to control the water intake. He would stabilize the flooding then radio a mayday signal. He saw that the aft EPIRB was missing as was part of the bulwark and resolved that after the pumps were working he would activate the forward EPIRB. Swift though Bryn's logical resolutions flowed in his brain, even swifter was the intake of water into the hull of the cruiser. With his shattered shoulder Bryn had taken several painful minutes to stagger to the main control station. The hole in the starboard side was taking water at several hundred litres per minute. The weight of each litre lowered the hull further into the water causing the water intake rate to accelerate.

Along the starboard side of the hull, the small hull fractures were increasing in size. The laminated hull material continued flaking off. Even the motors were conspiring against Bryn as hundreds of fine lines radiating crosswise beneath the hull were irrevocably increasing in breadth due to the vibration of the propeller shafts. Water dribbles grew into spurts, hundreds of them, and Panygyric's hull line steadily settled below that envisaged by its design engineers. Bryn struggled at the main control station. He speedily located the pump switches, started the independent motors and listened with relief at the characteristic thump of the pump and the whump of water forced out under pressure.

Although the weather had not deteriorated, Panygyric Five was steadily moving forward for some time and the shelter provided by being in the lee of Lady Julia Percy Island was no longer available. Moving sluggishly and lower in the water the long black liquid swell of the unsheltered, more turbulent ocean surface now began to dump over the transom and flood the cockpit, salon and engine room.

Bryn tried to trim the cruiser with some success at first and his pushing forward of the throttles to maximum with the altered trim offered a few seconds of hope until a large blacker wave dumped tonnes of foaming hissing water into the cockpit and the salon began to flood. The cracks in the cockpit floor caused by Erwin's bomb let water flow below deck. Water rose above the engine mountings. The shock of the weight of the water widened the small cracks transversing the hull beneath the cockpit and disaster became inevitable. Two more great black breakers hit the rear of the cruiser and a deep fissure developed right around the hull at the junction of the salon and the cockpit, the area that took the brunt of Erwin's self annihilating improvised explosive device.

Bryn heard as well as felt the tearing of the hull and panic began to emerge as he felt Panygyric settle suddenly to a level that blocked off the pump outlets. With a gurgling choke the pumps stopped. Abandoning the control station Bryn painfully pulled himself upwards against the terrible starboard list of his disintegrating cruiser. He made for the upper deck lifeboat. Bryn was almost clear of the cabin when a deafening snap followed by a sickening lurch riveted his gaze rearwards. The entire aft section of Panygyric was pulverised beneath a gigantic black wave and torn away from the remainder of the cruiser.

The widely undulating remainder of the hull could be seen for only a moment longer because water flooded the engines, short circuited the reserve batteries and Panygyric began to roll throwing Bryn overboard. Bryn's hands moved without conscious thought to pull the tagged cords that activated the release of compressed gas to inflate his retro-reflective PFD. He managed to inflate one side and that proved sufficient to raise his head above water to gasp air. With his functioning hand he fumbled for and found the other tag. The inflation of the other side propelled him above the churning water.

Panic immobilised Bryn. The realisation that he was in the most shark infested water on planet Earth overcame his momentary paralysis and made him lift his half frozen, dangling legs. The sudden lift brought him a few more seconds of horrific life. The Great White shark spearing up from the dark depths intended to rip off the entire appendage it sensed dangling down in the black water but the sudden retraction meant that only Bryn's foot was bitten off in the swift upward strike.

Bryn experienced the dull pain of the rippling away of his foot. The impact of the mental turmoil was greater. Bryn knew with shattering horror that he was to be eaten alive. A second Great White confirmed his belief as it took off most of his other leg. He felt as if a gigantic cricket bat had slammed into his thigh. The smell of Bryn's blood or the vibrations of his agony may have attracted other sharks or it may have been the first attacker returning for another bite who took an arm and most of his right side. The nylon PFD proved no obstacle. What was left of Bryn, his head, shoulders, damaged left arm and torso piece were shared by two voracious sharks.

Nothing of Bryn remained. Bryn's Will had specified that he desired to be buried at sea. He achieved his ambition. Only a few hundred metres away, the body bits of Erwin, washed from the remains of Panygyric Five, made meals for a myriad of smaller varieties of fish.

CHAPTER FIFTY

DURING PAUSES BETWEEN BOUTS OF highly athletic sexual activities Bryn had told Stephanie that he would be away a couple of days on important business and may not be in regular phone contact. Bryn did not specify what type of business and Stephanie's only attempt to draw him out was delicately rebuffed with kisses and touches that made her forget to press for details. Two days had passed with no call. That was most unusual. Stephanie had tried calling Bryn's mobile several times only to hear the message that the phone was switched off. The radio phone to Panygyric Five was unresponsive too. A call to ECARUT provided no comfort and the list of phone numbers and email addresses on the computer in Bryn's home office produced negative results.

After one more night alone Stephanie became sufficiently worried to contact Bryn's lawyer for advice. The lawyer was a specialist in commercial law not police matters. He telephoned a policeman friend at the St Kilda Road Police Complex for advice. The friend was a Superintendent and promised to do a "mirror job". That is, he would look into it. The Superintendent had a spare, intelligent, young Detective Senior Constable wasting his time on general duties and in view of the commercial importance of the missing person and to give the Detective something more interesting to do, the Superintendent assigned Detective Senior Constable Jason Lyons the task of enquiring into the whereabouts of Bryn Hamley.

When he received the assignment sheet, Jason Lyons stared at it for some time wondering if the apparently routine assignment masked something more significant. He asked himself whether the ATS had influenced his selection for the job. Confronted with a problem with obvious potential for complications, Jason decided he needed advice. He felt comfortable with Detective Senior Sergeant Jarvis on the recent surveillance job so he phoned Jarvis. Over the phone he was guarded but what little he had to say interested Jarvis who agreed to meet him for a coffee in a café not far from the Police Complex.

Neither knew that they occupied the very table at which Ian had once espied Ray Woodbury. Jarvis listened to his young colleague, asked several pertinent questions then used his mobile phone to call the ATS.

The overburdened ATS Intelligence Office who took the phone call from Jarvis treated it like a lotto win. The ATS had lost all contact with Dormunt and Hamley and any help from Lyons and the dependable Jarvis would be appreciated.

The ATS Intelligence Officer asked that Jarvis act as the contact and that through him Lyons should submit a duplicate of every report on a regular basis. Jarvis was advised that the Vicpol Superintendent need not be informed of the duplicate reports. The ATS aspect should remain on a "need to know" with a Victoria Police Assistant Commissioner to ensure both Jarvis and Lyons were covered at high level.

Jarvis was satisfied. Any high level influence was acceptable to him as he aspired for promotion to Inspector. Jarvis passed on to Lyons word for word the information from the ATSIO. He pointed out that the undeserved cloud over Lyons, caused by failure to convict Erwin, would more rapidly be dissipated with some higher level influence on side.

In the Vice Squad unmarked car the two policemen drove to St Kilda Marina. Erwin's four wheel drive vehicle, the Beast, was parked where last observed. They went to the office and spoke to the attendant. Lyons left his card with the request that if anyone was seen taking an interest in the Beast then he be phoned immediately. Jarvis told Lyons they would leave it there another two days. If no movement by then, Jarvis would arrange to have it towed to the police garage.

On his return to his work station, Lyons phoned Stephanie. He told her that he was assigned the task of locating Bryn and arranged an appointment for later that day. Jason Lyons assured Stephanie that all inquiries would be discreet and that it would be premature to attribute anything serious to Bryn's delay. The Superintendent saw Lyons working on a "to do" schedule and was pleased to notice that the despondency that had earlier settled on Lyons had disappeared. The Superintendent had felt guilty at the orders he received from higher up, transferring Lyons from a prestigious position to a general duties role. The Superintendent considered how he might get Lyons to join his lodge.

The titled blue-blood gentleman, the pillar of Melbourne society who Bryn had invited to join the board of ECARUT was perplexed. Sir Mervyn had accepted, with reservations, Bryn's explanations about a possible business predator using anonymous poison pen letters to foil the ASX listing. Bryn's explanation were logical, true. But the poison pen letters accusations also had the ring of truth, made more concrete by the fact the several of the persons named in the letters also appeared to have disappeared without trace. For three days now there had been no contact, no telephone response, no email response and no fax. The cultured voice of a young lady answered Bryn's home phone, his fiancée, she claimed, and she sounded genuinely worried at being unable to make contact with Bryn.

The acquisition and recognition of power is absorbed via a process, akin to osmosis, within the elite blue-blood circle. The prospective director of ECARUT sensed the absence of power. He knew that power is useless unless it is asserted. He resolved to assert his own power; he coveted ownership of ECARUT for its wealth. He called several trusted cronies and discussed the methods by which they might advantage themselves as directors of ECARUT in the absence of Bryn.

The concept they contrived was simple. They decided to assert that they were appointed, relying upon their prestigious positions in society to overcome anyone who challenged by demanding such mundane peccadilloes as documentary proof. Even if Bryn returned, the blue bloods felt that their combined prominence may cower this young unknown upstart, against whom serious accusations remained unresolved, into buckling and allowing them to wrest control from him. After gaining control, they would issue an extraordinary number of one cent paid but fully voting shares to each other. With that voting power they stood a good chance to "legally" bully Bryn off the Board and out of significant control of his extraordinary affluent company.

Tactics of this nature had been used several times in Melbourne and Sydney when the founding entrepreneur of a company died and members of the elite establishment successfully bullied beneficiaries out of their proper inheritances. They did not call it theft by intimidation rather they called it "acquisition by exercise of elevated intellect". That's why they are called "elite", they steal undetected behind a voluminous vocabulary that confuses legitimate heirs and leaves them bereft of their inheritance.

As a preliminary step to implementing a scheme of "legalised" theft, Sir Mervyn drove to Mornington in his chauffeured Rolls Royce. At ECARUT he commandeered Bryn's office, told everyone that he was the temporary Chairman and had minutes drawn up to show that he and four cronies he named were properly appointed as directors. His arrogant manner and the deference usually accorded to men with the prefix "Sir" before their name, soon had an overawed stenographer typing furiously to provide the draft minutes he dictated.

Four senior ECARUT managers, the Legal and Compliance Manager, Chief Financial Officer, Manager of IT and the Personnel Manager were initially intimidated. The intimidation was partly due to the Rolls Royce car parked immediately and illegally outside of ECARUT's front door. The blue blood "Sir" could not care less about parking infringement notices because the Rolls Royce was registered in the name of a company he invisibly owned in the Bahamas. He parked anywhere except tow-away zones and the Bahamas Company never paid any parking fines. However, after half an hour of being ordered to produce reports of various types, the ECARUT senior managers met in the board room, summoned their commercial courage and decided to seek proof of the authority of the titled interloper to give orders.

The Legal and Compliance Manager fronted Sir Mervyn and asked by what authority he sat in Bryn's office. He was aggressively told that Bryn would not be back and that the Board of ECARUT would be changed. When asked if any senior executives of ECARUT would be considered for Board positions, as Bryn had indicated some time ago, "Sir" arrogantly and loudly told him that staff must learn that they have an inferior place in the organisation and should not aspire to be elevated to a level above their station. The voice of Sir Mervyn was so cuttingly loud that everyone in the entire office heard the depreciating reproach.

"Sir" had obviously passed his use-by date. A censure of that type worked wonders in the past but when flung at the new breed of technocrats, justifiably proud of their achievements, it failed miserably. The Personnel Manager, abandoning all caution, called the police. Arrogance, which had been part of his power for decades, was Sir Mervyn's downfall although he did not know it at the time. The Personnel Manager had just replaced the telephone handset when his Personal Assistant told him of an incoming call from a Victoria Police Detective named Lyons who wanted to talk to the Chairman of ECARUT. The Personnel Manager took the call and told Lyons about "Sir" who claimed to have taken over from the missing Bryn. Lyons was surprised at hearing of the attempted take over because it indicated that Bryn would be away for some time. It raised suspicion as to the reason for the absence. When he heard that the local police had been summoned Lyons requested that they contact him immediately upon arrival at ECARUT.

Lyons knew not what to do. Likewise he knew what not to do and that was to let a potential source of information, Bryn's records, be contaminated or destroyed especially as the ATS interest had elevated the importance of the case. Bolstered by the assurance of the ATSIO that higher authority would watch over him and that unascertained terrorist links seemed to be involved, Lyons acted decisively. When the local cop, a Senior Constable, phoned him a few minutes later, Lyons ordered that Sir Mervyn be detained to assist with inquiries. Lyons ordered the impoundment of the Rolls Royce into which he was told some files were loaded. The chauffeur was not arrested but requested to assist the Police in their enquiries. Lyons phoned Jarvis, told him what he had done and was relieved to receive approval. Jarvis, in turn, phoned the Sergeant in charge of the Mornington Police Station, a colleague of many years, and endorsed the orders of Lyons.

Consequently the ECARUT staff were treated to the appearance of half of the plain clothes and uniformed staff of their local Police Station congregating to arrest the person who claimed to be the new head of their organisation and the towing away of the elegant Rolls Royce car. Sir Mervyn spent two hours in the Mornington lock up, outraged, blustering and threatening in a raggedly dignified voice. The phone call he was permitted to make to his lawyer produced some action but nowhere near the expected result. "Sir's" lawyer phoned an Assistant Commissioner of Police to protest the illegal restraint of his titled client. The protest was based on false arrest and was being treated seriously until the lawyer mentioned that "Sir" was attempting to restore order and consumer confidence because of the disappearance of a person named Bryn Hamley. Scarcely an hour before, the Assistant Commissioner was at a briefing where he was told by the ATSIO that Bryn Hamley was a "Person on Interest" in relation to a violently anti-social organisation reliably known to have distributed detonators to its members after a lesson on bomb making.

The lawyer was astounded when he was abruptly told that Victoria Police hierarchy would not interfere with the action of its Mornington officers. In thirty years as a lawyer a refusal at that level within the force had never occurred. When the phone call ended the lawyer was firstly indignant but paused to examine the situation. If top brass police refused to assist such a well known member of the Melbourne establishment as Sir Mervyn then something was amiss, and it must be serious. He phoned "Sir" to say that he and an experienced criminal law colleague were heading forthwith for Mornington. "Sir" was definitely not amused at being held in a common lock up until their arrival.

He was even less amused when later the duty constable gave him a menu from McDonalds from which to choose his meal.

Jarvis and Lyons were well on the way to Mornington by the time Sir Mervyn received the highly unsatisfactory call from his lawyer. Jarvis had made a short stop at an inner city bank to collect a thick envelope from a safe deposit box. He made no comment to Lyons as to the contents. By secure radio, Jarvis had left a report with the ATSIO on recent events connected with the company owned by the missing Bryn.

"Sir" felt insulted when he was escorted by a Senior Constable to the interview room and introduced to a Detective Senior Sergeant and a Detective Senior Constable, neither of whom seemed concerned by his refusal to sit down and his tirade of sneering abuse. He expected a Commander at least to perform the apologises and his release. He was even more insulted to be addressed by his first name "Mervyn". No one who valued their commercial prospects in Melbourne had used that name without the deferential "Sir" to him for twenty five years. He was remonstrating with the Sergeant when the Constable, at a nod from the Sergeant, left the room. The Sergeant took from the inside pocket of his jacket a thick envelope. From the envelope he took fifteen post card sized coloured photographs, that he casually spread in front of "Sir".

Sir Mervyn could not know that Jarvis had expropriated the photos from three automatic cameras concealed behind screens in an establishment located in a luxury city high rise apartment. Jarvis had led the raid and obtained ample other evidence to make convictions stick against the operators so he kept the shots taken of earlier clients. Obviously they were intended for blackmail and just as obviously the operators of the establishment raided made no complaint when they found the photos to be absent from the police evidence list. Jarvis, a cautious man, had kept them for over eight years on the grounds they may be of use some time in the future.

Sir Mervyn looked sick. His aging eyes lost a lot of ferocious fire and filled with tears. He asked Jarvis what he wanted for the photos in words spat from between his beautifully white expensive dentures. Jarvis deliberately and methodically put the photos back in the envelope before he answered. Typical technique; let the person in custody stew a bit. Jarvis told Mervyn that Detective Lyons would come back in, the recorder would start and Mervyn would tell everything he knew about Bryn to the tape. With mental reservations, Mervyn reluctantly consented.

Sir Mervyn talked for fifteen minutes. Nothing he told the two detectives was incriminating nor was it terribly helpful. He knew little of Bryn either socially or commercially. Bryn was a successful entrepreneur who sought elevation to a level in society beyond his breeding and Bryn was missing, so Sir Mervyn had altruistically intervened to protect the jobs of the workers. He barely paused when told that his lawyers had arrived. Jarvis recognised it as aristocratic bullshit. The interview ended. The tape stopped.

Jarvis nodded Lyons to leave. Sir Mervyn and Jarvis spoke briefly. Sir Mervyn agreed to break entirely with ECARUT and forget all about everything connected with his visit to Mornington. Jarvis agreed to release his impounded Rolls Royce and destroy the incriminating photographs in one year provided Sir Mervyn and cronies kept clear of ECARUT. No charges, no counter charges, no record beyond minimal, which would state that a mutual misunderstanding had occurred. Sir Mervyn walked to collect his chauffeur and Rolls Royce whilst ignoring his two annoyed and confused lawyers.

Jarvis and Lyons walked innocently into the office of the local Sergeant to advise that all was forgotten and forgiven. Jarvis told his old friend that should he require higher sanction for the events that had occurred, then a phone call from an Assistant Commissioner could be arranged. The Sergeant was thankful but declined to take matters further.

Jarvis wanted Mervyn out of the equation. Despite his title and position in society, once Jarvis saw Mervyn starring in the group sex session photos then Mervyn became just another perverted low life. Jarvis thought of him as "Perving Mervyn". Jarvis had no reason to protect ECARUT. But ECARUT was connected to this Hamley character who in turn connected to Erwin. The less people to cause complications in anything connected to Erwin then the safer Jarvis felt. Jarvis had no contempt for caution.

CHAPTER FIFTY-ONE

THE VIEWS FROM THE HUGE window walls in the high rise apartment were stunning. In clear weather Stephanie could see the coastal town of Mornington where Bryn's company ECARUT had its registered office. In another direction the purple/blue ranges that fringe the Melbourne basin could be seen. To Stephanie the only view she wanted was a bird's eye view of Panygyric Five. She pressed her nose to the window to look downwards. The sight of the vacant mooring made her cry again. The intercom chimed to signal a visitor at the ground floor and when Stephanie heard it was a policeman making enquiries about Bryn she activated the security entry. She noted that the detective looked a lot like Bryn on the screen colour monitor then went to the bathroom to apply cosmetics to repair the damage done by her tears.

Detective Senior Constable Jason Lyons was unprepared for the beauty of the woman who met him at the elevator. She was a stunner despite evidence of recent crying. For her part Stephanie was unprepared for the resemblance that Lyons bore to the missing Bryn. Several years younger and with a few less social graces but otherwise a replica was how she later summed him up.

Lyons had a lot of fragments of information about the missing Bryn but nothing substantial or hopeful. He imparted a few facts then asked questions then more facts and then more questions over several cups of coffee. Stephanie never realised the mass of information Lyons extracted from her during the conversational interview. Lyons established that nothing was missing from the apartment except items that Bryn normally carried for a day's boating. Stephanie showed Bryn's passport to Lyons together with details of Bryn's unused bank accounts, credit card statements and untouched massive investment portfolio records. Bryn's cars remained in the subterranean garage. When searched later by Lyons the cars yielded nothing. So far as Stephanie knew, Bryn would be away overnight on Panygyric Five for business purposes. She did not know where he was going or with whom. Bryn was not secretive about aspects of his business, it was just that he felt business would be boring to an artistically inclined young lady.

Stephanie learned that Bryn had stopped Panygyric Five at St Kilda Marina to pick up a man then had sailed to refuel at Mornington. The Coast Guard reported his exit from Port Phillip Bay and other sightings confirmed that he was seen travelling west to the Southern Ocean into a mild storm front. But for a cruiser of the size and power of Bryn's craft the storm was not considered a hazard especially in the light of Bryn's expertise as a mariner.

Stephanie screwed up her pretty nose when Lyons mentioned the name of Sir Mervyn and said she did not like him. He was too quick to put a hand on a lady's knee on short acquaintance. She had told that to Bryn and he registered anger but prevailed on her to await the listing of ECARUT on the ASX then Bryn would dispense with services of Sir Mervyn. Lyons wondered whether the greed of Sir Mervyn may be linked to Bryn's disappearance. The attempt to gain control of ECARUT certainly justified this suspicion. However Detective Sergeant Jarvis had said he would investigate anything to do with Mervyn and he had not yet completed his inquiries. Lyons urged Stephanie to seek protection by involving Bryn's lawyer immediately. It was with considerable reluctance that Lyons left.

Shortly after leaving, Lyons reported to Jarvis that he was certain that Stephanie had never heard of Erwin Dormunt and that she was not an immediate suspect in the absence of Bryn, given that both Jarvis and Lyons had witnessed Bryn's departure. Lyons also reported no evidence what-so-ever of any link to the Knights of Socialist Australia. In fact Stephanie's response to that question from Lyons was the nearest she came to a smile in her current situation. Lyons felt a tinge of guilt at the thought, no the hope, that Bryn might never be found.

Stephanie and Jason Lyons met several times over the next week. For both it was more of a social meeting because no new information surfaced. Stephanie said that Bryn's lawyer had obtained a Court Determination and several senior executives of ECARUT had been appointed as interim Directors to keep the company running. The proposed ASX listing was postponed indefinitely. Sir Mervyn had terminated his association with ECARUT. Stephanie learned from the lawyer, with a mixture of relief and regret that she was the sole beneficiary of Bryn's estate.

When Stephanie told the fact to Lyons, his professional training caused him to ask himself the question, Qui Bono? Who benefits? As a matter of routine Lyons had to elevate Stephanie several steps higher on the list of possible suspects in relation to Bryn's disappearance, but his heart was not in the spirit of the elevation.

Lyons was confronted by an impenetrable wall of nothing. No sightings of Panygyric Five at any port within range of its fuel tanks. No reports of any additional refuelling, docking, or wreckage. No EPIRB transmission of distress, no use of any credit cards, no withdrawal from banks. And although the blank response was reported by Jason Lyons to Stephanie, he did not reveal to her that a similar blank slate existed for Erwin. Stephanie had no need to know.

In execution of the warrant Lyons led a team consisting of the forensic crime scene examiner who had attended an earlier search plus two uniformed officers. Erwin's residence had a fortnight's layer of dust. Items in the rubbish bin were furry with mould. The bomb making ingredients and detonators indicated that Erwin had constructed one explosive device. During the course of typing out a report on Erwin, Detective Lyons received a Coast Guard message that wreckage located on an isolated beach may be of interest. Lyons made the five hour drive to the wreckage site in the company with forensic examiner and a representative of the maritime insurance company that carried the multi million dollar insurance cover on Panygyric Five. By the time they arrived many more pieces of wreckage, cushions and floatable kitchen items were discovered on the shore. Lyons phoned Stephanie to report a possible identification of wreckage of Bryn's cruiser. His consolation call lasted over twenty minutes.

The laboratory of the Forensic Science Unit of the Victoria Police, working in conjunction with a private laboratory engaged by the insurance company, took ten days to establish that the wreckage was part of the hull and superstructure of Panygyric Five beyond doubt. The two laboratories also independently established that the wreckage clearly indicated an explosion had ripped apart the rear section of the hull and that fragments of the explosive matched the bomb ingredients located in Erwin's residence.

Over the next month several air/sea searches turned up nothing. Bryn's former lawyer, now acting for Stephanie, obtained further Determinations following a preliminary Coroners Court hearing, that appointed Stephanie as the Administrator of Bryn's estate. With increasing assistance from Jason Lyons, Stephanie took control of Bryn's financial empire. She was pleasantly surprised at the warmth and loyalty shown to her by the senior executives at ECARUT who were confirmed as executive Directors. According to the lawyer and auditors the business was thriving.

Sir Mervyn's thoughts settled down from a vortex of red hot hatred of Jarvis to a cold black dagger of revenge. Enlisting the help of several cronies to conceal his involvement, Sir Mervyn began to stir up negative opinion against Jarvis. He did not get far. Jarvis was awarded a police medal in recognition of his exemplary service in breaking a twenty four man paedophile ring. Shortly afterward he received the anticipated promotion to Inspector. Sir Mervyn's cronies became curiously reticent when they perceived that he wanted to tangle with Inspector Jarvis using them as proxies. Sir Mervyn's attempt at revenge fizzled out. Sir Mervyn wondered if Jarvis had his cronies by the balls too.

Sir Mervyn never got his photos back. He died of a heart attack later that year brought on by over exertion at what was described in the press as a "late evening private party".

Lyons found himself assigned to the Vice Squad working under the direction of the newly appointed Inspector Jarvis quite often. Both had received thanks from the ATSIO and been counselled on the advantages of developing selective amnesia so far as the ATS working hypothesis that the secretive Hamley and the deadly Dormunt may have been amateur terrorists who scored an own goal, that is, tried to make a bomb and blew themselves up in the process. Neither Jarvis nor Lyons believed the hypothesis but as it closed the file on Hamley and Dormunt, both presumed dead, then neither police officer raised any objection. Especially Lyons.

No one seemed to miss Erwin. Eventually the Trustee of his trust account sought court permission to wind up the estate and distribute the proceeds to five charities. In appreciation, one charity erected a memorial plaque to Erwin in the narthex of a church. Any unknowing passer-by reading the dedication would have assumed that Erwin died the death of a religious martyr. Lenny was disconsolate for several minutes when it became obvious that Erwin was highly unlikely ever to write any more cheques to him.

Jason and Stephanie found a mutual irresistible attraction over the months following the disappearance of Bryn. Stephanie was hounded by a section of the investigative media who dug deep and uncovered a few unsavoury aspects of Bryn's business. They proved that some people close to Bryn inexplicably disappeared. Jason proved adept at shielding Stephanie and deflecting hurtful questions from the more rabid members of the feral media tribe. Stephanie berated herself at times because she could not make up her mind about her deepening attraction to Jason. Was it because he resembled a slightly younger Bryn? She felt increasingly unsettled about her continuing platonic association with Jason.

Speculation in the media about the absence of Bryn and Erwin ranged from eye-witness accounts of them being beamed up by an alien space craft, certified true by the Oceanic Division of the Friends of the Alien Universe Society, to the theory that they escaped together from an inhospitable society for a life of gay love. The proponents of this theory were members of a gay club with a propensity for dressing in public as bare bottomed fairies. A weirdly dressed supporter of Erwin tried to convince anyone who would listen that Bryn was about to prove that Erwin had been set-up in a recent murder trial. That proof would precipitate the collapse of the entire capitalist system said the heavily tattooed black lipsticked spruiker. From the more raucous of these mad, but not mad enough to be locked up demonstrators, Jason provided Stephanie with protection and comfort.

It was not a one way street so far as comfort was concerned. Jason found working in the Vice Squad to be of enormous interest with challenges to his character and integrity daily. He observed the absolute bottom of the barrel of human scum. Stephanie's irrepressibly optimistic presence assisted in the preservation of his mental equilibrium. A full year after Bryn's disappearance, Stephanie stopped self analysis about her feelings for Jason and rewarded him for his patience. The handsome couple celebrated the end of their platonic friendship at a luxury hotel at the inland city of Alice Springs, about as far away from the sea in Australia as is possible.

Jason Lyons resigned from the Victoria Police. He became an executive Director of ECARUT in charge of security. Eventually he became an acknowledged expert on mortgage fraud but that did not occur for many years by which time he and Stephanie were married, living in a Mornington beach front mansion containing exquisite artworks and were parents of three children. The newly promoted Police Superintendent Jarvis was Godfather to the first born. Police Commander Jarvis was Godfather to the second son.

Ian had watched the Beast. Every day it stood where Erwin had left it. Ian watched the Panegyric Five berth. Every day it was vacant. Ian had no way of knowing what happened aboard the cruiser and what became of the cruiser. He saw the police contractor tow away the Beast. From listening to the Coast Guard radio he absorbed snippets of information about wreckage found on the Victorian coast. Ian made a mental quantum leap to conclude that the essence of his plan had come to fruition. Two killers had killed each other.

For his ravaged grandson Ian had achieved revenge by remote control. Ian decided to quit the investigation industry and had no difficulty in selling his investigation company for a reasonable figure. The electronic vehicle tracking device he crushed and disposed of. He had no use for the illegal five year old battery operated signalling device. There was no need to run the risk of being caught in possession of an illegal device, as better devices based on newer technology would soon experience the inevitable price decline. He doubted his need for a device in the future but knew where he could always obtain one. The files on Bryn and Erwin he shredded then burnt the shredded strands in the outdoor brick barbeque.

Ian had no compunction, compassion or remorse for contriving the deaths of two men. He held that the world would have been better had these two been drowned at birth. Ian and his family had scars seared in their souls by the terrible murder of their cherished grandson and those scars allowed for no compassion for murderers. Ian would devote the rest of his life to his wife, children and grandchildren to help ease the pain of the scars. Philosophically Ian accepted that human life was a juxtaposition of humour and horror but philosophy provides no protection against the unknowable future.

Ian chose not to dispose of his two hand guns. He had no contempt for caution.

ABOUT THE AUTHOR

DUDLEY FLINT IS THE PSEUDONYM of a semi-retired Melbourne, Australia, author. In his civilian career he had over 40 years as General Manager, Trustee or Consultant to Australia's top government, semi-government and industry superannuation funds, with over 15 years as a Councillor of the Victorian Division of the industry's peak body, the Association of Superannuation Funds of Australia (ASFA).

In the wider field of business, he served as a Director of a Bank, a Motel Chain, and a joint semi-government / Bank multimillion dollar property trust and was Chairman of an ASX listed property development company. As a licensed Private Inquiry Agent he draws on decades of experience to detect and resolve, mainly by common sense negotiation, "irregularities" within the superannuation industry. Restitution before retribution is his strength.

Parallel with his business career, he served as an Officer in the Australian Army Reserve rising from a humble National Serviceman to Officer Rank and receiving the ED (Efficiency Decoration). His last posting was that of Divisional Artillery Intelligence Officer for the Third Division. The author's qualifications and vast experience make him the only person capable of writing this unique book.